Kirkus Reviews (February 15, 2012)

An American teen encounters monsters both fantastical and human in the land of his birth. After a fire destroys their home, Tomas and his parents move to Slovakia, a country Tomas hasn't seen since he was 5 years old. He's unconcerned about the move; scarred from a childhood fire and painfully shy, Tomas hasn't got any friends to leave behind. Trencn, at first, seems wonderful. There's a truly fabulous castle, and he's made his first real friend: his cousin Katka. But Katka is dangerously ill, and Tomas' attempts to help are complicated by his first experiences with racism. In the United States, Tomas is "white"; in Slovakia, the olive skin he inherited from his Roma grandfather marks him as a Gypsy and a valid target for abuse. Nothing can help Tomas--and more importantly, Katka--except the mythical creatures Tomas started seeing almost as soon as he landed in Slovakia. It's unclear whether he can trust the watery vodnk or the fire vla, but they both promised to help. A first encounter with racism blends well with a compelling fantasy adventure (although Tomas's family, lacking any Romani culture or traditions, reiterates some of racism themselves; his mother explains how they are worthy of praise because they are "not like other Roma"). A shy boy blossoms in this surprisingly witty debut. (author's note, further reading) (Fantasy. 11-16)

VODNÍK

VODNÍK

BRYCE MOORE

Tu Books

AN IMPRINT OF
LEE & LOW BOOKS
New York

Text copyright © 2012 by Bryce Cundick, whose pseudonym is Bryce Moore
Maps copyright © 2012 by Isaac Stewart
Interior reaper illustration © Ozan Tekin

TU BOOKS, an imprint of LEE & LOW BOOKS Inc.
95 Madison Avenue, New York, NY 10016
leeandlow.com

Manufactured in the United States of America
by Worzalla Publishing Company, March 2012

Book design by Isaac Stewart
Book production by The Kids at Our House
The text is set in Minion Pro

10 9 8 7 6 5 4 3 2 1
First Edition

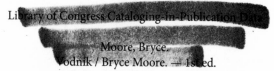

Library of Congress Cataloging-In-Publication Data

Moore, Bryce.
Vodník / Bryce Moore. — 1st ed.
p. cm.
Summary: Sixteen-year-old Tomas and his Roma family left Slovakia because of mysterious attacks on his life when he was a child, but when they return, the same creatures of folklore begin to strike again and Tomas, aided by his cousin, will have to bargain with Death herself to set things right.
Includes bibliographical references.
ISBN 978-1-60060-852-0 (hardcover : alk. paper) —
ISBN 978-1-60060-881-0 (e-book)
[1. Supernatural—Fiction. 2. Mythology, Slavic—Fiction. 3. Cousins—Fiction. 4. Death—Fiction. 5. Romanies—Fiction. 6. Slovakia—Fiction.] I. Title.
PZ7.M78227Vod 2012
[Fic]—dc23
2011042996

For Denisa, who made it all possible. I love you!

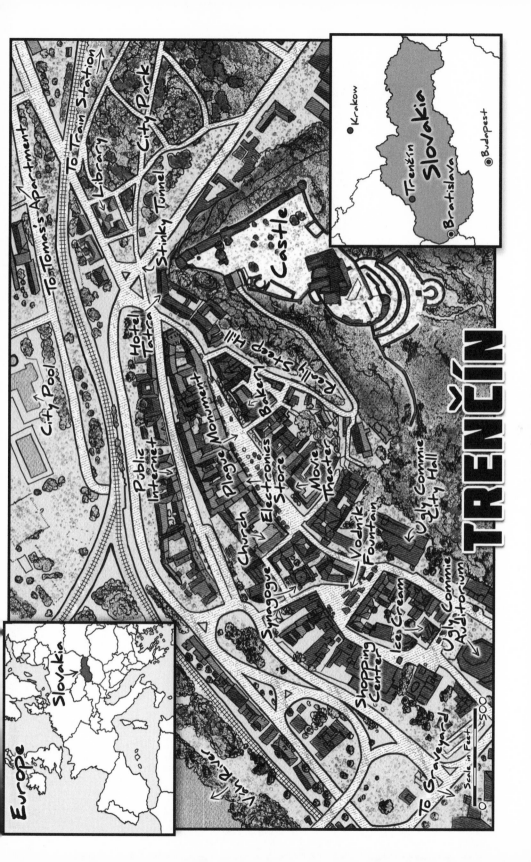

PRONUNCIATION GUIDE

Ajax	EYE-axe
Alena Kováčová	AH-len-ah KOH-vah-cho-vah
Katka	KAHT-kah
Lesana	LESS-ah-nah
Ľuboš	LOO-bohsh
Matúš Čak	MAH-toosh chalk
Morena	MORE-en-ah
Ohnica	OH-neet-sah
Starenka	STAH-ren-kah
Tomas	TOE-mahs
Trenčín	TREN-cheen
Víla	VEE-lah
Víťazoslav	VEE-tah-zo-slav
Vodník	VODE-neek
Zubatá	ZOO-bah-tah

CHAPTER ONE

ASH

Fire vilas can be treacherous to deal with if you get on their bad side. They're unpredictable, vengeful, and have memories that last centuries. Often the simplest approach to dealing with them is to bind them to flame instead of trying to kill them. Once bound, a fire vila typically becomes much more docile.

Waking up in a hospital bed is never a good thing. I coughed, and pain shot through my lungs. My eyes felt raw, like they'd been sandblasted.

"Tomas?" Mom came over to the bed and put her hand on my forehead. An oxygen mask covered my mouth, and they'd clipped a pulse monitor on my left forefinger. The room had a television and dresser, but no window. Fluorescent lights glared down from the ceiling, making my parents look pale and worn. It didn't help that they both had smudges of ash at the edges of their faces.

Even with tired eyes that betrayed a lack of sleep, Mom still managed to stay in control, with her hair in a tight ponytail and her back straight. Her complexion was normally as dark as mine, but now her olive skin looked washed out. Less vibrant. "How are you feeling?"

I blinked. My thoughts started to click together. When I spoke, I could still taste the smoke, and I couldn't seem to take a full breath. "The house.

What happened?" The oxygen mask made it sound like I was talking through a towel.

Dad swallowed before answering. "It's gone. The firefighters' response was quick, but . . ."

What could I say to that? The scene flashed through my mind again: the smoke, the smells. Fire eating the hallway, cracking the glass in picture frames. "Everything?"

"Everything but us," Dad said. "And that's all that really matters, right?"

We were all quiet after he said that, the only sound coming from the steady *beep* of the pulse monitor—well, that and my breathing. I'd make Darth Vader proud, with all that wheezing. I knew Dad was right, but my mind conjured up images of the living room engulfed in flames, the computer, all my movies, Mom's recipe books. Dad spoke again. "I—I'm sorry, Tomas."

"For what?"

He ran his fingers through his hair, something he only did when he was stressed. "I should have been there for you. If we hadn't decided to go to the midnight movie . . . When we got home, the fire was already in full force. Your mom and I rushed in to get you, but the firemen stopped us. I couldn't . . ." He trailed off, his throat practically convulsing as he kept swallowing. He pushed his glasses up his nose, and for a moment, he seemed like a stranger. Completely powerless.

"It's okay, Dad," I said, feeling guilty and not sure why. A bout of coughing hit me, and it took a moment to continue. "It worked out. I'm fine. No worries."

He nodded, but didn't say anything. Mom's face was lined with concern.

"What happened?" I asked Mom, giving Dad some time to think. "I could have sworn I was in the middle of the fire. How am I not hurt?"

A voice spoke from the doorway. "That's what we'd like to know too." A doctor entered dressed in a white lab coat over street clothes. He held a clipboard, which he tucked under his arm as he walked over to me and shook my hand. "I'm Dr. Geld. Glad to see you up and awake again."

"How long have I been out?" I asked.

He smiled. "About eight hours. Enough time for us to get some oxygen into you and for your body to have the rest it needed to start recovering. You inhaled a lot of smoke. Do you remember much of what happened?"

"No. I woke up and tried to get out, but there was so much smoke . . ." I checked my old burn scar that covered my right arm and then some, the skin mottled and rippled like a melted candle. "It wasn't even hot."

Dr. Geld cleared his throat. "Yes," he said. "Well then, that's that. The firefighter said he found you in your bedroom, surrounded by flames. But since you say the temperature inside wasn't too high—and your body confirms that for us—we'll have to just say you're a lucky young man."

"Yeah," I said, coughing again. "Lucky." Twice now in my life I've been this "lucky."

"Right." Dr. Geld made a couple of notes on his clipboard. "I did have one question for you—or your parents. We ran a few basic tests to make sure your son was all right. There seems to be some extensive scarring in his lungs. Healed already, but if you could just confirm—"

"He was in an accident when he was little," Mom said. "He almost drowned. The scars are from then."

Dr. Geld frowned and flipped through his papers. "From drowning? I would have thought they came from when he was originally burned. The charts—"

"It happened at the same time," I said. "When I was five, I almost drowned, and they found me with third degree burns on my right arm and side of my torso. It's on my records, if you'd get them from my doctor."

"Oh," the doctor said. I knew what he was thinking: how does someone get third degree burns while they're drowning? I wish I knew. "That explains that," he continued. "You'll need to stay with us for another day or two before we can release you. Sometimes smoke damage can take a bit to fully manifest, but I think you're out of the woods now. You'll be free to check out soon enough." We went through another round of hand shaking, and he left.

An uncomfortable pause followed the doctor's departure, filled only by the unrelenting beeping coming from the machine next to me. The place smelled like biology class, and the bed was too soft. "Free to check out," I said at last. "Check out to where?"

"Well," Dad said, sitting down in a chair and not meeting my eyes. "About that. We've been on the phone with the insurance agent, and it wasn't all good news."

"What's the problem?" I asked.

"Housing costs have soared in the last few years," Mom said, coming over to the bed to take my hand. "And . . . well, your father and I have discovered our insurance hasn't kept up."

I stared at them. Insurance? I'd never spent a moment in my life even thinking about the word. Maybe I should have. "What do you mean?"

"We were under-insured," Dad said, finally looking up at me. "Badly. We can't afford to both replace our belongings and purchase another house."

"But that's what insurance is for, right?" I said, drawing on what little I knew of the subject. "To pay you back for all the stuff you lost. Don't the insurance people make sure you've done things right? They probably—"

"The area became too expensive," Mom said. "The insurance will pay our mortgage off, cover the loss of the Explorer, and maybe give us some money left over, but not enough. So your father and I can find new jobs somewhere else, or . . ."

"Or we could try something more drastic," Dad finished.

"Drastic?" I said. My shortness of breath seemed to get even worse. Had someone turned off my oxygen?

Dad nodded, then licked his lips. He stood up. "How would you feel about moving to Slovakia?"

"Slovakia" and "Tomas" weren't two concepts that got put together much anymore. Ever since we'd moved from Slovakia when I was five, right after the accident, I'd always shied away from it. Mom and Dad had gone over a couple of times, but something had always come up to keep me away. And yes, if someone were to really press me, they might discover the Atlantic Ocean had more than a little to do with my reluctance. Didn't the Titanic teach anyone a lesson?

"What?" I said.

Mom glanced at Dad, who gave a little shrug. Mom sighed, then said, "Our savings would go much further there, and we'd be able to keep our standard of living. It's something we've thought about doing for years, but there was always a reason to stay in America. Now . . . your Uncle Ľuboš said he could find a job for me. He knows someone at an ESL school, and they're hiring teachers."

"What about Dad?"

"I could try writing again," Dad said, coming closer to the bed to hold on to the metal side rails. As he talked, some of the worry lines faded from his face. Where Mom now hesitated, he was excited. "That's what I wanted to do years ago, but so many things got in the way—my job took so many hours, and I never had the time to really dig into it. I know you're just finishing your sophomore year and—"

"Fine," I said.

They blinked in unison, eyes wide in matching expressions. "Just like that?" Mom said. "Fine?"

"You guys are trying to be nice to me, and I appreciate it. But it's okay. We're in a tight spot." Another round of coughing hit me. It felt like my body had issued an eviction notice to my lungs. Once I could breathe again, I said, "So . . . fine. It's not like I'll be leaving anyone behind."

That caused another awkward pause. My struggle to make friends had been a popular dinner table conversation over the years, with them always suggesting I try different things: sports, drama club, karate. Anything but movies and TV, which is what I really loved to do. Movies didn't stare at your scar or make you flounder for something to talk about. What was so wrong with that? My parents were in touch with only about three people from their high school days. What did it matter if I never had friends at school?

I could watch movies in Slovakia just as easily as I could watch movies in America. My mind was still numb from everything that had happened. What I needed right then was a television, a remote control, and about five hours of nothing to do.

Dad was watching Mom, his jaw clenched in defiance for some strange reason. If there was an Oscar for staring contests, my parents were gunning for a nomination. All at once Dad cleared his throat and asked, "What do you remember about Slovakia?"

She didn't answer. He broke the gaze and turned to me, repeating the question.

"Oh," I said, taken aback. "You meant me?" I shrugged, trying to force myself to concentrate. "Not much. I was five. There were a lot of trees, and there was a playground near our house. That's about it." I only remembered the playground because there was a picture of me at it on our piano. No—there *used* to be a picture of it on our piano.

"Well," Mom said, glaring at my dad. The room, which was small enough to begin with, had gotten even smaller. Had somebody wheeled in another beeping machine? "That's enough questions for now." She had gone from fine to pissed in about five seconds, and I wasn't sure why.

"What is it?" I asked.

"Nothing," Mom said.

Dad's face hardened. "It's not nothing. If you're so worried about it after all these years, I don't want us moving back at all. Let's just ask him. If he doesn't remember, then we can drop it. Okay?"

Mom's lips pressed together, but she stayed quiet.

Dad fiddled with my blanket as he spoke, unable to meet my eyes. "When you were in Slovakia before—when we lived there those three years—you had a very . . . active imagination. It got you into no end of trouble. And even though you were always an honest kid—as honest as kids get, of course—you would swear you were seeing the wildest things. *Škriatokov. Víly.* Myths."

I hardly recognized the Slovak words. Dwarves? Fairies? Mom never told me Slovak folktales—this must be why. "So what?"

He glanced up at me for a half second, then focused on the metal side railing on my bed, shaking it to see if it was loose. "It wasn't just that. At the end, you had that . . . accident. Your mom—we—thought it might be connected. We couldn't stay there and risk anything happening again."

"Oh," I said, not sure how else to respond. I started to massage the burn.

"So you don't remember any of it?" Mom asked.

"Not much. The accident's a total blank, and everything else from then is just flashes and pictures. I was five, remember?"

"See?" Mom said, trying to sound bright. She walked over to the lone dresser in the room to get her purse. "We shouldn't have worried. Now we'll get out of your hair so you can get some rest."

I wasn't letting it drop that easily. "Why did it stress you guys that much, then?" I asked.

"What?" Mom asked, pausing with her purse over her shoulder.

"Dad, you're sweating like a pig."

He wiped his brow. The guy was turning into a spaghetti western extra. "It's just hot in here."

"Spit it out."

"It's not just that," he said. "Your mother's mother."

"I think that's quite enough for today," Mom said. She grabbed Dad by the arm and practically dragged him to the door.

"You mean Babka?" I said, even more confused. "What does this have to do with her?"

Mom smiled and stepped back to sit at the side of my bed. She stroked my hair. "You're tired. It's been a horrendous day. Let's leave it at that, okay?"

"What does Babka have to do with any of this?" I asked.

Mom swallowed, then shrugged with one shoulder. "I miss her. I don't like people talking about her—it still hurts too much. She died when I was in high school, and going back to Slovakia again . . . it won't be the easiest thing I've done. Your father's just concerned about me. Now stop worrying, and get some sleep."

And with the pulse monitor beeping, the oxygen mask over my face, the rawness of my eyes, and my persistent cough, sleep sounded really good right then. My house had just burned down. My parents had picked an odd time to fight about obscure family history, but then again, their house had just burned down too. Did I really want to get into an argument over this? I was tired. I was confused. I still felt like I had a point. Mom was uncomfortable talking about it, but what about *me*? She always pulled something like this. Didn't I deserve some straight answers?

Even if I did, it was clear I wasn't going to get them without a fight, and I wasn't up to a fight right then. Besides, I'd probably be confused by the answers if I got them. All of this was making my head spin. I leaned back in my bed. "Okay."

My father went over and picked up his keys from the dresser. He looked stiff—upset. But he tried to sound chipper. "All right then," he said. "We need to see about restoring some order to our lives. You stay here and rest. We'll go out and get you some new clothes."

Of course. My entire wardrobe had gone up in the blaze. The memory of my T-shirt and shorts smoldering on my skin came back in a flash. "Dad," I said. "My clothes were burning. I remember that. How is it I'm not touched?"

He looked at me and shrugged. "I don't know. All I can say is that it was a miracle. That's the only explanation we're likely to get."

CHAPTER TWO
BREAD AND CHEESE

The ability to interact with mystical creatures is typically hereditary, although an experienced Death can grant this to humans at will on a temporary basis. Having trouble telling your friends and acquaintances what you do for a living? Turn to Appendix M for more information.

The next month was a whirlwind of activity. My parents were waist-deep in paperwork and planning, both of them on the phone with people in Slovakia nonstop. We were going to live near my Uncle Ľuboš and his daughter, Katarina. His wife had died years ago from cancer.

The doctors were surprised at how quickly I got over my smoke inhalation. Within twenty-four hours, my cough was gone, and the redness in my eyes had disappeared. I could even breathe normally.

We still didn't know what had caused the fire, although the fire department guessed it had started in the office. It wasn't a stretch to see the fire starting in my imagination. A spark at the wrong place, and a flicker appeared, small at first, then spreading. Taking over the desk and my dad's books, and all the time I was upstairs, sleeping while my parents were out at the late movie.

What if I had been awake? I could have put out the fire right when it started. Or called 911 earlier. It didn't seem right that something that had such a big effect on our lives could have been stopped so easily. Why hadn't I stayed up later that night?

Each morning I woke up in the hotel, confused about where I was. I'd lost everything I had. My Indiana Jones box set. The original *Star Wars* poster Dad had got me for my twelfth birthday. The huge hard drive I'd taken days to back up all my movies on—gone.

Forever.

Once they let me go back, I went through the last week of school in a sort of muffled daze. I'd asked the principal, Mr. Hannigan, not to announce anything about what had happened. What was the point of letting my "peers" know the freak had been in another fire? They would have just increased their jibes. Having a huge disfiguring scar across your whole right arm and chest doesn't do wonders for your social life, in my experience. As it was, I still got hit in the neck with a spitball during first period (physics with Mr. Hubble) the day I returned. Classy.

People didn't like me, no matter what I tried. Each new year, I'd do my best to make conversation with the guys in my classes. (With girls, I was lucky if I could string a sentence together longer than three words without stuttering.) I'd force myself to try to branch out. It never worked. They were all *Scary Movie*, and I was *The Exorcist*.

American high school wasn't something I'd miss when I grew up, and that bugged me. It was something I was supposed to love. Where was my *Breakfast Club* moment? My *Clueless* clique? I wasn't even a Pedro for any Napoleon.

My mind kept drawing to what Mom had told me about Slovakia over the years. It had been Communist. It was mostly white, and people had a thing against Roma, which was one quarter of my heritage. *Roma.* That was the PC way of talking about Gypsies. I thought being a quarter Gypsy was cooler than being a quarter Roma. No one at school had a clue what Roma meant, but people thought Gypsies could tell fortunes, had dark good looks, and helped a hunchback now and then, if they felt like it. They were people from grand, adventurous stories.

Despite only being a quarter Roma, I was olive skinned like my mom. Would the Slovaks hold my skin color against me?

Would I have a thing against them?

All I wanted was a place where I was accepted and fit in, where I could live a normal life. Someplace where I wasn't so self-conscious about my burn, and where I found some good friends.

Was that too much to hope for?

By the time I'd endured a white-knuckled airplane trip over an entire ocean just waiting to drown me, I was willing to settle for a long sleep and a promise that I'd never see the ocean again. And don't get me started on the layover from Hades and the encore plane ride. When we landed in Bratislava, it was pitch black outside, despite my watch telling me it was six in the afternoon. I didn't want to see another plane for years. My legs ached, my eyes were parched, and my head felt crusty, like teeth that haven't been brushed in weeks.

The airport was a quarter of the size of the mall at home. The rental we ended up with was like a clown car. There wasn't enough room in the trunk for our luggage, so I was stuck in the back seat with a suitcase as big as me. Did I mention the car only had two doors and smelled moldy?

"See?" my dad said. "This is much better than the plane ride."

"You're in the driver's seat," I said.

Mom laughed. "It's only an hour and a half to Trenčín."

I grunted and leaned my head against the window, doing my best to zone out while the miles rolled by. I must have fallen asleep, because the next thing I knew, Dad was saying my name.

"Tomas. Tomas! Wake up. We're here."

I opened my eyes and blinked.

Dad had stopped the car next to a large ghetto-ish five-story apartment building. It wasn't well-lit, but from what I could make out, the whole thing was made out of gray slabs of cement. "What happened?" I asked. "Did the car break down?"

Mom cleared her throat. I was getting pretty sick of that sound. Any time my parents made it, bad news followed. She turned around and smiled. "This is where we're going to live. Isn't it wonderful?"

I checked out the window again. *Wonderful* wasn't the word that sprang to mind. *Commie project housing* was closer. I was rather proud of my restraint, though. All I said was, "In an apartment?"

"Not just any apartment," Dad said. "One of the nicest apartments in the city. Only ten minutes from the town center and right by the canal. It's going to be great."

Was "right by the canal" supposed to comfort me? It was like telling someone with arachnophobia that their house had plenty of spiders nearby. "Okay," I said. Maybe it was better on the inside. Or maybe I never should have agreed to move to Slovakia.

Mom got out, and after some fumbling around, I flipped the switch that leaned the front seat forward, letting me out too. Dad locked a big yellow bar to the steering wheel. "Get all our bags. We'd better not leave them here."

I glanced up and down the street. Not a soul in sight. None of the windows even had light coming from them. I had to ask. "Who's going to steal it? A squirrel?"

"Just get your bags, Tomas," Mom said.

"Whatever."

We tromped up to the main door of the building. It was battered and scraped, and it could have used a new coat of brown paint. I would have preferred taking my chances sleeping in the car instead of risking my life by going into that place this late at night.

I surveyed the area while Dad was still fumbling for his keys. Across the street from us, there were some trees and a small playground, then a small hill that must have blocked the canal from sight. Thank goodness for small blessings. No other buildings, and the air smelled fresh, for a city. At least we weren't crowded in on all sides. The moon came out from behind the clouds, casting everything in a silver light.

Someone stood between the trees off to my right, watching us. I stared back, and that's when I noticed I could see a reflection of the moon off the person, almost as if they were made entirely out of water. Could I see through them too? A chill ran down my spine. The person—thing?—flicked out its hand toward me, and a fat drop of *something* cold and wet landed right in my eye. I jerked my head back and blinked to clear my vision. When I could see again, the person was gone. Another drop of something landed on the sidewalk next to me, and then another. Rain. Maybe going inside was a better idea. I was obviously too tired, and if I didn't get some sleep soon, I'd start seeing the things my dad worried I'd seen before.

Dad had unlocked the door, and we went inside. A set of stairs went all the way to the top, with landings at each level, each with two apartments. "Where's the elevator?" I asked, my voice echoing off the walls.

"Not so loud," my dad said in a hushed tone. "There isn't one. Our place is this one on the left." He locked the main door behind us, then opened our apartment and turned on the lights.

I went in with low expectations, but I was still disappointed.

The entryway had bare walls and worn flooring tiles. There was a hall to my right, and a small room to my left. The walls were plastered, but they still looked like cement, and the plaster was cracking. Strangest of all, the whole place had twelve foot ceilings. It was a hole, but it was trying to be a high-class hole, at least.

Mom was beaming. "Wonderful."

Dad nodded. "Just like old times, huh?"

I dropped my bags and walked down the hall. It led to another small room and the living room. Or, the living room, dining room, and kitchen, all jammed into a space as big as our kitchen had been. The fridge was ancient, the stove seemed ready to blow up if we tried to use it, and the floor was linoleum that was old enough to apply for Social Security. Someone had laid out bread and cheese on the table, I assumed in preparation for our arrival. There was another bedroom off the living area.

I faced my parents, who were grinning and holding hands. "We can't live here," I said.

Their smiles drained away. "Come on, Tomas," Dad said. "It's not *that* bad."

"Yes," I said. "It is."

Mom came up to me and hugged me. "Give it a week, a bit more furniture, and some paint, and you'll see what we see. I promise."

I gaped at her. "Mom, no offense, but it's going to take a whole lot of paint to make this place be a quarter as good as our house was."

That brought silence. Curse it. I hadn't meant to say that, but it was still easy to forget home was nothing more than charred timber.

Mom forced a laugh. "Get ready to sleep. Your room is down the hall on the right just as you come in. We'll worry about getting the place more livable in the morning."

"It'll be great," Dad said. "Just picture it. A big screen TV on that wall.

Surround sound speakers there and there. Couch right here. The room back in the hall will be my office. You'll love it, Tomas. Trust me."

Maybe it could work. But I was tired, and Dad's enthusiasm wasn't exactly contagious right then. I couldn't help thinking that agreeing to move had been a mistake. I rolled my suitcase into my room, which did indeed have a bed, although it was hot as an oven in there. I cracked the window—no air-conditioning. Outside, the rain had picked up and was now pelting the ground in earnest. At least it brought some cool breezes. I rifled around until I found my toothpaste and toothbrush and headed to the bathroom. Another problem—no toilet.

"Mom!"

She came in after a moment. "What's the matter?"

"Where's the toilet?"

"It's the next room over." She stepped out and pointed. Why did an apartment as small as this one devote two whole rooms to something that only needed one?

"What's it doing there?" I asked.

"It's just the way they do it here. Look at it this way. You won't have to wait to go to the bathroom when someone else is in the shower. If you think of it, it makes more sense than how they have it in America."

"Seems dumb to me."

Mom stomped her foot on the tile. "Would you drop it? Do you realize this is the city—the country—I grew up in? It's so much better than it used to be. If you ever had to experience what I had to go through. My family had to wait ten years to get a car. Three-hour lines for toilet paper. No fresh fruit. We . . ." She shook her head and left without another word. I felt about two inches tall.

I stood there for a moment and then went about getting ready for bed by rote. Before I knew it, I was lying down with the lights out, staring at the ceiling and touching my burn while I suffered through AC withdrawal. Mom was right. Maybe I had been thinking too much about myself. They had given me the choice of coming here or not, and this was what I had chosen. I would have to live with this, even if my bed had no springs and my room was a quarter the size of my old one.

Whether I liked it or not, there was no going back.

CHAPTER THREE
WATER

Vodniks have an aversion to fire or heat of any kind, and if left without a source of water, they have been known to drip to death. They are allergic to salt, which acts as a mild irritant. They do their best to appear harmless, and many an Assassin has fallen prey to them over the years.

Time to get up."

I opened my eyes, then squinted against the sun. My room had a big window, and only some sort of lace thing for a curtain. Dad was standing by my bed. "What time is it?" I asked.

"Eleven. We'll have to hurry if we're going to make it." He went to leave.

"To make what?"

"You'll see." He closed the door behind him.

A large part of me wanted to go back to sleep. When I checked my watch, I figured out why. It was 5:00 A.M. back in Pennsylvania. If it hadn't been for that promising tone in my dad's voice, I would have closed my eyes immediately. As it was, I stumbled up and headed for the shower. If I had to face the day and the public, I could at least look half decent doing so. Of course, once I realized that the shower was some sort of handheld thing, a simple baseball cap was more tempting. Still, when you have a disfiguring burn that covers your whole right arm, you need every little bit of better-looking you can get, even if it involves water.

I got in the shower.

How did a guy who was deathly afraid of water manage to clean himself on a daily basis? Uncomfortably. It had taken a lot of parental persuasion (and a great deal of mocking at school), but there came a time when I'd had to acknowledge that deodorant could only do so much. Weekly showers couldn't cut it anymore, and I had to up it to daily. Never baths, though. And always as fast as I could get it done. Which turned out to be not so fast that morning.

Sixteen years of experience cleaning myself wasn't enough to prepare me for how to do it when one of my hands was always occupied with the showerhead. Water kept spraying everywhere, and it was only a matter of time before I hit my face with the stream. My eyes flooded; my ears even got doused. I gasped, and everything went strange.

Really strange.

With a sound of rushing wind and a flash of blinding white, I wasn't in the shower anymore. I was in a fat white eight-year-old body that had never been mine, sitting in a boat on a river—a river!—I had never seen, and I was wearing clothes that came straight from Ye Olde Medieval Faire: a white shirt, white pants, black vest, and a white coat—all of it with enough colored embroidery to keep a room full of grannies going for a year. The coat alone had multicolored flowers stitched along every seam and pocket outline.

"Where to?" someone said.

A white girl—maybe sixteen—was sitting across from me. She was dressed similarly, just with an apron and skirt instead of vest and pants. All white.

I leaned back and kicked my feet up, getting precariously close to the river. "Let's just float," I said. "The wedding will last forever, and there's nothing to do anyway."

What was happening? My phobia was somehow dulled. Normally I think I'd be hyperventilating if I found myself in a boat. Still, all that water was making it hard for me to concentrate.

The girl leaned back as well, tilting her head up to the sky and smiling. She was pretty. Long brown hair that fell well below her shoulders, with eyes that matched the river and a nose that was just a size too big. She glanced behind her at the shore, then said, "I told you we'd find something to keep us busy."

I laughed, my voice high and piping to my ears. "Busy, or beaten if whoever owns this boat ever finds us."

She opened one eye to peek at me, the blues in her embroidery making her eyes seem brighter. "Beat us? They wouldn't dare. Besides, it's bound to be some stuffy merchant who wants to pander to Father anyway. They'd be overjoyed to let his two children go out for a ride. Why worry?"

"Right," I said. "Well, shouldn't we see if there's anything interesting in this thing?"

"Steal?" she asked.

"No. Borrow." There wasn't much in the boat. A quick search turned up a solitary leather satchel.

"Anything?" The girl had sat up and was leaning forward to see what I came up with. Not much, unfortunately. Some hard rolls and a sausage, a few handkerchiefs, and—

"Look at this!" I had caught a glimpse of something shiny and went after it. She leaned even closer and smiled when I took out a gleaming bracelet. It was made of polished copper fashioned into a series of flat tight spirals.

"Beautiful," she said.

So was she. Why did I have to be her fat prepubescent brother in this dream? I held the bracelet out to her. "For you."

She took it with a grin and a gleam in her eye. "You shouldn't have. It's—"

The boat hit something in the water and sent the two of us rocking. The girl's expression changed from mischief to worry, and I clenched the side of the boat. "Sandbar?" I asked.

She shook her head and scouted behind us. "The river's deep at this part. There shouldn't be any—"

The boat rocked again, tilting so much that water splashed inside. Part of me—the not-an-eight-year-old-boy part—was still freaking out from all that water. "We didn't hit that," I said. "That hit us."

"Ondrej, what are you talking—"

"Something hit us. Something big."

She went for one of the oars and passed it to me. I took it one-handed, not willing to let go of the boat with my other. She hefted the second oar, ready for a swing. And then we waited.

Nothing.

The breeze riffled through my hair. Birds chirped in the distance. Nothing broke the surface of the river. Maybe it had just been something on the bottom after all. A sunken ship? In a river?

After a moment, the girl leaned over the water, peering down.

Something grabbed me by my coat and jerked me backward. I screamed in surprise and the oar clattered to the boat bottom, but I held tight to the gunwale, so that instead of being pulled out, I was still half in when the girl whirled to see what was happening.

She gasped in surprise and lunged over to beat at whatever had me. All

I could see were two grimy wet hands gripping my coat and pulling as hard as they could. This was human?

A spout of water shot out from behind me and hit the girl right in the face, pushing her off balance and back in the boat. One of the hands let go of my coat and pried at my fingers, its flesh cold and soggy, with sharp nails that dug into my skin. I yelled and jerked my head back to knock the thing in the face, but I was in a kid's body. I was no match for it.

It got my hand free just as the girl was getting up from where she had fallen. She had time for a final swing of the oar, but it went wide. "Lesana!" I yelled, and then was wrenched back over the gunwale and into the river.

The last thing I saw was the girl's panicked face, and then a hand covered my eyes, and there was only darkness and water.

And coughing and sputtering.

I was back in the shower, blinking my eyes and shaking my head free from the water that had hit me in the face. I put down the showerhead and grabbed my towel and just stood there, staring at the wall.

Could that have been jet lag? Sleep deprivation? Didn't some tumors bring on visions? But where would I have come up with that scene? And that girl—Lesana? No. Severe sleep deprivation. My hands were shaking.

"Tomas!" It was my dad from outside the door.

"Coming!" I'd ignore the vision. If it happened again—after a full night's rest—then I'd worry about it. But for now, with all the changes that had happened in my life, who knew what stress and no sleep could do to my body. Maybe dreaming you were a fat eight-year-old was a typical response. Either way, I forced myself to think about getting ready, and tried to put the water-induced *whatever* behind me.

Five minutes later, we left the apartment. The daylight assaulted my eyes, and I had to sneeze twice before it was better. We had gone out the back door, which led to a courtyard with trees and another playground.

People were out and about, shouting in Slovak and staring at me as much as possible. Enough that I started to wonder if I had a flashing neon "American" sign above my head.

"Ready?" Dad asked as Mom came out the door. "Or should I say, *Si hotový?*"

"Ha ha. Where's the car?" In the sunlight, it was easier to believe that the vision had been some sort of fluke. An overactive imagination, maybe. Nothing to do with the things I'd seen when I was five.

"We're not driving," Mom said. "The castle's in the city center. No cars allowed, and the closest parking would still be a long walk. Your father was serious. We're going to have to start talking Slovak. *Angličtina nám tu nepomôže. Ideme.*"

I understood that last word: let's go. I mulled over the other sentence as I followed my parents toward the center of town. Usually Mom slowed down when she talked to me in Slovak, but that had been said at a normal rate, which meant that most of it sounded like one long word. With some effort, I deciphered it: *English won't help us much here.* Maybe not, but I'd pick up the Slovak in no time. All I needed was a bit of brushing up.

We passed row upon row of gray apartment buildings, each one with similar battered doors and nosy people who all paused what they were doing to gawk at us. I actually saw one mother grab her child and keep him from coming near us. Mom had warned me things were different here. Through all those years of Communism, there had been Slovaks and Roma—no other races, and here in western Slovakia there weren't even many Roma. So I guess it made sense we stood out, but it still made me feel like I was on the sex offender list. I was used to being stared at for my scarred arm, but I could usually turn that off by wearing long sleeves.

You can't exactly "turn off" your skin color.

Maybe I was being sensitive—looking for racism when there really wasn't any. Maybe people were just checking out the new neighbors. Nothing strange about that.

I studied the city as we walked. It was odd to see all these signs in a language I had (sort of) spoken all my life, but had never really seen as important.

Lekáreň, Slovenská Sporiteľňa, Kvetinárstvo. And it wasn't just the words that were strange. The logos, the fonts—the signs themselves were weird. Foreign. Duh.

I kept glancing up, each time expecting to see the castle, but it was never there. When it did appear, it was like it had sprung from the earth. One minute the buildings had nothing above them but sky, and the next the castle was looming over us like it had never been hiding at all. It had a main tower with several outbuildings and a series of walls that hunched up around the central keep like an army protecting its king. Some parts were crumbling, true, but that only added to the sense of age. It was easy to picture an army camped around it, laying siege for months at a time. It could have come right out of *Lord of the Rings*. I mean, it was no Helm's Deep, but it was an easy Helm's Shallow. That castle alone made me regret never having pressed Mom to find out more about Slovakia. Why didn't I remember it?

From far away, the main tower gave the biggest impression, rearing up over the rest of the castle like a dragon surveying its hoard. I could make out specks of birds flying around it, as well as dots of color: people walking around an observation platform. The top of the tower, instead of being open to the air, was covered in wood, like it was wearing a square hat. But it was an old square hat, so it managed to fit in with the rest of the structure.

My dad caught my shirt, stopping me before I stepped into traffic. I barely noticed—the castle was too interesting.

"Are we going there now?" I asked, sounding like a kid waiting to go to the toy store. I couldn't help it.

"Yes," he puffed. "Just keep walking."

We walked under an overpass and out into a park, and the billowing trees blocked further view. The park led to the base of the castle's hill, and we descended into another tunnel that crossed beneath the street. The graffiti-laced walls stunk of cigarettes and urine, and a group of guys a bit older than me were hanging out toward the far side, smoking and laughing. They quieted when they saw us coming, elbowing each other and nodding in our direction with some half smiles. Mom and Dad didn't seem to pay them any attention, and the guys didn't say anything to us specifically, but when I glanced back at them after we had passed, they were still watching us. Me. The one in the middle reminded me of Draco Malfoy. Thin, blond, and snide. He flipped me off before I turned and caught back up with my parents.

I was happy to be out in the fresh air again, although when we walked up the other side, we were too close to see the castle anymore.

The roads on this side were narrow and made of cobblestone, which wasn't the most comfortable surface to walk on. It felt like I was moving over a road made of solid bubble wrap.

The street went up steeply to the right, and then switchbacked to the left. Now I could see the castle again. Closer, it was clear that some of its walls were crumbling. There was a giant steel construction canopying the road, protecting it from a chunk of wall that had slipped down the hill.

When I'd first gone to Disney World, I'd been pissed that the castle was just a glorified gift shop and tunnel. But this was no Cinderella's castle, and it had the ruins and safety hazards to prove it. Not to mention the steep hill. No wonder no one would attack a well-built castle on high ground. I was winded just walking there.

The road ran straight through a stone arch in the outermost wall, and a man sat in a building by the gate, idly reading a magazine. No one was in line to buy tickets. Inside the entrance gate (a huge affair of aged metal and rivets) another man shouted to us and waved. Mom smiled and waved back, then walked up to talk to him. After a bit of chatter, Mom came back and we continued up the hill, which only got steeper.

"Okay," Dad said. "You've got to close your eyes from here on."

"What?"

"I promised your uncle he'd be able to give you the castle tour himself, but he can't meet us just yet. So close your eyes, okay?"

I sighed, but my leftover guilt from yesterday made me cave. I closed my eyes, leaving them open a crack so I could at least not stumble into anything.

Dad guided me by pushes after I refused to hold his hand. (What was I, two?) We kept walking, and the path leveled out. I waited to hear the crowds. A castle this awesome had to be packed to the rafters with tourists, but all I heard was our footsteps and Mom and Dad chatting.

We went up some more and then stopped, and I heard what sounded like a wooden beam being taken from a door, followed by the sound of the door opening.

"Watch your step," Dad said.

I tripped over a big step but managed to not fall down. Then I was allowed to open my eyes.

We were standing outside the castle walls, the city spread out before us in a patchwork of buildings, with a river cutting through it. It looked so different from home. All the roofs were red tile, and the buildings snaked together, the alleys forming mazes below.

This was Europe.

Dad put his hand on my shoulder and said slowly, "*Prídeme tam neskoro. Poď.*" We'll be late. Come.

I took a last glance at the city, then nodded. There would be plenty of time to explore later. The path we were on hugged the outside of the castle wall, leading to a ruined staircase that was a lawsuit waiting to happen, but it fit in with the surroundings. Halfway down it started to smell horsey, and at the bottom lay a clearing about as big as half a football field. Three quarters of it was filled with a fenced area full of loose dirt by the outer castle wall. It was lined with lances, shields, and banners, all brightly painted. The area had a long fence running through the center, turning it into a giant loop. The rest of the clearing had rough bleachers with all of fifteen or twenty people sitting there, looking almost apologetic for being so few in number.

"It's a joust," Mom said as we climbed the empty bleachers. "Your uncle is part of this group. It's his job. Well, in addition to being one of the night watchmen here at the castle."

It wouldn't be his job much longer if no one came to the performances. Maybe their group sucked—they'd come out in tinfoil armor and papier-mâché helmets. I settled into my seat. It wasn't the most comfortable thing in the world—wooden planks and a metal frame that radiated the summer heat. Way more rickety than the solid American quality I was used to.

Just as the show was starting, an olive-skinned girl came to sit next to me, smiling. Long dark hair, gorgeous brown eyes. Model-level hotness.

I stared for a moment, managed to eke out a smile in return, and tucked my right hand against my side. Maybe there was some Roma camaraderie thing at work, but if she caught sight of my arm, any friendly feeling would disappear faster than I could sneeze. The girl grinned even wider and waved. Her hair reached halfway to her waist, and her features were a mix of Disney's version of Esmeralda in *Hunchback* and Angelina Jolie. Just younger. I nodded and scooted a little farther away from her, then acted like I was more interested in the joust.

I was such a wuss.

A man came out dressed in a red robe and cloak with white fur on the edges, and I breathed a sigh of relief. No tinfoil. The outfit was completed with a white cap, leather belt, and leather bag on his side. He strode onto the field and started talking in Slovak. "*Vítame vás na turnaji . . .*"

My parents had sat in front of me, but Mom craned her neck around to translate for me. "He's welcoming us, and he's excited for the battle that's about to begin. A"— she paused as she listened to the man some more—"challenge has been declared between the Slovak knights and some visiting French knights. They've decided to settle it today by the typical contests."

Mom and I were both startled by a voice to my left. "I can translate for you, if you'd like."

I looked over to see the girl. She had sidled closer while I was focused on listening to my mom.

Mom beamed. "Oh! Hello! Thank you so much. That would be wonderful."

I couldn't believe it. My mom was willing to just shove me off on a stranger? A beautiful stranger my age who had one of the most enticing accents I'd ever heard, and skin color just a shade darker than mine? With perfect cheekbones, a sculpted nose, full lips—I tried to stutter out a thank you, but she stopped me by placing a hand on my shoulder. She was touching me!

"Don't worry about it. Let's watch. Oh—and you can call me Katka."

Why had I ever worried about going to Slovakia? She leaned in close to me and began to translate, her voice low and right in my ear. For the first while, I couldn't pay any attention to what was going on in front of me. She had a mellow voice that was perfect: not too squeaky and not too low. And every now and then, her breath would tickle my ear. I had to fight the urge to peek at her, forcing myself instead to concentrate as much as I could on what was happening on the field. I kept my right arm so close to my body it might have been glued there.

Six riders galloped onto the field, each of them decked out in a different style and color of armor, and each of them going full blast, their horses tracing the edge of the ring and kicking up clods of dirt. Mom turned around to me and pointed at the knight dressed in blue and yellow with white griffons. "That's Ľuboš."

I gawked at him, my mind on overload—there were too many cool things at once. He was everything a kid could wish a father to be, but I'd settle to claim him as an uncle. His horse was a monster, decked out in an outfit that covered its head and body down to its hooves, all blue and yellow, just like my uncle's armor. Most of the knights' armor was covered in cloth, but from the glimpses I got and the pieces that weren't concealed, I could tell this was the real deal. The steel was solid and well used. My uncle had curly brown hair that fell to his shoulders and a beard that would have made King Arthur proud. For being half Roma, he was pretty darn light-skinned, especially compared to my mom and me.

The next hour and a half flew by. We were so close to the action I had to wipe dirt from my face twice. Nothing about this was fake. When my uncle and the knight in red started to duel with axes and shields, I thought for sure someone was going to get maimed. They were hacking with all their strength, splinters and hunks of wood flying from their shields with each blow. But they were both good enough that neither penetrated the other's defenses until my uncle rushed the red knight and knocked him to the ground. His axe was at the fallen man's throat in a second, and the red knight yielded. Katka cheered just as loudly as I did, but I wished there were a throng of people to roar with us.

It hadn't taken me long to forget about being nervous in front of her. She had a laugh that was infectious and an easy manner that melted my fears. Before I knew it, I was pointing with my right hand at something on the field. I froze, my eyes riveted by the sight of my scarred arm, its white and red and yellow mottled pattern held out in the open for anyone to see, practically right in front of her face.

It didn't faze Katka for a second. I could tell she had seen it—I saw her eyes pause for a moment at my arm. But instead of the usual expression of disgust or "I want to look away but I just can't," she ignored it, pointing at something else and continuing the conversation.

I felt like I had died and been reborn as Brad Pitt. Moving to Slovakia was worth every bit of worry and mental anguish. Maybe it was a bit premature, but I couldn't help thinking that for the first time in my life, I had a shot at a girlfriend.

The tournament ended to enthusiastic applause from the bleachers, but there was no way fewer than thirty people could make the cheers sound properly loud. All the knights saluted each other and their audience and galloped back to their tents.

My parents smiled at Katka and me. I felt a goofy grin spread all over my face. "Did you have fun?" Dad asked.

I nodded. "It was a blast."

My mom patted Katka on the arm. "Thank you so much for helping translate."

"Don't worry about it," she said.

Meanwhile, my uncle had emerged from the tents and was headed toward us. He had some of his armor off, and he was sweating more than a fat kid in gym class. He took my mom in a bear hug. She groaned, and I thought I heard a few ribs crack. Then he slapped my dad on the shoulder, shook his hand, and beamed at Katka and me.

He barked a laugh. "*Tomáš! Vyrástol si.*" You've grown. "*A vidím, že si sa už skamarátil so sesternicou.*"

He was speaking too fast.

Katka leaned toward me and translated. "He's happy we've become friends so quickly."

I frowned. "Why?" I asked at last.

She laughed. "Because I'm your cousin, silly. Katarina."

CHAPTER FOUR

COKE

Appendix E.3.4. If you believe you've had a run-in with a Rasputin, take a moment to analyze the creature. Do you see the telltale scarring? If not, you're most likely mistaken. If the scar's not grisly or noteworthy, it's not a likely candidate. If you have been unfortunate enough to encounter a real Rasputin, please contact your supervisor immediately.

My smile went from genuine to forced in a heartbeat, though I tried to not let it show, no matter how confused I was. My cousin was this little girl in a picture in our living room. Or she was before the picture burned up. Sure I'd known the picture was old—but in my mind, she was seven years old. Whoops. I gave Katka a big hug (something I never would have done if she'd been the stranger I thought she was) and let Uncle Ľuboš grab my right hand and inspect my arm.

"*Nevyzerá to zle. Môžeš tým pohnúť?*" He studied me with such a serious expression that I worried he knew I'd been checking out his daughter.

Katka translated, "Can you move it?"

"Oh," I said. "Yeah." I took my hand out of his and swung it around, moving my elbow and fingers and feeling like the tin man showing he didn't need oil. It had taken years of physical therapy to get it so mobile, and all the doctors raved about what a miracle case I was. Usually with a burn that bad, the skin tightens, meaning your movement is hampered.

Even so, the skin grafts had never worked to smooth out the scar, I had trouble feeling with it, it didn't sweat, and it stung in the cold.

My uncle nodded. "*Vedel som, že sa ti to zahojí. Maš dobrý koreň.*"

Everyone laughed, so I assumed that was something good. I tried to laugh with them, but all that came out was an uncertain grin. The adults started chitchatting in Slovak, and I got lost. There seemed to be a debate going on, with my parents protesting and Ľuboš sounding reassuring, but it was hard to tell emotions in a different language.

Finally Ľuboš clapped his hands. "Come," he said in English. English! "I go change, but you meet my friends."

We trailed after him to the medieval tents. The jousting group members were milling around, hosing down horses, putting equipment away and changing into normal clothes. A woman walked past me in her underwear, and it took quite a bit of focus not to stare. I was in Europe. They probably went out for dinner in their underwear.

While Ľuboš disappeared into a tent of his own to change, Katka introduced me to his friends, a series of bearded men with names I promptly forgot. I was too impressed with their swords. One of them—Adam?—offered me his, and I took it carefully. It was heavier than I expected, but between the weight of the blade and the pommel, it balanced itself out.

I pointed the sword at Dad. "Hello," I said. "My name is Inigo Montoya. You killed my father. Prepare to die."

He laughed, but Mom rolled her eyes and said, "Put it down, Tomas. It isn't a toy."

Katka frowned. "I don't understand. How could your father kill your father? It is a joke?"

I blushed and tried not to appear hurried as I gave the sword back to

Adam. "No," I said. "Just a movie quote."

Adam flourished the blade and then pointed it at my chest. "To the pain," he said in accented but clear English.

I instantly liked the man. I'd have to educate Katka about fine American cinema later this summer.

"*Dobre*," Ľuboš said from behind me. He was coming out from his tent, just finishing pulling on a T-shirt. Even in normal clothes, he still seemed ready to do some serious damage. He handed me a Coke, which I took gratefully. It wasn't cold, but it was wet, and I was thirsty.

"Tomas," he said while I drank. "I have question."

"Yeah?" I said.

"You want job?"

"What?"

He sighed, then pointed up at the castle. "Castle Trenčín. We give tours, but we not have English tour guide. Katka does some, but we need native. You want job? I am night watchman here. I know boss, and I can get you job."

I looked from him to the castle and back, afraid I wasn't understanding. "You want to know if I'd like to work at the castle?"

Ľuboš laughed and shook his head, causing my heart to plummet. "Sorry," he said. "Too fast."

Katka explained in Slovak, and my uncle grinned. "Yes. You like to work at castle?"

I beamed. "I'd love to." Then I recalled who I was standing with, and I turned to my parents. "Can I?"

They nodded.

Ľuboš clapped his hands. "*Dobre.* Then I give you tour. Meet me in courtyard in fifteen minutes. Katka will take you." He babbled some stuff in Slovak I didn't catch.

My parents said their good-byes, and Katka grabbed me by the arm and dragged me back toward where I had come in. "He made me promise to get you to close your eyes again." She stopped in the middle of the path and smiled even broader. "I've never had cousin before. I have been planning this since I first hear you coming. I'm very happy you are here."

I was surprised her English had gotten worse so abruptly. During the tournament, it had been flawless. The change in her speech was endearing. Sure, it was like she was doing one of my dad's Boris and Natasha impersonations, but it gave her a flaw, which made her more approachable. We reached the door back to the main castle complex, and Katka opened it for me. I dutifully closed my eyes, still feeling kind of silly, but willing to endure it. She took me by the shoulders and led me through the door.

"So when did you start learning English?" I asked, trying a stab at conversation. Jet lag was starting to catch up with me, and I didn't want to let it.

"When I was eleven, although I don't have much chance to practice it except here at the castle."

So maybe she memorized those speeches, which would explain the sudden change in language ability. "How long have you been giving tours?"

"Two years."

We walked in silence for a while, her giving me nudges to keep me from running into anything, and me wishing I could think of something to talk about.

At last we stopped. "You can look now, but only one direction. No turning around."

I opened my eyes to see her smiling at me. I couldn't help smiling back, and in the process, I felt a little more comfortable. I was facing the main entrance. It was still as dead as it had been before. Three guys about our age were huddled over by a modern building made from steel and glass, which stuck out amid all this history like a drama kid on the football team. They waved at Katka, but they ignored me.

"Where are all the people?" I asked.

Katka glanced past me, back up toward the castle. "Don't bring that up when my father comes, okay? It's . . . difficult, especially on days like this. Usually, we have better crowd, but it's getting worse. After wall fell down—" She cut off in midsentence, her face suddenly twisting in pain. She put a hand to her right temple.

"Are you okay?" I asked.

She shook her head, but didn't say anything.

"What's wrong?" Was someone nearby who could help?

"Just a headache," Katka said. She was back to normal, her face pain free.

Right. In my experience, headaches didn't come and go at the drop of a hat.

"Anyway," she said, ignoring what had just happened, "my father worries enough about the crowds already. If we don't get more people here, we might lose castle."

That jolted me from my train of thought. "What?"

"It belongs to the city now. If we can't keep castle in proper shape, it will be sold to someone who can."

"Like who?" I asked.

She frowned. "Can we talk about something else?"

I nodded, my mind racing to come up with another topic. I was saved by an interruption.

"Excuse me."

A short man—maybe a slice over five feet—walked up from behind me, coming into view to look up at me. Two other things stood out about him besides his height: his wild, bushy hair and the fact that he was wearing a dark turtleneck despite the heat. He had eyes that were straight out of Santa Claus: twinkling and merry was the only way to describe them. Better yet: he'd spoken in English.

"Yes?" Katka said, also in English.

"I don't mean to interrupt. I mean, I know it's rude and everything to come up to complete strangers and just start talking. Just start blathering away. But I heard you speaking English. Not that I was eavesdropping. Never that. But the language does stick out a bit. I'd say like a sore thumb, but with less pain. That *was* English, wasn't it? Not Dutch or Swedish or Swahili?"

I smiled. English! "Yeah," I said. "It was English."

He chuckled. "American English, no less. How impressive. Are both of you American?"

Katka seemed to be having a hard time following the guy's words. He had an accent, but I couldn't place it. Some place European, probably.

"No. Only me. I just got here yesterday."

"Allow me to welcome you to Slovakia. I'm Víťazoslav. Víťo for short." He thrust out his hand, and I shook it. It was soft and moist, like he slathered on hand lotion.

Víťo adjusted the sleeves of his turtleneck. Now that I'd seen him for a bit, I noticed he had some huge sweat stains going on in that thing. You could have wrung it out and gotten a half gallon. "I don't mean to intrude," he said, "but I wanted to be sure to speak with you before you scurried off somewhere. You never know, with Americans. Will you be here long?"

I nodded. "We moved here."

He rolled his eyes in exaggerated joy. "Oh! Yes! Fantastic. Superb.

Will wonders never cease? And now, for the next question. You wouldn't, by any chance, have anything against a strange man coming up to you when he sees you in the city or the castle, would you? And when I say strange man, I mean me. And when I say come up to you, I mean come to practice English with you. Would you be opposed to such a situation?"

"I . . . guess not?" I kind of wanted to say no, but couldn't think of a polite way to do it.

Víťo smiled again. He had a big mouth. You saw more teeth in his grin than you expected. "May the moon of peace and prosperity shine down upon your posterior. Or is that posterity? I get the two mixed up. See? I need the practice." He raised his hands in the air. Thankfully, BO didn't accompany the pit stains, or the whole castle would have been a biohazard site. "But enough. Enough, Víťo. You've taken enough of the kind lad's time. I'm off. We shall see each other again, good sir. Certainly we shall. What was your name?"

"Tomas."

"Of course it is. What else would it be? Well, Tomas. A token for your generosity, and a down payment on next time." He flipped a coin in the air toward me, and I caught it. I tried to turn to thank him, but Katka stopped me as Víťo rushed past me up the hill.

"No turning around. Besides, my father is almost here."

I nodded and examined the coin Víťo had given me. It was well-worn and shoddily minted. It had a picture of a shield on each side, with some hard-to-read writing circling the edge. The date was clear, though: 1690.

A hand clamped down on my shoulder. "Who was that man?" Ľuboš asked, coming to stand in front of me.

I shrugged. "Some guy. He wants to practice English with me, and he gave me this."

Ľuboš took the coin from me and studied it for a moment. "This . . . Kreuzer. Old. Good condition. Maybe fifty dollars. The man, he spoke English?"

"Yeah," I said, still marveling that someone had casually tossed me fifty bucks worth of coin. "Do you know him?"

He frowned. "No. Probably here snooping for Germans." He trailed off, and if anything, I could have sworn he growled. Whatever his thoughts were, he shook his head and clapped his hands loudly. "No matter! Time train new American ace tour guide. Please turn around and meet your new job."

CHAPTER FIVE
SPIT

Spirits aren't to be confused with vilas. While vilas each have their own element and are formed by ancient forces of nature, spirits are simply souls that lost their way at one point or another, becoming bound to an element in the process. A spirit might be tied to an element, but a vila *is* that element. It's a slight but significant difference, as you'll no doubt discover in time.

The castle plateau was as big as my high school grounds back home, and almost every bit of it was old. There were trees as thick around as five of me, and a large amphitheater lay ahead with an enormous stone well by it.

Ľuboš pointed at the modern building where the teens had been hanging out. "See that?"

I nodded.

"That is stupid," he said. "Look at where we are. This castle was built by at least 179 AD. There were trees. There were rocks. There were no steel I beams and plate glass. The first thing you must know about Trenčín castle is that Communists restored it. They were more interested in making new style of architecture than doing good restoration."

His voice grew louder, dropping into a singsong pattern that indicated this wasn't the first time he'd said this. Plus, his English was much better when talking about the castle. "Now," he continued, "we are having many troubles with maintenance. The Communist work is falling apart. In some cases, this is very bad. We don't have money to make repairs. In other cases, this is very good. Get rid of bad renovations for free. If only stupid glass building would fall down. Hot in summer. Cold in winter. Stupid gift shop that sells no gifts."

Katka and I followed as he strode across the terrace, weaving between the amphitheater's wooden benches, and to the well. It had a waist-high stone wall with wooden beams supporting a pointed roof. I didn't get much closer. After all, wells meant water, and even if the thing was covered with an iron grate, I didn't want to risk falling in.

Ľuboš saw I was still ten feet from the well and motioned for me to come forward. I shuffled a foot or so more, but he would have to pay me to go farther. He laughed and shook his head. "Whatever." He gestured at the well. "This is Well of Love."

"Is that like, the tunnel's mother?" I asked slowly.

Ľuboš creased his forehead in confusion. "Not tunnel. Well. Legend says it was built long ago by man named Omar. His love, Fatima, was captured by the lord of the castle then, Stefan Zapolsky. When Omar found out, he rushed to Stefan and offered him anything—Omar was very rich, and he had much to trade. But Stefan said only thing the castle lacked was water, and that if Omar could give him that, he would let Fatima go.

"Omar and his men dug for three years, eighty meters straight down, before they reached water. In the process, almost three hundred of his men died. When they found water, Stefan was so happy, he let Fatima go. To this day, people come to well and throw in coins for luck in love."

"Eighty meters," I said, edging a bit closer to the well to show I was impressed. "Cool."

Ľuboš gave a half smile and walked over to stand by me. "And the whole story is lie. Actually, the well was started in sixteenth century. It took workers forty years to dig down eighty meters, and by the time they got there, they still hadn't found water. But with rainfall, the well collects enough water to act as artificial . . ." He frowned, then said, "*Umelá nádrž.*"

"What?" I asked.

"Place for water—about fifteen meters deep usually, but all fifteen meters of it is bad for drinking now. Too many minerals from rock walls. As tour guide you must know the legend of the Well of Love—very popular tourist attraction. We clean the coins out twice a year. Good for money. Let's go. Much to see."

He led us on a whirlwind through the armory and some outbuildings, and then we headed up the hill. The path curved past a murky pool on the right before it led to another gate in a wall. I stopped at the pool and stared at it, the wind blowing through my hair. Something about it was familiar. I started massaging my scar. Ľuboš and Katka stopped as well.

"Is this where it happened?" I asked.

Katka translated for her uncle, and he nodded. It was hard to believe something so small had affected my life so much. My scar tingled, like it could still feel the heat of the fire.

Ľuboš pointed at the pool. He spoke in Slovak, but Katka translated. "That is runoff from castle gutters. No doubt it is hard for you to see, but you will work at the castle now. You need to be comfortable, or else tourists won't be. We need the money. So don't think of that pool as the place you almost died. Think of it as castle runoff."

Katka patted me on the back, and they continued up, giving me a bit of space. The water in the pool swirled, and for a moment, I thought I saw a head staring out at me. The eyes in particular seemed well formed, two evenly spaced tight swirls that gazed up at me with an unreadable expression. I blinked, and it was gone.

Enough with the trip down memory lane.

Right before the main entrance to the keep, Ľuboš stopped on the wooden ramp's corner and pointed in front of him. "The wall fell away here a few years ago. Probably because of water damage. One night, I woke up in morning to see it was gone. I was just worried at first that I had done something. I was very glad to know it wasn't my fault, and that no one was hurt. Construction is working on it, but to replace the wall is very expensive. It will take many tourists to earn it back. Many." He trailed off, his face lined with worry.

Ľuboš didn't stop long, though. He shook his head and resumed his cheerful demeanor, taking us through a barbican and into the main castle, the central tower looming over us and blocking out the sun. The next hour was filled with him talking and us listening. In each building we entered, he'd pause and mutter something, then bow. Finally I asked, "What are you doing?"

He stopped and studied at me. "When I first started working at the castle, some of guides told me it was haunted. But of course people will say it's haunted, I thought. Good for tourism." His English here was pretty good, so I figured this was part of the tour too. He continued.

"One night, I was going on my watch route. The dog was out, it was late, and castle was empty. Normal. I was outside in the courtyard when suddenly the alarm goes off. Very loud. I find out what set it off, and it says something had been in one of the tower rooms. So I investigate with a flashlight. This was my first time dealing with the alarm going off, so I am very nervous. I search the building from top to bottom. No one was there.

"Then the dog starts to bark again and I see what he is barking at.

Across the courtyard, I saw a woman made out of water. Clothes, skin, hair—everything. I blinked, and she was gone."

A shiver ran down my back. That sounded just like the person I'd seen last night outside our apartment. Ľuboš continued.

"I didn't know what to do. I knew I had seen someone, but what if it was an intruder? I was not paid to be scared. I was paid to protect castle. So I took Stallone—the dog—with me and went to where I had seen the woman. When I got there, there was a puddle. Nothing was near the puddle. No leaky faucets. No pipes. It had not rained for days, yet there was the puddle.

"I look back where I had come from. Where I had been standing, a man was watching me. He was short, and dressed in full suit. He made no movement—just stared at me. I blinked, but he didn't disappear. Stallone didn't bark at him. I should have yelled to him. Asked who he was. What he was doing there. I am night guard. But I could not. I was shocked. Scared. We held that position for a minute, then he walked away.

"After I got enough courage, I searched the castle again. The whole complex, from the entrance gate to the tower. No one was anywhere. No locks were undone. No windows open. I didn't sleep for the next three days."

Ľuboš finished his story, and I remembered to breathe. I almost told Ľuboš about my experience from the night before, but then a quick glance at Katka made me hold my tongue. "Who do you think they were?" I asked.

My uncle sighed, then spoke in Slovak with Katka translating. "I will tell you something I don't tell tourists. And you are not to repeat it."

I nodded.

"Many believe Trenčín is cursed. Of course they blame Roma. When do they not? Stupid. But it is fact: there are more drownings here than anywhere else in Slovakia, and that is even with many people avoiding water. I think the man and woman are connected to these deaths. Maybe angry spirits from the castle's history."

The town was cursed? And of course it would be drowning. I shuddered.

"Come," Ľuboš said, breaking my train of thought. "This is not talk for happy day. The tour continues. You asked what I say each time I enter a new building. I greet the real owners of the castle. This is not ours. We just use it. Remember that, and you'll be fine. And now, more tour."

Ľuboš led us to a stairwell going up. As he walked, he continued to talk. "No matter what else a castle was built for, whether beauty or sport, its main reason is always defense. In real castle, at least. Maybe Disney castles are different. Stupid."

We emerged to another chamber, one with low wooden beams. Ľuboš pointed at another doorway off to our left. "That is where the stairs continue. To an attacking army, this would be very confusing. They would not know the layout, and so they would become lost. Come."

The next stairwell was thinner than the first, and my elbows brushed either wall. "In tight space," Ľuboš said, "the person above on stairs has big advantage over the person below. Easier to defend and attack. Spiral stairs always go clockwise as you go up in castles. Defenders coming down can use their sword arms. Attackers coming up can't." He gestured with his arms showing how the central pillar of the spiral staircase would block a right handed person from swinging a sword if they were facing up.

This stair exited into an all white room with gothic windows. But for some strange reason, the doorway was shorter than the rest of the stairs, height wise. I almost banged my head on it before my uncle stopped me.

"Watch your head," he said, then moved to one side of the door and pretended he was holding a sword over his head, ready to strike. "The attacker would come through door and have to stoop. A defender could chop his head off easily, because by stooping, the attacker exposes weakness in his armor. Understand?"

"Yes." Medieval people were sick and sadistic, but they were good at what they did.

"Come," Ľuboš said. "Higher."

The stairway was now super thin, and I felt like I needed to breathe in just to keep walking. My elbows kept scraping the stone walls. This time, we exited into the open air. We had reached the wooden observation tower.

The entire city stretched out around us: the river snaking through the middle and weaving its way past a public pool and soccer stadium, the city center resting at the base of the castle, and the industrial and residential areas rearing up around it like younger but uglier and taller siblings. Birds flew around the tower, sweeping past in a flutter of wings and soaring low enough that we were looking down on them at times.

I might have had phobias of water and fire, but heights had never fazed me. I leaned as far as I could over the chest-high wall separating us from a fall. Then I spat. It was caught by the wind almost immediately, and I lost track of where it went.

Katka snorted, but Ľuboš laughed. I had thought he would. I smiled at him. "Trying to hit stupid tourists," I said.

His laughter deepened once Katka reluctantly translated for him. "Just don't do it too often," he said through her. "Bad for tourism, and we need money. And don't do it on tours." He sighed and pointed out around us. "That is the tour. Finished."

I cleared my throat. "So, uh . . . when can I start work?"

Ľuboš slapped me on the shoulder. "I give you tour script, and you memorize it. Study, and I will test you whenever you like. Once you pass, then you can do tours."

"Oh," I said. That was kind of a downer, but I should have expected it.

"Do you have any questions?" Ľuboš asked.

"Who owned the castle?" I said.

Ľuboš said something that sounded like a Slovak curse, though I had no clue which one. "I forget part of tour. Very bad example. Matúš Čak was main owner of castle. He was like king of entire area in 1300s. He died with no children, and his empire was broken up. But even though he had much money, it was never found and neither was his grave. There are rumors of secret tunnel beneath the castle that leads to his grave, where all his treasure lies.

"When Communists were renovating the castle, they discovered the castle's foundation rock was unstable. Many small caves and holes. So they filled them all with concrete. Stupid. Archaeologists have found tunnels beneath the city center, but they have never found any that lead to the castle. In my opinion, Matúš has a very simple grave that is unmarked. He was Catholic, and they didn't believe in fancy graves. He might be in a monastery somewhere. I don't really think it matters."

He held up a finger. "All that matters is legends bring in more tourists, and—"

"We need money," Katka and I said at the same time. We all laughed until I stopped because it felt a little too sitcommy.

Still, the thought of a buried king lying in mounds of gold was more than appealing. "What if the treasure were here?" I asked.

Ľuboš snorted. "Treasure. That's for children and fools who come here trying to dig up the property."

"What about all your talk about needing money for the castle?" I asked.

"Stupid," Ľuboš said. "We will not save castle with fairy tale. But enough of that. We go down now. I am hungry. We have barbecue at castle soon."

A barbecue sounded good. Before I left the tower, I took another look at the city around me. I could barely believe that just yesterday I'd been surrounded by the normal life of America. Slovakia was different, but there were definite perks. And who knew? Maybe underneath where I was standing, deep within the rock, lay a king's ransom in treasure.

CHAPTER SIX
KLOBÁSA

Even rarer than the ability to see mystical creatures, being able to actually interact with them—be affected by their actions—is both a blessing and a curse. Probably about five percent blessing and ninety-five percent curse, but studies thus far have been inconclusive. It doesn't help that most humans who can interact with these creatures end up dying quite quickly, or turning evil.

The tour had taken longer than I had thought. By the time Ľuboš had found the tour materials for me to memorize (which, granted, took a while—he wasn't the world's most organized person), the sun was already setting. We met my parents at the castle portcullis, the iron grate that slid down to block off the main keep from invaders.

Dinner was klobása with rolls cooked over a campfire made from castle wood scraps. The parents stayed by the fire. Katka kept me company twenty feet away. There were times when I hated myself for being so chicken. It wasn't like the fire was going to blaze up and burn everything down in an instant, but I couldn't force myself to have anything to do with flames. Even twenty feet away, I felt nervous and tied up inside, knowing my family was that close to such a big fire. Thankfully they were family and more than understanding. Ľuboš cooked the klobása himself and brought it over to us.

I had thought I had been eating klobása all my life—it was called Polish sausage in the States. Except now that I ate this, I realized what my mom had meant whenever she complained she couldn't get any good klobása. It was like every time I had ever eaten it, it had just been a glorified hotdog. This was *real*: it was filled with spices and the taste of smoke, and it hissed and spat when held over the fire to cook. Wherever the grease dripped into the flames, a tiny explosion shot up to the sky. I caught myself rubbing my burn quite a few times, and had to keep reminding myself to stop.

Above us the clouds had blown away to be replaced by the few stars strong enough to shine through the city lights. For a moment, I could almost believe we were living back in the medieval days, holed up in Trenčín castle and having an outdoor feast. True, the tower was lit up by gigantic floodlights, but I could eliminate those in my mind.

Katka and I talked in English while my parents discussed things with Ľuboš in Slovak. I caught my mom frowning at me a couple of times—she was still big on the Speak Only Slovak kick—but other than that, it was a relaxing evening. After a while, the adults left to go to another part of the castle Ľuboš wanted to show my dad. Katka and I kept chatting.

I was still stunned by how well the two of us got along. I'd never had a conversation this long with someone my age. Ever. And I hadn't even known her at the beginning of the day. Now I was telling her all about the finer points of *The Princess Bride*, Rob Reiner films, and William Goldman scripts. And maybe she wasn't understanding everything I was saying, but she seemed to genuinely care.

It was awesome.

In the middle of explaining the Dread Pirate Roberts, I saw a flash of light out of the corner of my eye. I turned to see the flames shoot up, doubling in size for a moment. I jerked backward. "Did you see that?" I asked Katka.

Katka looked over at the fire. "See what?"

It did it again, except this time, the fire burst up in a column into the sky, almost coming halfway up the castle tower and bathing the entire courtyard in orange light. Oddly, the flames didn't add any extra heat to the surroundings. Now I completely lost all sense of dignity. I grabbed Katka and dived for the only cover I could find: in this case, a bench near the picnic area. Katka shook me off, staring at me like I'd gone nuts, despite the fact that the fire was towering over her. I pointed. "That!"

A woman stepped out of the flames. Her skin, hair, clothes—everything about her was made up of solid fire. Her hair was a burning red in the shape of a woman's long locks, but where normal women would have strands of hair, she had strands of fire, each strand pulsing and flickering with the same light as the campfire. Her skirt had stripes, alternating shades of flame, and her blouse was the blue of the inside of a candle. Her skin was a lighter shade of orange, with her features well defined and beautiful. The air shimmered around her, like it does above pavement on a hot day.

A whole person, made of *fire*.

"What are you talking about?" Katka asked, raising an eyebrow in blank confusion with the woman five feet in front of her and the entire area lit up enough to see every cobblestone in minute detail.

So much for sleep deprivation and jet lag. It was at this point that I could no longer pretend I wasn't seeing things, or that nothing supernatural was happening. When you're standing bathed in the light emanating from a woman of flame, and the person you're with can't see a thing, either you're on drugs, or something's up.

"It's a woman made out of fire," I told Katka. "And she's standing right there." My cousin was craning her neck, scanning the entire area to find what I was talking about. In the firelight, I noticed a disturbing fact: Her widened eyes were still dilated enough for darkness, even though they should have been at pinpoints by now.

The woman peered at me. "Tomáš?" she asked, using the Slovak pronunciation, TOE-mosh instead of TOM-us. When she spoke, smoke came out of her mouth. Her voice, on the other hand, was normal.

I had no saliva in my mouth, and all I could manage was a nod. Would she burn me to a crisp? And how had she known me? Of course, who cared if she knew my name or not if all she wanted to do was fry me?

A *whole person* made of fire.

I wanted to run farther away—run anywhere—but I had no control of my legs. I couldn't even straighten up out of my crouch behind the low wall.

Her brow furrowed, the flames inside bending to the new shape of her forehead, creating small blue creases. Whoever heard of folding fire? She became . . . darker. Redder, like the color of glowing embers instead of a forest fire. Her dress and shirt turned black with red accents, and her hair was now just a dark auburn, with a tiny flicker of yellow every now and then, almost like highlights. I had to blink to readjust my eyes.

"Why have you returned?" she said. "And to the castle of all places. He will kill you if he finds you."

"Kill me? Who?" And how was she speaking English?

"What's happening?" Katka asked, narrowing her eyes as she stared intently in the direction I was looking.

The fire woman glanced at my cousin and sniffed, then snapped her fingers. Katka froze in place, not even breathing.

"What did you do to her?" I asked.

"Nothing. I did it to us."

I licked my lips, trying to get some saliva flow going in my mouth again. The fire woman gave off a muted sound of flames: hushed crackles and snaps that made me think of bonfires and witch burnings. "Um . . . who are you?"

She raised her eyebrows. "You do not remember?"

I shook my head. "Should I?"

She laughed. "I would hope so. I risked my life to save you." She took another step forward, and I retreated again.

"Are you trying to fry me?" I asked.

That stopped her. "Of course not. Why would I—"

It occurred to me that if she knew me when I was in Slovakia before, she might know what I couldn't remember. "You say you saved me—did you give me this at the same time?" I held up my burned arm.

The woman sighed. "Tomáš, I apologize, but it was for your own good. The vodník wanted your soul when he first saw you. He only pretended to be your friend. That is why I am surprised to see you back. He is not the kind to take failure lightly."

Vodník? If a gawk could be said to increase, that's what happened to me. "I was friends with you—and him? This vodník?"

"Of course you were. Don't you remember anything?"

A flash went through my mind—blazing white heat and water down my throat. "Tell me more," I said. Maybe if I had some more information, it would jog my memory.

She shrugged, sending small ripples of flame down her shoulders. "I don't know much more. It was here at the castle, at the little pool below. He lives here, of course—in the well. The humans were having a fair, and

I didn't arrive till late, once the bonfires were lit. When I did, he was already holding you under in the pool. I had to flare to save you, and I almost killed myself in the process. He wanted you so badly."

"Why?"

She pointed around us. "We cannot affect the world anymore. Before, yes, but something has changed since the old days. The vodník can still drown people. He can even still manifest to regular humans when he chooses. But his power is rare, and it's weakening. I cannot affect humans at all. Around you, it's different. It's like you let a piece of the old times live again. You're special."

Great. I'm lucky *and* special. "What's your name?"

"Ohnica." She looked up at the tower we were standing by, watching the bugs swarm the floodlights. I'd say one thing for a fire woman: she probably didn't have to worry about mosquito bites.

As I studied her longer, I began to get another tickle at the back of my thoughts. The image of me chasing after a ball made out of fire. Maybe I *had* seen her before.

"Well, Ohnica," I said. "Why are you speaking English? And why am I so special?"

"Language is irrelevant to us," she said. "We are understood in any tongue. And as to why you are special . . . I don't know. Some guess it's hereditary. But none of that matters. You need to stay as far away from this castle as you can."

"Do you mean the vodník guy?" I asked. "Why would he want to kill me so bad?"

"You escaped once. He does not forget that. If he decided to add you to his collection, he will keep trying."

"Collection? What *is* a vodník?"

Ohnica glanced at the fire, then back to me. "Time runs short. For the past decade or two, I am bound to active flames. Before, I could wander at will, as the vodník does. I am weakening. If you could build a large enough fire, I might be able to break free. Then I could be of more use to you. In the meantime, stay away from here. Get answers from the humans—they can tell you about *vodníkoch*."

"But I just got a job working at the castle," I said.

The fire woman sighed and headed back to the fire. "I cannot tell you what to do, Tomáš, and even if I could, you do not seem ready to believe me. If you insist on working at the castle, be prepared. Do not be alone near water, and do not get close to the well. When the vodník appears, you might have to kill him. I will come to help if there is fire nearby."

"Um . . . okay."

She considered me for a moment. "I understand this is all new to you. For now, know that I am your friend. If you need help, start a fire and I will come as soon as I can. Build one big enough, and I can do more. Hopefully we shall have some time to get reacquainted when you are less skeptical. I missed you. I hope you survive." With a final sunny smile, she disappeared back into the flames.

CHAPTER SEVEN
ICE CREAM

Some things really are just stories, of course. Many Slovak tales speak of Starenka, a woman who turns up to help heroes in their time of need. Despite how frequently she appears in these stories, our Investigations Unit has never been able to confirm her existence. We are reasonably confident she's just a figment of some storyteller's imagination.

The next day, Katka came over at eight—two in the morning back in Pennsylvania. Not that it mattered; I had woken up at seven on my own, and I hadn't been able to fall back asleep. Stupid sunlight. I'd managed to convince Katka last night that I'd just been kidding about the fire woman. I think she bought it mainly because of the culture difference between us. Thank goodness for that. My parents had taken me home—Katka had stayed at the castle with Ľuboš—and I'd been deep in thought since, trying to make sense of the mess I was in.

"Do you want to see the town?" Katka asked when I came to the door.

I looked down at the T-shirt and shorts I had on. "Why not," I said. There were advantages to sleeping in your clothes. I grabbed a baseball cap, slipped on some sandals, and off we went. The day was sunny and brisk, and the lawn in the park had just been cut, the air heavy with the scent of grass. It was nice to be outside and listen to the birds chirping in the trees.

When we got to the place where Mom and Dad had led me up to the left, toward the castle, Katka took me right. The street opened into a large plaza with a giant pillar in the middle. I pointed at it. "What's that?"

"It's a monument to the people of Trenčín who died in the cholera plague in 1710." Katka led me over to it. It had steps leading up to a square monument with a round pillar that had a tarnished statue of a man at the top. A couple of old women clustered around the base, hawking flowers and herbs. One of them walked up to me.

"*Kúpiš si bylinky?*"

I shook my head. From the look of her, she should have been in a nursing home. Her back was bent like a candy cane, and she was dressed with enough layers of skirts to make her hips jut out like a shelf. It was a wonder she hadn't melted yet in the heat. The skirt was patterned in black thread, and she wore a maroon blouse, with a black scarf covering her hair.

She inspected me from head to foot, shielding her eyes from the sun while she held her basket of herbs in her other arm. "*Nenechaj sa núkať. Viem, že ma vidíš. Treba ti kúpiť bylinky. Je vás dnes už tak málo.*"

I cleared my throat and looked for some help from Katka. She ignored me, staring off in the distance and rubbing her temple instead. Maybe this was her way of forcing me to speak Slovak? "I . . . uh—*Nechceš.*" *I don't want.* Sure, it was caveman speak, but it ought to give the granny the picture.

She babbled some more in Slovak and then laughed and smiled wider and nodded before prattling on some more. The woman was loony. She shoved a bundle of herbs toward me.

I held up my hands. "*Nechceš. Nechceš.*"

The smile left the old woman's face, reducing the wrinkles somewhat.

She said something else, her tone ominous. But maybe that was just me being confused. At last she sighed and tucked the herbs back into her basket, hobbling off.

"Ready to go?" Katka asked.

I glared at her. "Why didn't you help me out there?"

"What?"

"That old crone who just tried to pawn off some weeds on me."

"Crone?"

"The old lady." I went to point her out, but she was gone. The other grannies were there, but no crooked woman in black. "She was right here, rattling off Slovak that I couldn't understand a word of. No thanks to you." I was grumpier than I should have been, but I felt stupid and unnerved that the woman had disappeared. That was the problem with old people: they were always wandering off.

Katka sighed. "I don't know what happened. Maybe I was lost in thought. That happens with me from time to time. In any case, you are fine. No harm done. Come—we have more of the city to see."

At least it hadn't been a fire woman this time. Just a little old grandma, and there really was a lot more of the town to explore. At the same time, Katka seemed disturbed by what had happened too. She kept putting her hand to her head—just like she'd done yesterday, although her face wasn't pained this time. Then she noticed me staring, and I focused on the town.

In America, if something dated back to the 1800s, it was bordering on ancient. Here, people lived in buildings that had been around that long and didn't bat an eye. The city center ran in a large L-shape, with churches and town gates and fountains peppered throughout. There were some butt-ugly buildings too, made out of ten parts concrete and one part glass that Katka said had been put up by Communists. Masters of architectural atrocities.

We reached the bend in the L, coming to another open square where a tarnished copper statue sat: a man in a well, water shooting from his mouth in a steady stream. "What's that?" Where the water hit the ground, it leapfrogged to another spot, where it leapfrogged again, like he was skipping spit instead of stones. A couple of children were playing in the water, squealing and scampering around. How they could feel so safe around water was beyond me.

Katka smiled. "That's the vodník."

I froze. "The what?"

"A creature from Slovak legend. Like vampires, but with water and no fangs."

We walked around the square, giving me a better view. The man in the well was little bigger than a young teenager. He wore a top hat and had hair that burst out from underneath it, like the Mad Hatter. His empty eyes stared out at the square with a cold regard. Beyond creepy.

Katka explained. "They live in bodies of water and lie in wait to drown humans. When they do, they steal their victim's souls and put them in teacups, which they collect."

It's one thing when you hallucinate, but hallucina*tions* usually don't know things the hallucina*tor* doesn't. I had been *friends* with one of these vodníks? My left hand snuck over and began to massage my scarred arm. I snatched it away. "Teacups?"

She gave a slight shrug. "So?"

"Teacups," I said again, miming as if I were drinking tea.

"Yes. Teacups. With lids."

Of course. "And *why* does he store them in teacups?"

She shrugged. "It's make believe. For children. Why are vampires afraid of garlic?"

Maybe she had a point, but still. "You have a statue devoted to a thing that kills people, and you put it in the middle of town where kids can play with it?"

She shook her head and smiled. "It is only myth—even children know that. Let's go somewhere to sit down in shade. Want some ice cream?"

Anywhere away from that statue. There was an ice cream shop around the corner. The place had quite a line going, with people laughing and enjoying themselves.

When Katka and I queued up, the laughter stopped.

People edged away from us, clustering and murmuring among themselves. Katka noticed—how could she not?—and rolled her eyes. "Do you believe this?" she said. We were still speaking English, so it wasn't like most people would be able to understand us.

"What are they doing?"

"Slovaks do not like Roma. It does not help that there are so few of us here in the west. The people only hear of Roma. Lazy. Thieves. Filthy. Dishonest. And they believe it. Every time I go into store, I must prove I have not stolen anything. How do I steal ice cream? Stupid." She glared at the people around us, crossing her arms tight to her body. "Stupid," she said, louder.

And it *was* stupid. Katka and I had done nothing to irritate anyone. The same trio of guys I'd seen yesterday in the stinky tunnel were hanging out a few yards off, the Draco lookalike shouting at one of his friends, who bore an unfortunate resemblance to Gollum. Sunken eyes that bulged a tad much, and a slight hunch. Why didn't people give *them* the crusty looks? They were making more noise than half the crowd combined. We got through the line and ordered our ice cream. The vendor counted the bills Katka gave him twice.

This was worse than being bullied for my scar. Way worse. At home, the troubles I'd had were confined to school. I might see some of the jerks at the mall or the movies, but they usually left me alone then—there were other people around. Plus, these people would be sued sideways back in the States. Wouldn't they? I hated having all those eyes on me, all of them untrusting. All of them guarded. Now that I was noticing it, it seemed everyone was watching me. Draco and Gollum—were they making fun of us? Was their fat friend mimicking me by rubbing his arm, or did he just have an itch? (Come to think of it, he looked kind of like Jabba the Hutt. Not quite *Return of the Jedi* Jabba, but definitely a *New Hope* deleted scene candidate: wormy, large, and hairless.) That couple leaving the ice cream parlor—was it because of us? Had we ruined their afternoon? I'd had nightmares better than this.

"Come," Katka said. "Don't pay them attention. They're not worth it. Idiots."

She led me around the corner, where we sat across from a fountain (one without a human-drowning-creature motif). I tried to focus on my cone. The scoops were the size of golf balls, not baseballs, but the ice cream itself was fantastic. Creamy and smooth and unlike anything they had in the States. I'd gotten six scoops: two straciatella (chocolate chip), two chocolate, and two banana. The last had been on Katka's suggestion, and even though the concept seemed wacky (banana ice cream?), the taste was great. It was like a banana split without the bother of adding fruit. If only I could get over the racism as easily as Katka seemed to.

"So?" she said, taking a lick of her single scoop. "Why are you acting so strange?"

"What?"

"You've been upset all morning, and last night at castle, you shut down after your little fire woman joke. What is wrong?"

Would she believe me? I didn't think I could stand keeping it secret any longer, though. Sooner or later, someone would have to know. Why not Katka? "You have to promise not to make fun of me."

She rolled her eyes, and I sighed. Better to spit it out. "I've been . . . seeing things."

"Things?"

My mouth was dry. I ate some ice cream to collect my thoughts. "Strange things." I told her about the person made out of water I'd seen the first night, then about Ohnica. She took it all in stride.

"I knew you were serious. What did this Ohnica say when you talked to her?"

I blinked. "Um . . . that we used to be friends, that she was the one who gave me this burn, and that there's a vodník who lives at the castle and wants to kill me. Or put me in a teacup, I guess."

"A vodník?"

"Yeah. That's why I thought it was kind of freaky for you to have a sculpture of one downtown. So . . . you believe me?"

Katka shrugged. "You were like this when we were little too. I always thought there was something different about you, and you have no reason to lie now. I certainly believe you believe. I suppose you might be crazy."

"You remember me from back then?"

"A bit. Enough to remember the adventures you were always coming up with."

I was grateful she was accepting my story, but I wasn't crazy. Was I? Time for a change of subject. Maybe she'd open up some herself. "Tell me about your headaches," I said.

"No."

"Um . . . please?"

She just shook her head. So much for that conversation. I didn't quite understand Katka. She could be warm and friendly one minute, and then shut me out the next. We ate our ice cream in silence, while I tried to come up with a new topic. If we went too long without speaking, I might start freaking out. Family or not, Katka was a girl, and I had a horrible track record when it came to talking to girls. One day wasn't going to just erase sixteen years of bad experiences. I needed at least a few weeks before I'd feel on semi-solid ground. On a hunch, I asked, "What do you know about Babka?"

"Who?"

"Babka. My mom's mom. Our grandmother."

Katka raised an eyebrow. "Nothing. She's been dead since before we were born. Why?"

I took another lick of ice cream. "No reason. I just wondered if your dad had ever mentioned anything . . . strange about her."

She shook her head. "No, why?"

I was about to respond, but then I glanced back across the fountain. A woman in black stood there, still as the grave. She was off to the side of the fountain, and she wasn't the crazy lady who'd tried to sell me the herbs. This one's back was straight, and she wasn't wrinkly. She was pretty, even beautiful maybe. Long black hair, pale white skin.

But the thing that stood out, the thing that stopped me in midthought, was the fact that she was also holding a scythe and staring creepily down the street, like she was auditioning to be the grim reaper.

"Um . . . who's that?" I asked.

Katka followed my gaze. "Who?"

"The lady in black with the scythe."

"What?"

"The one right—"

A girl on Rollerblades whizzed in front of me, headed toward the fountain. She hit a cobblestone wrong and went sprawling, skidding forward to catapult face first into the fountain, her skates sticking up in the air.

Some people laughed. Draco, Gollum, and Jabba, who had come to lurk across the square, even clapped. But the skates didn't move, the legs didn't flail, and the girl didn't get out.

Katka and I dropped our ice creams as we rushed over to the girl. Each of us took a side of her as we lifted her out of the fountain. She was unconscious, her head dangling limply.

"*Polož ju*," Katka said, trying to steady the girl's head.

"What?"

"Lay her down."

I did, and Katka put her ear to the girl's chest, then frowned. After a moment, she started CPR. I heard a few gasps from the gathering crowd, followed by angry muttering. Surely they wouldn't mind a Rom helping someone in need? As soon as Katka started chest compressions, I stumbled back to a sitting position. This could not be happening.

In the distance, I could hear a dull murmur of the shoppers from the square. The cobblestones were hard and unforgiving beneath me, and the sand was working its way into my palms. Katka kept going.

"Do you need any help?" I asked. My mouth was dry as the desert. She ignored me.

Someone had called the paramedics, and an ambulance roared down the street seconds later. Katka continued CPR until one of the medics took over. We both watched as the girl was loaded into the ambulance. Two policemen showed up, running on foot. They cleared the crowd away, which had started to talk as soon as the officials were on the scene. People were gesturing wildly, and more than a few fingers were pointing our way. The policemen must have noticed how Katka and I were the only other ones wet, and they split up, each to talk to one of us. The ambulance switched on its siren, a low and whiny drone different from the high pitched wail they had in America. It sped off.

"*Ako sa to stalo?*"

I gawked at the officer. Instead of the black uniforms I was used to from the States, he was all in green.

"*Ako. Sa. To. Stalo?*" He asked it louder this time, obviously irritated. He had that overly patient tone parents use when they're trying to be obnoxious to their children right before they ground them.

It clicked in my head: *how did it happen?* I shook my head. "My Slovak's no good." Trying to express myself about something so traumatic in a second language was going to be too much.

He frowned, then said something else in Slovak.

"I'm American," I said. "I'm sorry."

He nodded and held up a hand to me, signaling I was to stay put, and then turned to help his partner question Katka. I stared off after the ambulance. Had all of that really happened? It wasn't until then that I thought to look for the lady in black again. She was nowhere to be found now. Had it been connected to the accident? It seemed like she had been waiting there to watch it happen.

I was having visions of creatures from folklore, and I just happen to see a woman with a scythe right before someone died. Coincidence?

Maybe scythes were a popular fashion accessory in Slovakia. Like purses.

Right.

How could a girl just *die* like that? Maybe she wasn't dead. It hadn't been a horrific fall—just something you'd see in a stupid movie. I hadn't heard anything break, and she hadn't been underwater long enough to drown. Had she? As I thought about it more, the image of the vodník sculpture leaped to mind, with the man sitting there staring out at the town square in an endless gaze, water spouting from his mouth and children laughing and playing in it.

Meanwhile, the police were grilling my cousin, peppering her with questions that sounded anything but polite in tone. She had folded her arms and clammed up, answering them with single syllables. Whatever she was saying, it wasn't calming the cops at all. They were getting more animated, pointing back in the direction the ambulance had driven off, then over to the fountain. Most of the crowd had dispersed, but a few clusters still hung around, glaring at us and muttering.

I stood up and walked over to stand next to Katka. "Hey," I said to the cops in English. "We didn't do anything wrong."

The police paused to look at me, then they chattered back and forth. Maybe if they'd been in real cop uniforms, I would have taken them more seriously. But in those green outfits, these guys looked like forest rangers with bad attitudes.

"Hey," I said again. "Leave her alone. She tried to save that girl's life."

"Stop, Tomas." Katka shook her head. "They are almost finished. Let them feel big. It will get this over faster."

And she was right. After another couple of minutes of what sounded like repeated questions, they were putting away their little notepads and nodding to her curtly. Then they started babbling at me in an admonishing tone. I bobbed my head to whatever they were saying to me, hoping it wasn't "Did you kill her, you dirty Gypsy?"

When they had left, Katka and I sat down across from the fountain, both of us staring at it. Now that the police and the body were gone, the rest of the crowd was disappearing too.

"It is ridiculous," Katka said. "They all saw girl skid and fall. We weren't even close. But they blame us. And they do not want me to help try save her life. Even police don't trust. They wanted to take us to station. Question us more. I think if you had not told them you were American, we would be there now."

"They really thought we had something to do with it?" Unbelievable.

"Of course. We are Roma. We cause all problems in Slovakia."

"It can't be that—"

"Did your mother tell you nothing?" Katka's face was flushed, her forehead scrunched and her eyes narrowed. "Do you know what they do to Roma in Eastern Slovakia? They wall us off from the rest of the city. Like animals in zoo. I saw it on the news. Then they complain they must deal with us, because we are too stupid and lazy to work for ourselves. They debate on national news why they must 'put up with Roma.'"

"Everybody's like this?"

She sniffed. "Some not. Some, if you get to know them, treat you fine."

I tried to think of something similar in America. Was there a town where they walled off African Americans? Everyone would get sued to death. But then again, there were all those burning crosses and white hoods and lynchings they taught us about in social studies. If people treated me differently just because of my scarred arm, what would they do if your whole body was different? In America, the local police didn't support racism. Did they?

"What did the lady look like?" Katka asked after a pause.

"What?"

"The woman in black. Was she carrying a scythe?"

"Then you saw her too?"

"Was she?" Katka repeated.

"Yeah—a big one. She was holding it and staring at the fountain, almost as if she—"

"You are not crazy."

"What?"

"In Slovak folklore, Death appears as a woman. She is always dressed in black, and must kill certain number of people each day. She carries scythe with her. This woman's name is Zubatá."

My stomach took a bungee jump off a very high bridge. This was exactly the line of thinking I'd been trying to avoid. "You mean you think I saw Death? Come on. I mean, it was a woman. She didn't even have a hood, and I could see her face."

Katka held up her hand. "Not Death. Not so bad. Just Zubatá."

I forced a laugh, then picked at the bench we were sitting on. The paint was peeling. "What a relief. You had me going there for a minute, but I should have known. I mean, the scythe thing is so cliché, and—"

"This proves what you are seeing is real."

Crap. I stood up and started walking back toward the church square. Katka followed. "You mean you actually *believe* me?" I said.

"Before, no. Now, yes. You did not know about Zubatá, but you described her."

"But I don't even believe it myself. It could be my imagination, or—"

Katka grabbed my right arm and pointed at it. "This is not imagination."

I jerked it back and stopped walking. "This was from an accident. Your dad was the one who saved me. I was drowning."

"Then how you get burned in water?" she asked.

I glared at her. "I don't know. But it didn't have to be from some fairy or troll or witch or Death wannabe."

This was always how it started in horror flicks. Guy sees freaky looking person with a hook (or scythe), and by the end of the movie, the guy has the scythe buried to its hilt in his eye socket. I wanted to believe that all I needed was some rest, and then I'd stop seeing little old ladies running around with farm equipment.

"Tomas, this is great opportunity. This Ohnica said a vodník lives in this town. A vodník still able to drown people. If we can prove he is causing the curse of the town, then maybe we can do something about it. Help other people. Get everyone to stop resenting Roma so much. Prove they are wrong."

I cleared my throat. "Didn't you hear me when I said it wanted to *kill* me?"

Katka nodded, her long ponytail bobbing enthusiastically. "All the more reason to know where it is and what it is doing. We will start at the public pool."

"The pool?"

"Yes," she said. "Many people have drowned there over the years. We can go and watch and see what happens. If we're lucky, we'll see the vodník, and then we'll know."

Since when was dying a spectator sport? Around us, hundreds of people walked by, none of them having to worry about mystical water creatures wanting to steal their souls. "I'm not going to go watch people get offed in a pool," I said.

"We won't let the vodník kill them. We'll stop it before it happens."

I fell back on my stubborn nature. I looked Katka straight in the eye and said, "There is no way in hell you're getting me anywhere near a pool if there's some insane mythological water guy out to kill me."

But arguing with my cousin was like dealing with a force of nature. It didn't help that I'm just a big pushover to begin with. What else was I going to do in Slovakia? Katka was my only friend. In about ten minutes, she had it all arranged. She was going to pick me up at my apartment the next morning, and we were going hunting for drownings.

Heaven help me.

CHAPTER EIGHT

SPRITE

Morena was inducted into the Death Hall of Fame back during the string of plagues in Slovakia in the late seventeenth century. Despite the tremendous extra workload during that stretch, she let only a single soul escape her grasp, a remarkable feat for a Death in any country. She is famous for her work ethic, her ruthless pursuit of victory, and her addiction to throat lozenges. Morena, we salute you!

Two weeks went by. Katka had explained to her dad that she wanted to help me study and needed time off, which she got. She had an interesting relationship with my uncle. With her mom dead from cancer and him working at the castle so much, she had free rein of the city. She didn't have a car, but in a European city, you didn't need one. Anywhere you wanted to go, you could walk or take the bus.

You'd be surprised how much language you can pick up in two weeks, especially when your mother did her best to raise you bilingual. After the first week, I was understanding pretty much what everyone said to me. After the second, my own Slovak had shaken off the rust and was improving. Almost all my conversations were in Slovak now. It wasn't that I'd never learned it—I'd just never had the desire to use it. Living in the country that speaks it does a lot for desire.

For one thing, Mom instituted an "Only Allowed to Watch Movies in Slovak" rule—one which Dad had the nerve to go along with. That was an enormous motivating factor by itself. Of course, I was stuck with what was on television—we didn't have the budget to get a whole lot of movies to own just yet. I quickly discovered that Slovak translations of English movie titles could get a little . . . strange. "Ghostbusters" is much different than "Tamers of Ghosts." I mean, it's not like Bill Murray was getting Slimer to jump through hoops in the circus.

But when you're dying of thirst, any water's better than no water.

The other main reason I wanted to learn the language fast was so I could understand all the snide remarks people made at me.

Don't get me wrong. It's not like the entire country was always frowning at me—it only felt like that. Going from a place where my ethnicity was only a matter of the occasional mistaken (for Hispanic) identity to one where at times it was seen as my defining characteristic . . . it made the transition to Slovakia a lot more difficult. Many people in the city seemed afraid to get close to me, as if I had leprosy or was going to pick their pocket. A shopkeeper once stopped me when I was leaving the grocery store and practically strip-searched me to make sure I wasn't trying to steal something.

There weren't many other Roma in the city, so we stood out quite a bit. You'd think Roma, at least, would be friendlier to us. You'd be wrong. I tried striking up a conversation with a Roma guy who was waiting for the bus next to me one day. He was friendly at first—confused by my accent, but open and congenial. Then Katka came to stand by me, and he shut down, nodding once or twice before apologizing that he had to go. After that, all the Roma I saw avoided me. Katka said it was because they all felt like we'd turned traitor—given into the Slovaks. Assimilated. Maybe the best comparison would be like an African American "passing" for white—a betrayal of your roots.

Great. So we weren't accepted by Slovaks, and we weren't accepted by Roma.

Having Katka there was the only thing that kept me sane. She'd been dealing with this stuff since she was little, and she knew how to handle it. And if being her friend didn't help me much with the Roma in the city, it did wonders for the Slovaks. She was well-known. Or rather, her father was. No one wanted to risk incurring the wrath of a trained knight with a whole arsenal of medieval whoop-ass at his disposal.

I didn't understand why people had such a problem with me. "What is it about being Roma that's so bad?" I asked Katka in exasperation about one week into my stay. "Why do people hate us?"

She took me to the train station. There were a few olive-skinned men sitting on benches, talking to one another and laughing, each with a bottle in his hand. Farther down, a few Roma kids were playing, their hair oily, their clothes clearly unwashed and raggedly patched in places. You could practically feel the resentment pouring off the Slovaks that passed.

Katka's green eyes were passionate. "When Slovaks think of Roma, this is what they think of. People who don't work, who live off the State. These Roma, they live in a rundown house near here. The government gave it to them for free. They have destroyed it. They drink, they steal, they're awful. But are they awful because they are Roma? Slovaks would have you believe we are born like them. It's in our blood."

"Are Roma here all like that?" I asked.

Her shoulders slumped a little. "Many. There are more in Eastern Slovakia. From what I read, the same problems are throughout Europe. Hitler didn't just send Jews to the concentration camps. Roma were sent too. But where Jews at least have Israel now, Roma still have nothing. No place where they are accepted and treated as equals. No jobs. Unwelcome at school. Would they still be like that if they were given a real chance? This is not genetics any more than your street gangs in America are genetics."

I watched the children playing, their parents completely ignoring them. They were climbing on the fence bordering the train tracks, shaking the chain link and howling with glee. What chance did they have to grow up to become fully functioning members of society? At the same time, I wanted to yell at them—to tell them to wash up. Stop being so wild.

Stop making life harder for me.

Katka and I left the train station, but it was several days before I could get the image of those children out of my head.

When Mom checked on me before she went to bed that night, she asked how things were going. I unleashed a bundle of pent up frustration on her, all of the experiences I'd had pouring out of me, like they'd just been waiting for her to ask before they all came to the surface.

She gave me a half smile and sat down on the bed beside me. "It'll get better."

"What do you mean?" I said. "How?"

"You're new right now. People only know you for what you look like. Trenčín doesn't have many Roma, so we stick out. They see you and wonder if you're going to be like all the Roma they hear about on the news. Make problems. Bring more Roma with you. They'll get over it. Slovaks aren't bad people. They just aren't used to diversity, so it's easier for them to fall back on prejudices. When I was going to school here, it took time to make friends. Longer than it would have if I were just Slovak, but friends still came."

"Katka doesn't seem to have many other friends."

Mom shrugged. "Katka . . . is different. She takes it all too personally."

"And how is that wrong? How can you give the bigots a free pass like that?"

"It's not a free pass, Tomas. It's complicated. Look at me. I've already made friends at the school where I'm teaching. People see me, and at first they wonder how a Rom could get a job like this. But then they get to know me, and they judge me for who I am, not how I look. They see I'm not like other Roma."

I slapped my bed in frustration, looking down at my burned arm. "So you get to be the token Roma friend? People shouldn't make assumptions about you based on a single glance. And maybe the 'other Roma' deserve the same courtesy."

Mom started tracing the quilted lines on my bed's throw. "People shouldn't do a lot of things they do."

No kidding. We were quiet for a bit, then I asked. "How did our family end up okay?"

"Okay? I don't know if you can call it that. Alena—my mother—married a Roma man. Her parents disowned her. Her siblings stopped talking to her. My father died when I was three. I don't remember him and I don't know the Roma side of our family very well. They didn't like him marrying a Slovak woman any more than Mama's family did. Mama had been married to him a little less than six years. She had to press forward after his death. Raising her two children, providing for us . . ." She trailed off, her expression pained.

At last she continued, sounding artificially bright and cheery. "I don't want you to make up your mind about Slovaks yet. Yes, they have some issues, but aren't we doing the same thing to them that they do to us, if we dismiss them all as bigots? Get some sleep. You'll feel better tomorrow."

Typical Mom: avoid real discussion by ignoring it.

Typical Tomas: let her get away with it.

Still, the persecution against me lightened up some once word got out I was Ľuboš's nephew. I had to endure scowls and "accidents" now and then, but compared to the first two weeks, life got better. Even being around the pool felt like a relief. Well, *around* was a relative word. I stayed near the fence, about as far as I could get and still be at the pool complex. It was a mixture of pros and cons. It had a football field–sized amount of water, but it had plenty of string bikinis too. There were no women made out of fire, no scythes, and no crazy candy cane–backed grannies. Then again, it also had plenty of old fat men in Speedos, and what has once been seen can never be unseen. Like I said: pros and cons.

It also helped that Katka wore a bikini to sunbathe. Not that I was checking her out, but all the guys who liked to make fun of Roma didn't miss a good opportunity to ogle one when the opportunity arose. Next to all that hotness, I might as well have been invisible. The first day, I'd been sure everyone at the pool would point and stare at my burned arm. I even debated going in a long sleeved shirt. Once we got to the pool and Katka stripped down to her swimsuit and lay out in the sun, I might as well not have existed as far as guys were concerned: I was scrawny, short, and forgettable. You didn't bulk up much by watching movies.

I'd lie next to Katka while I studied the tour routine. It wasn't overly complicated, but I was never a genius when it came to memorizing, so it was slow going. Every now and then I'd glance up to see what was going on at the pool—death watch, so to speak—but other than that, I buried myself in the tour. The less I had to look at all that water, the better.

It must have been in the high nineties that Thursday, and I had my scarred arm all lathered up in lotion and sunblock to protect it. I was in my swimsuit and barefoot. Katka had sent me off to get the refreshments, though how anyone could call a pint-sized can of Sprite with no ice *refreshing* was beyond me. Still, a person had to drink, so I'd gone fairly willingly.

Techno music was blasting from speakers set up around the pool, the bass line thumping out beats in a never ending stream of booms. Draco, Gollum, and Jabba were hanging around the snack bar when I walked up. It took them a bit to spot me, but when they did, smirks broke out all around. Together, they got in line behind me.

"I didn't realize the pool had gotten so bad lately," Draco said. "Seems they have an infestation problem."

Jabba bumped into me from behind, knocking me forward into the girl in front of me. I flashed an apologetic smile at her, but she frowned at me and edged farther away.

Gollum snorted up some snot and laughed. I wondered how bad this might get. They weren't smoking, at least. No burning embers to worry about.

A voice spoke to my right—in English. "Greetings, young Skywalker."

Adam from the castle had walked up. The trio noticed him too. Funny how fast they were able to find something else to do.

I beamed at him, relief flooding me. Talk about a knight in shining armor. The guy knew all his English from geeky movies, and he never passed up an opportunity to try out lines. "May the Force be with you," I said.

He grinned and continued in Slovak. "How are you doing? Adjusting to life as a Communist, or are you still set in your capitalist pig ways?"

I glanced around him to see the Bigot Gang heading off. Hey—I could call them the BeeGees for short. BGs. It was the little mental victories that kept me going. I smiled some more. "Doing great, Comrade. What are you doing down from the castle?"

He nodded over toward the far end of the pool area, where a woman was playing with two small boys. "Here with the family." Back in English: "All work and no play makes Jack a dull boy."

I waved good-bye to him, wondering if he knew how creepy that last line had sounded. Probably not, but it would be better to keep him away from any axes for the time being.

On the way back, I discovered why the BGs had been so ready to retreat. They'd laid an ambush in the form of an impromptu game of soccer between me and where Katka lay out in the sun. I tried to skirt around it, but no matter which way I went, the soccer game seemed to follow. The ball smacked into my chest, and Gollum ran up to field it. "Oops," he said, smiling. He kicked it back to Jabba, who returned it. Once again, Gollum just missed it, and this time it hit my shoulder. Passive-aggressive taunting of the Roma kid. Fun incarnate.

I had to make a choice: I could either skirt closer to the pool than I was comfortable, or I could walk all around the water in the opposite direction. For once, personal pride won out over my phobia. There was no way I was going to let those chuckleheads think they'd gotten the best of me. Stick up for myself—that's what Katka kept telling me to do. Why not start now?

After all, it wasn't like I'd lose my balance walking on a level stretch of land, and the water would still be feet—not inches—away.

I swallowed and headed toward the pool. It seemed like somebody turned up the sun. I started sweating, and my stomach roiled with nausea. If I blew chunks in the pool, I'd never live it down. Maybe personal pride shouldn't have won out over my fear of water.

The ball hit the back of my head, and I heard more laughing behind me. I kept walking.

Keep calm, Tomas. Just a few more feet, and I'll be past the pool and on my way back to Katka.

I was halfway there, and I was beginning to get confident. I was doing it: beating my phobia. It was actually possible. Maybe I'd just need the right motivation to—

Someone shoved me from behind.

The Sprite went flying, and I teetered on the edge of the pool. The water stretched out below me, blue and deep and rushing to meet me. I fell with a splash.

Freezing water was everywhere. I couldn't think straight, couldn't breathe. My arms and legs flailed around, connecting with something that was either the floor or the side of the pool. Above everything else, my mind was shouting one question: why had I never learned to swim?

And then there was nothing but rushing wind and blinding light.

I wasn't in the body of the fat eight-year-old this time. I was in the body of someone bigger. Someone underwater: that much was clear. When you're on dry land, the sun doesn't undulate and the air doesn't ripple. I glanced up toward the sun, and outside the surface of the water, I could see a river-bank. I'd never been swimming (if you didn't count what was even now happening to me at the pool—was I drowning? Was this what death was like?), and so the effect of looking out of water was new and strange to me.

Disturbing.

And I could breathe underwater.

Someone was on the riverbank. I recognized the long hair and the dress: Lesana, the girl from my last water vision. My body moved toward her, my legs trailing behind me, with only my hands touching the riverbed, the rocks smooth and cold on my fingers. I breathed out, and a stream of water came out of my mouth, not bubbles. I was like a living garden hose.

As I got closer, I saw she was holding a flower. She had no shoes on, and her feet were dirty, with dried mud going clear up to midcalf. A shapely calf, at that. Lesana stepped toward the river and threw the flower in.

I reached out a hand ever so slowly, inching it out of the water and toward her leg. She stood there, apparently oblivious to my presence. Was I invisible? Instead, she gazed at the flower as it drifted away, carried by the current of the river.

My hand got closer and closer. Two feet away. One foot. With a lunge, it shot out and grabbed her by the ankle, and I jerked backward, throwing her off balance and into the water. I tried to stop myself, but I had no control. I plunged my other hand into my suit jacket and came out with a lidded teacup.

Lesana thrashed in my grip, water flying every which way, but I was too strong for her. Inhumanly strong.

I focused on her with an almost clinical attitude. As if I wasn't killing her, just observing. My hands began to tingle, and I had a feeling of . . . something, moving from her and into the cup.

Lesana struggled even more. With one hand holding her and the other holding the cup, I had no way of defending myself—a fact she noticed. She changed her efforts from fighting in general to beating my face and gouging at my eyes.

I cried out and let go of her ankle. She was on the attack now, not trying to escape, but increasing her assault. Coming straight on at me, I got a good *look at her face, and my body froze. No doubt it was Lesana: that nose was a dead giveaway.*

She punched me in the face. I snarled and bit her hand in response.

Lesana jerked in pain and swam backward.

I let her go.

Then someone had their arms around my chest, and my head was above water. I floundered, trying to touch something—anything—solid. I managed to clutch at my rescuer, in the process almost sinking both of us. It wasn't until I had the edge of the pool in my hands and was being pushed up out of the water that I realized it was Katka who had saved me. The BGs were nowhere to be seen. No one else had come to help me, but then again, I had only been in for a moment before Katka had come to the rescue. Her skin was even darker wet, her hair plastered back against her scalp. When she smiled at me—seeing I was all right—her teeth were a stark white against olive skin.

She was out of the water in an effortless push. "Trying to learn how to swim?" she asked.

I didn't think I was in a mood for humor, but I found myself laughing anyway. It was such a relief—each breath going into my lungs and bringing sweet air with it. I was alive. Actually, I must not have been that close to drowning, after all. I wasn't coughing up water, and I'd never really felt myself breathe any in. It took the two of us a moment to realize people shouting and pointing to the middle of the pool. A boy was floating facedown. He couldn't have been older than ten.

A couple of lifeguards were already on their way to him, paddling for all they were worth. I surveyed the pool area. Sure enough, on the opposite side, I could just make out the form of a woman dressed in black, the sun glinting off the scythe in her hand. "She's there," I whispered to

Katka, and nodded toward the apparition. "Zubatá."

Katka looked, but she couldn't see anything. "Any sign of the vodník?" she asked.

I had already been searching, but I shook my head. "No one in a suit and top hat." This was more than morbid, talking about the poor dying kid as if he was already a statistic. The lifeguards had reached him by now, and they were bringing him back to the side, pulling his motionless body behind them. The boy's face was out of the water, his eyes shut and his mouth lolling open. "Isn't there anything we could do to help?" I asked.

"You've already seen Zubatá," Katka said. "She doesn't show up for fun. The boy is dead. Just watch and see if anything strange happens. Trust me. These people will only get angry if Roma try to help with a drowning. Let the lifeguard do his job."

From what we'd experienced the past two weeks (especially the incident with the poor girl at the fountain), she was probably right. The lifeguards had the boy by the side of the pool and were administering CPR. Somebody cut the techno music, and the pool went silent. Everything was just like you would expect to see it, with the exception of Zubatá walking over to stand by the side of the scene, her scythe at the ready. Now that she was walking, I saw that her black outfit was really just a long cloak. Underneath it, she was wearing a plain white dress. Maybe all black all the time got old after awhile. It was hard to tell her age. She had raven black hair without a hint of gray, but she didn't seem young. Not wrinkled, but still. Old. A bright white light came out of the boy's mouth to float in the air above him. I couldn't make out its shape or size—the light was too intense to see clearly, like a marble-sized sun, floating in the air.

"Do you see that?" I whispered to Katka.

"Don't talk," she said. "Tell me about it when it's over."

Zubatá reached down to grab it, but before she could take it, the bright light—the boy's soul?—started swirling back down, sucked into an invisible vortex. At first the movement was slight, and then it increased, the light spiraling more quickly until it exploded.

Death didn't take the change well. She scowled at the boy and swept her scythe down at him.

It passed right through one of the lifeguards, to continue on unchecked through the boy's body. Nothing happened. The lifeguard just stood there, watching the other perform compressions on the boy's chest.

Zubatá tried a couple more times, but it was like watching a coach in a baseball game kick dirt at the umpire: more a gesture of protest than actually getting anything done. She eventually turned, took a few steps, and disappeared with a swirl of her cloak.

The lifeguards kept trying until the paramedics arrived and took over. The two men stood up—one of them tall and strong, the other shorter and more average, though we were too far away for me to make out any real features. They watched as the boy was loaded into the ambulance, then the taller one walked off, his shoulders slumped as he went back to his post. The shorter one glanced around, walked over to pick up a bag that had been sitting on the ground near them, and then he walked off as well. The other lifeguards were closing down the pool. Not that they needed to do much: people were streaming out of the gates, packing up and leaving en masse.

"Well?" Katka said. "You're staring like a fish, so you must have seen something."

I shook my head, and the two of us went back to get our stuff. "Give me a second," I said. We'd just seen a boy die. Even after seeing the roller skating accident two weeks before, I wasn't ready for this—especially not on top of that strange water vision I'd had while I was drowning.

Katka was too anxious. "What did you see?"

"I don't know," I said, remembering. "There was this bright light that came out of the boy. Zubatá went to take it, but she couldn't get it. It . . . exploded. She tried to scythe the kid a couple of times, then she walked off and vanished."

"That sounds strange," Katka said. "Maybe the lifeguard managed to save the boy's life. Maybe he'll get better."

I shrugged. "With two lifeguards so close, you'd figure the kid would never have drowned in the first place."

Katka stared at me. "Two?"

"Yeah. Both of them were—"

"Tomas, there was only one."

"No," I said. "There were two." I scanned the area. The bigger lifeguard was back in his chair, but the shorter one was gone. "Maybe he went inside, or he's off duty now. He had a bag with him, and he might—"

"A bag?" Katka asked.

"Yeah. So maybe he was done for the—"

"That was the vodník."

It was those sorts of thoughts I was trying to avoid. "He wasn't in a suit."

"Don't be an idiot. Vodníks can change. Maybe they learn to adapt. You said he had a bag—it must have had his teacup inside."

Now that I thought about it, Zubatá might have been trying to slice the lifeguard with her scythe instead of the boy. And her scowl could have been directed at him, as well.

"How did you fall into the water?" Katka asked.

Honestly, that fact had slipped my mind right then, even though I was still drenched. "I—someone pushed me."

Her voice was grave. "Vodník."

I was quiet for a moment, then said, "Come on. There's about a hundred people here who would love to see the Roma kid take a dunk. Why does it have to be the vodník?"

She didn't answer. As I thought about it, it did seem to be too big of a coincidence, me getting pushed and then a boy drowning right after.

"So he tried to drown me, and when that didn't work, he took the kid?"

Katka nodded.

That meant the whole bit about trying to save the kid's life—crouching by the lifeguard's side and doing lifeguardly things—had been to trick me. To make me not suspect anything. If I'd spoken up, could I have changed things? And had the vodník stolen that soul from Zubatá? That couldn't make her happy. What sort of creature taunted Death?

"Well," Katka said after I didn't speak. "That proves that. A vodník. I knew there was no such thing as a Roma curse. Now, we just need to think of a way to stop him."

Right. And while we were at it, we should just find a cure for cancer and the common cold. Something told me there'd be no "just" about this.

CHAPTER NINE
ROLLS

Despite their human appearance, vodniks have more than a little amphibian in them. They can go without water for quite some time, but sooner or later, they need a good dousing. Even then, tests have shown it takes more than three years for one to actually die from lack of liquid.

The next morning, Katka called to see if I wanted to go into town with her to see a movie. Some classic she said I'd love. And maybe some foreign film would be just what I needed to take my mind off everything that had happened at the pool. Dad hadn't been able to get the home theater thing working yet—something about a delivery delay on the surround sound. (We had the big screen, but who *actually* uses the tinny speakers on a TV set?) Going out to the movies would be cool. A bit of needed familiarity.

As I got ready to go, I could hear my dad typing away at his computer. He must have heard me open my bedroom door, because his typing stopped and he peeked out from his office.

"Up already?" he asked.

I shrugged. "Yeah."

"Going out with Katka?"

Something about him—the set of his shoulders, the tone of his voice—sounded off. "To the movies. Why?"

"Just wondering." He paused, thinking. "If you were going to write a book, what would it be about?"

I blinked, stunned. Dad never asked for help with his writing. Usually he squirreled it away until he was ready for people to evaluate it, but for him to ask for suggestions in the middle of something he was working on was unheard of. "I don't know," I said.

"Neither do I." Dad paused, then ducked his head back in the office. A moment later, he was standing in the doorway, fingers massaging his temples. "I'll admit it. I've come to an impasse."

"What have you been working on since we got here?" I asked.

"Garbage. Nothing's flowing. I started a piece about a talking alpaca, but it took me nowhere. I tried another one, about archaeologists battling the spirit of Matúš Čak in catacombs beneath the castle. Too derivative."

Talking alpaca? Dad was really getting desperate. I swallowed, a pit in my stomach. "Why not, uh, try to write a book about us?"

"What?"

"You know. A family's house burns down and they move to Slovakia."

"Too depressing," he said.

"But that would just be the background. You could make it about the son, who starts having strange things happen to him when he gets there."

Dad checked the main door, as if he were worried Mom might come in. He faced me again. "What's going on?"

"Huh?"

"Two weeks at a pool every day? That's quite out of character for you, and judging by your hair yesterday, you actually went *in* the pool. What have you been up to?"

I thought about telling him all of it. The vodník, Ohnica, Zubatá—just getting everything off my chest. But what would that have done? We couldn't afford to move back to America—not after having spent all our insurance money investing ourselves in Slovakia. And even if we found a way to move back, I didn't want to. I liked hanging out with Katka, and Trenčín was cool—even taking into account the Bigot Gang. I mean, it had been more than two weeks, and I hadn't watched more than a handful of movies. At home, I sometimes averaged two films a day, more in the summer. The castle was incredible, I had a new best friend, and I was finally getting the language down. Why should I let some watery loser force me to move again? So all I said was, "Nothing."

Dad gave me a flat expression. "Really?"

I nodded.

Silence.

"But you'll tell me if something does happen," Dad said. "If you're in trouble or anything."

I nodded again.

More silence.

Dad stepped back. "Okay. If you need anything, just holler. I'll be in the back, slamming my head against the wall." He returned to his office, and I went to finish getting ready.

Because really, what could Dad have done? Called the police? Picked up witchcraft to try to deal with the vodník? This was something I'd have to do on my own.

For better or worse.

Katka showed up fifteen minutes later. I paused to yell bye to my dad, then ducked out before he could add any errands. I was already supposed to pick up bread, and that was enough in my book.

Once we were safely away from the apartment, I spoke—in Slovak, of course. We were all Slovak all the time now. "I . . . I had this sort of vision thing."

She looked over at me, her expression neutral. "Vision thing?"

"Actually, it was the second one I had. The first one was in the shower. The second was yesterday, in the pool. With everything that happened with that kid, I forgot to tell you about it."

"What did you see?"

"In the first one, it was like I was this eight-year-old boy, hanging out with his sister. We were in a boat, and then something snatched me and pulled me into the water. In the second vision, I think I was a vodník. I was in the water, and I tried to grab the sister. She fought me and got away."

"And this all happened to you in the shower and the pool?"

"Yeah."

We were quiet for a while. Katka seemed quieter than normal. Subdued. Overhead, the sky was overcast, and thunder rolled in the distance. The park was empty except for a couple of homeless people lying on benches.

Katka spoke first this time. "I have no idea about that. But these visions haven't harmed you, correct?"

"Harmed, no," I said. "Disturbed, yes."

"Then maybe we focus on the real vodník first, and worry about shower visions later."

I shrugged. "All right. What do we do about the vodník?"

We headed into the tunnel that crossed under the main road. Someone had used it as a toilet. Recently. I kept an eye out for the Bigot Gang, but so far so good.

"They need water to stay alive," Katka said. "We could use heat lamps, or lock him in a sunny room. He'll evaporate."

"Evaporate." Was she serious?

She nodded.

"Isn't there some easier way?" I asked. "Like silver bullets or a stake through the heart? Evaporation sounds like a . . . *Bond villain's plan.*" I finished the sentence in English, unsure how to express it in Slovak.

"What?"

"Too complicated and likely to fail."

Katka sighed. "You and your movies. This is real life. Our folktales are much less violent than your American action films—at least as far as vodníks are concerned. In the tales, they are basically friendly and mischievous."

"Sure," I said. "Right until they drown you."

"But even then, vodníks are just doing what they do. In our stories, the make-believe creatures are the way they are. They do what they are made to do. It is the people—the humans—who are good or bad. There are no stories about vodník slayers, so I'm having to make it up from bits and pieces."

"What about their bite?" I asked. "Is there something bad associated with it, like with vampires or werewolves?"

"Not that I know of. There are no stories about vodníks biting, but then again, I never talked to someone who actually saw one of the creatures—or was one, or whatever. So maybe all the stories are wrong."

We were both quiet again. This vodník problem was too large to deal with, and I don't think either of us was ready to tackle it, now that we'd had time to think. Imagining saving the town from a curse was one thing; figuring out how to actually do so was entirely different. We were out in the fresh air now, and a fat drop of water splashed down in front of me. "Come on," I said. "We can talk more inside when we get to the movies."

Katka didn't respond, and I glanced over to see her holding her head and frowning. "Katka?"

She blinked twice, then looked at me and forced a smile. "Coming." She started walking again.

"Are you okay?" I asked.

"I'm fine. Just a bit of headache."

"Again?"

"Don't worry about it. There's the theater."

I thought about pushing harder, but decided against it. Maybe the headaches were just from stress. The vodník problem was a tough one, and that could be how her body reacted.

The movie proved to be about as far removed from American cinema as you could get. Apparently it was really popular back in Communist days, although why was beyond me. It focused on three guys who each got a special power from a gnome: one could make anything he wanted appear in his hat, one had a bottomless bag of gold, and the other could strum a harp and make people materialize to do his bidding. It was a cool premise, but the finale was a fifteen minute scene with a woman's nose growing out of her face like a snake, then going on a cross-country tour from Slovakia, through the Czech Republic, into Austria, and then on up to Germany.

Her nose.

Still attached to her face.

I am not making this up.

Katka thought it was great.

"Next time we go to the movies," I said when we got out, "I get to choose."

My cousin shook her head. "I don't see what your problem is. That film is a classic."

Clearly the definition of "classic" varied depending on your native country, but I let it slide.

Katka had to run a few errands next. The two of us walked through the square and into the closest thing they had to a mall in Trenčín—just a big drugstore, really. Everything in Slovakia was smaller than I was used to. The shopping carts, the food portions, the cars, even the people. When we reached the meat section, Katka took some time sniffing at different sausages to find one she liked.

Finally I asked, "How do you tell which one is good?"

She handed me a package. "Smell."

I did. It was a sausage. "And?"

She handed me a different one. "Now try this."

Still a sausage. I shook my head.

Katka smiled. "You can't tell a difference?"

"No."

"Well, you'd taste one. These aren't nearly as good as we could get from *mäsiara*, but they're too far away. Still, we can at least get rolls from *pekárne*."

I looked back down an aisle we had passed. "There're rolls right there. Why not buy those and save ourselves a trip?"

Katka shook her head. "Those will be stale. The ones across town are much better."

We were on our way to pick up the rolls when I saw Gollum lurking outside the electronics store by the plague monument. He hadn't seen me yet. "I'm hungry," I said.

Katka nodded. "We can get a few extra rolls."

"Not for rolls. Isn't there something else?"

Gollum blew his nose into a tissue, then dropped it on the ground.

Katka shrugged. "There's a *bagetaren* back the way we came. You might like it."

"Great," I said. "Let's go." Gollum was just starting to turn our way when Katka and I did a one-eighty.

It had rained while we were shopping, leaving the ground slick and the air heavy. As we walked, I noticed Katka massage her temple when she thought I wasn't looking. Her headache again?

The *bagetaren* was nestled into a row of shops with apartments above them, right off of one of the main squares. The food was okay, although I could have gone for an all-out hoagie instead of a weird tasting version of Subway. Strange deli meats with flecks of who-knew-what in them. Katka had sardines on her sandwich. A sardine sub?

We took our food out and ate underneath one of the huge outdoor umbrellas scattered around the square. Technically, it belonged to one of the bars and we weren't supposed to sit there unless we bought something, but what was the point of being a teenager if you didn't act ignorant and stupid sometimes? Besides, someone was sure to shoo the dirty Gypsies away sooner or later. Katka was all for fighting the Man whenever possible.

"So," I said after taking a bite of my sandwich. "What's up with your headaches?"

The question sat between us like a two-ton gorilla. I wasn't used to confrontations—especially not with girls—and holding Katka's gaze was more difficult than I thought it would be. It must have been hard for her too—she broke away first, eyes dropping to her sandwich.

"We should tell my father."

"Excuse me?"

"About your visions and the fire víla. Ohnica."

"Don't change the subject," I said. So that's what Ohnica was—a fire víla? "What's the matter with you?"

She ignored me. "He knows lot about folklore—he'll be able to help us figure out what to do."

What could I do? If she didn't want to talk, she wouldn't. I knew that much about her by now. We ate in silence for a minute or two, but I had to try one more time. "You're not going to budge on this, are you?"

Katka stood. "Let's get you your rolls."

Whatever. I liked Katka, but she could really get on my nerves some-times. She had to have things her way. Always. And she had a tendency to treat everyone like they were against her. Maybe it had to do with growing up in a city where so many people really were.

We walked in silence to the bakery. I could wait her out—she had to talk to me about the headaches eventually. I could be stubborn too. We went inside, and Katka sighed. "They're almost out."

I checked the shelves. What was she talking about? They were loaded with every kind of bread I could imagine and some I couldn't. Whole wheat, white, braided, with or without raisins, loaves or rolls or ba-guettes—you name it. "I'm sure something here will work. It's just bread."

"Still," she said, "maybe we should have gone here first. I should have remembered."

The lady behind the counter was short and as wide as she was tall. True to Slovak form, she stared at both of us. Rudely gawked would be a closer description. Katka ordered for me, and in a few more minutes we were back on the street with a bag of rolls, the sky threatening rain again.

"So should we head home?" I asked. When Katka didn't respond, I turned to see she had her hand up to her temple, and she was frowning. "Katka?" I said. "You okay?"

She shook her head slightly. "I—I think I need . . . to go—" Before she could finish the sentence, she dropped her bag and fell to the ground, rolls flying everywhere. I was at her side immediately, but there was nothing I could do. She was convulsing, her arms and legs jerking and flailing back and forth, and her eyes rolled up inside her head.

Katka was having a seizure.

CHAPTER TEN

BELT

Sooner or later, we all need help. Maybe you've got a demon that keeps eating your souls before you can get them, or there's a witch who casts an entire city into endless slumber. That's why we encourage every Death to have his or her very own hired assassin. We get it. You're busy. Death's Assassin can step in to take care of those trouble spots while you take care of business.

Help!" I called out in English. *"Pomoc!"*

A crowd had gathered, but no one stepped forward. What the hell was the matter with these people? I tried to remember anything I'd heard about seizures. Didn't people swallow their tongue and choke? Or bite through it? Katka convulsed so badly that only her heels and shoulder blades touched the ground. Her scream rang down the street; her mouth clenched wildly. I unbuckled my belt and tried to slip it into her mouth so her teeth gnashed it, not anything else. On the third try, it worked.

Everyone was still watching. What was I supposed to do? Katka had a cell phone, but I didn't know how to call the equivalent of 911 in Slovakia. So I did the only thing that made sense—I tried to protect her from herself.

I took the bag with the few rolls left in it and put it under her head so that she had something to cushion the blows. I caught her shoulders and tried to keep them as still as I could, hoping that by doing that, she might stop convulsing so much. Trying to control her was like trying to hold back a pit bull. Her expression was blank, one cheek twitched uncontrollably, spittle streamed from her mouth.

Just when I thought they'd never end, the spasms slowed. First I could hold her down more easily, and then they stopped altogether, leaving me breathless and drained. I glared at the people around me, but they were already dissipating. An ambulance pulled up. How long had the whole thing taken?

Then the paramedics were out and helping Katka. They took out my belt and rolled her on her stomach, putting her face to the side so she could breathe freely. A line of spit hung from her mouth, pooling on the cobblestones beneath her. I had to look away. I felt embarrassed for her, and mad for feeling such a useless emotion, and stupid that I had been so clueless.

When I turned back, Katka was coming to herself. The medics checked her eyes and mouth, and she sat up. One of them stood and came over to me.

"What happened?" he asked.

I shook my head. "She just collapsed. I don't know."

The man nodded. "We know her history. Take her home. Let her rest. She'll be fine." He grabbed his bag and headed for the ambulance.

Katka was blinking. She seemed like she was back from wherever her mind had gone during the seizure. I stepped over to her. "Hey," I said.

She wiped her mouth with her hand. "Hi." She stood and brushed herself off. Her clothes were wet from where she'd fallen onto the rain-soaked cobblestones.

"Do you—are you sure you should be getting up this soon?"

She sighed. "I know what I'm doing. This isn't the first time this has happened."

Would she mind if I asked what it was? Or what I should have done? If I were in her shoes, I'd want to be treated normally, like nothing had happened. But I had no idea how to do that.

"Come on," Katka said. "Let's go home."

I frowned. "Shouldn't we go to the hospital or—"

"I'm fine." She stared down at the rolls, half of them on the street and the other half squished in the bag. "Although we'll have to get some more *rožky*."

Just then, the lady from the bakery came out with a bag full of the bread. She offered it to Katka. "For you."

My cousin started to refuse, but the woman insisted. Katka took it. "Thanks."

The woman nodded and went back inside. I watched her go, my mouth open in surprise. Had someone just done something nice for a Rom? Maybe there was hope for the country after all.

Katka started off. I followed.

We walked in silence at first, our footsteps splashing through puddles and taking us back toward the park. Only after we'd gone through Smelly Tunnel did I feel ready to talk. "What was that?"

It took her awhile to answer. "A seizure."

"Why did you have it?"

Katka took a deep breath, then blurted it out. "I have a tumor in my brain. Untreatable. I'll die within a year."

I stopped.

She stopped.

A truck roared by behind us, belching exhaust into the air.

"Were you going to tell me about this?" I asked.

"Yes."

"When?"

"I—I was afraid to. When people see what happens to me, they change. I didn't want you to find out too soon."

It was a novel concept: a girl scared I wouldn't be friends with her. "I had no idea what to do to help. You could have been hurt."

She paused, then nodded. "You're right. I should have told you. I'm sorry."

We walked in silence. I was trying to think about how to find out more information without being too tactless. I switched over to English, not sure if I'd be able to handle the Slovak vocabulary. "So . . . have they already tried chemo—"

"Yes," she said.

I swallowed. "And they can't—"

"No."

"Wait a minute," I said. "You didn't even let me finish my sentence."

"I didn't have to. I went to doctors for the past four years. Nothing worked. When you see so many different doctors, and all of them start out optimistic but end up shaking their heads, why go to another?"

"Why not?" I asked. "I mean, you can't just die."

"Things work differently here in Slovakia. Maybe in America, I could keep trying. But we can't afford to."

"Isn't the health plan here all socialist and whatever? My social studies teacher always talked about how great Europe was for that. That you don't have to pay all the bills."

Katka scoffed. "The bills are not problem. It's the bribes that add up."

"Excuse me?"

She explained in Slovak. "My mother had headaches, just like me. We went to the hospital to run some tests. They put her in a room and said they would start as soon as the doctor had time. But it never happened. Every morning, it was the same. Emergencies had come up, and the doctor would have to run the tests later. Finally my father asked what was happening. The nurse was nice. She told us the doctor was waiting for extra money before he did the tests."

Katka paused. We had left the park and were into the residential area, the apartments looming over us, gray and somber. She swallowed. "My father took my mother home. He doesn't make enough money to pay for silly bribes. That's what my mother said. She was full Roma, and the bribes were even more than they would be for a normal Slovak. My father let her talk him out of it. Four weeks later, she had her first seizure.

"We paid the bribe then. Tumor, they said. We paid another bribe to operate. Unsuccessful. More bribes to get radiation treatment. Unsuccessful. She died soon after. The treatments had left her shattered and us poor."

What do you say when someone tells you that? "Whoa" was all I managed. Across the street, two toddlers were sitting in an apartment window, staring at us.

"Right," Katka said. "So when I started getting the same headaches, your parents helped pay for the bribes. But it was like before, except now we're all out of money. There is no point in going to doctors. I'd rather *live* the rest of my life than be frail, sickly, and bald when I die."

It wasn't possible. She seemed so healthy. "Didn't any of the treatments help your mother?" I asked.

"Not a bit," Katka said.

"What can I do?"

She tried to smile. "What you've been doing. I haven't had a real friend in years. I have a hard time trusting Slovaks, after what happened to my mother. People in school either dislike me because of my race, or I dislike them because of how their friends treat me. Don't let knowing this change you too."

I swallowed. "I won't. What do you do now?"

Katka started walking again, her footsteps fast and sure. "Rest. I'll be fine. The doctors—when we were still talking to them—said I shouldn't feel much pain or even notice many differences up until the end. Maybe a day or two of coma, and then death."

"How can you—"

"It's something I've learned to deal with," Katka said. "I might as well enjoy what I have. Having you come has really helped."

It wasn't every day somebody told you that you made their life better. In the end, I just nodded. "I'm glad to be here too."

We reached Katka's apartment building, and she waved before going inside.

I went straight to my place and into my room, grateful for the chance to think. Katka was going to die. This was even worse than the house fire. I knew something terrible was going to happen, and there wasn't a thing I could do to stop it.

Things had to work out. We were in the twenty-first century—somebody should be able to fix her. But what did I know about Slovakia? Those bribes were crazy, and to go back and get things done right in America would cost money.

Money we didn't have. Damned money. Money money money. Everywhere I turned, I needed more of the stuff. It might not buy happiness, but it bought just about everything else.

Dinner was quiet. My parents must have found out I knew, because we all sat there moving food around on our plates and avoiding conversation.

"We wanted to tell you," Mom said finally.

"She asked us not to." That was Dad.

I shoved my plate back. "Yeah? Well that makes everything okay, then. At least you wanted to tell me something for once, but couldn't, instead of just not wanting to tell me anything at all."

"What do you mean by that?" Mom said.

I glared at her. "I mean communication in this family sucks. There are secrets. I know there are. You know I know. So why don't we just put them all out on the table? What else aren't you telling me?"

My parents exchanged glances, then Mom spoke. "Tomas, have I told you I'm proud of you?"

What? I frowned, but didn't know what to say.

"I am." She put her fork down and leaned forward, her elbows on the table. "You've really been coming out of your shell since we moved here. It's what your father and I always wished would happen. It's been three days since you even asked me when the surround sound system would be delivered. You've been dealing with all these changes so well. Yes, there are some things we haven't told you. We have our reasons. Can't you just trust us?"

Trust her? I wanted to. But I also wanted to yell at them. Demand answers. Instead, I did neither. I stood up from the table without another word and went back to my room. My parents came after me. Knocked on the door. I ignored them. Let *them* be the ones wishing I'd talk to them for once.

Part of me felt guilty. Katka was the one who was going to die—what place did I have for feeling sorry for myself, just because I was going to lose the closest friend I'd ever had? I'd still be able to go to college, get a job—do all sorts of living stuff.

Katka wouldn't.

Hours later, my mind was still going in circles. I'd been lying there for too long, and I still couldn't fall asleep. When I checked the clock, it was past midnight. Too late for a movie, but there were other options. Lying there was doing nothing but make me crazy.

I left the room, doing my best to walk quietly. It wasn't as hard as it was back in America. Our apartment here had all tile floor—cold as Pluto in the morning, but no boards to squeak. My parents' door in the living room was closed, so I flicked on a reading lamp by the couch and started going through some books Uncle Ľuboš had sent over when we moved in.

Librarians like my dad seem to need books around. By now, he had cataloged them all and put call numbers on their spines for easy organization. Way to go, Dad.

I browsed the call numbers, searching for something that might at least pass the time and feel quasi-useful. The 940s (European history) and 929s (family history) would be snoozeville. The 398s were more promising, though: folklore. Maybe I'd find something about the vodník that would help at least one of my problems. I grabbed three that looked most interesting, then glanced over at my parents' door. I wasn't doing anything wrong, but then again, I didn't want them to find me nose deep in Slovak legends at two in the morning. Too many questions. Only the son of a librarian would be worried about getting caught reading illicit books in the middle of the night.

I took the books to my room.

The first two were duds, but when I opened the third, a yellowed envelope dropped to the floor. I put the text down and picked up the envelope. It wasn't sealed. Inside was a collection of Slovak newspaper clippings, brittle and old. I took out the first.

New Evidence Points to Murder in Mysterious Disappearance

Trenčín. Police have uncovered what they believe is a crime scene involved in the disappearance of Alena Kováčová.

I sat up. That was Babka's name. I scanned the top of the clipping for the date: June 17, 1985. I kept reading.

"All along we've been skeptical of the events as we understood them," said Kapitán Martin Zajac. "For a family woman to disappear without a trace and with no reason—it just didn't make sense. Now, the clues are falling into place, and we feel confident enough to change the classification from disappearance to kidnapping. Possibly murder."

The scene was discovered when office manager Rudolf Novotný went to change fuses in the basement of his building. He came across a purse that was found to have belonged to Kováčová. Having read about her disappearance in the paper a week earlier, he immediately phoned the police.

After a thorough investigation of the basement, they came across signs of a struggle, as well as extensive water and fire damage, although they refuse to go into detail about exactly what was found. "The case is wide open," Zajac said. "Some things, we need to hold back."

I kept reading, eventually poring over every article in the envelope. They all had to do with Babka's murder/disappearance. After I'd read it all, the course of events was pretty clear.

Babka had gone into work early that day, leaving Ľuboš in charge. Apparently they had all planned on taking a trip to the mountains for the weekend, and Babka wanted to get an early start.

She never came home. My mom was the one who called the police. Until they came across the crime scene, no one had any clue what had happened to my grandmother. And then, after the discovery, people still had no idea. The police couldn't make heads or tails of the water and fire damage (although exactly what damage was done was never described), and their leads dwindled. The articles came further and further apart and got shorter, until by the end there were just some side stories about how Mom and Ľuboš were faring, parentless. Ľuboš was already eighteen at the time, though, so apparently they did fine. The last article in the clipping was about my mom moving to America to go to school.

I put the clippings back in the envelope and sat back in my bed. How had I not been told about this? It was all I could do not to go wake my parents up and demand an explanation.

That was too brazen for me, but I got up and left my room, and while I put away the Slovak legends books, I wasn't exactly quiet about it, nor was I gentle. If there were a superhero for books, that would have been my dad. He could hear a book being abused from miles away.

Sure enough, the door opened, and he poked his head out, his hair all over the place and his glasses crooked on his face. "What's going on?"

"Can we talk?"

He checked the clock on the oven. "It's three in the morning. Can't it wait?"

"No."

Dad thought about it, then nodded. "I'll put on my robe. Meet me in my office."

I brought the clippings with me and put them on his desk where he'd see them. His office wasn't big, and the shelves were bursting with more books (the reference section, non-circulating). He kept his desk clean, though. A minute or two later, he came in and closed the door behind him.

"Now," he said. "What's so important that it couldn't—" His gaze fell across the desk, and he froze. "Jiminy Christmas." He picked up the envelope, then plopped into his chair. "Your mom is going to kill me."

"Why I wasn't told what happened to Babka?"

He sighed. "It wasn't my decision. I know you're upset—I can relate. Your mother didn't tell me at all. I found out from Ľuboš when I came to Slovakia for the first time, and she flipped when he told me. When we had you, she made it clear I was never to let on about what happened to Alena."

That was garbage. "But why not? Why not just tell me?"

He shrugged. "It's a sensitive subject with your mother, let's just leave it at that."

"No," I said. "What's up with her? Why is it she just ignores problems? Why do you let her?"

"Let her? What do you think I am, Tomas? Marriage is a complex thing. I can't force your mother to do something she doesn't want to do. I wouldn't want to if I could. People are complicated. I love your mother, but you're right. Any time there's a sensitive subject, she does her best to avoid it. Pretend it doesn't exist. Some of that has to be from whatever happened to her mom. That can do a lot to a person. Some of it . . . who knows? I've wished I knew for the past twenty years, but I've never been able to figure it out. We have to be patient with her."

"Maybe if we both—"

Dad peered over his glasses, his eyes strong. "What would you do if it were Katka? Would you pressure it out of her? What about you—don't you have some secrets you'd rather other people not know? Secrets can be important, Tomas. Sometimes it's best to leave them alone."

A pang of guilt shot through me. Should I tell my dad about the vodník? That was different. "What else do you know?" I asked. "All I got from the clippings is that Babka disappeared and was maybe murdered."

Dad nodded. "That's about all there is to the story. They never found a body, never even had a single suspect."

"What about the water and fire damage?"

He spread his hands. "I don't know. Your uncle looked into things at the time, but it's not something I ask about these days. Ľuboš was obsessed with it for years until he finally swore off it. Your mother made him promise not to tell you, and if she found out I was discussing it with you now . . ." He glanced at the door, then back to me. "I'm sorry you had to learn this way. It wasn't my idea. And I know you have a lot of questions about it. The thing is, there are no answers. Trust me. Now you know, and let it end there. End of discussion."

Yeah, right. "This is ridiculous," I said. "Why does Mom have the right to be dictator whenever she feels like it?"

"Because her mother was murdered. That gives her the right."

"No it doesn't," I said. "I'm a part of this family too. Alena was my grandmother."

"Tomas," Dad said. He was giving me his Serious Expression. "I mean it. Don't bring it up. I've been dealing with this for almost twenty years. Don't ask Katka about it, either. With her health, she doesn't need any surprises. I want you to promise me not to bring this up."

"But—"

"No buts."

I grunted. "Fine," I said. "I won't bring it up. But if anything pops up in conversation, I'm not going to stick my head in the sand like you. I'll talk about it."

He nodded. "Fair enough. It won't come up in conversation. Your mom and Ľuboš have too much practice pretending it didn't happen." He stood up, still holding the clippings envelope. This was probably the last time I'd ever see it. "Good night, Tomas." He left the room without waiting for a response.

I went to bed, but I lay there for what must have been hours. I was thinking about what Ohnica said, how the ability to see mythical creatures was hereditary. Had Babka been seeing things before she died? What about my mom? Katka couldn't see them. Could my uncle? My anger and frustration with my mom had a big streak of fear running through them. Fear that maybe she knew something I didn't. Something important. Should I be as scared about this as she was?

And I was thinking about extensive fire and water damage. Why had the clippings been in folklore books? Was there a connection between Babka and the vodník? Could I get Ľuboš to tell me more? And this was on top of the news about Katka. When I fell into an uneasy sleep at last, my dreams were filled with fire women, green water, and a Rollerblader's skates sticking out of a fountain.

CHAPTER ELEVEN

TEARS

Love's first kiss (LFK) is actually a very underrated commodity, especially these days, when those kisses are happening sooner and sooner. It used to be when you needed a good LFK, you could just whisk by the local village for a lovelorn farm boy up for an adventure. Now you're lucky if you can find a teen who hasn't made it past first base.

I woke up when my door opened. The moon shining through my window traced the outline of a woman as she walked in, highlighting the slope of her shoulders, the curve of her cheek. I could see through her. Was this a dream?

She wasn't a ghost—no crazy auras around her body, at least. She stood there by my closet, and I could see the closet handle behind her, rippling slightly as if it were underwater.

"Hello?" she said, coming closer.

I was in that half-awake, half-asleep phase, my mind foggy. This had to be a dream. I could see she was made out of water, much like the thing I'd seen my first night in Slovakia. Where Ohnica had been crafted from different shades of fire, this woman had no variations. Her skin looked the same as her clothes and her hair. All of it rippling, all of it clear. If it weren't for the angle of the moon and the way she reflected it, I don't know if I could have made out her features.

As it was, the nose gave it away: the girl from my water visions.

"Hello," she said again. She reached out to touch my face.

Her skin was very wet, and very real. Not a dream. I gasped and bolted upright in bed, then did what any able-minded sixteen-year-old would do if a strange water creature loomed over him in the middle of the night.

I screamed.

She slapped a hand over my mouth. Droplets of water sprayed from her palm and splattered on the wall. She tasted like tears. "Calm yourself," she said in a low feminine voice. "No one can hear you, and I'm not here to kill you."

What a relief. I shook off her hand and backed up in bed until I was against the wall. "Who are you? What are you? What have you done with everyone else?"

"My name is Lesana, and I've slowed down time for us. The vodník said that you'd had that happen before, so it shouldn't be too much of a surprise for you."

"The vodník?"

She nodded, then walked over to my dresser and ran a finger over the top, as if she were checking for dust. "That's why I'm here. He wanted me to tell you something."

"What are you?" I asked. "Are you like Ohnica?"

She frowned. "That deceitful víla? We're as different as night and day. She's bound to fire now, thank goodness. I am free to walk where I will."

"Are you the vodník's messenger?"

"Whatever you want to think," she said. "He wants to meet with you. Soon."

"More like he wants to kill me."

"If he wanted to kill you, you'd be dead. He could have taken your soul at the pool, but he didn't. That was but a warning."

Now she was inspecting my closet door, opening it and closing it for some bizarre reason. "How did you fall in with him?" I asked. "I've been having these vis—"

"This isn't about me," she cut in, slamming the door shut and facing me. "It is about you and him. When you're ready to talk, he'll wait for you by the castle well."

"The Well of Love?"

She frowned, the moon tracing out each line on her face. She didn't look any older than she'd been in my water visions. She was angry. She was also beautiful. "I loathe that name," she said. "It sounds like something from a cheap carnival. But yes, that's the right well."

"Why didn't he just come here himself?" I asked.

"Because he did not wish to. I don't have to justify his decisions. I only deliver the message. So may I consider it delivered?"

Talk about grumpy. "Sure," I said. "It's delivered."

"Good." She reached inside a fold in her skirt and took out something that looked like a marble, then threw it on the floor at my feet, where it exploded in a puff of mist. In an instant, she rushed over and jumped on top of me. If I had thought I couldn't get more surprised, I was wrong. Did I mention that where she landed, my pajamas soaked through at once? Cold.

Lesana put her lips to my ear and whispered, "I'm sorry it must be like this. He is ever watching. That dampening charm will distract him for a time, but we must hurry."

I tried to lean away from her, but she clutched me tight, further drenching my clothes. Actually, now that I was used to the wet, it was easier to notice how soft she felt. I was basically being straddled and held close by a girl in my bed.

And I tried to lean away from her?

"You need to stay near," she said. "If we separate too far, the spell won't work."

"What are you doing?"

"Don't interrupt. I need your help. If the vodník finds out what I am doing . . . I've been his captive for so long. If you can't help me, I don't— I'll never be free. I've been sending you the water visions whenever I can. It's the only way I can communicate. When he sent me to spy on you the first night, I established a connection with you that let me send the visions without him seeing them."

She paused for a breath, and I spoke up. "What do you mean help you?" I asked, my voice breaking. "What am I supposed to do?" Where was I supposed to put my arms? Around her? By my side? Concentrating on the damsel's cry for help was difficult when you were easily distracted by damsels in general, let alone by damsels in your lap.

When Lesana spoke again, her voice trembled. "I don't know. Something. Anything. Just get me away from him. Do not trust him, and do not trust whatever I say when I am not whispering to you like this. Will you help?"

What was I supposed to say? She was a watery Princess Leia, and I was her only hope. "I'll do what I can," I found myself saying.

"Thank you," she whispered. Without another word, she got up and left the room.

CHAPTER TWELVE
KOFOLA

2.25.1—There may come a time when you need to prove you aren't insane, despite the cautions listed later in 7.3. On the whole, humans can be a suspicious lot, but have no fear: a quick potion will make this book visible to even the most skeptic, and once they've read something, humans tend to believe it. It goes without saying that you should refer to Appendix D2 for instructions on filing appropriate paperwork.

The next morning, I had another water vision.

This time, it was on purpose. I filled up the bathroom sink with water, and got ready. The reasonable part of my brain had to do some convincing before the incredibly-afraid-of-water part decided to go along with the plan. What if I hit my head and fell unconscious? What if my head got stuck in the sink? What if—

I stopped thinking and dunked my head in.

Rushing wind, blinding light.

This time I was old and overweight, dressed like Bach and striding through pouring rain and flashing lightning up to Sleeping Beauty's town house. It had a tower with a pointed roof, complete with banner flying in the wind and parapets.

I burst through the main door, up a staircase, and straight to Lesana.

"I can't believe this!" *I roared.*

The room had low ceilings with beams crossing close to my head. Lesana stood in front of me, her right hand bandaged—the one the vodník had bitten. Her eyes were sunken, from stress or the vodník bite, I didn't know. Her skin was a bit green, as well. Then again, there was that storm raging outside the window, and much of the room was greenish. Either way, she looked better than she did when she was totally made out of water. I remembered her on top of me. I should have put my arms around her then.

Focus, Tomas.

"I don't see why your opinion enters into this," *Lesana said. Despite her appearance, she still managed to put a whole lot of vigor into those words. She put her unbandaged hand out to hold a chair next to her—to steady herself?*

"Of course my opinion matters," *I said, my voice high and whiny.* "A Gypsy? No daughter of mine should even be in the same room with one, let alone married to one. They're animals, not people. Would you marry a bear? I'm not going to be the fool of the city at my own expense. There are plenty of other* nápadníci *who would—*"

"I've made up my mind. I love him. He's a good man. If I need to, I'll leave without your approval."

That stopped me mid-rant. I patted down my clothes until I found a pipe and took it out. Thankfully, I didn't light it. Instead, I stared at Lesana—my daughter, apparently. "I've already lost a son," *I said.* "I refuse to lose a daughter."

She seemed to relax, her face going slack and her shoulders slumping. I continued, "If I must, I will lock you in your room until you see reason. I would rather see you dead than married to a common Gypsy."

Lesana fainted, collapsing against the chair before crumbling to the floor. I sighed and set my pipe down and walked over to her. I knelt down beside her and stroked her hair. The more I saw Lesana, the more I liked her. I wanted to get to know her better.

My hand stopped and I studied the girl. Something was wrong. She was too still for having fainted. I leaned forward, my heart rate increasing, and put my ear next to her mouth. She wasn't breathing.

I coughed and shook my head. That had been a short vision, and it had left me with a lot of questions. Easy to fix. I blinked the rest of the water out of my eyes, looked back at the sink, and dived in again.

And got a face full of water.

I sputtered and cried out in surprise before stumbling back from the sink, dripping water everywhere. Why didn't the visions come every time?

Maybe because Lesana was afraid of getting caught.

I gave it another shot, just in case. No dice. Whatever the reason, I wasn't going to find out now. I hurried through a shower, got ready, and was about to call Katka when I saw I had a message on my phone.

"Hi Tomas, it's me. The castle called today, and one of their guides broke his leg. I need to go back to work. Vacation's over. But as soon as you can pass the tour off with my dad, you can come with me. I'll see you later."

I sighed and sat down. Her voice sounded strained, and as soon as I'd heard it, I remembered her cancer. How was I supposed to be there for her if she was at the castle all the time? Enough was enough.

I had the tour close to memorized already—I'd just been stalling out of fear of actually giving a tour. It's one thing to work at a castle. It's another to have to be in front of a bunch of people.

I holed up in my room and memorized until my eyes bled. Well, I took time to watch *Back to the Future* for a break. (Why could I recite lines from that film after not having seen it for a year, but I couldn't remember what year the Well of Love was built?) But other than that, it was memorizing. Before Ľuboš left for his night shift the next day, I got the green light.

"But," Ľuboš said, "I have told Katka to go with you at first. It is easy to memorize, difficult to perform." He'd invited me over to his place for some dinner while I showed off my memorization skills.

I cleared my throat. Something else had been bothering me, and I didn't feel right starting the job with it still up in the air. "Uncle Ľuboš, if the castle is in need of money, and there are hardly any tourists . . . wouldn't it be better if I didn't get hired? Save the castle some expense?"

He frowned and exhaled sharply, his bearded cheeks puffing. "You shouldn't worry about that."

"Maybe," I said. "But I do anyway."

Ľuboš's face was lined with stress and age. It was as if all the energy he seemed to have was just a show, and that inside, he was worn out. "Look at it this way," he said. "We need tourists. If we can tell tour companies we have a native English-speaking guide, then perhaps more will come."

"Is it that bad?" I asked.

He nodded and sat back in his seat, pushing his bowl of soup away. "If we don't do something to increase the tours by the end of summer . . . it will be too late. There's already a German corporation trying to purchase the castle. That Víťazoslav you met earlier—I am convinced he has been sent to make an offer."

My jaw dropped open. "A corporation?"

"They want to make it a vacation spa resort. The city wants them to keep it open to the public, but Trenčín needs the money. Any tourists would be better than no tourists. I am just the night watchman. If I . . ." Ľuboš swallowed, then stood. "Just be the best tour guide you can be, okay?"

"What do you know about vodníks?" As soon as I said it, I hated the way I'd broached the topic. Talk about a change of subject.

Ľuboš grunted and picked up his spoon again. "Fairy tales. Why do you ask?"

Could I tell him? Katka had said we should go to him, and if the vodník really were after me—and I was heading to the castle tomorrow—maybe I should have some support in place ahead of time. My uncle was into all that folklore stuff anyway. I could trust him. "I thought I might have seen one," I said at last, figuring that was safer than saying I thought one was going to kill me.

I could almost watch the wheels in Ľuboš's head turning. His eyes went to the door, then the phone, then back to me before sinking to the table. "Why do you think that?"

Better to get it all out at once. "Because I've been seeing mythical beings since I arrived. A fire víla, and Zubatá, and a water spirit, and—"

Ľuboš's eyes snapped back to mine, and he cut me off. "Tomas, you must not let . . . I promised your mother . . . Go to your parents. Talk to your mother about this."

"Do you believe me?"

"I believe you believe. But this isn't the first time our family . . ."

That was opening enough for me. "Babka," I said. "Your mom. What do you think happened to her?"

He sighed and put his spoon down again. "Who told you?"

"I read it in some of the books you loaned Dad. There were newspaper clippings."

He leaned forward to rest his elbows on the table, the wood creaking with his weight. "I will say only this, and then you will leave and not ask me about it again, for all our sakes. My mother, she was a good woman. But we have a history in our family. A streak of madness. My great-grandfather, my great uncle. My mother. The doctors think it is some strange hereditary schizophrenia. See things. Hear voices. We were worried it was happening to you when you were little, but you moved to America, and it went away. Maybe you should not have come back. You need to talk to your parents about this. Not me."

He stood up and left the room without another word. I sat staring at his bowl. Crazy? I wasn't crazy, was I? I rubbed my scarred arm. That wasn't seeing things. And Zubatá—I saw her before the girl died. I still had nightmares about that.

No. I wasn't crazy. And something about Ľuboš's attitude told me he didn't think I was crazy either. The way he shut the conversation down so quickly. How he couldn't quite meet my eyes. How he insisted I talk to my parents about this. One thing was certain: I wasn't talking to my parents until I had proof. Something they couldn't argue with. Because otherwise, my mom would just pull a "don't talk about that" stunt, and that would be that. Well, that or she'd put me on antipsychotics. Neither a good option.

I hardly slept that night, too anxious about the next morning on top of all the other things happening to me. The thought of taking groups on tours—having them listen and watch me for an hour or more nonstop—was the stuff nightmares were made of, not to mention the fear of what would happen if the vodník tried to act. I wasn't crazy. This stuff was real, no matter what anyone said. And then there were the castle's finances. I couldn't imagine why more people didn't come to Trenčín. It had everything a town should have, and the castle was incredible. Was it that stupid rumor of the Gypsy curse, given extra credence because of the vodník's drownings?

By the time Katka knocked on my door, I had been dressed for two hours and was sitting by the front door, staring at it. I stood and went into the hall. Katka looked better than she had in a week. The color was back in her cheeks, and she was as full of energy as ever. That was something, at least. We headed into town. The farther we went, the more it felt like my stomach was trying to make diamonds out of whatever was left in there from last night. Way too much pressure. "What if I forget what I'm saying?" I asked as we exited our neighborhood and entered the park.

"I'll take over," Katka said.

"What if they're too grossed out about my burn?"

She didn't even glance back. "They won't care. And if they do, why should you care?"

I wished I could do that. Not care. "It's easy for you to not worry about people thinking you're a freak. You're gorgeous."

"Tomas, people only treat you like a freak because that's how you act. It's how you treat yourself. So you have a burned arm. So what? It's much more important to you than it is to everybody else."

Whatever. I didn't want to think about the terrors of the day and be psychoanalyzed by my cousin at the same time. The castle reared up higher and higher above us. I started dragging my feet, and Katka groaned in frustration.

"We're going to be late! Come on."

One way or the other, we made it there—and without even a trace of the Bigot Gang. The other tour guides introduced themselves. I had my burn covered at first, worried about how people would take it, especially if they already had a problem with Roma. But the more people smiled and shook my hand—with no winces or stares—the more I opened up and relaxed. Not only did they not mind my burn, but they didn't pick on me for being a Roma, either. This was Ľuboš's home turf. It made sense people would be more accepting of Roma—or at least of his family. Why had Katka and I not been coming here?

Oh yeah—we'd been too busy hunting for drownings at the pool.

Almost all the other tour guides were high school aged. From what Katka had told me, it was considered a fun summer job for most people, and students would come up and talk to each other and relax in between tours.

I had trouble with the Slovak names: Miloslav, Svetozár, Ľubka. Who was supposed to keep all those straight? Adam was there too—ready with his pop culture lines that were such a contrast with his appearance. It was like he had the soul of a film geek in the body of a bearded action star.

He shook my hand and smiled. "Go ahead. Make my day," he said in English.

I grinned at him. "That one doesn't quite work."

He shrugged, and the smile stayed on his face. "So you finally convinced your uncle to let you come."

I nodded, and he slapped me on the shoulder. Not terribly hard, but I could see how he was friends with Ľuboš. "How are things going in Slovakia? Do you enjoy it?"

The question in Slovak took me by surprise. So far he'd usually just used me as an English sounding board. "Uh . . . good. I like it fine."

"What's your favorite part?"

"Are you kidding?" I said. "This castle."

He laughed. "Good answer. I've got to go help get the joust ready for performance, but I'll talk to you later, okay?" He switched back to English. "Remember: do or do not. There is no try."

And then he was gone. Someone cleared their throat behind me. I turned to see Víťo, the short turtleneck guy. The probable German spy.

"Hello," he said in English. "Fancy meeting you here again, and on such an auspicious occasion too."

I frowned in confusion. "Huh?"

"Huh, he says. Huh. As if he didn't know. As if he were unaware of the brilliant tour guide career that he was about to unleash on the unwitting, unknowing people of Slovakia."

"Oh," I said. "That. How did you know?" It was kind of hard to take him as a real threat. Maybe he was just a nosy guy with a wide smile and overactive sweat glands. Once again, his turtleneck was sopping wet. I watched it drip onto the ground, bringing "disgusting" to a whole new level.

"I am nothing if not well connected," Víťo said. "And a fitting day for an American tour too."

"Why?"

"Surely you jest. You must be. I expected you to have fireworks ready to shoot off at a moment's notice. Aren't you Americans all wild about the Fourth of July?"

It was the Fourth? "Uh . . ."

Katka came up to me, frowning at Víťo. "We've got to go," she said. "Now."

"By all means," Víťo said. "Just wanted to wish the boy good luck. Break a leg. Or don't. Take a break instead." Laughing at his lame joke, he walked away.

"What day is today?" I asked Katka.

"July . . . third? No. The fourth."

I failed as a patriot. Oh, well. "What do we do now?"

"Nothing. I just don't like that man, and I don't want to encourage him being here. Now we rest and wait for the tours to show up."

I swallowed. "Okay."

For once, it was a busy day. Each group that headed up the hill was another exercise in torture. Would they be foreigners? I was nauseous. Katka tried to keep a conversation going with me, but all I could concentrate on was what language was being spoken by whoever was walking up the hill. And it finally happened.

English.

I heard it long before I saw them. Loud, cacophonous talking that sounded more like a flock of seagulls than people communicating. Katka and I turned at the same time to see a group of twenty making its way up the hill, all of them dressed in bright colors and stupid hats, all in stars and stripes. It was the first time I'd ever looked at a group of Americans and seen them as other people might. Were we all that obnoxious?

Katka chuckled. "Ready?"

My stomach had already dropped, and my palms were sweating. The left one, at least. Scars don't sweat. "I need a drink."

She didn't say anything in response, just stood up, reached in her bag, and passed me a bottle of water. It was warm, but I barely noticed.

"Come on," Katka said. "We'll meet them over there." She pointed to the glass and steel monstrosity, where even now the Americans were congregating. One family was having a meltdown, with a boy that couldn't have been more than four screaming that he wanted to go to the zoo. Trenčín didn't have a zoo.

I followed Katka, my mind in a daze. Suddenly I couldn't remember how the speech started, or where we were supposed to go first, or if we went into the armory before or after we went to the tower. My cousin must have noticed how rigid I had become. She patted my shoulder and whispered. "They're strangers. And remember to talk in English, not Slovak."

I nodded and stepped out in front of the group. "Uh. Hi. Welcome to the castle. We—"

"You speak English?" The woman who spoke up had a loud, brassy voice and a spray-on tan. It's not often you see geriatrics the color of an Oompa Loompa.

"Yeah," I said. "I'll be your tour—"

"Good, then maybe you can explain why I had to pay ten times as much as Slovaks do to get in here."

"Excuse me?"

"It's highway robbery! What—they think Americans are made out of money?"

"No, it's just—"

"Because I'm not made out of money. I'm on a fixed income. I'm retired. I want to pay the cheaper price. I want a refund."

What she wanted was a good swift kick in the butt. "I'm sorry. I'm not sure. I—"

Katka cleared her throat. "The Slovak government decided to make that a rule. The economy in Slovakia is much different than the rest of Europe or the United States. If they charged the same price for every-one—the higher price—then Slovaks wouldn't be able to go to their own national heritage sites. I'm sure you noticed, though, that our prices are still a fraction of what you'd pay to visit similar sites in the rest of the European Union."

The woman opened and closed her mouth, reminding me of a frog. Then she said, "Oh. Well why didn't you say that?" She faced me. "Are you not a real tour guide? If I'm going to pay the American price, I better be getting the best tour guides they have, not some amateur."

The tour didn't improve from there. The woman threw me off my game. I forgot my lines five times. Each time, Katka was there to correct me. She even took over on three different occasions for whole rooms at a time, and once I led the group into an oncoming tour on its way back from the tower. If Katka hadn't been there, I might have told that woman exactly what I thought of her, which would have gotten me fired. Who would have known giving a tour was that complicated?

When it was finished and the Americans were on their way, I was about ready to give up my passport and become Slovak for life. "Are we all like that?" I asked Katka.

She smiled over at the departing group. "No. Sometimes Americans wear hats that match."

I sighed. "What do we do now?"

"Celebrate," Katka said. "You did it!"

"Ha ha. I practically ran over a toddler, and you talked almost more than I did."

Katka motioned with her head that I should follow her, and we went off to the break room. "Don't be so hard on yourself," she said. "My first time was worse."

"Not possible."

"Want to bet?"

"What did you do?" It couldn't have been worse than my day today.

She laughed. "Until you put money on it, I'm not saying."

We entered the break room, which was back behind the glass building. "I don't have any money with me." And now I wished I had some.

"Your loss." Katka went over to the refrigerator and took something out. "I've got you a surprise."

She handed me a large bottle. I read the label. "Kofola?"

Katka nodded. "It's the Slovak equivalent of Coke. We had it during Communism. I even got it chilled for you—aren't I nice?"

"A lifesaver." I opened it up, it hissed out the extra air and I was chugging it before you could blink. I stopped in midswallow, and stared at her, my head tilted back and my eyes wide. I slowly took the bottle down and forced myself to finish swallowing.

"What do you think?" Katka asked, a bit too innocently.

"It's very . . . Communist." Rancid.

She laughed. "That's one way to put it. Most people say it tastes like Coke with beer. It's an acquired taste." She held out her hand for the bottle, and I was more than happy to give it back. Katka drank deeply. When she finished, she grimaced. "It's better warm."

I shuddered to think of it. "Can we go back outside?" I asked. Usually on a hot day I would have been glued to a chair someplace cold, but habits change when there's no air-conditioning.

Katka nodded, and we went out and back in the direction of the main keep, just walking for the fun of it. Ľuboš passed us as we headed up, a broad smile plastered over his face. The joust must have finished while Katka and I were giving the tour. "Fantastic, Tomas," he said, gesturing to the crowd around us. "Six groups in one day. You're a good luck charm!"

At least he had something to smile about. He slapped me on the back and continued down to the tour station.

"I threw up," Katka said out of the blue.

"Excuse me?"

"On my first tour, I got so nervous I threw up over the side of tower.

I almost hit another group in the courtyard, and the grounds crew had to wait for it to rain for the stain on the side of the tower to completely disappear."

No. Way. "Are you just saying that to make me feel better?"

She shook her head. "It's the truth. I wanted you to hear it from me before you asked my father about it. He still teases me."

Who wouldn't? "Well . . . thanks for sharing." I didn't feel like such an oaf anymore.

We reached the ramp leading to the keep's main gate, and we paused at the corner. Below us, the construction team was hard at work on the fallen wall, using pulleys and ropes to move building materials from inside the castle walls to the construction site itself. I could see Adam talking to one of the construction workers, pointing at some of the materials and then over to the wall.

"You'll get better," Katka said.

I nodded. "Right." I couldn't get much worse. And maybe I hadn't done such a bad job after all. If it weren't for that granny-from-hell, it would have been great.

Katka cleared her throat. "Well, what do you want to—"

My right hand shot out to grip her arm, cutting her off in midsentence. On top of the wall, right next to where it had crumbled away, a new figure had appeared. Her black cloak was easy to make out, contrasting with the blue sky behind her. The scythe in her hand caught the sunlight and sent it shattering back to me as she gazed down toward the construction zone.

"What is it?" Katka asked, but I ignored her. As soon as I had seen the woman, my eyes had leaped to the construction site. If I could see what the danger was before it happened . . .

Adam had finished his conversation with the man and was making his way over, smiling and waving at us as he navigated through coils of rope and building materials.

I held up my hands. "Stop!" I shouted. "Don't come any farther."

He stopped for moment, his head tilted in confusion. As he put a hand to his ear to show he didn't understand, a loud cry came from the workers. I glanced over to see a rope holding one of the loads of rubble had broken free. The entire container shot down through the air and crashed to the ground in front of Adam, just missing him. Over a thousand pounds of rock exploded in a cloud of dust and shrapnel.

I looked back at where the woman had been standing. She was still there, but she was no longer staring at the area below us.

She was staring at me, her eyes blazing with fury.

CHAPTER THIRTEEN
ME

If you do happen to miss a death, be warned! You must recapture that soul as soon as possible. Failure to do so will have serious consequences. Ever heard of the Trojan War? You wouldn't have if Thanatos had done his job right. That one single slip resulted in decades of overtime in the Mediterranean.

I stumbled back in surprise, and Katka caught me from falling to the ground. When I checked again, the woman in black was gone. For a moment, Katka, Adam, and I stared at one another, then he unsteadily continued toward us. We went down to meet him.

Death shouldn't have been pissed at me. I saw someone in trouble, and I did something about it. People save people's lives all the time. But that look hadn't been one of annoyance. It was pure malice.

"How did you know?"

I blinked and focused on where I was. We had reached Adam, who was exuding relief and confusion. I cleared my throat. "I—uh . . . saw the rope slipping, and thought you might get hurt."

He watched me for a few heartbeats. One of the rock shards had hit him in the cheek. He was bleeding. "I'd be dead if I'd taken one more step."

I glanced at Katka. She shook her head. I cleared my throat again.

"Oh—you probably could have dodged out of the way," I said. "Maybe gotten hit by some rock shards, but nothing serious." Right. And jumping off the Empire State Building would leave you a little sore, but fine.

Adam gazed into the distance. "Probably."

I waited for him to speak again, but he seemed way too disturbed to manage conversation.

Katka spoke. "We need to get back to the waiting area. Another tour might come."

Adam nodded, but stayed quiet.

"Do you need any help?" I asked.

That got him to meet my eyes. "Thank you, Tomas."

"You're welcome." What else was I supposed to say?

Adam shook my hand and left without another word.

"Come on," Katka said to me after a moment. "I want the whole story."

We went back to the castle plaza—the one with the Well of Love. A juggling troupe was performing, and a group of maybe forty had the benches half filled. Katka and I sat at the back, and I checked around one more time before speaking.

"Zubatá," I said. "She was on the wall, staring down toward the construction, and I didn't think. I just . . ."

Katka smiled. "You just saved Adam's life."

"Katka, she was looking at me . . . after. She didn't seem too thrilled with what I had done."

The smile left her face. "Oh." We watched the jugglers, but for some reason, a bunch of whirling knives and flaming brands weren't comforting.

I shrieked when a hand fell on my shoulder, causing the jugglers to stumble in their routine, one of them narrowly dodging a knife before it clattered to the cement. The crowd turned to see me, and I turned to see who had me by the neck. At first all I saw was T-shirt. I craned my neck up to see beard, and above that, Ľuboš's eyes drilling into me. He had a hand on Katka too.

"We need to talk," he said, and practically pulled us to our feet. The crowd murmured as we left, herded back toward the tour guide break room until Ľuboš let go of his daughter, pulled out his keys and opened a different door. Behind it was another room, full of boxes and cloth-covered who-knew-whats. Ľuboš closed the door behind him and studied me. I wondered if he knew how intimidating he could be. "Now speak," he said.

I cleared my throat. "About what?"

"I just ran into Adam, and he had a very interesting story. I want to hear your side."

"Nothing," I said. "I saw he was in trouble, and I warned him. That's it."

"That's not it," Katka said. "He saw . . . Zubatá."

Instead of scoffing this time, my uncle asked, "You did?"

He was taking me seriously? "Yeah," I said.

He sighed, then shook his head. "What you have done might have been very stupid. To know if it is stupid, I must hear the whole story. Now speak."

"Wait a minute," I said. "Now you believe me?"

"Did you talk to your parents, as I told you to?"

"No."

"Stupid. But it might make things easier now. Why do I believe you? Adam said you yelled before there was an accident—before anyone could have known. It makes your tale more believable. And remember, I have seen things at the castle too. Your mother, she will just have to deal with this. I cannot always do as she wishes. Speak."

I crossed my arms. I'd known I wasn't crazy. "Fine. You want the story? I saw Zubatá, saw Adam was in trouble, and warned him. He lived. The end."

Ľuboš groaned. "As I thought. Very foolish. Very stupid."

"I saved his life!"

My uncle nodded. "For now, maybe, but one does not cheat Death lightly. What if she decides to get revenge for this trick? What if she kills you, instead? Yes, you saved his life, or extended it for a few hours. I will mourn if my friend dies, but what if now I must lose you too?"

The fact that I had been thinking the same thing only made my reaction worse. My legs gave out, and I plopped down on the floor. Ľuboš and Katka were there right away, fanning me.

"Breathe," Ľuboš said. "Don't kill yourself. Make her do it, if she insists."

I glared at him. "Is that supposed to make me feel better?"

He forced a smile. "No. Just make you think better."

In that case, it had worked. "You know, these warnings would have been a whole lot more use if you'd brought them up last night instead of saying you didn't believe me."

Ľuboš sighed. "This is all more complicated than you realize. Besides, there's no question of belief now. I *know*. You are in big trouble."

"What can I do?" I asked.

My uncle pointed a meaty forefinger at me. "Don't tell your parents. Your mother thinks all of this is insanity, and there's nothing they can do anyway. I'll call them and tell them you're staying with me tonight at the castle. It's my shift. Whatever Zubatá decides to do, it will most likely be tonight. None of the stories says she has a long temper."

"What will she do? And what can you do to stop her?" I asked.

Ľuboš shrugged. "I don't know. Hopefully something will come to us."

Katka and I spent the evening hiding in the storage room, talking about the old stories, with her telling me as much about Zubatá as she could think of, though nothing had helped. No clues about how to escape her or deal with her. She was death incarnate: not known for making compromises. When ten o'clock rolled around and Ľuboš said Katka had to leave the castle, I thought I was going into cardiac arrest. She'd been the one person keeping me sane.

"Why does she have to go?" I asked Ľuboš.

"Because I said, and I'm her father. So she must go." Ľuboš stood his ground, which was some pretty impressive ground, given his stature.

There wasn't much I could say to that kind of logic.

Katka protested, but Ľuboš wouldn't budge. He didn't want her in danger. He left to escort her to the door, and then the room had just me, piles of boxes, some unknown objects covered in sheets, and a whole lot of shadows. The only light came from a naked bulb hanging from the ceiling. I had to stay hidden because Ľuboš didn't have permission for me to stay the night.

I tried to keep calm. If Death was so ticked off with me, she probably would have come and smote me right then. Or was it smitten? Smoted? Unless Death liked to make her victims sweat before she got around to smiting.

All those sheet-covered things in the room didn't help. I stood up and walked over to one. My footsteps echoed on the tile floor, and my breathing was labored. The object was about my height, and sort of human sized, although it was bulky. Any other day, I would have whisked the sheet off in an instant, but there in that silent storeroom, all alone. . . . In a horror movie, it would be the ideal homicidal maniac hiding spot. Throw a sheet over himself, then wait for the first scantily clad teenager to come and take it off, or (if he was lucky) for two oversexed teens to start making out in the room, and then *voomp*, off would come the sheet, and down would come the machete.

I swallowed, no longer sure whether it was better to leave the sheet on or take it off. Then again, I was neither scantily clad nor making out with anyone. Still, I couldn't turn my back from the sheet. But what if the killer was behind me, even now creeping up step-by-step, the knife raised high—

I whirled. No one was there. I spun back to the sheet and ripped it off, then screamed at the long-nosed troll leering at me.

"What's the problem?"

I screamed again and whipped around to see Ľuboš coming through the door. He walked over to the troll and knocked on it. "Wood," he said.

Sure enough, it was only a statue, and a badly carved one at that. You could see where the blade had sliced away the wood, leaving the troll as blocky as an eight-bit video game. Big nose, funky hair, potbelly. It's amazing how fast you can go from scared out of your skin to feeling stupid. "Oh," I said. "Right."

Ľuboš sat down on the floor and patted the spot in front of him. "Please. Sit."

I did as asked, happy to not be alone and even happier not to have a scythe sticking out of my head. "Is Katka gone?" I asked, more to hear the sound of my own voice than to know.

He nodded. "We must speak. I had you stay at the castle so that if anything should happen, chances are less that Zubatá will kill someone else in addition to you. Better for you to be alone now."

"What?"

"Think about it. Do you want her deciding to make a gas line explode and kill your mother and father too? Or an entire city block? Tomorrow will be better. If she decides to kill you, it will be tonight. She must make an example out of you, and to do that, the response must be swift, so no one can say it was an accident. The longer it is, the less likely she will kill you. In fact, it is already late enough. You are probably safe."

"What if she wanted me to get really nervous first?"

He grunted. "I had thought of that, but decided it would be best not to bring it up if you didn't."

"Uncle Ľuboš, you'd just give up on me like this?"

It took him a moment to answer, and when he did, his voice was tight. He was holding back tears. "No. I would not 'give up' on you. But there is nothing I can do. I have thought, and thought, and thought, but I can't . . ." He stood up and cracked his neck, then turned away. "You can leave this room and walk around the grounds, but don't come into the keep. Stallone is out, and he would attack you. I'll be back to check on you in a couple of hours."

Without looking back, he left. I realized the position he was in, and I was touched he was so concerned. It didn't do squat for my current predicament, and it was one case where the thought definitely *didn't* count, but at least I knew he'd cry at my funeral.

Enough. It was time to think better thoughts, and time to be out of this sheet-infested room. If I was going to die tonight, I wanted it to be under the stars. I walked outside.

It was cloudy.

CHAPTER FOURTEEN
THROAT LOZENGE

Humans like to make deals with Death. It comes with the territory. And while you might be tempted, we discourage you from entering into such pacts. Unless they involve really good dark chocolate. Because some deals are just too good to pass up.

I sighed and went down to the amphitheater to walk off some steam. Ľuboš was right: I wasn't dead yet, and I wasn't going to die. If some Slovak version of Death wanted to eat me for dinner, she would have—

Laughter echoed through the amphitheater, low and cackling. I froze, and the laughter stopped. It hadn't sounded close, but it was hard to tell where it had come from—too many buildings for sound to bounce off. The castle floodlights did a great job of making the walls bright, but provided terrible lighting for actually seeing anyone near me. Now all I could hear was the sound of cars passing by below. Somewhere, someone was having a cookout: I could smell smoke.

When I moved, the cackling started again. It came from my left, back in the direction of the well. The well with the vodník. The well I was supposed to stay away from. Fine by me. I headed the other direction. Vodník or Zubatá—either one was bad for my health. But when I crept up the hill toward the main keep, I heard something move in the ruins to my left. Something big. Big enough to cause the earth to shake, as if stones were grinding against each other deep below us.

Maybe going to the main keep was a bad idea too.

Weren't castles built to make people feel safer? So why did I feel so trapped?

I turned back to go to the tour guide break room, only to see a figure silhouetted in the floodlights, standing twenty feet away. It wasn't the vodník: the scythe was a dead giveaway.

Zubatá had her hood up. She was going for the full freak out. She walked toward me, and I was so scared I couldn't move. If she was going to kill me, there wasn't a thing in the world I could do but stand and watch. I hoped I didn't cry and beg.

The figure kept coming, almost gliding across the flagstones. A breeze brushed across the path, but it left her dress untouched. She took the scythe in both hands, no longer using it as a support. Only ten feet separated us. Five feet. Three.

"Please don't kill me!" I begged. So much for dying stoically.

She drew the scythe back, then paused and cocked her head, an unspoken question.

"I won't do it again," I said, not even thinking about what I was saying. I just spoke anything that came into my head. "I learned my lesson. Knowing is half the battle. I'll pay you back. I—"

The scythe sliced forward. I closed my eyes and braced myself to be torn in two. There was a puff of air, a twitch at my side, and then—

"Did I scare you?"

I opened my eyes. I was still standing there, and I was all in one piece. I looked down at my feet, worried that I'd see my dead body staring up at me—that I was already in the afterlife, and that Zubatá was just waiting around to gloat.

No dead body.

"Did I scare you?" she asked again. She had a raspy voice, but with a touch of warmth. Sort of like a benevolent chain smoker's voice. She drew her hood back, revealing her long hair. Up close, I still couldn't tell her age. She had a hooked nose and high cheekbones. She reminded me of Morticia Adams, with a shot of Elvira and a dose of generic grandmother. She looked slightly different from each angle.

"Excuse me?" I asked.

She whipped the scythe back and forth past my head. Each time I was sure it would cut me in two, but each time it passed with little more than a tickle. A disturbing tickle, but nothing to cause lasting physical damage. "The scythe," she said. "And my laugh. Was it scary?"

Scary? I'd be standing in wet pants if I'd had anything to drink earlier. "Y-yes," I said. And when that didn't sound like an adequate answer, I added, "O great and powerful Zubatá."

The smile slipped away from her face immediately. "Don't call me that."

"What?"

"Zubatá is a character from a children's movie. Those damned Communists make one lousy kids' movie in 1985—1985!—and the entire country starts thinking I'm this woman with gold teeth and a scythe. It's an outrage!"

What? "Gold teeth?"

She sniffed. "You haven't seen it?"

"Seen what?"

"*Perinbaba. The Feather Fairy.*"

"No." If it was anything like the movie with the woman's nose that takes an international vacation, I didn't blame her for being upset.

"Good," she said. "My name is Morena. Not Zubatá. I'm the goddess of death, thank you very much. And winter, when I feel like it. But these days, mostly death. Don't forget it."

Had I lapsed into blissful insanity? I was still there on the castle grounds, a pool of light spilling out from the break room door twenty feet to my right. Then again, what did that have to do with being sane? "What do you want with me?"

"Mind if I put this down?" she asked, and gestured with the scythe. "Technically it doesn't weigh anything, but carry it around long enough, and you'll swear that's not true." She let it clatter to the ground, then she stretched and cracked her neck, the movement revealing her white dress again. "Come on over here—let's sit down." She gestured at the amphitheater seats and headed toward them.

I held back. "I don't know," I said. "My uncle—"

"Won't notice a thing. I've messed with time."

"Well, still. I don't know if I should be . . . talking to . . ."

"Death?" she said. "Ol' Morena? Why not? You can see me, and you seemed comfortable enough screwing around with my job earlier today. Why not have a little chitchat?" She narrowed her eyes. "There are other things I could do instead. My scythe can be wonderfully sharp if I want it to be."

I rushed to sit down across from her so fast I stumbled and almost fell. She laughed again, though this sounded much warmer and less freaky than before.

"I've forgotten how easy you new ones are to scare," she said. "It's so much fun."

I lowered myself slowly to the bench, not wanting to make any sudden movements and risk making her reconsider her apparent decision to not slice me like a salami. "You're not going to kill me?" I asked.

"Maybe not. It depends on how this chat goes. Unless you pull another stunt like that one you did earlier. I couldn't believe it! Oh, I was peeved at the time. But I got to thinking, maybe it would be nice to talk with another human. It's not every day I find someone able to see me. Anyone I'm not about to kill, of course." She snapped her fingers, and the image of a skull and crossbones appeared above her hand. "Interfere with my work again, and it won't be the same story, no matter what happens tonight."

"Oh. Um. Sorry." Because that's what you say when Death tells you off for saving people's lives.

"No, you're not. But that's all right. It's already taken care of."

"What do you mean?"

"Adam choked to death this evening on a piece of steak."

It felt like someone had just punched me in the stomach. "Are you serious?"

She nodded, took out a compact, and checked out her reflection, primping her hair just a tad.

"Why?" I asked. "Why did he have to die?"

"Rules. Everyone has a time and place they're supposed to die. It's my job to make sure that happens. There's a bit of room for error—enough that I can fix situations like today, for example—but on the whole, every-thing has to be just so. If it's not, I never hear the end of it from the higher ups. Throat lozenge?" She reached inside her cloak to put back the compact and take out an ancient paper-wrapped candy.

I shook my head, too numb to think. Adam was dead? Dead dead? What would happen to his wife? I saw her at the pool with their children. Their *children*.

She ate the candy herself. "Death used to be much simpler a hundred years ago. I could keep everything organized just up here." She tapped her head. "Now, it's all a rush. Did you know six people die every hour in Slovakia? On average, of course. There are good times and bad times, but I haven't had a real vacation in decades. The only time I get is like this: when I stop it. And you can't do anything then. Everything's frozen stiff. It's awful."

Now that she mentioned it, it hit me. Everything was motionless. Even the trees were still, stopped in midbreeze as if they were in a picture. A bird was frozen in place above the glass building. I turned back to Morena, angry. "Death is something natural. It just happens. You don't need to stick your nose in and murder innocent people."

She laughed. "Whatever you want to believe." She reached back inside her cloak and took out a leather packet, brittle with age. Morena opened it, revealing a series of yellowed bound papers that looked like a primitive day planner, like one Benjamin Franklin's great-grandfather might have had. "Miss a death, and worse things happen. Famines, wars, pestilences. Even seemingly inconsequential people like your Adam can have a huge effect. They say something they shouldn't have said. Have a child that was never supposed to exist." She tsked. "No no no. It won't do. I have here the death times of everyone in Slovakia. Everything has to be done in order—you can't go back in time, of course. If I miss just one death, it can throw my entire schedule. Look."

I took the planner gingerly, afraid it would break or I might kill someone by holding it wrong. It didn't seem possible for it to hold much information; it wasn't thicker than a paperback. It had very thin pages that, despite their age, felt sturdy in my hands. And there were lots of tabs: day, week, month, year, and decade.

"Go ahead," Morena said. "Browse through it."

For Death, I supposed she was technologically savvy. She could have still been writing on clay tablets. I found today. Sure enough, right at 18:09:53, Adam was listed as dying by a crushed skull, then that had been neatly crossed off and corrected with the real time and manner of death.

I flipped through the days and weeks, trying to make sense of it. So many names, so many places, so many ways to die. "Can you know when specific people will die?" I asked. "Is there an index?"

She laughed. "I'm not going to tell you how you die, or when. It only works for others."

"Not me. Anybody."

"You say a name out loud, and the corresponding page lights up."

I didn't waste a moment. "Katka Kováčová."

A page lit up. I flipped it open to read.

August 25th, 23:57:09, death by brain cancer.

"What year?" I asked.

"This year."

It was already July fourth. That was less than two months away. "This can't be right. She's only sixteen."

Morena plucked the planner from my hands. "That's when she's slated to go."

"Take me, instead." I said without thinking.

"No. I don't do deals. I tried it in past, and it didn't turn out well. Far too much work on my part, and humans are never appreciative enough. Besides, one life doesn't equal another. They all do different things, have different effects on the world. You can't trade one for another."

"Give her more time."

She shook her head and let the planner go back to nonexistence, then leaned down and picked up her scythe again. "I run a tight ship. No exceptions. If she doesn't die then, that means someone else has to go. And that someone else always has his or her own family and friends who whine and complain about how they don't want their loved one to die. It's not worth the trouble."

I stood up. "Come on! There has to be a way. Anything."

Morena stood up too. "Anything?"

It almost sounded like she was waiting for me to say that. That made me pause. "You mean you have an offer?"

She walked around me, smiling as she wove her way between the benches. She hopped up on one and walked across it, using her scythe for balance, her long black hair flowing out behind her. "I like you, Tomas. You've got spunk, when you're not wetting your pants. Spunk is good. I won't accept your life instead of hers. You're more valuable to me. It would be nice to have someone to talk to on a regular basis. But I might accept someone else's soul instead."

"Do you mean . . . if I kill someone else, then Katka could live?"

"That's the way it works. Someone's got to die then. Find a substitute before the deathday, and she's free."

"Would she still have the cancer?" I asked. "I don't want to save her just to have you kill her the next day."

"If you fill your part of the bargain, I'll take care of the cancer. She won't live forever, but I'll guarantee a death of old age."

This wasn't a decision I could make right on the spot, but Morena took care of that.

"I have to go," she said. "Time will only wait for so long. But my offer stands. You don't need to sign anything. No contracts in blood; my word is binding. It'll be interesting to see what you do."

She disappeared. The wind finished brushing through the trees, the bird flew off undisturbed. I sat down on the bench, wondering what in the world came next. My mind was a car put up on cinder blocks, the accelerator jammed down. Running wildly, but going nowhere.

Some time later, footsteps from the path leading to the castle broke me out of my trance. "Tomas?" It was my uncle. I raised my head, but I didn't turn around from where I was slumped on the bench. I followed his footsteps by ear, listening as he left the dirt path and walked through the grass to where I was.

"What happened?"

"I met her," I said. There was no need to tell him about Katka. Knowing the exact date wouldn't help anybody—not unless I could do something to stop it.

He sat down next to me. "What did she say?"

"Adam's dead."

Ľuboš bowed his head. "As I said, you don't cheat Zubatá."

"Morena," I said. "Her name's Morena. Zubatá is just a character name from some Slovak movie."

"Oh."

We were both silent. He was taking it much better than I had thought he would. Then again, what would my reaction have been if someone told me the Grim Reaper was real, and that they'd just angered him? I'd probably think whatever resulted was as inevitable as an earthquake. "Is she done with you?" he asked.

I nodded. "She told me she'd kill me if I did it again."

My uncle put a meaty arm around my shoulders. "This is not your fault. You tried to do what was right. How would you have felt if you

142

stayed silent, and Adam died in front of you? He was going to die one way or another."

I felt bad for using Adam this way, but I was thankful that Ľuboš had something to explain my depression that didn't involve revealing Katka's death date. I sat up straighter. "That's true."

"Of course it is," he said.

We stared across the lit up city. I didn't know what Ľuboš was thinking, but I was going over my current situation. If I did nothing, and Katka died, how would I feel? But I couldn't kill someone—I wasn't a murderer. But if I didn't find a way out of it, I knew I'd feel just as responsible for Katka's death as if I had caused it.

"Of course it is," I echoed, more to say something than to express any real meaning. I had a month and a half. I would think of something.

CHAPTER FIFTEEN
PRIDE

While there has been a movement of late to romanticize the vampire, the reality leaves much to be desired. Vampires are a lazy, slovenly lot, prone to long bouts of diarrhea and cursed with some of the worst body odor on this plane of existence. Their public relations effort, on the other hand, is top rate.

I woke up early in the morning, having had a half night of crap-for-sleep. When Ľuboš came to get me, the sun had not yet risen above the castle walls. "You should go home," he said. "I must prepare for the joust, but maybe you'll be able to sleep better in your own bed." He looked tired as well, though that might have been from being up all night keeping an eye on the castle. When did the man rest?

My feet felt like bricks, and I struggled to keep my eyes open, but I couldn't stop thinking as I walked down into the city. The place was practically a ghost town, with no sounds but my footsteps echoing from the walls to either side of me. What was I going to tell Katka? What I knew was important to her, but telling her might give her false hope. What if I couldn't fill the pact, and she died anyway? But maybe by telling her, she could help me, and we'd solve the dilemma. But if we didn't—

Someone tripped me, and I went sprawling face first to the cobblestone. That woke me up. I shook my head and turned to see Jabba step out of a storefront, laughing. "Clumsy Gypsy. Had a bit too much to drink?"

Just what I needed. I stood up and brushed myself off, then moved to keep walking. Ignore the jerk. But Gollum and Draco had appeared in front of me. The three of them must have seen me coming and planned this. The street was little more than an alley connecting the path to the castle with downtown, and the place was deserted.

Prime real estate for an ambush.

"Listen, guys," I started.

"No, you listen." Draco stepped up to me and poked a finger to my chest. "No wannabe knights are going to save you this time."

"Why?" I said. "What is it you have against me?"

Gollum started a laugh that morphed into a cough. "Don't talk to us like you're our equal, with your American money and your fancy English. You still reek of wagon and horse, Gypsy."

"Give us your money," Draco said. "And maybe we'll leave you alive."

Were they serious?

Jabba rushed forward and punched me in the stomach, hard. I *oofed* in pain.

Definitely serious.

It took me a second to recover from the blow, but once I did, I reached into my pocket and took out my wallet, fishing through it for all one hundred of the Crowns I had on me. That was less than five bucks, American. Gollum plucked the bills from my hand.

"Can I go?" I said.

Gollum and Draco laughed. Jabba punched me in the stomach again. I bent over in pain, my insides feeling like they were on fire. I stumbled away from him, but Draco shoved me back. Jabba's fist slammed into the right side of my jaw. My vision clouded, and I fell to the ground.

That's when the kicking started.

I curled up in a ball, protecting my head while every other part of me got treated like a soccer ball. My legs, my shoulders, my arms. The kicks that fell on my back were the most painful. I could barely think, but I was clear enough to panic that they'd kick my spine the wrong way and paralyze me. I rolled to my back, and the kicks dug into my sides and shoulders, continuing for what felt like forever.

I had to get out of there. They might kill me. No one was there to stop them. What could I do to make it end? Tears were streaming down my face, and I realized I was sobbing, my eyes clenched closed.

At last, the kicking stopped. Two of them spat on me, huge wads of phlegm. Gollum had a lot of mucus to go around. I opened my eyes. Jabba and Gollum were walking back down the street, laughing and slapping each other on the back. Draco was still standing there. I could see his skinny jeans, but I didn't look up at his face.

That's when he peed on me.

And I just lay there and suffered through it. Another human, urinating on me, and I did nothing about it. Once he was finished, he followed his cronies.

I lay there in the middle of the alley, hurting, humiliated, and crying. Why had we moved here? Why had our house burned down? Why did I have to be Roma? Was I so different? I'd thought I knew how this racism thing worked. It was like bullying, but without the school walls.

This was more than bullying. This was mindless hate.

At last I tried standing. My sides and legs hurt, but I could put weight on both legs. Still, I wasn't going to walk all the way back to my apartment in this condition. I limped back to the castle.

Ľuboš was unlocking the main doors when he saw me. He hurried forward and put his arm around me to support me. "What happened? Was it Morena?"

I shook my head. "A group of guys," I said. My cheek hurt when I spoke.

My uncle's face hardened. "Come. Let us get you fixed."

He took me back to the watchman's apartment, where he had a bag full of herbs and bandages and—more importantly—a shower and a change of clothes. "Sometimes there are accidents at the joust," he explained while testing my injuries, probing with his fingers into my side, checking my eyes with a flashlight. A half hour later, I was feeling a bit better, though my pride would take longer to heal. Pain still lanced through me when I moved my torso too much, but Ľuboš hadn't found any major injuries. It had helped that they'd been wearing sneakers instead of boots, he said. It could have been much worse. I worked my jaw back and forth. It wasn't broken, but it hurt.

Katka walked in while he was putting away the last of his healing supplies. She gasped when she saw me. "What happened?"

"Those three idiots from the town," I said.

Ľuboš frowned. "It will not happen again. I will see to it."

"Really?" Katka said, her face darkening. "What will you do? Beat them up? Get them arrested? Who will believe a Rom?"

"I will make them believe," Ľuboš said. "I have friends—"

"Even if you got the police to do something, do you think that would help? They would give the bigots a slap on the wrist, and it would put a target on Tomas's back for every other Roma hater in this city."

"Then what do you want to do?" Ľuboš asked.

"Nothing," I said, speaking before Katka could answer. "I'll just do a better job watching where I'm going. I shouldn't have let myself get cornered like that. It won't—"

"Don't be silly," Katka said. "This is not your fault. We will—"

"No." Ľuboš stood to his full height, looming over Katka. "Tomas must handle this problem on his own."

I blinked. "Come again?" I hadn't expected him to go along with my suggestion.

Ľuboš's face softened some. "We will not abandon you. I will have words with some of my friends. These three boys who attacked you, there will be consequences. But if Katka and I solve this for you, it will not help you. You must learn how to handle this."

"How to get beat up?" I asked, dumbfounded.

"No," Ľuboš said. "How to fight. How to defend yourself. If you are dangerous, these boys will not hurt you."

An image of me unleashing medieval wrath all over Draco's smug face was more than comforting, but I gestured down at my body. "Defend myself? How?"

"Body size can change," Ľuboš said. "It is not difficult. It just takes time and effort. But you must do it. Do you understand why?"

I nodded. My uncle was right. I wasn't sure if I'd be able to do it, but I had to at least try to stick up for myself more. And if it involved a war hammer, so much the better.

Over the next half hour, Ľuboš and I worked out when I'd be able to come down and get training from his joust buddies, who were out today mourning Adam's death but would be back on the job about the same time my bruises healed. Katka wanted to come along, but Ľuboš shook his head, explaining he didn't want to put undue strain on her body. It was a somber reminder of what I'd found out from Morena the night before, and it quieted me down. Too much was happening too fast. I wanted a break—a pause button. All I got was the day off from Ľuboš. He said he'd cover the tours for us today.

At last Ľuboš headed off to keep getting the castle ready, leaving Katka and me staring at each other. I tried to act normal, still not sure what was the best thing to tell her.

"What's wrong?" Katka asked after all of five minutes. Apparently I'm not as good at acting normal as I'd like.

"You mean besides seeing Death last night and having her tell me she killed Adam?" I hoped sarcasm would serve as a cover for my unease.

"Yes."

So much for that. "Nothing," I said.

"You're rubbing your scar."

She was right. "Mosquito bite."

"That's a pathetic excuse. What aren't you telling me?"

"It's been a long morning," I said, then winced and held my side. Maybe the sympathy card would work.

"You're hiding something from me. Why?"

And that quickly, I was sitting there with no more excuses and no idea how to get out of talking to Katka. I sighed. "Okay," I said. "Let's go to the park, and we can talk there." Maybe the fifteen-minute walk would help me come up with a way to break it to her. It would definitely help loosen up my body some. I didn't know which was making me tenser: my injuries or the pressure I'd been feeling all morning.

As we walked, I kept expecting the Bigot Gang to appear and finish the job. I knew Ľuboš had sworn they'd pay for what they did, but until I saw them and knew I had a bit of a reprieve, walking through the city wasn't going to be easy for me. The memory of lying in a huddled ball, getting kicked from all sides . . . I was still so embarrassed and ashamed and afraid. I'd see a flash of movement out of the corner of my eye, and I'd flinch. It happened four times during the walk across the city. How long would it be before I felt safe outdoors?

Katka was wise enough not to ask me any questions until we were sitting on a wooden bench in a corner of the park. It was big, with wide swathes of green grass framed by tree-lined paths. A gentle wind brushed through the treetops, the branches waving fifty feet above our heads. People were around, but none close enough to hear our conversation. "So what happened?" she asked.

I swallowed. I had made my mind up to tell her, but it still wasn't easy. How would she take it? "I'm not sure you want to know," I said.

"You saw Zubatá last night?"

I nodded. "Her name's Morena. She was very specific about that."

"Huh. Okay, Morena. And she told you something you don't want to share?"

"Obviously," I said.

She thought for a moment. "It's when I'm going to die."

I forced myself to meet her eyes and nodded again. "August 25th," I said.

For once she had no response. She just stared at a mother walking by with her child in a stroller.

"That's not all," I said. Giving a terminally ill person a straw to grasp at was bad, but when that straw might involve murder . . . Katka still deserved to know. "Morena said I could make a trade."

"What?"

"Soul for soul."

Katka sat back against the bench. "And you weren't going to mention this to me?"

I shrugged.

"Don't you think it concerns me?" Katka said. "That I had the right to know?"

A pickup soccer game was going about thirty feet away. I watched it instead of thinking, but it soon brought up too many mental images of my recent beating. Each time someone would kick the ball, I remembered lying in the street, Gollum's foot smashing into my shoulder, Jabba going for the soft spots. The sound of Draco's laughter.

"What are we going to do?" Katka asked.

I turned from the soccer game. "I have no clue. Do you think we should tell your dad?"

"Are you crazy? He'll just worry, and there's nothing he can do about it."

Exactly. I shrugged again, pain lancing through my side. "Fine."

"No, Tomas. I need you to promise me. No one else finds out about this unless I say so."

"All right, already." It was her call, and nobody in this family talked to anybody about anything, anyway.

She was quiet again, then said, "What do we do about the deal she offered you? There must be a way to fulfill it."

"Right. Know anyone who needs killing?"

My cousin was staring at the soccer game herself now. A vein was throbbing in her forehead, and I wondered if this would be enough to bring on another seizure. She stood up. "I need some time to think. Be alone. Will you be okay getting home from here alone?"

I nodded and stood as well. "It'll be okay, Katka. We have a month and a half—plenty of time to think of a way out of this."

"Maybe we'll talk later, okay?"

I tried to smile. "Don't get too down, though."

Katka shook her head and left. I had to keep reminding myself this was a good thing. If I hadn't talked to Morena last night, Katka still would have been slated to die. This way, at least we had a shot of saving her life.

But how? We couldn't involve any of our parents, and even if we could, what were they going to do? Kiss it and make it better? Heck—if we told Ľuboš, he'd probably arrange for an "accident." Someone else dies, and the problem would be solved.

I could think of three nominees right off the top of my head.

I rolled the thought over in my mind as I headed home. It didn't take me too long to get an answer: the one Morena had pointed out. Would I like to have it turned on me—have Katka killed so someone else's "someone you knew" could be saved? No way. Even the Bigot Gang must have families. Murder could not be an option.

And besides, how was I supposed to get a death for Death? It was like the old "what you get for the person who has everything?" dilemma, only a million times worse. Morena had talked all about how she couldn't kill someone before their time, but wasn't that what she was asking me to do? If she had rules to follow that I wasn't aware of, how could I be sure this deal was even possible?

Thunk.

I almost tripped over a package that had appeared out of nowhere in front of me. I glanced around me on the street. No one was near. The package was hefty and rectangular, wrapped in plain brown paper, tied with a white string with a note attached. I bent down and picked up the package, which weighed about twenty pounds.

The note was written in flowing black handwriting and had a simple message:

Thought you might like some help.
—A.

I looked around me again, just to be sure I was still alone. Who was A? Did Morena have a first name? She was the only one who knew about this, and she was the only one who could probably read my mind. But then why not sign it M? Nice and clear. I crouched at the side of the street to open the package, feeling like Charlie searching for the Golden Ticket, except way more morbid. I knew what it was before I opened it. I had been through enough Christmases to recognize a book when I felt it, though this one was more on the level of a tome. So I went straight for the cover:

Death in the Modern Day.

CHAPTER SIXTEEN
BARBECUE

Introduction

Congratulations on your decision to get involved in the exciting and fast-growing industry that is Death. No doubt you have realized that with the exponential growth of life today, the need for capable Deaths can only grow greater. This little book is designed to explain everything you need to know about the science behind the business of death. Your first step is to memorize all the simple rules in the chapters that follow. Once you have the basics down, you're sure to see how easy this profession really can be. If you have intelligence, education, and ability, so much the better, but remember that it's possible to kill things without any of these qualities.

I waited until I was in my room (and showered again) before I started to read the book. The walk had breezed by, despite the heavy weight I had to carry and the lingering pain. From the feel of it, I'd have some dark bruises on my legs and back. But I had too many questions to worry about the bruising, and I was too curious to think about anything else besides what information the book might hold. Better to be focused on this than what had happened to me this morning.

Luckily my parents weren't home yet. I locked the door to my room, settled on the bed, and got the package out.

The book was as thick as a dictionary and bound in smooth leather.

And it was in English, not Slovak. There were no locks, and the paper seemed to be just that—paper. Acid-free, even. No human skin turned into leather, no eyeball on the cover. Just a big book.

When your father's a librarian, you approach books differently—especially nonfiction. I evaluated the quality of the binding and design. It was excellent work. I scanned the table of contents, flipped through the pages, noticed the extensive index. It was organized by subject: *Introduction, A Brief History of Death, How to Manipulate Time, Death and You, How to Keep Track of Death*—even a *Troubleshooting* section. From the snippets of text I caught as I browsed, its tone was pretty casual, considering the subject matter. Not only that, but it had little illustrations peppered throughout, sort of like that Books for Dummies series. Except instead of helpful friendly faces, these pictures were of a little cartoon reaper showing the reader how to do whatever the text was describing.

When I read the introduction, it stopped me cold. People *became* Death? How? Why? I checked the index, but I couldn't find anything that answered those topics. The book was aimed at someone who already knew about becoming Death, however that happened. Maybe you were recruited, like for a spy agency. I flipped further in to check out some other sections, which were arranged into related laws and bylaws with so many notes and subnotes that it was practically impossible to follow.

There were some jobs I couldn't imagine anyone wanting to do. This one took the cake. Then again, thinking about Morena, maybe it just called for the right kind of person. Someone who, instead of telling you the time, points you in the general direction of a clockmaker. I had wanted to know how to fulfill this deal of hers, and she plopped the whole rulebook in front of me.

I started searching the book in earnest, looking for at least the general section where I might find some answers. The more pages I flipped, the more frustrated I became. There was practically no rhyme or reason to the way it was organized. Everywhere it was the same—that stupid cheery narrator talked about how easy all of this was, and about how successful I'd be, all the while ignoring the fact that it was impossible to even believe a tenth of the material, let alone put it in action. Meanwhile, that little reaper guy helpfully showed the right way to decapitate someone, or how best to intimidate victims. One page had instructions for a potion that would make the book visible to mortals: it involved tap water and dandruff (with an accompanying pic of Reaper Dude in need of Head and Shoulders). A five-year-old could come up with a better potion than that.

An hour later I took a break. I was over to Katka's apartment before I remembered how depressed she'd been. I thought about not knocking, but then did anyway. This was a development, and it might cheer her up—give her more hope.

She came to the door in her pajamas. "What is it?"

"I wanted to check on you."

She nodded. Uncomfortable pause.

"You okay?" I asked at last.

Another nod.

I took out the book and held it in front of me. "Listen, Morena gave me this. It's all about the rules she has to follow and tricks she can use, and I was thinking maybe one of them might help . . . you know."

Katka ran her fingers through her hair, trying to straighten it. Her eyes were red and puffy. Actually, now that I noticed, she looked pretty crappy. "That's a dictionary."

I checked. It was still *Death in the Modern Day*. Same cover, same everything. My shoulders slumped, but then I caught myself. "That's just because it's disguised. There's a potion in here for making it visible to you."

"Potion?"

"Tap water and dandruff."

That earned me even more skepticism. "Are you sure you're thinking straight?" she asked. "You had that hit to your head. Maybe you need some more rest." She started to close the door.

I stamped my foot. "Come on! Before this, you knew you were going to die sometime, maybe soon, maybe not—but it was going to happen. If we figure out a way to fill this deal Morena made with me, you get better. She promised you'd die of old age, not cancer. And now we have her rulebook? It's like an open-book test."

Katka stared at me. Either my speech hadn't been inspiring or she was still working on waking up.

"You know what I think?" My mouth had gotten me this far, so I kept going. "I think lawyers would have a field day with this agreement. There's got to be a thousand different ways to fulfill it. We have a month and a half. No problem. We just need to—"

"Come on," Katka said. "Let's sit down."

Well, that was a nice change. We went into her living room, and she turned the light on and went to the couch. "We make quite the pair," she said. "You being beaten this morning, me with a month and a half to live. But you're right. Sulking isn't going to do us any good."

I nodded. "The answer's in here. We just need to find it."

It took quite a bit of page flipping to find the stupid potion again. But I did at last:

Take 2 tablespoons tap water, add one of your own nose hairs and three flakes of dandruff. Mix thoroughly in a counterclockwise direction with a dandelion stem, and allow it to rest uncovered overnight. *In the morning, use a pure white feather to paint the concoction on the tongue of the skeptic. Voila. The book will then be visible in its natural state.*

I even managed to convince Katka to go along with it. What did we have to lose? We followed the directions exactly, finishing off the potion the next day before our tour shift at the castle. We snuck into one of the storage rooms the joust team used, surrounded by costumes, helmets, and swords.

Katka was reluctant to get her tongue brushed with a feather laced with my dandruff, but we all make sacrifices for science. As soon as the feather left her tongue, her eyes glowed purple for a moment.

She gasped, blinking, her eyes wide.

"Are you okay?" I asked.

"That was . . . strange. It felt like someone ran ice down my spine." She took out the book and thumbed through it. "But it worked. It's not a dictionary, after all. Who would have thought? What's up with all these cartoon pictures of the guy with the skull?"

Hallelujah. It was one thing to have people say they believed you, but another to have them actually experience the same thing. I really *wasn't* crazy.

"Never mind," I said. "Now we can get down to—"

Ľuboš opened the door and walked in. "Tomas. You're late."

"Late?" I asked, feeling like I should be covering up the book, then reminding myself that it would only look like a dictionary to my uncle. His crazy daughter and nephew, cramming themselves into a clothes closet with a dictionary, a feather, and a bottle of flaky water.

"Defense training," he said.

Oh right—Bigot Gang Ass Kicking Time. I glanced at Katka, who nodded at me. "I've got this here," she said. "Go."

Fifteen minutes later, I was standing in the middle of the joust arena, the stands empty. Ľuboš had found me some loose fitting clothes that made me look like a peasant in *Monty Python and the Holy Grail*. I felt stupid, but he'd pointed out that getting my street clothes dirty wouldn't be a good idea right before I gave a tour.

Ľuboš spent the first few minutes poking and prodding at me. The bruises on my back and legs hurt, but my jaw was feeling mostly better. At last, my uncle grunted in a vaguely approving way.

"Now, the basics." Ľuboš held his arms out to the side and shook them, rolling his neck to loosen up. "I do not know karate. This is not fancy. Knights were not concerned with being pretty. They wanted to do damage quickly and effectively. Get your enemy on the ground, then punish him. Break bones, and do it fast."

Break bones. Perfect. If the Bigot Gang wanted to mess with me again, I'd be ready.

Ľuboš continued, "But you are not ready for that yet. The first part of unarmed fighting is knowing how to fall."

What? I'd seen *The Karate Kid*. The first part was doing pointless exercises that ended up being ways to do karate. "Come again?"

"Fighting will hurt. You'll be thrown to the ground. Knocked around. You must learn how to do it correctly. How to absorb the blows." In a flash, he bent down, hooked a hand over my ankle and pulled. I fell flat on my back, the blow cushioned by the soft dirt we were standing in. "See?" Ľuboš said. "That was not the right way to fall. Do the same to me."

"What?"

"Trip me."

I bent forward, took his ankle, and pulled. He didn't move. I pulled harder. I might as well have been trying to tear down an oak tree. Ľuboš smiled. "One more time," he said.

I gave his ankle one last jerk. He flew up into the air and fell, rolling to the side as he landed. He continued his roll and used the momentum to get back to his feet. "That is how you fall."

The next hour flew by, as Ľuboš went over the basics of falling from different angles. Falling forward. Falling backward. Falling to the side. Getting tripped. Getting pushed. By the end I was out of breath, sweating, and aching. Ľuboš wasn't even clammy. He smiled at me and nodded. "Two things," he said. "First, you must get stronger. Much stronger. I have weights in my apartment. Have Katka show you where they are, and start lifting. I will show you how. Upper body and lower body. Second, you must practice what I've shown you. These sessions, they are training. You learn new techniques with me, and that is good. But you must practice those techniques on your own. Perfect them. Okay?"

"Sure." It felt good to be *doing* something.

"A final piece of advice," Ľuboš said. "I don't expect those bullies to bother you anytime soon, but if they do, you must have no mercy. You must fight dirty. Between the legs, the eyes, the nose—these are the soft spots of a man. The solar plexus, if you can find it. Be prepared to do damage, and do it fast. Okay?"

"But won't that make them more angry? Make them want to hurt me more?"

"Tomas, three against one . . . if they try to beat you again, they might do lasting damage. You fight to stay alive. You hurt them, and then you run like a rabbit. Forget pride. Forget teaching them a lesson. Disable them and get away. Okay?"

I hoped it didn't come to that. In the movies, I'd have a great scene where I beat up all three of them, triumphant music swelling in the background. But I still remembered them kicking me, spitting on me. Peeing on me.

This wasn't the movies.

The next two weeks were a mix of amateur hour at the local magic shop and a *Rocky* training montage. In our spare time, Katka and I took turns with the book. Well, she ended up looking more at the book than I did, coming to check in with me when there was a part where the English was too much for her, even with a dictionary. It was good she had time for it—I was too busy lifting barbells that were pitifully small (while watching Slovak reruns of 80s American TV shows) and throwing myself to the ground on practically every surface I could find.

And as frustrating as all that might sound, I could still see myself making progress. I had a problem, and I was doing something tangible to fix it.

It felt good.

Things weren't so good on the Morena contract front. The first thing to do seemed like a no-brainer: ask Ohnica. But when you've got a fire phobia, steeling yourself to summon up a friendly fire woman isn't exactly basic math. I was proud of myself for being willing to even consider it, let alone do it. Finally a few days later Katka and I made a small bonfire out behind the castle one evening (bringing some klobása along to make it look at least a bit like a barbecue). The castle had a large wooded area that belonged to it, but which was only accessible by a locked gate. A locked gate we just happened to borrow the key to.

Of course, when I say "we" built a fire, I mean Katka and I stacked all the logs up, and she lit it while I was a safe distance away, far enough back that I didn't feel the heat. That was my standard operating procedure, when it came to fire. I didn't hyperventilate or anything, but I wouldn't go any closer.

The víla appeared when I called her name, having waited for the fire to get to roaring speed before giving it a shot. The flames lowered, and Ohnica stepped out like she was coming from behind a curtain, glowing in the night air like Obi-wan when he appeared as a ghost to Luke. Except orange, not blue. Katka gasped and stepped back. Apparently that potion from *Death in the Modern Day* had made more than just the book visible.

Ohnica got right down to business, freezing Katka before turning to me. "What is it? Has the vodník attacked you? Have you killed him?"

"No. I haven't seen him yet. I haven't really been trying to."

She blinked, those burning cinders of eyes covered for a moment like cooling lava before bursting back to life. "He hasn't even tried to see you?"

"Well . . . he sent a girl. Lesana. She told me he wants to meet soon, but—"

"Do not test his patience, Tomas. He is unpredictable. If he said he wants to meet, you have no choice."

"That's not why I called you. I mean, sure, I'll meet with him. But do you know how to work a switch with Death, soul for soul?"

"What are you up to?"

"Never mind. Can you do it without having to kill another person?"

Ohnica shook her head. "No, and killing another person wouldn't do it either. Morena knows when everyone is going to die. Everyone. You can't surprise her—at least, humans can't."

I had thought this might be the case. "What about the vodník?" I asked. "What if I released one of the souls it had caught?"

"I don't know. It might. But I don't know of a way to do that."

"You can't just break a cup?"

"I told you. Humans have a hard time interacting with us, and we have a hard time interacting with them. It used to be different, but . . . And in any case, the teacups don't break. He has them specially made."

Right. Because spirit-stealing teacups weren't exactly made in Taiwan. Or maybe they were, by special Taiwanese monks. I stared at her, watching the flames ripple through her dress. "Is there anything else we could try?"

She sighed. "The only thing that can break them is a soul who escaped one, but since no souls *can* escape them. . . . It doesn't matter, Tomas. You're already risking your life by being here with the vodník. Must you add Morena on top of that? The woman is not stable. I don't know what deal you think she made with you, or why, but she does not do things on a whim. Everything is calculated with her. Everything has a reason. She's using you. I suggest you put her out of your mind."

"I can't," I said. "I need to—"

"Then I won't be part of it," Ohnica said, frowning. "I do not approve."

I was losing her. "What about my grandmother?"

She cocked her head. "Who?"

"About twenty or thirty years ago, my grandmother disappeared. There was fire and water damage where she lived. I thought . . ."

"I might know something about it?"

"Yeah."

Ohnica waved her hand dismissively. "Tomas, I can't be expected to know every bit of what goes on in this city. I'm sorry she disappeared, but you humans need to keep better track of one another. I told you before. If you really want my help and are serious about it, build a bigger fire. This is better than the last one, but I need a good house fire. Get me something like that, and if you're there, I might be able to free myself from these flames at last. Then I could protect you. Now, I can only wish you luck."

Like I'd ever want to be anywhere near a house-sized fire again. The bonfire flared to life, and when it dimmed, Ohnica was gone, the fire extinguished.

"Wait," Katka said, freed from her pause. "Where did she go? Is it done already?" She walked over and poked at the embers with a stick. Our klobása was burned to a crisp.

"She froze time," I said. "These creatures seem to be able to do that. Anyway, she didn't have anything useful to offer. According to her, even murdering someone wouldn't do it. Morena knows when everyone dies. So . . . what do we try next?"

Katka thought for a moment. "Did Ohnica say anything about what to do with the vodník?"

"Oh," I said. "That. She thinks he might get violent if I don't follow through on his request."

"What request?"

I realized I hadn't told her about Lesana's midnight visit—or the articles about Babka's mysterious disappearance. In the rush of starting the tours and Adam and Morena and my beating, it had all gotten pushed to the back of my mind. Time to fill Katka in.

We stayed in the woods late into the night, talking by the embers of the fire. She took it all pretty well. Curious and intrigued about Babka—and surprised her father had never shared those stories with her. Nervous and skeptical about what to do with the vodník.

Every so often, it hit me again: I was in Europe. Sitting there in the woods, talking with a cousin I'd never remembered, trying to figure out how to live in a new country and deal with mystical beings and not get beaten to a pulp by the local populace. A few months ago, I would have thought I was crazy. So much had happened since my house burned down. My life was so different. Better in some ways.

Worse in others.

I cleared my throat. "This is a bit . . . odd, isn't it?"

"What is?"

"We're talking about ways to cheat Death."

Katka tried to smile. "Do you think we shouldn't bother?"

"No. It's just every now and then, I take a step back and realize how crazy my life has become since I moved to Slovakia."

"*Your* life," Katka said, her face bland.

"I didn't mean it like that."

We were quiet again. I heard the high-pitched whine of a mosquito near my ear, and I tried to shoo it away.

"Do you regret it?" Katka asked at last.

"What?"

"The move."

So I wasn't in too much trouble. "Not really. I miss my house, but it's not like it's there anymore. And Slovakia's got potential—if we can get through this Death thing and the Bigot Gang."

Now her smile was genuine. "I'm glad."

I cleared my throat again. "Anyway, I think I'll keep avoiding the vodník for now. It's not like he's done anything to directly threaten me."

"Only shoved you in a pool."

Oh. Right.

Katka continued. "You can't keep running from your problems, Tomas. You need to face them. Stick up for yourself. Lesana said the vodník wants to meet with you soon. Put off the decision long enough, and you'll have no decision to make."

Was that supposed to be a good thing, or a bad thing? I changed the subject. "Other ideas about this Morena deal?"

Katka gazed at me for a full thirty seconds, silent. Thinking. What about? Before I could ask, she spoke. "There are some other things to try from *Death in the Modern Day*. Have you heard of Starenka?"

"Who?"

"A figure in Slovak folklore. There's a spell in the book for summoning her, although the book is a bit skeptical if she exists or not. It's a little unclear, but maybe it's just my English. Anyway, Starenka is an old grandmother who sells herbs and shows up to help heroes when they don't know what to do."

"Herbs?" I asked, my stomach dropping out from me.

Katka nodded.

"I . . . uh . . . remember back to when you were giving me a tour of the city?"

"Yes."

"Remember that old granny I told you about—the one you couldn't see?"

Katka's eyes widened. "Oh."

"Right," I said. "Maybe I've already met this Starenka lady, and I blew it. She didn't seem too happy with me."

"You didn't know any better. We'll try the summoning, and if she comes, you can apologize."

Anything was worth a shot, though how a geriatric could help was beyond me. Still, you're never supposed to make fun of ideas in a brainstorming session. "Fine. What about the vodník? What if we . . . killed him?"

Katka frowned. "Won't work. Mystical beings have souls that are handled differently than human souls."

"Why?"

"I don't know. The book has a whole chapter about soul equivalencies."

"It does?"

She nodded. "I remember, because I thought we could maybe go to an animal shelter and euthanize the dogs. That wouldn't work, either."

She had considered killing puppies? How far had we sunk? "How about Lesana?"

"The girl in your visions?"

"Right," I said. "We could release her."

"I don't know. Messing around with vodníks . . . it sounds more like something Death's Assassin would handle."

"Come again?"

"Did you even read the book?" Katka said, frowning.

"In a few days? It's like two thousand pages, and you've been hogging it."

"Death's Assassin is the person who kills magical creatures who refuse to die. From what the book said, Death can get too busy handling humans to be able to worry about trouble spots. That's where Death's Assassin steps in."

Sort of like a hit man for Death. I'd have to check that out later. "But I wouldn't be killing the vodník. Just releasing one of his souls."

"Still," Katka said. "It would be too dangerous. I'm not going to have you risking your life just for a chance at saving mine. Starenka will work. She'll have some advice for us—she always does in the stories."

I didn't say what I was thinking: we weren't living in a story. The conversation wandered from there, touching on other ideas, from the brutal (asking to help someone with a suicide) to the abstract (asking the sun and moon for help, apparently another tried-and-true Slovak folklore solution). At last we fell asleep under the stars, too tired to go home.

CHAPTER SEVENTEEN
TERMITE BLOOD

Care should be taken with these humans, because if you fail to properly kill them the first time, going back for a follow up visit can prove futile. In extreme cases, some have become immune to Death itself, essentially ceasing to belong to Homo sapiens and becoming something else entirely. The best known case is Rasputin, who was so hard to kill that even humans noticed, and it is after him that this type of phenomenon has been named. See Appendix E.3.4.

He's not very pleased with you."

I woke up to see Lesana staring down at me. Maybe "see" wasn't the right word for it. The North Star shone down on me through her face, but I could make out the rippling form of her in the night, as well. I sat up and checked on Katka. She was asleep. "What?" I said.

"He said he wanted to meet with you soon. He means it." She concentrated for a moment, and her body began to ice over. Little tendrils of frost blossoming on her skin, her dress, her face. I could have sworn the night air grew warmer. When she was done, she looked kind of like the Silver Surfer, only less shiny. And hotter.

Easier to see, at any rate.

"How did you do that?" I asked.

"I do what he lets me do," she said. She held a finger out, and it melted and elongated until it was three feet long and as sharp as a needle. Never mind the Silver Surfer—she was the T-1000. She pointed the needle at me, resting it against my chest. "I don't want to kill you," she said. "But I can't do anything about it."

Before I could call out, she drew her hand back and thrust it forward, like a rattlesnake striking. The needle plunged through my chest.

But there was no pain.

Lesana drew her finger back to show she had let it melt again. I hadn't been skewered, even if I'd almost wet my pants. What a relief. "Meet at the well," she said. "You have one week." With that, she evaporated, literally. First the ice disappeared, then the rest of her in a puff of water vapor that sailed off into the night sky.

I didn't sleep any more that night.

When Katka woke up at dawn, I was staring off at the castle, thinking about my options. Too many deadlines, and all of them were taking the "dead" part too literally. Katka tried to console me: maybe Starenka would have an idea when we summoned her.

But getting the old woman to show up was a complete bust. The potion involved was even wilder than the nose hair concoction, with ingredients ranging from termite blood (which I had to drink and then regurgitate—fun incarnate) to half a tadpole. It took us two days to get it ready, what with having to split our time between searching for ingredients, giving tours, and trying to keep our parents from becoming suspicious. And did I mention I was still training for weight lifting and medieval fighting? Ľuboš kept checking with me to see if I'd had any more run-ins with the Bigot Gang. I hadn't, but only because I turned and hid anytime I saw someone who remotely looked like one of them. He didn't need to know what a chicken I was becoming, though. I'd fight the Bigot Gang—I would. But not until I had a clue what I was doing.

When we finally had the Starenka potion, stored in a glass container in the shape of a globe, we went out to the same spot we'd made the fire. I threw it on the ground, just as the instructions ordered.

The glass shattered against a rock, sending shards dangerously close to Katka. Then we waited. No one showed.

"Maybe she's slow," Katka said. "Starenka is very old."

So we waited some more, but after two hours, she never came. She probably didn't exist, after all. Either which way, it was disappointing.

The days kept marching by. The deadline with the vodník was fast approaching. My falling won approval from Ľuboš, and he graduated me to learning a couple of basic arm locks and throws, admonishing me to keep falling in my spare time. He also asked my sparring partners to up the ante—get more physical on me. I certainly was getting used to being shoved around. The weights I was lifting didn't get any heavier, but I was able to do more reps with them, which was something. I also had used my earnings from doing castle tours to buy some real DVDs. *Lord of the Rings* and *Star Wars*. Just the bare necessities for now.

After one long training session (focused on getting a hip throw right), Ľuboš asked me to sit next to him on one of the bleachers at the joust stadium. "When you faced these bullies, how did you feel?"

Scared out of my mind, but I didn't want to admit that to him. "I don't know."

"Yes, you do. You were scared, yes?"

I hesitated, but nodded.

"And when you think about them now, you feel butterflies. Maybe your hands shake a bit."

"I wouldn't—"

"Tomas, it's okay. Listen. When I joust, I feel the same. When something goes wrong at the castle, when I have a confrontation with angry tourists, when I get into fights—always the same. Butterflies, jitters."

I blinked. "You?" The man was a mountain, constant as gravity.

He smiled at me. "Yes. Me. Everyone feels this way. You watch your movies, and you think it is all Bruce Willis and Sylvester Stallone. No fear. No jitters. But now I will tell you the truth. When you fight in real life, you don't just fight your opponent. You fight yourself. Your doubts. Your distractions. You get into a fight, and suddenly you are worrying about things you should not worry about. It does not matter how cool you look. How hungry you are. What past history you have with your opponent. You must be focused on winning and winning alone. Much of the time, the victor of a fight is the one who was in the moment the most. The one who ignored everything else.

"The jitters you feel. The butterflies. That is natural. Humans are programmed to feel this when we get into danger. It is your body's way of preparing itself. Sending adrenaline and energy to the core muscles. When you feel this, you are not falling apart. You are preparing to win. In this state, my mind thinks better. My reactions improve. Embrace that feeling. Accept it. Look forward to it."

He stood up and brushed himself off. "I have to go prepare for my evening shift. Think about what I said. You are improving. Keep up the good work."

I stared at the empty joust area after he left, remembering back when I'd first come to the country and seen Ľuboš joust. Everything had seemed simpler then. No worries about the Bigot Gang, the vodník, or deals with Death. But I wouldn't get anywhere whining about it. I had to *do* something.

First thing when I got home that evening, I dived into *Death in the Modern Day*, obsessively reading page after page. Katka was at her place, sleeping off a headache. My parents were out on a date. The apartment was quiet except for a clock ticking on the wall. I sat at the kitchen table, poring over the pages. There had to be something there that would help me or help Katka. Something.

Anything.

For once my hard work paid off. I found what was the best lead yet.

It was in the *Magical Powers and Persons* section, which detailed the various problems Death could have with mystical interference in the job. (And had little pictures of the reaper guy getting hurt in all sorts of ghastly ways.) A chill went down my back, and I leaned forward to reread the section I'd found.

> Rasputin: One of the most interesting traits humans can develop is the ability to resist magic, although this is even rarer now than it was in the past, since mortals who can interact with mystical creatures are few and far between. From time to time, a human will battle a creature of folklore. Usually, the result is a dead human, but sometimes through these terrible ordeals, something inside a human snaps. We're not sure exactly what it is or why, but they manage to pull through, almost dying but recovering.

I swallowed, then flipped through the book to find the right appendix. One sentence leaped out at me: *If the scar's not grisly or noteworthy, it's not a likely candidate.* A Rasputin developed a grotesque scar for each resistance he gained.

I studied my burned arm. Grisly for sure. Had that been why I hadn't been burned in the house fire? I had always been so careful to stay away from anything having to do with fire. I knew it was hot—I remembered getting burned when I was five, and all the years of therapy I'd had to go through. The skin grafts. That had been more than enough incentive to stay away from flames. I never even got close enough to feel their heat if I could help it, so how would I know if I was immune?

I put down the book and grabbed a box of matches. I took them back to my room and sat on my bed, staring at the little red-topped stick. This was silly—I'd get burned.

But what if I didn't?

When you have a phobia, trying to get the courage up to confront it isn't easily done. The thought of a live flame in my hand was enough to make me sweat. My hand shook so much I couldn't even get the match to light the first two tries. This was crazy. I didn't want to intentionally burn myself, did I? According to Ľuboš, my body was gearing up for some big-time fighting right then. I had butterflies so bad I felt like I was going to throw up.

The match hissed to life. The flame was small at first, and I held the stick to the side to let it get more fuel. Once it was big enough, I took a breath, and stuck my finger over the fire, prepared to jerk it back at the first sign of heat.

But there was no heat.

Well, maybe some pleasant warmth. But no pain.

I saw the fire curling around my finger, but it might as well have been air. When I blew the match out and checked my hand, it was untouched. I took the matches and went back to the kitchen.

To the gas stove.

With it turned up to high and my hand at the ready, I paused again. It was one thing to try things with a tiny flame, but if I stuck my hand in the burner, I could get seriously hurt. Better to do it slowly.

I held my hand a foot above the flames. Nothing. Inch by inch, I brought it down until my fingers were in the center of the fire. I might as well have had my hand in some warm water. I went from severe nerves to a rush of excitement.

My scar took on a whole new meaning. It was no longer a sign of embarrassment, but a signal of rank. I was a Rasputin.

This was too cool. It felt like I'd found a cheat code for real life. Immunity to fire? How awesome was that?

I rushed over to Katka's apartment through the night air, cool with the scent of rain. I buzzed her door until she opened up, coming out in the hall to frown at me as I bounded up the stairs. "What is it? I thought I told you I had a—"

"Check this out," I said, then walked past her to go to her kitchen. She followed, voicing some confusion and irritation, but all complaints ceased when she saw me shove my hand into the burner.

She yelped and leaped to hit my hand out of the flame. "Are you crazy?"

"No," I said. "Look." I held my hand in front of her face, and she grabbed it to inspect it more closely.

"How is this possible?"

"Magic," I said, then got her the book to show her the passage.

When she had read it, we were both silent. A car drove by outside, filling the silence. Finally, Katka asked, "You had to be attacked by fire, it says. Does that mean Ohnica attacked you?"

I shrugged uncomfortably. It was a possibility I'd been trying to avoid thinking about. We had so few allies right now, I didn't want to be suspicious of anyone who was helping.

Or seemed to be.

"I'm not sure it says that," I said. "It could mean that any near death experience is enough to trigger this Rasputin effect. Ohnica said she used fire to save me from the vodník."

Katka frowned, picking up the book and turning it over in her hand. "Maybe. Do you have other scars?"

"Nothing on the outside. The doctors noticed I had some scarring on my lungs, though."

"Maybe you're immune to drowning."

It was a thought that had occurred to me too. After all, when I'd been pushed into the pool, I hadn't taken in as much water as I thought I should have. No water, actually. But still . . . "No offense," I said, "But I'm not going to go try that one right now." It wasn't like I could drown "a little."

"I don't blame you," Katka said. She put the book down. "Still, it would be nice to know."

"Especially since I'm going to go visit the vodník."

Katka frowned. "Are you sure that's wise?"

"It's much wiser than trying to avoid him. I could be toast if we wait much longer. I've only got four days until his deadline's up. I have to get this over with, one way or another. Our attention needs to be focused on saving you, not split between that and figuring out what to do about the vodník."

She paused for a moment, as if debating whether or not to bring something up. "I've been thinking," she said at last. "Every summer, we clean out the well—get all the coins people have thrown into it over the year. It's scheduled for three days from now, on Tuesday the twenty-sixth. Tuesdays are slow tourism days, usually. I'll talk to my father and see if I can get him to let you be the one to clean it."

I froze. Me? Down an eighty-foot well? "So instead of meeting at the well, I meet him *in* the well? That's supposed to be safer . . . how?"

"Don't worry. They drain the well, you'll be in a safety harness, and there will be witnesses. I don't think the vodník would want too much attention on his home, if that really is where he lives. If we did it another way, you'd be meeting him alone, and he could do whatever he wanted. Besides, it's right before his deadline. You can't push it off anymore. This way is better."

Better.

Right.

I tried to remind myself that this was my idea, and that I had to do it one way or another. But it was one thing to come up with a crazy idea, and quite another to start thinking about how to get that idea done.

CHAPTER EIGHTEEN
SALT

A vodník bite is an alternate method of soul stealing, for when teacups aren't handy. It's much more painful, prolonged, and dramatic. First the wound begins to seep water, and then the human suffers dizzy spells which increase until he faints away completely, almost as if he died. If the soul isn't claimed by the vodník before this happens, the transition either continues, with the human eventually awakening as a water spirit, or subsides, with the human recovering (assuming other humans haven't buried him first). The healing process can take up to a month. Unfortunately, souls lost in this manner are almost unrecoverable by Death.

While Katka worked on convincing Ľuboš that I was the man for the well cleaning, I tried to figure out how to survive the upcoming confrontation. My uncle's fight training was great for bullies, but I had a hunch I'd need a bit more firepower to survive the vodník.

Death in the Modern Day had a huge section on killing things, particularly where it gave tips for Death's Assassin on how to deal with magical creatures. There was an entry for vodníks, discussing ways they could be dealt with, ranging from a theory about letting them drip to death over three years (while the little cartoon reaper kept watch) to other more outlandish ideas.

A popular theory states that their biggest weakness lies in their collection of souls. If one can be broken free from a vodník's hellacious teacup trap, it might in turn be able to free the others, who could then rise up and overwhelm the vodník. Of course, this is pure conjecture, since to date, no one has been able to free a soul from a teacup.

It went on to list some potions that could be used to provide some protection, but they were simple, three-ingredient things with names like "Viktor's Fairly Reliable Water Propellant" and "Daniela's Essence of Salt," that increased the amount of salt in your sweat. I had been looking for something more like "Tomas's Vodník-B-Gone Failsafe Water Creature Killer."

No dice.

Still, something was better than nothing. When Katka came by two days later to say she had the well cleaning all set up, I showed her what I had found. Neither of us were too crazy about my options, and Katka did her best to persuade me to give up.

"I've been thinking," she said. "There must be another way. Going into the vodník's lair? It's suicide. I was wrong to even suggest it."

"No," I said. "You were right. If someone . . . drowns . . . in the well, then there will be an investigation. Suspicion. The vodník can't want that. Besides, maybe I'm immune to water, just like I'm immune to fire. I'll be fine."

Probably.

While brushing my teeth the day before the well cleaning, I paused to consider the sink. I'd tried the water vision trick numerous times, hoping to get some more information I could use for the upcoming confrontation. It had never worked, but once more couldn't hurt. I filled up the sink and dunked my head.

Wind and light.

I was dressed like a monk: brown robes, rope for a belt. The whole getup. I was climbing down some stairs that were lit by torches, and I was sweating. Not sweating in an "I'm hot" sort of way, but more in the "I hope I don't get killed by something nasty" vein. Much more panicked and much less whiny.

At the bottom of the stairs, I was met by vaulted ceilings, stone boxes with statues lying on top of them, and enough atmosphere to satisfy the biggest horror-movie junkie. I was in a crypt. The air was damp and musty, and the torches bathed everything in a hellish light. Really, I could think of few places I'd less rather be.

Except maybe down an eighty-foot well.

Part of the crypt had been walled off recently: there was a wall with clean mortar and evidence of construction around it. That was where I was heading, my knees trembling and my hands clenching something that felt like tool handles.

I paused a couple of times to check around me. Nothing overtly dangerous. No demons. No lurking zombies. Then I was at the wall. I swallowed, raised my hammer and chisel and started carving something into the wall.

With each stroke of the hammer, rock flew back into the air, sometimes hitting me in the face. I narrowed my eyes to protect them. Dust filled the air, getting into my nose and mouth. It tasted like hard water. I kept carving, though I had to keep wiping my palms on my robe, trying to keep the sweat off and my grip firm.

As soon as I started to make the lower part of the L, I was sure of it, and starting on the E confirmed my belief. So Lesana had really died in my previous vision? That didn't seem possible. Had it been from the vodník's bite?

I paused in my work and looked around again, then shook my head and readied my hammer and chisel. Two pounds later, I heard something, or thought I did, at least.

Another pause. I strained my ears for any sound. All that came back was the crackling of the torches and a faint breeze from behind me. Just as I was getting ready for another pound, it came again, faintly from behind the wall.

"Help."

I fainted.

And found myself with my head buried in water. I panicked, forgetting for a moment where I was. Then it came back, and I lifted my head out of the sink, shuddering and shaken.

"Ľuboš," I said. I toweled off my face and went straight to my uncle's apartment, going outside in my pajamas. I buzzed his intercom until he let me in.

When I met him at his door, his hair was all over the place, and his eyes had trouble focusing. "What is it?"

I walked past him into his apartment and into his living room. "I need to know something," I said.

He followed me after a moment, closing the door behind him and stumbling to the couch. "Couldn't it have waited until the afternoon? I worked all last night."

"Do you know legends about Trenčín?"

He blinked. "What?"

"Katka says you study legends and myths and stuff. Have you ever heard one about a girl getting buried alive?"

Ľuboš sat up, ran his fingers through his hair and beard, and leaned forward. "Why?"

I stared at him. "Is there that kind of a legend then?"

A pause, then he nodded. "But after I tell you, we must discuss this."

"Deal."

He sighed. "Actually, there's a very specific story. It is supposed to have happened in 1796. A girl—the daughter of an earl . . . Andricky—fell in love with a man her father did not like. When her father found out, he went into a rage and swore he'd rather see her dead than married and penniless. She dropped dead at his feet. A doctor came, examined her. Dead. No question of it, but her body didn't stiffen. Didn't lose color. Many people did not think she was really dead. So instead of burying her, they laid her out in a crypt. Still her body didn't decompose. Finally, they chose to wall her into the crypt where she lay. Days later, when a man came to carve her name into the wall, he thought he heard something, and fainted. Others came back, but no one heard anything."

Ľuboš spread his hands wide. "So that is the story. Now what do you know?"

"The girl wanted to marry a Rom, and the man who came to carve her name—he was a monk," I said. "And he heard her call out for help."

"How do you know this?"

"I saw it. I was there."

My uncle breathed out and sat back. "How?"

I told him all about the visions with the water, and about my conversations with Ohnica and Lesana. He listened with a straight face, not interrupting me. When I was done, he puffed his cheeks and blew out through his teeth. "Very bad. Very bad."

"What do you mean?" I asked.

He leaned forward again. "I told your mother it was a bad idea for you to come back. Your father was at least open to the idea, but your mother has never believed. She refuses to."

"Believed what?"

"Your stories. The experiences you had when you were little. Something tried to kill you then. I told them to take you away and not bring you back. But when you grew up normal, and nothing had happened for so long, and with the fire . . . your father was able to convince your mother to bring you again. And now this. Morena appearing to you. Visions. A water ghost. Very bad. This is just like—" He cut himself off, then shook his head. "Very bad."

"Just like with Babka?" I asked, wondering if I'd finally find out more. But Ľuboš ignored my question.

This wasn't going like I wanted it to. It was supposed to be Ľuboš comforting me and telling me how to fix things, not talking doom and gloom, and he didn't even know about the vodník. I considered telling him, but that might lead the conversation toward Katka's problem, and I didn't want to betray her trust.

"Come on," I said. "It's not all that bad."

"You're being haunted, and you say it's not that bad?"

I tried to laugh. "I'm being haunted by a cute medieval girl. There are worse things in life, even if she *is* made out of water. Maybe I could save her or something."

Ľuboš tried to smile. "Maybe. It is good you are positive. But I think maybe you should not go down the well tomorrow."

"I'll be fine," I said, trying to sound like I believed it. "I'll have the safety harness on, and if anything goes wrong, you'll be right there to rescue me, right?"

He nodded but was still somber. "You tell me if you get into other trouble. Okay? Anything."

I hated lying. "Okay," I said.

My uncle patted me on the back. "Get some sleep tonight. You have a big day tomorrow."

Tomorrow.

Tomorrow I'd go down the well. Maybe it'd turn out the vodník didn't live there after all, and instead I'd find Lesana and get to talk to her. It'd be like expecting to get executed but ending up on a hot date instead. Unless of course that hot date decided to stab me on orders from higher up.

The day went by slowly. Work was practically dead—only one tour group the whole day, and they were Slovak. We kept stealing glances at the well, where some of the jousters were doing double duty draining it. Katka and I didn't approach the well—we just kept pretending we weren't worried. One way or another, I lasted through the remaining hours. I was so nervous, I forgot to keep an eye out for the Bigot Gang on the way home, something I realized only once a large guy my age passed in front of me in the park.

I froze, convinced it was Jabba, and that I'd walked into another trap. But it was just a stranger. Sufficiently chastened, I was more careful the rest of the way. I hadn't had a run-in with the Bigots, but a large part of that was due to how well I'd been avoiding them. I'd take them on when I was ready. Maybe in a few more years.

Sleep that night was restless. I kept dreaming about the well. I was in a harness, getting lowered down and down and down, all the while knowing that at the bottom, I would die.

Uncle Ľuboš was supposed to pick me up at 5:30 A.M. I was sitting next to my apartment building when he came by.

He smiled at me while I stood up. "That excited?"

"Sure." I couldn't tell him I was scared out of my gourd. So scared I had downed some nasty-tasting potions made out of strange household ingredients—and a lot of salt—and now felt like I'd been an entire day swimming at the beach. I had even taken along the salt shaker, just in case.

Ľuboš stopped for a moment and sniffed. "Do you smell something?"

"What?"

"Like . . . ocean?"

I frowned and shook my head. "No. Nothing."

He shrugged and headed off. We spent the walk to the castle going over how the cleaning process worked: strap a guy into a harness, send him down on a rope, and have him use a bucket to gather up all the loot.

"What about all the water?" I asked. "Is it totally gone?"

Ľuboš shook his head. "Not dry, but most of it. The water should be just like if you were standing in a shallow pool. Maybe your knees, maybe your waist. Not deep."

Easy to say for someone not afraid of water. *Remember, Tomas—this was your idea.*

When we got to the castle, Ľuboš went to set everything up. I headed over to check out the well again, standing in the courtyard while I waited. It should have been a harmless thing—just a circular waist-high stone wall and a wooden roof. And (more importantly) a sturdy metal grate over it to keep anyone from falling down into the water. Eighty feet straight down and *kerplunk*. Now the well seemed more like a giant mouth, waiting to swallow some aquaphobic fool dumb enough to go into it. Buckets went down wells, not people.

I wanted to say I wouldn't do it. Forget the vodník. I couldn't go down there and get stuck with the water, with no way out except a rope. But then again, I couldn't forget Katka. And after all, Ľuboš had already told me they had taken out most of the water. There probably wasn't even enough to drown in. As long as it didn't start raining. The sky was clear, the sun was out, and I had my uncle to look out for me. I took a deep breath and tried to focus on what I'd say to the vodník.

We had been friends before. Ohnica had told me that. But he had tried to kill me. Why? It was a question I'd thought of again and again since first meeting the fire víla, and maybe today I'd get an answer. Or get killed.

Ľuboš showed up and slapped me on the back. It felt like a love tap from a gorilla. "We're about ready."

He led me closer to the well, lecturing as we went. "Remember, the water down there, it's dead. They never reached any spring. Everything that's down there is from the rain, and it leaches bad minerals from the rock wall around it. We don't use it for anything. Don't swallow, and don't get it in your eyes."

I ran my hands over the stone wall. It was rough and jagged. Would the inside be like that too? The thought of getting scraped and banged up did little to make me any more excited to make the trip down. I sniffed, imagining I could smell the stink already, dank and moldy.

I peered through the grate down into the shaft. It was too dark to see anything farther than a few feet. It reminded me of that movie where the girl drowns in a well and then kills people for revenge. Why would a vodník want to live down there?

My uncle unclipped his keys from his belt and jangled them as he found the right one. He unlocked the grate and opened it, then continued his preparations. I took a few steps back. I didn't want to fall in by accident; a rope was better than nothing.

I searched around the grounds for a rock, not finding one near. People probably threw them down all the time. There were some over near the rough path that led up to the main keep. I came back to the well, held my arm out as far as I could reach without actually approaching the edge, and let the rock go.

It was uncomfortably long before I heard the *plop*.

"Here we are." My uncle was ready at last. Before I knew it, I was strapped in and Ľuboš and some of his friends were holding the end of the rope attached to the harness. I felt like Peter Pan, just without the tights.

I crept onto the edge of the well and perched there, waiting. Team Ľuboš had the rope pulled tight and shouted for me to start. I held my breath and slipped over the edge.

I didn't fall to my death. In fact, they were maybe being overly careful. They must have been trying to make the descent more comfortable. As it was, I just had more time to think about the bottom and feel the harness dig into my butt. It was basically just some straps that fit around my waist and legs, and it hurt.

The walls weren't round. That was surprising. They were square. Dry at first, becoming slimy and covered in moss and algae as I went farther down. They weren't rough, but I did my best to not touch them anyway. It smelled like I was headed toward a sewer. What else did people throw down here besides coins? I started to breathe through my mouth, but it was so bad I could taste the smell. At least it got cooler the lower I went.

I kept a tight grip on the rope; my scarred hand didn't feel the fibers of the rope very well, but my left hand started to get raw as I kept adjusting my grip. It felt like the air was getting thicker—harder to breathe. My heart was trying to pound a hole through my chest.

Don't look down. Don't look down. I repeated the phrase in my head like a mantra. I focused on the rope or on the light from the hole above me that kept getting smaller each time I checked it. On second thought, maybe focusing on the light was a bad idea. Despite the cold air, I was beginning to sweat. My grip grew looser. What would happen if I slipped? Nothing: I had the harness. What if the water was too deep? The harness would support me and I'd call out for them to stop. What if . . .

I couldn't resist anymore. I glanced down to see the bottom still shrouded in darkness. I'd barely gone down twenty feet. It had felt like eternity.

Lower.

Lower.

I looked back above me. The light seemed as small as a tennis ball now. Any minute I'd be down to the bottom. Down to the water. Down to something that might be waiting to kill me.

Time to risk another peek below me.

The bottom was only a few feet away, and someone was waiting for me there, standing waist deep in water and looking none too pleased. I gasped in surprise.

It was Vito, the strange sweaty guy.

And he threw a knife straight at me.

CHAPTER NINETEEN
RAW SEWAGE

Union dues are to be paid at the end of each decade. Late fees will be assessed at thirty percent interest a month for the first year, followed by ritual dismembering for each month thereafter. Participation in the union is mandatory.

The rope snapped like an old guitar string.

I dropped the remaining few feet into what turned out to be ice-cold sludge, splashing it everywhere. It tasted like someone had boiled brussels sprouts, blended them with dirty socks, rotting melon, and a generous dose of raw sewage, extra chunky. And don't get me started on what it felt like in my eyes.

I panicked.

No matter how much I flailed my arms and struggled, I couldn't seem to get above water. I was going to drown. And then someone grabbed my hand and pulled me to the surface.

"Put your feet down," he said, but I was so pumped up on fear that I couldn't understand him until he repeated himself.

The bottom was just a few feet down, muddy with what felt like a fair number of coins mixed in. My panic subsided to a dull roar, and I stood in water up to my waist, spitting out everything in my mouth and trying to throw up and gasp at the same time.

"Anything happen to you?" Uncle Ľuboš's voice echoed down the shaft.

Víťo—the vodník—wiped at my face, fresh water streaming from his fingertips and cleaning my eyes far better than I could have done. He scowled at me, pointed upward, and then put his finger to his lips. I got the hint. My first fear had been that he planned on killing me on sight. That didn't seem to be the case.

"Uh—I'm fine!" I spat out more sludge. "The rope snapped, but I'm okay."

There was a pause, then he swore. "Don't get the water in your eyes or mouth. We'll lower more rope, and you tie it to the harness. Can you make a good knot?"

"Y-yes," I called back. And to think I had once said Boy Scouts would never come in handy.

"Good. Fill up the bucket, and then jerk on the rope when you're ready."

"All right!" I yelled back, then focused on the vodník. It was dim down there, but as my eyes adjusted to the light, I could see the turtleneck was gone. He now wore a green top hat and an olive three piece suit. His hair had turned green, and it flowed out from under his hat like a spring bursting through a rock.

"Víťo?" I asked, edging my hand into my pocket to feel for the saltshaker. It was gone.

"You can still do it," he said, sounding envious. Greedy.

I stared at him. "Do what?"

"Never mind." And then he was silent. And silent.

At last I said, "What was that for?"

He cleared his throat and glared at me. "What? That's it? You finally meet me as I truly am. I haven't seen you for, for, for ten years or whatever and the first thing out of your mouth isn't 'hello' or 'how are you' or 'oh, it's you.' No. It's 'what was that for?' Great. That's just great. Fantastic."

Now I was really confused, and all this water everywhere wasn't helping any. "Um. You cut my rope."

He took off his hat and ran his fingers through his green hair. "Cut your rope? Of course I cut your rope. I had to cut your rope. If I hadn't cut your rope, who knows what would have happened. My life—my existence—was in danger. You came here to kill me, after all. Didn't you? Didn't you?"

I took a step back through the sludge. "Well, no."

That stopped him. "You didn't? You seriously mean that—"

"No, I did not come here to kill you. I came because *you* threatened to kill *me*." I came to break one of your teacups, or at least try to free poor Lesana. Poor homicidal Lesana.

Now he put his palm to his forehead and scrunched his eyes closed. "But what about Ohnica? She told you—told you to kill me. I know, because I heard, because I was there."

"Then you know she said I *might* have to kill you. And besides, how *would* I kill you?"

The vodník brightened up. "That's a very good point, because we vodníks, we're very hardy. Sturdy. I'd say we had excellent upbringing, except for the fact that none of us are ever brought up. But you never know. Maybe you would find a way to kill me, or hurt me or even harm me. After all, I mean, you've been talking to that witch of a fire woman, and you can talk to Death to boot. When you're on a first name basis with the Great Beyond, you might get a wink and a nod and a—" He brought his hand across his throat and made a little death noise.

"You knew I was talking to Morena and Ohnica too?"

"Knew? Of course I knew. It's my business to know. That's why I had to cut that rope of yours. I had to tell you that I'm working on getting the answer. I know all about it, and I know what you can do to get out of this deal she's made. The one about your cousin."

Everything was going too fast for me. The rope Ľuboš was letting down hit me in the head. He called out from above: "Did you get it?"

I glared up, then lost my irritation when I remembered just how far down I was. Did I mention I was *standing* in *water*? My clothes were soaked, my socks were squishing in my shoes, I was cold and covered in toxic slime. Why did I think this was a good idea? Life sucked just about then. "Yeah," I called back.

"Good. Don't worry," Ľuboš said. "You have plenty of time."

"Okay," I said. "Everything's going just fine."

"Good." And that was it.

I turned back to the vodník, forcing myself to take deep breaths. I should have been filling the bucket with coins, but I was too scared to move. "So you don't want to kill me?"

He raised his eyebrows in surprise and put his hat back on at the same time, jamming it on with both hands. "Kill you? Kill my old friend, my best comrade, my old partner in crime? Why would I want to do that?"

I scrunched my forehead in confusion. "Didn't you have Lesana threaten me? And didn't you try and drown me when I was a kid?"

"Drown you," he said in disbelief. "Drown you. Of course I tried to drown you. But that doesn't mean I'd kill you. Never that. Not for Tomas."

"Isn't it the same thing?"

"No. No no no no no. Is a work by Warhol just a snapshot? Is a symphony by Smetana only somebody plunking at strings? Drowning by vodník and death are two very different approaches to the afterlife. With death, you have a very unpleasant heart-to-heart with ol' Mrs. Sickle, followed by something that goes far too deeply into religious debate for me to want to answer off the cuff like this. With vodník drowning, you find yourself safe and snug in a luxury teacup. No worries, no cares, just philosophy and debate for the rest of eternity. It's even better than life, if you can overlook the brief shortness of breath it takes to get there."

"Doesn't sound so much fun to me," I said. My feet were getting very cold and uncomfortable, but I wasn't dead yet, so all told, this expedition had been a success so far.

The vodník sniffed. "Not so much fun. Well, your alternative was getting charbroiled by Ohnica. She already had your arm crisped when I got to you. Besides, back when I knew you before, drowning was all you wanted. I told you and told you that your parents would be upset. But you wouldn't listen. You just had to be drowned. Is it my fault that I couldn't say no? That I wanted to fulfill your every whim?"

So Ohnica claimed one thing, and the vodník claimed something else. Who was I supposed to trust? My fear was subsiding, and I started eyeing the water. That bucket wasn't going to fill itself. "I was five. You knew better."

He shrugged. "I see. Such a simple answer. I'll keep that on file for the next time a kid tells me he wants to go under. If only I'd been half as smart as you are now. But I wasn't. That's no reason to kill me, though. Right?"

"Of course. I mean of course not. I mean, right. It's no reason to kill you."

"Phew!" He wiped his brow in relief. "Of all the ways to go, I thought that death by best friend would have been one of the worst." He looked down into the water and crinkled his nose. "Not salt. Surely my old best friend wouldn't have brought salt with him. Not into my home."

"I, uh . . ."

He rolled his eyes. "Oh well. Perhaps it was to be expected. And at least you didn't bring a lot of it. I can't stand the stuff. It aggravates my allergies."

And indeed, he did seem to be getting puffy around the eyes. "Hold on," I said. I swallowed, then plunged my hand into the water, feeling around for loose change. There was plenty down there, slimy and slippery. I grabbed a fistful and took them out of the water. Most of it was sludge. It was going to be a long job. I eyed the vodník. "You're really not going to kill me? Or drown me?"

"For you, Tomas—anything. You say the word. No killing, no dismembering, no drowning, no vivisecting. No nothing. I'm just glad you're back, and I'm glad I can be in a position to help you." He poked a finger into the water, and small jets of liquid shot into the air, each of them carrying a coin and shooting right into my bucket. In a matter of moments, the bucket was filled with slimy currency. Watching water do unnatural things made me want to throw up, but it was better than rooting around in a pool of it all on my lonesome.

I cleared my throat. "Oh. Uh. Thanks."

"Tell your uncle to lift it up. There's plenty more where that came from. I usually keep a percentage back from the greedy buggers, but in your case, I'm willing to let that go. I'll even throw some extra in on the side."

I tied the rope to the bucket and gave it a few quick jerks. After a moment, it started rising up the well toward daylight above. I looked back down, blinking away the brightness of the sky. "So . . . do I call you Víťo? Is that really your name?"

He snorted. "Víťo. It's a ruse. A guise. A simple pretense. I'm a vodník, not a name. I'm bigger than names. Names don't begin to describe me."

"Nuts" didn't begin to describe him. "What was that you said about knowing how to fulfill Death's bargain? Do you have a plan?" This was unexpected. Maybe I wouldn't have to come up with a way to ask him to see a teacup without raising suspicions. Sure, Ohnica had said they were unbreakable, but I'd figured it was at least worth a shot. Besides, Ohnica didn't seem like she had a monopoly on truth. But avoiding that whole scenario wouldn't be a bad thing.

The vodník smiled, all teeth, but in a denturish sort of a way. "Well, I wouldn't quite call it a plan. Not yet. I have lots of ideas. Many ideas."

"As in?"

He patted his chest. "I'm taking notes. Writing down the ideas. Every single one. While you've been out gallivanting around, I've been working, thinking, coming up with ideas to help you. And then you repay it by trying to murder me in my own glum home. I mean, it's not much, you know, but it's something. It's all I have."

I examined the walls. "Not much" was an understatement. "Hellacious pit of stench and despair" was closer to it. And water was *everywhere*. I had to take deep breaths. *Think about the vodník, not the water.*

He fluttered his hand at me to catch my attention. "Not that it's always this bad, of course. When the water's full, it's not as dank, and there's more room to stretch, and it's much wetter."

And that was supposed to make me more relieved? "Where are your teacups? All the souls you've collected."

"The souls? That's a very personal question. I don't just go up to you and ask you to see your life's greatest achievement, do I? Why do you have to be so nosy? Stay focused on what matters to you. The plan." He patted his jacket pocket again. "You're a bit earlier than I would have liked, I must admit. It's not completely ready. Only semi-ready. Quasi-ready.

But I'll have it for you soon. It's going to be fantastic. Supreme. Magnificent, even. Not that my ideas right now are bad, mind you. I mean, generally speaking, I'm a genius. I wouldn't say I'm a god among men, but I am. You don't kill gods, you know."

"What about Lesana?" I asked. "Where is she?"

His eyes narrowed, and he cocked an eyebrow. He was probably going for benignly amusing, but it came off as sinister. "First the souls, and now my girlfriend. What is it with you? How about I start taking an unhealthy interest in Katka. Would you like that?"

I shook my head.

"Right," he said. "Then don't you worry about Lesana. She's off limits to you. Strictly secretarial work when it comes to humans. But I'll be in touch with you soon. No well involved. Just don't bring any salt again. I'm practically breaking out in hives. And no more plotting to kill me." He sunk beneath the water, just as if the bottom of the well had given out and sucked him under, leaving me very much alone.

And wet.

Deep breaths, Tomas. Deep breaths.

The bucket klunked into my head, and when I grabbed it, the jets of water shot up again, filling the bucket with coins again. I repeated the process three more times before I was finished. When the vodník had been with me, it was easier to keep my mind off where I was. Alone, it was much worse.

I tried to convince myself that it had gone well. The vodník seemed much nicer than I expected (or at least more insane than violent), I wasn't dead, and he had a plan to help Katka. So nothing had gone according to plan, but things were still looking up.

If I could bring myself to trust the vodník.

Every time I thought of him being helpful, the image of him drowning that boy and stealing his soul flashed into my head. How could I work with someone who could do that?

It didn't make sense. He sent Lesana to me weeks ago to ask me to come to meet him here, and then he sent her again to threaten me. It was so urgent, it seemed. But when I showed up, he tells me he didn't expect me to come so soon.

Every time I hoped I'd get closer to some resolution, something popped up to push me further away.

And we were running out of time.

CHAPTER TWENTY

COBBLESTONE

While they present a unique set of problems for the aspiring Death, ghosts also present an interesting set of possibilities. Because their souls have not yet left this world, they are essentially "live deaths" – deaths just waiting to be completed. If you get behind in any of your tallies, and nothing seems to be working, finishing off a ghost might be the answer.

Eight days from when I talked to the vodník, we weren't any closer to a solution. He hadn't come forward with his "great plan," and no amount of searching the book helped us come up with new ideas. It was already August third.

We only had twenty-two days, but every way we turned was a dead end.

I thought I was going to go crazy. Always before, when there was something wrong, I could do something. Anything. Study harder for a test. Practice more. Talk to someone. Not this, though. Every idea had led to a dead end.

We couldn't kill another person—Morena knew ahead of time who was dying when, and she would inevitably beat us to the punch. We spent three days trying to finagle our way to a castle in Orava that was supposed to be haunted, but when we finally got there, we found no evidence of actual ghosts. And even if we had, we weren't entirely certain how to kill one. *Death in the Modern Day* had more than a little to say on the subject, but apparently killing a ghost depended a lot on how the spirit had become a ghost in the first place. We didn't have time to turn this into a *Supernatural* episode.

We tried other haunted places. Graveyards. Museums. I went over that cursed book backward and forward, and when I wasn't using it, Katka was. We came up with zilch. It didn't help that it was so hard to find anything in it. Death didn't make a deal with you that she knew was impossible to meet. Did she?

Maybe she did.

The questions were going to make me bonkers if the waiting didn't. At times Katka and I would manage to forget the looming storm cloud over us, but it inevitably came back with a vengeance. Katka would have a splitting migraine for two days, or she'd disappear into her apartment for an afternoon and not want to talk about what had happened.

She was getting worse.

It didn't come as a comfort that I was now practically a professional when it came to falling down and getting shoved, and even the dumbbells I was lifting were getting bigger. Progress in only one area—the least important one—felt like no progress at all. I'd rather get beat up again and have a guarantee that Katka would live than have her die and never have another run-in with the BGs.

It was my day off from giving tours. When I woke up, Katka had left a note on my door saying to meet her at the plague monument at noon. Ľuboš was gone on a trip with the jousting group in an attempt to raise enough funds to hold on to the castle. Tourism had gotten even worse. In any case, Katka asking me to go into the city today wasn't in the normal routine, and I hoped it might mean she had a lead of some sort.

It was pouring rain, with wind gusting hard enough to make my umbrella feel ready to go airborne. Among its other flaws, cobblestone acts like a great water retaining device. My feet kicked up drops with each step, and the wind made up for the rest. By the time I got into town, I was soaked from the knees down, and the rest of my body was more than damp. I wasn't so much panicked as just plain miserable. My phobia only got really bad when water started pooling. In the rain, I could tell myself it was just like taking a shower, only with more water retention.

The city center was empty enough that it took less than a glance for me to see Katka wasn't at the plague pole like she said she'd be. Maybe she didn't have an umbrella, and had gone inside one of the stores to wait. I made my way from shop to shop around the square. No Katka, though I did get a glimpse of Gollum walking out of the pizza place over by the clock tower. I was careful to duck into a store before he saw me.

"You!" the storekeeper snapped as soon as I walked in. "What do you want?"

I looked around. It was a dress store. "Uh . . . something for my mom?"

"Get out! You're getting water everywhere with your umbrella."

So much for that. But Gollum was gone, so mission accomplished. I checked my watch: 12:15. She could be running late. Or maybe she'd had a seizure, or . . . I'd wait another fifteen minutes, then go to the castle and check there. There was no place to sit down, and judging by the reception I'd just gotten, going into stores wasn't going to win me any friends, so I stayed outside to wait, against my better judgment.

Probably as a throwback to Communism, customer service wasn't a big thing here. In fact, the motto seemed to be "the customer is always wrong." From what Katka had told me, in the Cold War, shopkeepers had it cushy. If someone wasn't nice to them, then they wouldn't let that person buy the good stuff. No wonder a free market pissed them all off.

Then again, it could have just been more racism. Part of me really wanted to pick up shoplifting as a hobby. Everybody thought I was doing it anyway. I wished I could just walk through town and not feel like an outsider—not have the nasty looks from people I passed. I didn't have the plague. I was just like everybody else, only darker. And burned. What did that matter?

A Roma family walked by me: a father, mother, and a little girl that couldn't be older than five, eating an ice cream cone under her little umbrella. She waved at me. The parents just nodded stoically and kept going. At least it wasn't outright hostility.

Katka didn't show—not fifteen minutes later, not a half hour later. There was only so much "I'm sure she'll come round the corner the next second" I could take. I was worried, and that made me even grumpier. She'd get an earful from me when I found her.

If I found her.

The memory of her seizure leaped into my mind, the way her body had convulsed. The spittle. What if she were out there right now, alone in the city? Would anyone help a Roma girl, or would people just shrug it off and assume the girl was doing it to get attention or increase her haul when she went begging later?

I tried to take my mind off that train of thought. That's when I saw them.

Across the square, Gollum had cronied up with Jabba and Draco. They stood there staring at me through the sheets of rain. I wanted to slink away somewhere and hide. A knot of fear settled into my stomach. I'd been able to avoid the Bigot Gang until now, but there would be no escaping them now. Not unless I wanted to try running away.

And all of a sudden, I didn't. What had Ľuboš said? Embrace the fear. Focus.

I kept my gaze steady. They weren't going to make me cower, though a big part of me wanted to. I felt at my side where I had been bruised for days after their attack. Not again.

Time to leave. I gripped my umbrella tightly and trudged up the hill toward the castle, walking right past the Bigot Gang on my right. They spat at me as I walked past. I ignored it. Running wasn't going to get me anywhere. Yes, Ľuboš had said to run like a rabbit if I got attacked, but he'd also told me to stand up for myself. If they kept their malice to spitting, I could handle it.

On the slant, it was harder for me to keep my footing on the cobblestones, but I still tried to hurry as much as I could. Now that I was moving again, I was back to getting wet. I glanced back to see if I was being followed. Sure enough, they were there, walking side by side. Too cool for umbrellas. At least with all three of them behind me, I knew there'd be no surprises up ahead.

Then I tripped on the slick cobblestones.

Snap. Crunch. Splat.

I was face first on the ground. My umbrella lay beneath me, transferring all the water it had soaked up and making sure it finished the job of getting me drenched. I tried to stand, but someone pushed me from behind.

"What are you going to do, Gypsy?" Draco said, coming to stand in front of me. "Blame us for tripping too?"

I stared up at the three of them, surrounding me once again. I almost panicked. This was just like before. I had to control my emotions. I left the broken umbrella on the ground and stood up in a fluid motion. All that falling practice was good for something. "What are you going to do?" I asked.

To my left, Gollum coughed, then snorted up some phlegm. "We don't think you learned your lesson last time. Just like a Gypsy. You went running for your uncle and the authorities, full of lies."

On my right, Jabba moved to shove me. I stepped to the side of the blow and blocked it with my right hand, hooking around his arm and turning it into one of the arm locks Ľuboš had been having me practice, twisting his wrist so that his elbow was out straight in front of him. Using my momentum, I kicked Jabba as hard as I could between the legs, feeling a jolt go up my leg as I connected. He *oofed* in pain and bent over. I let go of his arm and ran for the hole he'd left in the circle around me. Draco stepped in to stop me, but I pushed him away. He stumbled to the ground, off balance. Gollum just stood there as I ran off up the hill.

It had worked. Even being soaked to the bone, I couldn't help smiling. Sure, maybe I'd just gotten myself into some sort of future trouble, but in the here and now, it felt great. Jabba would be talking like Mickey Mouse for a week. I didn't even mind being so wet anymore.

I slowed to a walk as I passed the main gate to the castle. The guy who was on ticket duty that day, Janči, nodded to me as if nothing were different. Like he always saw people walking in rain so dense you could drink it like a water fountain.

Up at the castle, I found Katka in the tour guide break room, lying down with a damp cloth across her eyes. That wiped the smile off my face. I knocked lightly on the door. "You okay?"

She took the cloth off her face and sat up. "Tomas? You're drenched. Didn't you get my phone message? I told you I'd meet you back at the apartment. I know how you hate getting wet."

Oh. "I didn't check the machine. What happened to you?"

"The usual, but I'm pretty much over it." She stood. "Wait here. My dad keeps a change of clothes in the other room." She returned with the clothes—including shoes—and some keys and headed outside. "There's an apartment over here where we let people stay sometimes. It has a shower that's more private than where you showered before. Don't worry. You'll be better in no time." In typical Katka fashion, she dealt with her problems by ignoring them. It must run in my family. I didn't bring up my encounter with the Bigot Gang.

When we went outside, the rain had stopped. Just like that. Stupid weather. We walked down the hill to the main entry gate, where a staircase led up the wall to a little square tower with a door recessed into the side. After a moment Katka found the right key, and we were inside.

The door opened to a short hallway, with a bathroom on the right and a large room straight ahead. It was furnished with four single beds, and two small windows let enough light in to make the place feel roomy. It would be a cool place for a sleepover. Rustic, but not medieval like the rest of the castle.

"Meet me back at the break room when you're finished," Katka said. "And lock the door behind you when you're done." She must not have been feeling that much better, since she was so quick to leave.

I sighed and headed to the bathroom. Everything would be better after a quick shower. I'd go and find Katka and cheer her up. But first the shower. A dry, clean Tomas was a better Tomas.

There was a towel already in there, and the shower was the kind with a bathtub built in, and—more importantly—a head that attached to the wall, which improved my mood. It had been forever since I'd had a real, hands-free showering experience. There was a window in the bathroom, but it was frosted glass, and I made double sure both it and the door were locked before I was ready to start.

I shucked off the soaked clothes and jumped in. Maybe it was the contrast with the wet pelting rain I'd just endured, but for once, I was able to forget my fear of water and just enjoy the heat and calm down.

At some point, a different sound intruded on my relaxation. Water was accumulating in the base of the tub, the shower stream now plunging into a growing pool. Just that quickly, my relaxation was ruined. My phobia started to kick in. Had I closed the drain? No.

It had to be a clog: old castle plus old pipes equaled plugged drain. I shut off the water. Or tried to. The knob spun loosely in its tracks, doing nothing. I spun it the other way, and the shower got stronger.

I swallowed, trying to remain calm while fiddling with the knob. The water pressure increased more. Now it was like hot needles jabbing into my skin. I'd get out and try fixing things without getting poked to death.

But the shower curtain didn't open. It might as well have been glued to the wall. My panic rose, and it got even worse when I saw a head emerge from the water, followed by shoulders and arms. It was transparent at first, but as it shot up, it gained color and form, water streaming down until I knew who it was.

The vodník.

CHAPTER TWENTY-ONE
SHOWER WATER

Remember: your scythe is not a toy. Anyone caught using it to pole vault, play baseball, or shoot pool will be punished.

He leaped toward me, hitting me in the chest and knocking me into the wall. My head bounced off the tiles, and the room began to swim. My feet slipped out from under me, and I made a wild grab at the shower curtain. It ripped off, sending me crashing into the growing pool of water in the tub.

The vodník had moved his hands up to my neck, and he was doing his best to shove my head under the water. I flailed wildly, my right arm caught in the shower curtain, and my left batting at his body. The water was getting deeper, helped by my body mass. If I had fallen in the other way—with my head toward the deep end—I would be submerged already.

If I didn't do something quick, I was going to die.

I struggled harder, forcing my right arm to beat at my attacker awkwardly, shower curtain and all. With my left hand I gouged at his eyes and was rewarded with a nasty bite. I screamed in pain and took in a lungful of water.

The vodník lunged down on me again, rapping my head against the tub. I was a sputtering, panicked wreck, and then the water slipped over my head, and everything was submerged into silence.

Totally underwater, it was easier to see, and I stared up at the face of my attacker. He was so calm. Like he was reading the morning paper over his cereal. Like none of this mattered to him at all.

Like we were still doing nothing more than chatting at the bottom of his well.

My vision dimmed. There was only so long I could hold my breath. If I didn't do something now, then I wasn't going to do anything again. With a last burst of effort, I focused everything I had into thrusting him off.

It wasn't enough.

My mouth opened almost on its own, sucking for air but only getting water. It poured down my throat and into my lungs.

And I kept breathing.

Sure, it was like I was breathing jello, but it wasn't killing me.

Just freaking me out beyond all expression. I breathed out and in again, still conscious. Still alive. Not choking and definitely not drowning. I relaxed just a little, still in the vodník's grip.

The vodník frowned at me in confusion, then dived back into the water and melted into nothing.

Even with his weight gone, it took a lot of effort for me to sit up out of the water. When I did, I breathed out, water gushing from my mouth like I was some medieval gargoyle. That wasn't enough for me, though. I got the rest of the way out and shook myself, like a dog trying to get dry. I *hated* water. Breathing it didn't make it cooler.

Though it did answer the question of whether or not my magic resistance included water.

My left hand was throbbing. There was a huge bite in it, right at the base of my thumb. It wasn't like a chunk was missing, but I could see teeth impressions, and it stung something awful. I had heard human bites were bad—what did a vodník bite do to you? After all, getting bit by vampires and werewolves wasn't something you wanted to have happen. I remembered Lesana getting bit by a vodník, and look what happened to her. Would I become a water spirit? Die? Be buried alive?

Confused-but-alive beat knowing-but-dead any day. The water was still running in the shower, but it was at normal strength now, and the clog—or whatever it had been—had cleared, too. The tub was almost empty.

I peeked out the door to see if there were any super-sized leprechauns waiting to ambush me. No one. I pulled my head back in and closed the door, turned my back to it, and slid to the floor.

I'm not sure how long I stayed like that, just enjoying being able to breathe normal air. Not getting burned by fire had been cool; this had been nothing but traumatic. Why had the vodník done that? The last I had seen him, he was nothing but smiles and stutters, and he hadn't appeared in eight days. Then *bam!* He tries to kill me? It didn't make any sense.

Finally, I stood up, took a deep breath, and jiggled my left hand—the one the vodník bit—trying to get some of the pain out. Enough thinking. It was time to do something. Exactly *what* was another question, but I knew the first step: get dressed.

Ľuboš's jeans had a tendency to lowride on me. I slipped the T-shirt on and checked the logo. *LA Lackers.* The colors were wrong, too: green and red. Did Ľuboš realize his shirt was a blatant rip-off?

I opened up the door all at once, figuring it would be better to surprise anyone waiting there and get the jump on them. The room was still empty, but I kept expecting someone to spring out from nowhere. Only after I had searched under the beds did I feel safe enough to sit and put on my shoes and socks. I needed to talk to Katka and find out every way possible to protect against anything unhuman. Whatever she named, I'd eat it, wear it, convert to it, or arm myself with it.

When I went outside and locked the door behind me, I felt like a clown in baggy clothes. The shoes flopped around on my feet just enough to make walking awkward. Still, it was better than being wet. The sun was out, and the water on the ground was already evaporating. Slovakia's weather could be strange.

Katka was outside sitting by herself on one of the amphitheater benches. The place was empty—cleared out by the earlier rain, no doubt. She smiled when I walked up. "Feel better?"

I held up my bit hand. "The vodník tried to kill me."

"What?"

"When I was in the shower, he attacked me."

She rushed forward and took my hand, bending over it as she examined it. "How did you get away?"

I grunted. "I'm immune to drowning, I guess. When he found that out, he ran off."

"Why did he do it?"

"I wish I knew. It wasn't like he said anything before he went for me."

She let my hand go and stepped back to check out the rest of me. "But you're all right?"

"Shaken up more than anything. And there's this." I waved my bit hand again. "Do vodník bites do anything bad?"

"Psst!"

I scanned to see where the sound had come from. It wasn't too hard.

The vodník was standing across from us in the well courtyard. He waved to me.

I jerked back. Was he going to attack again?

"What's the matter?" Katka asked.

I nodded toward the vodník. "It's him."

She saw him. "Víťazoslav."

"Just vodník," I said. "He's not human. He doesn't deserve a name."

The vodník gestured for me to come over. Like that was going to happen. I shook my head, and he made an exaggerated sigh, then held up his hands as if he was surrendering. It would have looked better if he could have gotten his arms all the way above his head, but either his suit coat or his lack of fitness wouldn't let him. It was all just an act—I knew that now. He'd had no problem moving when he was trying to kill me. Or "save me for later," as he'd probably phrase it. Drowning was drowning, no matter where your soul ended up.

"He wants us to go over there?" Katka asked.

"I guess. Should we?"

She shrugged. "As long as we stay together, and in the open. If he wants to talk, we might want to know what he has to say. Better to find out now. And maybe he has a teacup with him."

Maybe. "Fine," I said, and the two of us headed over.

As we approached, the vodník backed up to the armory door. When we were close enough for him to speak without shouting, he opened the door. "Geez. It took you like forever. What did you have to do—have a vote or something? Come. Come in."

Katka and I stopped where we were. "What do you want?" I asked.

He sighed. "I just thought we could get together and talk things over, you know. Just talk. And it's not like we need to do it out here, out in the open, out in the heat where we're practically melting. A bit ago when it was pouring, that would have been fine. Comfy, even. But what is it out here now? Boiling? I swear I'm evaporating just standing here. I might faint."

"Then faint," I said.

He put his hands over his heart, like he was hurt. His suit coat was damp and dripping. "So harsh. So cruel. I guess I can see why you might be a little sour with me. A little annoyed. But would you get mad at a bear if you walked into its den when it was hungry? Would you tell a fox off for trying to get something to eat if a chicken walked into its home?"

"You're not a fox or a bear."

"That's right," he said. "I'm worse. I'm a fox or a bear with a conscience. I feel bad about trying to do what I do. It pains me. I see a shrink about it twice a week. I'm heavily medicated. I've got to take so many pills, I consider them my daily lunch. Stuffed with anti-depressants. And all I was trying to do was sneak in and take some of them. I need to take pills around lunchtime, like I said, and I was late, and so I took a shortcut through the pipes—but you don't want to hear about that. You just want to be mad at me. I only want to apologize."

"Great," I said. I pointed at the bite mark. "Is this going to do anything to me?"

"What? Like are you going to start howling at the moon or craving blood? Of course not. Just go get a Band-Aid and some iodine. I'm sorry. Aren't you sorry for trying to gouge out my eyes and hit me in the head?"

"No."

His eyes were a deep green and much older than the few wrinkles on his face would have you believe. Finally he gave a nervous twitter and adjusted his collar. "Right," he said. "Why would you be? On to business then. The important thing—the reason I wanted to talk to you so urgently, even if it was awkward right this second—is that I have the idea to end all ideas. I mean, this is it. This one—oh yeah. Perfect. Wonderful. Wait until you hear it. You're going to faint. You sure you don't want to come inside where it's cool?"

"Yes," I said, as Katka said, "No."

The vodník cocked an eyebrow. "Do you want a minute to confer about it? Maybe ask for a recount? Because I could—"

"Why can I see you?" Katka asked. "I saw you before too. Before I took the potion that let me. I didn't see you at the pool when you drowned that boy."

"Drowned is such a nasty word," said the vodník. "I prefer 'saved.' I saved the boy. And as to why you could see me sometimes and not others, what can I say? I still have some talents left. I've always been naturally gifted. Head of my class at vodník school. Straight A's in—"

"Fine," Katka said. "What are you here for? Spit it out."

"Right. Just like the vodník statue you humans made in the town square. What is it with mortals and spitting?" He held up his arms again in surrender. "I know. I'm going to tell you. Here it is. You know that water girl I sent to see you? Lesana?"

I narrowed my eyes. "What about her? You told me not to ask about her."

The vodník laughed. "'What about her,' he asks. You see, this is why you should be glad you have me on your side. I'm practically only brains. I've got teacups and teacups full of ideas. My own little think tank. I'll tell you 'what' about her. She's the key. She's the answer. She's a soul just waiting to go home. Free her, and you've filled the bargain." He spread his arms out as if waiting for applause.

Katka looked hopeful, but she was trying not to show it. Would the vodník let us do what we had been planning to do anyway? What Lesana had been asking me to do for her? When the vodník had warned me away from her the last time we talked? The offer was suspicious to say the least.

I turned back to him. "How do we do that?" I asked. "Just break the teacup she's in?"

He dropped his arms. "A little gratitude can go a long way, you know. I mean, it's not like I'm coming up with these ideas for my health. How about a thank you, or a 'what a great idea'?"

"Thanks for the idea," I said. "How do we do it?"

He grunted, then reached inside his coat pocket and took out a sopping wet folded-up piece of paper. "Well for starters, you forget about breaking teacups. Sacrilege. I might as well say, 'Can I burn your flag now?' It's beyond rude. It's criminal. And Lesana isn't in any teacup. Teacups, no touchy. She's something else, and I thought you might be reluctant to go for this one, so that's why I took the time and effort and strain to write you out a set of instructions. Foolproof. It works because of who you are. You're special, Tomas. Not necessarily unique, but rare. When people like me are around you, we can do things we haven't been able to do in years. Decades. Centuries, even. And from what my sources say, you being able to do that makes this whole potion possible. You just do what this tells you, and everything will be all right. Maybe then you'll trust me. Maybe it'll be like old times again."

Special? Why did he wait until now to tell me this? I edged forward and plucked the paper from his fingers. Even getting that close to him made me nervous. Sure, he seemed harmless now, but after seeing him in action, I knew he was a steel trap. Innocent—until it sprang.

The vodník sighed. "Well, maybe it'll still be some time before you and I are playing water polo again. That's okay. I'm patient. I can wait. Just don't say I never did anything for you, okay, Tomas?"

I grunted. "If this works, I'll owe you one."

He smiled. "It'll work. I've had two wizards talking back and forth to each other about this plan for a week straight before they settled on it, then I let a witch pore over it and check it for accuracy. It'll work. And when it does, you'll owe me six or seven, not just one." Without another word he *melted*. It wasn't like he turned into a puddle, but he sank into the ground and slipped under the door leading into the armory, leaving me confused.

Typical.

CHAPTER TWENTY-TWO

PIG URINE

A vodník is made when a child is drowned. Not always, of course, but often enough that you should take extra care when handling the drowning of anyone under eight.

So far it had been a strange day, and for *me* to say that meant it had been a real doozy. But things were looking up. After all, the vodník had tried to kill me and couldn't. Maybe he was scared of me now, and that's what made him decide to tell me how to fill the contract with Morena. Maybe we just had to follow his plan, and everything would be fine.

Assuming it wasn't a setup.

The plan was frustratingly simple:

Step One: Make this potion. (He had then included a lengthy list of directions that fit the typical bizarre potion pattern we'd seen so far).

Step Two: Pour it on Lesana's grave.
Step Three: Win.

When we got back to my apartment and I could double-check with *Death in the Modern Day*, the vodník's plan was confirmed. Or at least the fundamental concept was. It was in the troubleshooting section, under ghosts, which we'd been toying with already.

I started to read it out loud. "Because their souls have not yet left this world, they are essentially 'live deaths'—deaths just waiting to be completed."

Katka interrupted me. "I saw that before. A bunch of outlandish ways to release ghosts. But I thought we couldn't do any of them. We checked when we went to Orava, remember? Besides, the vodník's potion isn't listed."

"Maybe, but it's better than nothing."

"I suppose." Katka sighed. She stood up from the table and paced around the living area in my apartment. "But it makes me nervous, doing what the vodník tells us."

"Do we have any other choice? We only have three weeks, and we haven't come up with any other options. At least with this we can prepare for any problems that might arise. We know he's bad. We're in the driver's seat here. And even if this doesn't work, maybe we can convince him to let us see one of his captured souls or something, then release it instead. Let's just focus on what we have to do. I'm going to go get something for this bite, and then I'd like you to read that list once more."

"Fine," Katka said after a moment. I got up and puttered around the bathroom, returning with bandaging supplies. When I sat down at the kitchen table again, she cleared her throat and studied the transcribed list I had made for her when we got back. The paper the vodník had given us had been practically falling apart, the ink smeared and running. Any longer, and it would have been illegible.

Coat a vial with the enchanter's first morning breath. Fill the vial with virgin spring water.
Seven hours later—on the same day—add to the vial three blades of thyme harvested by the light of a full moon.

Let rest for three days, and then transfer the mixture to a basin made of pure crystal.

Use five counterclockwise strokes to stir in thirteen grams of a single Dubak mushroom.

From a hundred-year-old Persian walnut tree, extract a whole, unbroken nut from its shell. Add it to the mixture in the noon light of a cloudless day. Break it apart using twelve jabs with a silver fork, then use that same fork to stir the mixture—five clockwise strokes.

At midnight that night, add only five drops of blood (one from each right-hand finger), given freely by someone other than the enchanter. Place the basin outside, uncovered, for seven days.

At dawn on the seventh day, transfer the mixture to a wooden cup carved from the heartwood of a cherry tree. Pour the mixture on the intended's remains (the grave site will do). If everything has been done correctly, the result will occur after sixty seconds. Failure to follow these steps precisely can have serious consequences, so great care should be taken.

"It could be worse," I said after she finished. "There's no dandruff involved."

Katka focused on wrapping the vodník bite. "We have three weeks, and this potion takes at least ten days to perform, and that's assuming we get a cloudless day. Does it really mean that? Completely cloudless?"

I shrugged. "You got me. It says we've got to be precise, though, so I'd go for completely cloudless."

"But that makes no sense. There are always clouds *somewhere* in the world. What if you just can't see any? If they're blocked by mountains or—"

"Katka?"

"What?"

"It's a magic potion to release the soul of a girl trapped as a water ghost. It doesn't need to make sense. I'd be more worried about finding Lesana's grave than anything else. It's a good thing the vodník has her on hand to ask. My dad's told me what a pain it is to do research for specific stuff like that. We don't have a Scooby Gang to go run errands for us. Worse yet, what do we do if this potion goes wrong—or if it's not intended to go right in the first place? After we go through all this junk, we're not going to have any time left to try much else."

"We'll follow Plan B: break one of the vodník's teacups."

I sighed. "Yeah. I keep trying to ask him about them, but he always avoids the question. I say we go along with the vodník for now and hope either his idea works or we get an opportunity to do the teacup thing. It's not like the potion will do anything bad until it's—"

A brick sailed through the window, shattering the glass, hitting the table and crashing to the floor. Katka and I screamed and leaped back. I rushed to the window. The street was empty, but it didn't take a genius to figure out who'd thrown that.

The Bigot Gang was upping the ante.

I hefted the brick. If that had hit one of us, it could have done serious damage.

When my parents came home, Katka and I took the blame for the broken window ourselves. We'd cleaned up the glass and ditched the brick. Getting my parents all worked up was only going to complicate matters. We needed free run of the city in order to complete this potion in time, and my guess was my parents wouldn't exactly give their blessing to city trips if they knew three hooligans were out for blood. So I suffered through a lecture on being more careful and responsible, then agreed to pay for the broken window myself. Maybe the BGs would feel like they'd taught me a lesson now and stop there.

I hoped.

It's better to feel like you're doing something than to sit around and feel helpless. Tours at the castle had slumped off to the point they were almost nonexistent. Ľuboš let us go to "on call" status, since sitting at the castle staring at the empty entrance gates was about as unproductive as you could get. Normally, I'd have stayed there anyway. Better to be at the castle than putting up with the crap we took in the town when people identified us as Roma. But now we had a Mission, capital M. A special purpose.

The first thing we needed to do was find out where we could get everything. And what was a virgin spring? Katka helped me with some of the other terms. That's how I found out that a Dubak mushroom was this type of mushrooms Slovaks all went crazy over. They used it in soups. Mushroom hunting was a national pastime in Slovakia (which said something about Slovaks), but it made getting that ingredient much easier.

Katka took a trip into town and came back not only with a cup carved from the heartwood of a cherry tree (bought from a local Roma wood-carver) but also knowing where we could get our walnut.

"Persian walnut is the common kind," she said. "And the trees usually live about 65 years, but the man at the carvers said he could get us some nuts from older trees, though he was curious why."

For the crystal basin, we found one Ľuboš had inherited from his mother—Babka. It was sitting in a cabinet gathering dust, so we didn't think anyone would mind if we used it.

Although we had success with most of the items on the list, some things were more difficult to find, like the thyme harvested under a full moon. We'd missed the actual full moon by one day, and there wouldn't be another one until September. I failed at astronomy. Have you ever tried going to a grocery store or farmer's market and asking when their thyme was harvested? It's not like people write these things down. We got a bundle of herbs we were 85% sure had been picked at the right time, but we couldn't be certain.

It would have to do.

And then there were all the other problems we were facing. For one thing, my bite wasn't healing. I didn't mention it to Katka—she had enough on her plate already—but no matter how much I disinfected it or cleaned it, the teeth marks stayed an angry red, the skin around them puffy and swollen. But it didn't seem to be getting worse. At least not at first.

One night as I was getting ready for bed, I was sitting in my room changing the wrap. I had to do it when I was alone, since my parents thought all I had done was sprain my wrist. The Ace bandage I used to keep the bite hidden wasn't perfect for treating the wound, but it was better than the questions that would come if either of my parents saw it. A thunderstorm was raging outside, rattling the windows now and then. We'd had rain for the past two days.

When I took the wrappings off, they were wetter than usual. I examined the bite more closely.

The wound was seeping water.

Over the course of a minute, I watched a bead of water form, grow larger, and then run down my hand and onto my wrist. I steeled myself and then tasted it. Just water.

I sat back on the bed and stared at the ceiling. Another bolt of lightning flashed outside, followed by a rumble. The air smelled like ozone.

For the last few days, I'd been doing my best not to think about the vodník's attack. I had wanted to put it behind me: the bite, the vodník, the un-drowning. If the wound had been getting better, maybe I could have ignored it. But leaking water? How serious was it? Would it have any Rasputin effects? Only if it almost killed me first.

It didn't help that the only person I could think of who had been bitten by a vodník was now a water ghost hanging out at the castle. In the vision I'd had of Lesana when she died, she'd had her hand bandaged too. I didn't know how much time had elapsed between the attack and the confrontation with her father, but was it the bite that had killed her? Or rather, waterfied her? The more I thought about it, the more I decided it had to be.

I went over the events I'd seen in the water visions. Girl gets bit by vodník. Girl gets weak and faints, apparently dead. Girl gets buried alive. Girl is now water spirit, hundreds of years later.

Time to check *Death in the Modern Day*. With no small amount of page flipping and index checking, I came across something that seemed to apply. As usual, it was buried in the footnote of some obscure reference that only loosely had anything to do with vodníks, which is why I'd missed it the first thousand times I read the cursed book. Apparently the vodník could steal souls by biting, not just teacups. After describing everything right down to the bite seeping water, the book listed some symptoms: dizziness, weakness, and apparently a tendency to fall into a fake death that could take a month to recover from. Then it talked about potential cures.

If they're already too far gone, I'd suggest giving them up as a lost cause. Totally curing them requires a potion made by a mortal able to affect both the magical and the physical plane, which is almost always too much of a bother to try. If you manage to reach the victim before the bite's effects have gone too far, try having them drink a teaspoon of pig urine mixed with a teaspoon of salt each day for a week. That should do the trick.

So maybe that's why the vodník wanted me to do the potion: I was the only route he had to get Lesana into a soul-stealable form, since I was "special." But that didn't account for why he had bitten me. Was I feeling dizzy? I could just picture me fainting and getting buried alive. Had the vodník done this on purpose? He knew what could happen—he'd done it to Lesana already.

Another sentence in the same paragraph caught my eye. *A vodník is made when a child is drowned.* So the vodník hadn't been trying to collect me when I was five—he was trying to make me one of him? Beyond creepy.

Don't get me started on the pig urine.

I got up, wrapped my hand up in the bandage, grabbed an umbrella and some shoes and walked over to Katka's. It helped living so close to your best friend. She answered the door in her pajamas, brushing her teeth. After jerking her head to signal I should come in, she disappeared into the bathroom to finish. She had the windows open, and the apartment had a damp feel to the air.

"What's up?" she asked when she came into the living room.

I didn't say anything—just took off the bandage.

She sat down next to me on the couch and leaned over to check the wound. "Uh-oh."

"It gets worse," I said, then got out the book and opened it to the right page. "Read."

She grunted after she was done. "You're right. Definitely worse."

"Well?" I said. "What if that happens to me? Those aren't good options. Either I 'essentially die' or I get buried alive."

Katka smiled, but I could tell she was forcing it. "Don't worry, Tomas. I won't let you be buried alive. Besides, medicine has advanced. Everyone will know you're not dead."

I wasn't so sure of that. "But what about becoming a water spirit? I can't do that." It would be like a person scared of heights being transformed into a falcon, or somebody scared of spiders becoming a tarantula.

"That's what the pig urine is for."

I shuddered. "Where are we going to find that? The book only says that works if you start it in time. What if it's too late? What if—"

"Then we already have a cure for that," Katka said. "It's what the vodník's having us prepare for Lesana, right?"

"Yeah, but Lesana's *dead*."

"Tomas, I don't know the answers. Tomorrow, we'll find pig urine. They must have it at a farm, or a butcher's. Or at least, they can get some. All they need is a pig. Then you'll start drinking. And we can make two potions from the vodník's recipe, just in case. Finally, if you fall down like you're dead, I'll be sure to tell the doctors you're not. What else do you want me to do?"

"But don't you get it?" I said. "This doesn't just hurt me. What happens if I faint or die or whatever before the potion's finished? Even if I recover, I could lose weeks. A month. What if I wake up, and you . . . you're . . ." I couldn't bring myself to say it.

Katka sighed and repeated, "What else do you want me to do?"

"Maybe we should go to our parents."

Katka bit her lip in thought. "Maybe we should. But what would happen then? Your mom doesn't have a good record of handling these visions well. Your dad, what could he do? If we tell my father, it will only worry him. I saw him go through that with my mother. I do not want my last days with him to be like that."

Her last days with him. That was a sobering thought. "We can try Ohnica again."

"Why?" Katka said. "We don't know if we can trust her to begin with, and we know what she'll say anyway. Build her a house fire so she can get her powers back. Are you ready to do that?"

Not hardly. At last I shook my head. "You're right. I just wish . . ."

"Get some rest," Katka said. "Everything's worse when you don't have enough sleep."

That sounded like good advice. But once I was alone in my room, I couldn't stop thinking. Everything was going wrong. We had less than three weeks until Katka died, I was being manipulated by a vodník, I was going to turn into a water spirit, and I had to drink pig piss to top it all off. Couldn't it at least stop raining for a few days? Sleep was a long time coming.

In the morning, the sun woke me. No rain. I was tired but optimistic, a mood only slightly damped when I headed over to Katka's, and she already had the pig urine. At least when it was combined with salt, its original taste was overpowered.

Then again, it's the thought that counts.

Eight glasses of water and four rounds of mouthwash later, we focused on finding out about virgin springs, with little luck. The vial was all set and ready to go—we had gotten one and I had breathed into it as soon as I woke up for three days straight. One of those breaths had to count as the morning's first. We spent a couple hours skimming through every page of Katka's fairy-tale books and the folklore section in my living room, but it was nowhere to be found. The vodník wouldn't show at the castle, and there was no sign of Lesana, either. If they disappeared like this, how would we even find her grave? I made a mental note to ask either of them the next time I saw them. Better safe than sorry.

And did I mention that our TV had broken? Something to do with the LCD light. It was under warranty, but I was going to be without it for at least two weeks. My practices with my uncle's friends (Ľuboš was still away on his jousting tour) were my only release right then, giving me a chance to work out my frustrations. I'd been doing it long enough now that some of it was becoming second nature. Falling was a lot easier, that was for sure. But I also knew the basic moves enough to start to be able to choose which one was best for a specific situation. When Ľuboš came home from his trip, he'd be pleased.

Even the Internet let me down. It took all of five seconds for me to learn two things. The first was that doing a search with "virgin" in it isn't the best idea in the world. The second was that *Virgin Spring* was a movie by Ingmar Bergman. Neither of these gems of knowledge helped. When I stood up from the desk after my Internet search, the room tilted. I stumbled sideways, right into the desk, almost knocking the computer over before I caught my balance. After I let go of the desk, it still felt like the room was spinning, but it was manageable. Was that pig potion working or not?

Maybe a short rest would help. I staggered over to my room and opened the door.

The old granny—Starenka—was waiting by my bed.

CHAPTER TWENTY-THREE
TONGUE

Virgin springs grant healing powers to the first human to drink from one. Of course, since this power is used up in the drinking, almost no virgin springs are still in existence. This is a good thing, since killing a human who has taken a spring's virginity can be a real pain in the ass.

t's about time."

"What are you doing here?" I asked.

"You summoned me. I came."

"I summoned you forever ago."

Her eyes narrowed to a sea of wrinkles. "Don't disrespect your elders, boy. I'll smack you so hard on the head you'll be comatose." Her voice was low and gravelly. She poked me in the stomach with her cane.

Now that the shock of her appearance was wearing off, the dizziness returned. I went to my bed and sat down.

"Hasn't anyone ever told you to stand for company?" she said. Another poke.

I slapped at the cane. "Stop that. I'm dizzy."

She hobbled closer. With me sitting and her standing, we were just on eye level. Her face was a wrinkled prune, but less purply. "Why do you insist on making things difficult for me?" she asked.

"Huh?" My mind had still been on prunes.

"That's the problem with today. Ever since they invented airplanes, everyone's too busy being busy."

"What do you mean?"

She sniffed. "At least you can make coherent sentences now. Much better than repeating 'You don't want' over and over like last time. What I *mean* is that I did my best to help you earlier. Everything was ready, but you refused to listen."

"I couldn't understand you. I—"

"That's my fault? What do you expect me to do? Learn English?"

"No, I—"

"To make things worse, you summon me and then scamper around faster than I can keep up. The castle, the canal, city center, back home. Do you think I jog at my age?"

"I—"

"Don't you know anything?"

"No," I said, giving up. The dizziness was making me nauseous.

She nodded. "At least you admit it. Let me tell you how it works. You need help, and I come and give you what you need—usually information that makes it possible for you to complete your quest. It's the way we've been doing things for thousands of years. It's my job to know you're in trouble. It's your job to be easily found."

My jaw dropped open. "So that's it?"

"What?"

"You're just going to tell me what to do to fix things?"

She shook her head and smiled with a glint in her eye. "It can't be that easy. But I'll tell you two things that will help. First, a virgin spring is a spring that hasn't been found by humans before. Second, the vodník knows where such a spring is, and if you dump enough salt in his well,

I'm pretty sure he'll show up to answer any questions you might have."

I leveled my best "get real" stare at her. "I've been at home plenty. I check my email. I have an answering machine. Did you have to meet me in person? Couldn't it have been a bit earlier?"

"Don't push it," she said. "I'm old. That makes me right. Oh." She snapped her fingers. "And here's this. You didn't want it before, but no doubt you've changed your mind." She reached into her cloak and took out a bundle of herbs. "Thyme harvested by the light of a full moon. Now stand up and get to work. Don't be so lazy."

"I'm not being lazy. I'm sick. The vodník bit me."

"What?" she said. "Where?"

"On my hand." I unbandaged my hand to show her the seeping wound.

She tsked loudly. "Damn foolish of you to let him bite you. Damn lucky that you'll be going to a virgin spring soon."

"I'm taking pig urine and salt for it," I said. "That's supposed to—"

"Pig urine? Do you know where that stuff comes from? Just drink some of the virgin spring. One of its properties is that it grants the power to regenerate. With the wound this far gone, pig urine's just going to give you indigestion. Idiot. Get to that spring tomorrow, or you're going to be sorry. You'll die for sure, and then what good will you be? Even as it is, if you don't get it soon enough, it'll be lights out for you for a few weeks—maybe even a month. Get to it in time and follow the vodník's directions precisely, and you have a chance of fixing everything." She tottered out of the room. I blinked a couple of times, then checked the herbs in my hand. Dead or unconscious for a month? Not good.

So much for resting. And drinking *pig urine.*

I got up and went over to see Katka, telling Dad on my way out that I'd be eating with my cousin that evening. Mom had evening duty at the

ESL school, so we were in scrounge and forage mode. Dad just grunted when I told him. Writer's block.

When Katka opened the door, I handed her the thyme Starenka had given me. "I got the answer."

She didn't take it nearly as well as I thought she would. "Tomas, you look terrible. Come in and sit down."

I went in. "Didn't you hear me? I know what the virgin spring is."

Katka nodded, then ushered me to the couch. "We can talk about that in a minute. First, there's something I need to show you."

"What?"

"See what I found." Katka reached down by the end of the couch, picked up a dusty book, and handed it to me.

I opened it to see copious notes all over the margins, all written in dense handwriting that was as close to indecipherable as you could get. The text itself was a standard legend book, similar to the ones I'd already seen around our house. I squinted at the notes, trying to make one out. It didn't help that Slovak writing was illegible to begin with—they all were taught one way to write, and it was a cursive with a whole lot of loops and lines that looked like loops. It looked borderline psychotic.

"What is this?" I said.

"It's my father's. I found it when I was searching through his piles of junk for something about the virgin spring."

"And what's it about?"

Katka grabbed the book and flipped through it to find a particular passage: a legend about a vodník. "Read that. I want to see if you think it says what I think it says. Dad's handwriting is awful."

It took me a minute, and it wasn't until I figured out the two key words that the sentence made sense. Water and fire. It clicked in my head, and I read the phrases again.

Oheň v suteréne—z tohoto? A čo voda?

I froze, then swallowed and read it out loud. "The fire in the basement—maybe from this? But what about water?"

"I think my father believes Babka was murdered by a mythical creature."

Just then, the door to the apartment opened and Ľuboš came in, home from his trip. He was early and had a huge smile on his face. A smile that vanished when he saw the book I was holding. He rushed over and snatched it from my hands. "This is private," he said. His face was red, and it wasn't from blushing.

I cleared my throat and wiped my palms on the couch. When had it gotten so much hotter in there? "We—uh—we—"

"We were just looking for something to read," Katka said. "Sorry."

Ľuboš put the legend book behind his back, then nodded. "Ask next time. You can read any of those history books."

As soon as I had figured out what those handwritten notes were about, my first thought had been to ask Ľuboš about Babka—this was the opening I had been waiting for. But now that he was looming over me in that small apartment, I wasn't sure. He'd always seemed so friendly and harmless, but now he seemed wild. Dangerous. There was a reason he qualified for the night watchman job. Katka was staring at the floor and blushing too.

"Uncle Ľuboš?" I asked.

"What?"

My mouth felt like the Sahara. "You think your mother was killed by a vodník."

Ľuboš checked behind him, almost as if he were afraid someone was going to come in. He faced us again. "I don't want to talk about this."

"Why do you think that?" Katka said.

Ľuboš sighed. "I don't think the vodník killed her. I think he saved her from the fire víla."

My jaw dropped. "What?"

Ľuboš folded his arms. "When you were little, Tomas, your mother found out I had been asking you for information about these mythological creatures. She blamed me that it got as bad as it did. After you were burned and almost drowned, I promised not to talk to you about them again. I felt too responsible. But you are old enough to make your own decisions now. You asked. You pestered me. So there you have it—my answer. From what I gathered from you when you were little, I believe the vodník saved my mother's life when she was attacked by a woman made of fire.

"I spent more than a decade of my life obsessed with it. Just look at those notes. I was losing my mind. I finally had to put it aside or go mad trying to find answers that wouldn't help even if I found them. When you said you were seeing things . . . I still didn't want to believe. Then, with Morena, I had to admit something was happening. But I can't go back to that mystery. It would consume me. Now. Is there something you two aren't telling me?"

My uncle's expression was solemn under that nest of a beard. I shrugged. "We were just looking up stuff about Morena and came across this. Sorry."

Ľuboš nodded. "Well, stop causing trouble for yourselves. You should be practicing self defense, not digging up family secrets." He left the room.

I slammed my hand down on the table and frowned at Katka. I kept my voice to a whisper, but it was as furious as I could make it. "We should tell him."

She shook her head and whispered back. "No. He thinks he wants to know, but he doesn't. You didn't see him after Mom's death. He tries to pretend he's strong, but he isn't. I don't want to put him through that again."

"What's up with this family?" I whispered fiercely, wishing I could shout. All this emotion made my head whirl more. "Do none of you talk about anything important?"

Katka seemed taken aback. "Where is this coming from?"

"You not letting me tell anyone about our deal with Death is some of it. My mom refusing to let anyone say anything about Babka is another." I swallowed, unsure of whether or not I should say what I was thinking. I decided to go for it. "You know, if we fail, you're going to die, and he's going to go through it whether you want him to or not. Wouldn't it be better if he at least was able to have a chance at helping save you?"

"And if he fails then? It would be too much for him," Katka said. "No. We don't tell him."

"What about me? If we fail, I'm going to be left wondering what else I could have done just as much as he would be."

"Do we have to talk about this?" Katka's eyes were brimming up, but I pressed forward.

"Yes," I said. "I'm sorry, but my life is on the line just as much as yours now. We need help for this, and not telling your father the whole truth makes no sense." My head was still whirling, and I didn't have the energy to fight this. "Tomorrow night. I'm going to tell him if you don't. It'll be better if it comes from you, though. Will you do it?"

She hesitated, but nodded at last. "Okay. You're right. I'm sorry, Tomas. I didn't mean for you to have to risk your life. Thank you for all you've been doing."

Now she was crying in earnest. I felt like a jerk, but I was also relieved

I'd gotten her to agree to telling Ľuboš. I went and put my arm around her. "It's going to be okay. You don't have to apologize. I *want* to help. And anyway—I've got good news."

Katka wiped at her eyes and pushed away, back in control. "Right," she said, sniffing one last time. Her eyes were puffy. "The virgin spring? You told me you found it."

"Sort of," I said. "I know someone who knows where one is. We're going to need salt. Lots of salt."

CHAPTER TWENTY-FOUR

FISH

Huge, ill-tempered, but immensely loyal, sea monsters make some of the best pets a Death could want. True, the food bills do add up, but they can live on a diet of human flesh alone—something any Death can provide plenty of.

It's not your fault," Katka said. It was the next day, and we were on the way up to the castle, ten one-kilo bags of salt in tow, along with the prepared vial we had retrieved from my apartment, for when we actually got to the virgin spring. Katka and I had each spent most of the day in bed resting. Our health wasn't exactly the best right then. We'd gotten up around two and headed into town to get the salt. We might only have one shot at this—I hoped it worked out. We'd been careful to stay out of sight in case Draco and the gang were out. They weren't, but we didn't have the time—or the strength—to deal with them if they popped around the corner.

"What were we supposed to do?" Katka asked, rehashing our conversation of the night before regarding Starenka's appearance, "wait around and hope Starenka showed up? We couldn't know if she would."

"It doesn't matter," I said. "We know what to do now, so let's do it. If anybody deserves to get smacked about this, it's that stupid vodník." Too bad we had to involve the vodník at all, but our mission was clear: find the virgin spring, finish the potion, release Lesana, fulfill the pact with Morena, save Katka. It all started with getting that spongy freak show to tell us where the spring was.

Katka stumbled and fell to the ground.

I stopped and offered her a hand up. "You okay?"

She nodded, but she didn't say anything, and I narrowed my eyes. "Why'd you trip?"

"Just clumsy, I guess." She tried to smile.

"Are you close to having another seizure?" I asked. "We can go back home and do this later."

"No." Her voice sounded much stronger. "We do this tonight. It's four o'clock. The castle closes in two hours, and we can get this done. Didn't Starenka say you had to do this today? We can't wait any longer."

I hesitated, then said, "Fine. We're almost there, anyway." It wasn't like I had a leg to stand on, anyway. The waves of dizziness had gotten worse since yesterday, although I'd managed to hide them from everyone so far.

We huffed and puffed the rest of the way up, then headed into the break room to stash the salt and think things through until the castle grounds closed and we could pour salt into the well undisturbed. And we had plenty of things to think about. Regardless of what Ľuboš believed, the vodník was up to something. Otherwise, why hadn't he just told us where the virgin spring was to start with? If we could only figure out what it was, then we'd be able to turn the tables on him. But no amount of brainstorming helped.

As we were sitting there, I began to get a headache. It started in my left eye, intense and with sort of an aching throb that accompanied it. Soon after, the room began spinning again. When I closed my eyes, it felt like I was on a slow merry-go-round. Katka wasn't doing well, either. She was trying to act normal, but I could tell she wasn't feeling well. Too pale, and she laughed too hard at my lame jokes, even the pop culture ones I knew she didn't get.

At last the castle started closing, and Katka and I helped—free of charge—herding the tourists down the hill and to the city below. We returned to the well and hung out until the tour guides started heading home too. Being the relatives of Ľuboš, no one really questioned why we were there, and once the castle was closed, only one guard was left to worry about, and he headed off to do a final check of all the buildings, giving us plenty of time to salt the well.

We went to get our bags. Tromping around the grounds hadn't helped my head, and picking up a backpack o' salt wasn't something I was looking forward to. I gritted my teeth and lifted. The pain was intense enough to make me wince and put a hand up to my eye, and the merry-go-round in my head sped up. Katka didn't notice; she was weaving her way over to the Well of Love, none too steady herself. I hurried to catch up to her, doing my best to stifle the pain lancing through my head and into my arm. It felt like the vodník was gnawing on my hand, and the dizziness was making me nauseous.

I got to the well and raised an eyebrow at Katka, each of us with a bag ready to pour. "Ready?" I asked.

She shrugged and nodded.

Someone cleared his throat. The vodník had appeared behind me. "You could have asked, you know," he said. "I'd hate to see what you do when you want to see someone at a hospital. Probably cut the power, or fill the place with toxic gas."

I glared at him. "You didn't exactly leave a phone number."

"So write a note and drop it down the well. Don't poison me. Sheesh. The two of you have a real interesting way of showing thanks. I'd love to see what you give people for Christmas." He walked over to us, and I tensed. He laughed and gave another toothy smile. "I don't bite. Well, not under normal circumstances. To what do I owe the pleasure of this visit?"

"We hear you know where a virgin spring is," Katka said.

The smile left his face. "Who told you that?"

"It doesn't matter," I said. "Do you?"

"Maybe. It's in the realm of possibility that I might know the where-abouts of such a thing."

"And you decided not to tell us about it?" I asked.

"It's called independence, and your generation should really look into it. Nothing but a bunch of *pijavíc*. And anyway, the only spring I know of is off limits. Totally out of the question."

"What about you being my 'best friend'?"

"So now I have to do things for you to prove friendship?" the vodník asked. "I already told you about the potion and Lesana. Don't you understand how few virgin springs there are left in the world? Anytime one of you humans finds one, *poof*: one less."

"But we need the virgin spring to get the potion to work," Katka said. She was ready to fall over, her face pasty and pale, her knees trembling.

"If a human finds a virgin spring, doesn't it cease to be virgin?" I asked.

The vodník sighed. "Of course it does—to everyone but that human. You can sort of take its virginity, a metaphor I would really rather not explore with the two of you right now. That's more of a go-ask-your-parents sort of a question, don't you think? Or maybe they teach it in schools these days? In any case, I have an idea. You give me a container, and I'll go get the virgin spring water right now. How's that?"

Katka had closed her eyes and hung her head, clearly in no condition to do much talking. I faced the little man. "I think I'm supposed to get the water myself."

"But then it wouldn't be a virgin spring anymore," the vodník said. "As soon as you see it, it's not one. Rather paradoxical, wouldn't you say?"

I was just about to say that he had contradicted himself when another voice came from the direction of the vodník, this one muffled and hard to hear. "That's part of the point of the spell. Sacrifice the properties of the spring and transfer them to the recipient."

The vodník jerked up straight in surprise, then clapped his hand against his right pants pocket and made a big show of coughing loudly.

"What was that?" I asked.

The vodník kept coughing.

"Someone spoke from your pants," I said.

The vodník coughed even louder. He pointed at his mouth and kept hacking away, then shook his head, like he couldn't talk, but his hand was still firmly attached to his pants.

I forgot my fear of him and strode toward him, grabbed his hand, and jerked it away from his pants. As I did so, a jolt of pain seared up my arm—it was the hand that had been bitten by him before.

The pants-voice came again. "Don't try to hush me up. You asked for my advice, and you're going to get it."

"Who's that?" I tried again.

The vodník stopped coughing and put on an angelic expression of ignorance. "I don't hear anyone."

"Liar," the voice said.

"Shut up," the vodník fake-coughed.

I addressed his pants, feeling silly, but wanting answers. "Who are you?"

"Don't remember," the voice came. "I knew once, but it's been too long to pay attention to such trivialities."

The vodník glared at his pants. "You'll be quiet if you know what's good for you. Ungrateful little—"

"Or else what?" the voice said. "I'm already in a teacup. It's not like things can get much worse. I'm too valuable for you to let me go."

I froze. This was it: a teacup at last, right where I could break it. I cleared my throat. "Are you one of the spirits who came up with the potion?" I asked.

"Of course I am. And you were right. Only the enchanter can harvest the virgin spring water, and the enchanter must be human. Of course, none of it's any good unless the human can interact with the spring, and it has to be human, or old Soggybottoms here would have done this years ago. That's why your . . . abilities are so useful in this case. A few centuries ago, this spell would have been easier. Now, hardly anyone is alive who could perform it."

The vodník reached inside his pocket and drew out a lidded teacup, sort of like one you might use to store sugar. He rattled the cup up and down and glared at it. "Enough. Teacups should be seen, not heard." He grinned at me. "You'll have to forgive my cups. They tend to prattle on. Normally I don't take them out for walks, but I was talking to him right when I found out you were going to dump salt in my well, so I brought him with me in the rush to stop you."

"Could I see it?" I said.

"See what?" The vodník was in the process of putting the teacup back in his pocket.

"The teacup."

He smiled, showing all his teeth. "Oh, I get it. This is the part where you somehow trick me into letting you get your grubby paws on a cup, and then you stumble into something and accidentally drop it, shattering it into millions of pieces and *oops!*, you've released a soul and fulfilled your pact with Death at my expense. You're so transparent, Tomas. Here. I'll save you the trouble." He took out the teacup again and threw it on the flagstone courtyard.

It bounced.

"See?" he said, then picked the cup back up and bounced it again before putting it away. It protested loudly—the voice complaining about the jostling—but the lid didn't even fall off. There was nothing visible keeping it on. *Magic.* "What?" the vodnik asked. "You think I'd store my most precious possessions in something that's fragile? These are the best teacups money can't buy. Indestructible. So forget about it. Shall we go?"

I was still staring at where the cup had fallen. It felt like someone had taken my heart and ripped it out through my mouth. Breaking a cup had been my ace in the hole—I'd been convinced it would work, and now it wouldn't. "Fine," I said at last, then turned to Katka. I had to shake her shoulder to get her attention, and when she looked up at me, her eyes took a moment to focus. "I've got to go."

"Go?" she asked.

I nodded. So did the vodník. "Of course," he said. "Tomas and I were just about to go down to the virgin spring."

Katka rubbed her temple again. "What about me?"

The vodník laughed. "Well, we can't have two humans go. If you see the spring first, then the spell could be ruined."

I supposed that made sense. It was hard to focus, when I was still feeling so let down. "Where is this spring?" I asked.

"The only place it could be," he said, and pointed at the well. "Down there. Where I live."

I stared at the well, a sinking feeling in my stomach adding to my confusion. Last time I'd gone down there, it hadn't exactly been peaches and cream. This time, I was dizzy, depressed, and afraid. Could it get any worse? It was almost enough to make me forget about my headache. "I've been down there. Nothing's there but dead water."

The vodník scoffed and adjusted his collar. "You didn't really think I stay there all day? Where would I keep my cups? No. That's just the doorstep. Kind of grimy, but necessary. Convenient." He snapped his fingers, and water squirted up from the well and onto the lock holding the grate closed. With a click, the lock opened. "Shall we?"

I swallowed and looked back at Katka. "Stay here."

"What?" she said. "You can't go down there alone."

"I don't have a choice. Didn't you see the cup? This is our last option, and he's got a point about why you shouldn't go down. It's not like I can drown down there." I licked my lips, then asked the vodník. "How long will this take?"

He sighed. "You humans are all so obsessed about time. It's like some sort of impulse. It won't take long, but if you want me to break it down to you in seconds, or minutes, or hours or something, I can't do that. Not long. Short. Very brief. You'll be back before she can miss you."

"Fine. Katka, if I'm not back in fifteen minutes, call your dad."

She shook her head. "I'm not letting you go down there without someone other than him."

The vodník groaned. "Sheesh. Where's the trust in the world? You want a friend with him? How about Lesana? I suppose I could dredge her up somewhere on the way down. Vodník's word of honor. Does that work?"

She nodded.

"Let's go," the vodník said.

I peered over the edge of the well to see the water had risen to the top. That was a lot of liquid. It was one thing to know you couldn't drown, but water still freaked me out. "How do we get down?"

He hopped onto the well wall and stepped into the water. It held him up as if it were solid.

When I tried, the water held me too. It started to sink like an elevator going down. I gave Katka one last forced smile before she and the rest of the world disappeared, replaced by darkness.

The vodník clapped, and the sides of the well flared to life in long vertical strips of blue light, casting everything in a rippling glow. "Better?" he asked.

I grunted.

He sighed. "For a sixteen-year-old, your vocabulary hasn't advanced much from when you were five, you know."

The rippling light pattern intensified, and part of the water surged into the form of a woman standing next to us. Lesana.

"See, Tomas?" the vodník said. "A replacement for Katka. Feel better?"

Lesana frowned at him. "Why did you have me trapped?"

The vodník cleared his throat. "Trapped? Me? I'd never dream of such a thing. It was a mistake, I swear."

She tried to respond, but all she got out was "But you—" before her voice disappeared. Her mouth kept moving, but no sound came out. She stomped her foot in apparent frustration, then came to stand on my right side and glare at the vodník.

"What was that?" the vodník said. "I can't quite hear you." The water stopped moving down, and the vodník grinned. "Here we are."

In front of us, the blue lights formed a circular pattern on the wall, sort of like a cross between a spiral and a bull's eye, with some Celtic ornamentation thrown in for good measure. A door.

The vodník said, "Turn around."

"What?"

He sighed. "There's a trick to opening my front door, and it's one I haven't let anyone find out for hundreds of years. I'm not about to change that now. Crime's awful these days, and you can't be too careful. So turn around, and no peeking."

Whatever. But he stared at me until I did as he asked. I tried to watch what he was doing in the reflection cast from Lesana, but she was too ripply to make anything out. After a moment, there was a *hiss*, and a blast of frigid air escaped into the summer heat. "I like to keep things cool," the vodník said. "Chilly is so much nicer, don't you think?"

I turned to see the open door leading to a tunnel lit by torches that burned with more of the eerie blue light.

"I'm not going in there with you," I said. "I don't trust you."

The vodník rolled his eyes. "And I suppose you trust that fire witch, instead? Whatever. I can see when I'm not wanted. Besides, I've got places to go, people to preserve. Just go down this tunnel, and head straight. The spring is at the end. And no drinking! Just get some water in your vial, and that's it. Lesana, watch him." He jumped backward out the door and into the well, leaving me staring at Lesana. Why had the vodník been so willing to run away like that? The whole thing screamed "setup."

It must have been even colder than I'd thought. Lesana was becoming ice again—fast. Maybe mystical water creatures froze quicker than normal. I watched as ice crystals crept over her body like ivy, spreading and connecting until, within seconds, she was a living, breathing ice statue, with the ice moving and flowing from one shape to another without cracking or shattering. Liquid ice, almost.

"Don't go in, Tomas," she said. "It must be a trap."

"I don't have any other choice. If I don't do this, then my cousin dies. Come on." I didn't mention the fact that if I didn't have some of that virgin spring water soon, I'd be as watery as Lesana. My head was spinning and felt like it was about to explode. I started walking down the corridor.

Lesana followed. At first we walked in silence, then she said, "He wants to kill you. He told me so himself—that he wants your soul for his collection. You let creatures like him have more power over the physical world somehow. He wants to be able to control that, and he'll kill you to do it. Steal your soul. The only thing stopping him is that he's not certain if you'll still be able to do it without your body. Whatever he's told you doesn't change what he wants."

I glanced over at her from the corner of my eye. Her forehead was crinkled in worry and fear, little wrinkles in the ice. Pretty cute, really. If only she wasn't just a water spirit. *Focus, Tomas.* It was nice that she was concerned for me, but I didn't trust myself to respond on that topic. I was in a foul mood, and I'd probably say something I'd regret. The tunnel appeared to be some sort of modified cave, like someone had taken a naturally-occurring cavern and evened out the floor, shaved the stalactites off the ceiling, yet left the walls rippled and rough. Torch sconces lined the walls every twenty feet or so, giving some light, but not enough to make you comfortable. About fifty feet in, there was an offshoot of the tunnel that led to the right, and soon after that, another one going left. Both were blocked off—the two tunnels were flooded, the water held back by an invisible, impassable wall.

The blue torches in the tunnel continued, though—even down the flooded passageways—and I could see glimpses of ornate furniture in the offshoots. This was much more like what I thought the vodník's home would be like. Comfort, not misery. Dracula's castle meets Atlantis.

I wondered if down one of those tunnels, the grave of Matúš Čak waited, entombed in water. The original owner of the castle, submerged forever with his treasure. Certainly down one of the tunnels was a collection of teacups, each one filled with a human soul.

We kept walking.

"So where's your grave?" I asked. We'd need to know that eventually to know where to pour the potion and release her soul.

She shook her head. "I can't remember."

"Can't remember?"

"No. It's been too long. The vodník likely knows. Ask him."

Weird. How could you not know where you were buried? It seemed like something a ghost would obsess over. "Have you been down here before?" I asked. The tunnel seemed like it wasn't going to end. We weren't walking quickly—this didn't have the feel of a place where you're comfortable just striding in anywhere—but we'd been walking for at least a quarter of a mile. The tunnel kept curving to the left, leading deeper and deeper under the castle.

"Of course," Lesana said. "This is my prison, usually. When he hasn't sent me off on some errand."

"How well do you know him?"

"You'd think I'd know him better after all these years. For the first few decades, he tried to befriend me, but I don't approve of his hobby. Those teacups." She shuddered, and small chips of ice went flying from her body and sprinkling to the floor. "Until you came, we hadn't been talking much anymore. He orders, and I must obey."

A few yards farther down, I stopped. "Do you smell that?"

Lesana sniffed a few times, her seemingly frail ice nostrils moving with the effort. She shook her head. "Ice isn't good for smelling. What is it?"

"Smells like . . . a fish market." I hated fish, and I was an expert when it came to telling a restaurant that served it. This had the same aroma, only without the cooking.

"Oh," Lesana said. "That's Ajax."

"Ajax?"

"He's too hard to explain. Just keep walking. You'll see him soon enough."

Soon the tunnel turned and widened into an actual cavern, the ceiling at least thirty feet tall, and the chamber itself as big as a small concert hall, filled with a light mist. An enormous chandelier hung in the middle of the room, the light from a thousand blue-flamed candles casting flickering shadows in the corners. The floor was covered in about an inch of water, but we could walk on it just like the vodník had let me stand on the water when we went down the well. Even more curious, this water seemed arranged in a pattern. In the castle, they had parquet floors, different shades of hardwood floors arranged in a pattern that makes the floor look like a wooden patchwork quilt. In this room, the pattern was made out of different shades of blue, some of it the clear blue of natural water, some the white shade of pure ice, and others in between.

At the other end of the room sat an incredible fountain. When I was twelve, my parents had taken me to Disney World. At EPCOT, there was this system of leapfrogging fountains that shot water into the air over your heads and into other fountains across the way. This fountain was like the grown-up version of that, except that the fountain *itself* was made of water, in the same way the floor was. Everywhere I looked, water was jumping and shooting from one spot to another, never staying still.

And in the middle of the fountain hunched the source of the fishy smell—a sea monster.

CHAPTER TWENTY-FIVE

TOMAS SANDWICH

15.2.93—Of course, everyone makes mistakes. It even happens to the Grim Reaper, though I wouldn't ask him about that. Just remember: don't panic. Should the soul not arrive at its intended destination and you must resort to the options outlined in 15.1, please fill out form 872i in triplicate and submit copies to your immediate supervisor (white copy) and to Records (blue), keeping one copy for yourself (goldenrod).

The monster was a cross between an eel, a shark, a stingray, and a dragon: lots of body (blue on the backside, white on the belly), a strong tail, thick winglike things, four stocky legs, and a snout with plenty of teeth. It was contorted into one of those Chinese dragon poses, with its legs splayed out and its long body twisted into a series of curves. The water jets were shooting every which way around it and on it, creating a mist that had spread through the whole room.

"Is that Ajax?" I asked.

Lesana nodded. "The vodník's pet. He should do what I tell him to, though. Unless the vodník's told him otherwise of late." She faced the beast and shouted. "Ajax?"

Ajax blinked an eye and cocked his head at us.

"Stay," Lesana said.

The beast grunted, then turned his face toward the wall.

"He's very obedient," Lesana said. "Just don't make any sudden movements, and do not make eye contact with him. Oh—and if he starts to attack, stay still. He can only see things when they move."

Right. Easy. I couldn't help thinking the vodník had decided to try killing me by monster, since drowning hadn't worked. "Let's just do this and get out of here," I said. We approached the fountain together. It had to be the virgin spring, even if it was different from anything I'd pictured. This was the end of the tunnel, for one thing, and for even more proof, the water vapor was . . . different, like ocean air, but more invigorating.

My whole body tingled with each breath I took, my limbs stronger and my thoughts clearer. I could feel my emotions more fully—the fear and the excitement. My senses grew sharper too. I felt the water and the touch of my clothing on my skin, felt the cold more keenly. I heard the ice crackle softly next to me whenever Lesana moved, and under everything was the noise of Ajax breathing. And it made the dizzy feeling subside.

I kept my eyes on the beast the whole time. Just because he hadn't moved yet didn't mean he couldn't, although what I'd do if he did was beyond me. Standing still didn't seem like a great idea. Closer, he was even bigger—the top of his back was at least three times as tall as me, and his head reared up to scrape at the ceiling thirty feet above. His eyes still followed us, but he hadn't done anything but breathe yet.

"Where do you think we're supposed to get the water from?" I asked.

Lesana shook her head. "I'm uncertain, but I think we should find the source—the place where the first water emerges from the rock."

I stared at the whole fountain, with all the leapfrogging spurts of water. It was a lot of the wet stuff, but nowhere deep enough for even me to be worried about drowning. And anyway—I was drown-proof now. "How do we tell?"

"Look and see," she said.

The two of us spent the next fifteen minutes inspecting the fountain. After a bit, I could tell that the water was going in a pattern, with one spout accepting a burst of water and then passing it on to the next. So it became a task of trying to trace back the spouts to the original one. It was simple to study one and note the pattern, but when we started trying to follow individual bursts of water, it was difficult to keep track of them, with all the crisscrossing and confusion and time delays in the chain. Not to mention the uneven light that blue-flamed chandelier gave us. It was like trying to find a missing bulb on a strand of Christmas tree lights, only with a time limit and the constant threat of impending death.

The longer I was around the monster, the harder it became to ignore his gleaming gaze. He didn't attack, though, and I remembered Lesana's admonition to not make eye contact. Ajax seemed hungry for a Tomas sandwich.

Finally, we discovered the source of the water—a small round spring cut into the rock directly beneath a coil of the monster's tail. Water came from there, but even after watching for a minute or two, we couldn't see it entering from any direction.

"So what?" I said. "Are we supposed to walk under there and get some water?"

Lesana nodded.

Right. Just waltz under Ajax and scoop it up. He wouldn't even have to try to kill me—he'd just have to shift his weight. Then again, if I didn't do it, I'd lose Katka for sure, and I'd probably become a water spirit, like Lesana, if Starenka was telling the truth. What was my world coming to, when I couldn't even be sure I could trust little old ladies?

Even being as terrified as I was, I was almost eager to try. The drips of spring water I'd gotten into my mouth were better than tasting the mist had been, and the closer we had gotten in our search for the source, the more powerful the effect had become. My headache had almost completely disappeared, for one thing. At this point, both my hands were tingling with some sort of energy. I didn't know what it was, but I really wanted to feel more of it.

I checked the monster again. True, Ajax could have swallowed me without having to chew, but he hadn't moved. He wasn't going to. I stepped closer to it, put out my hand, and touched him.

His skin wasn't oily like a fish's. It was smooth and rippled and solid as rock, like a snake. I had worried Ajax would whirl around and snap at me, but the beast didn't even twitch when I made contact. I turned back to Lesana. "Come on." I said. "Let's do this."

The water dragon's body arched above us as we examined the source. The actual device that shot out the water was different from the other ones we had seen. Like them, it was made out of the same solid water as the floor (it *rippled* in a way glass didn't), but I could see through this one. Beneath it was a hole leading down into the ground. The spurts of water coming from it were intermittent—only one every minute or so—but long. In the times when it wasn't spouting water, I tried to pry off the cover, but it wasn't moving.

"Oh well," I said. "This is probably close enough."

Before Lesana could respond, a black piece of paper appeared next to the spout. Written on it in white ink was one sentence:

It isn't. —A.

I felt a wave of relief wash over me. This was the first I'd heard from

Morena in what seemed like forever. If she was replying to my efforts again, it had to mean I was on to something. Yes, she seemed to be ill-tempered and big on pranks, but I didn't think she'd lie about this. To have her tell me I had to get the actual spring water—not what was coming from the spout above it—validated our plan even more than Starenka's assurances. I grabbed the piece of paper, looked up at Lesana and smiled. "This is going to work!"

She grinned and nodded encouragingly.

Of course, it would only work if I got the actual spring water. I tried twisting, pulling, scraping—everything I could think of, with no luck. I sat back and sighed. "Do you have any ideas?" I asked.

Lesana frowned. "I could try something, but I don't know what the vodník would do about it. He made this fountain. If he wanted us to be able to get water from the actual spring, he would have let us. If I break his construction, he'll know right away, and he'll be angry."

"He'll blame me. I'll deal with the consequences. Do it."

Lesana nodded. "Fine." She reached past me and hovered over the fountain. Her right arm changed to liquid and poured down the spout. She bit her lip in concentration and closed her eyes. After a moment, there came an audible *click*, and she stepped away. The earth began to rumble.

Ajax was growling.

"It is done," Lesana said. "But hurry with whatever you must do."

With the cover off, water was bubbling up from the ground and over the edges of the hole. The vibrations from Ajax's growl rumbled like an earthquake, causing my teeth to chatter and the spring itself to visibly move. If he was growling already, what would he do when I drank it— doing exactly what his master had told me not to?

First things first. I got the vial out and filled it. Inside the vial, the water glowed subtly, giving the glass a slight purple tint. When it was safely zipped in my bag, I looked from the spring to the vodník's bite. Which would be better? To become a water spirit later or get squished right now? If I didn't drink, I might pass out, and then who knew how long I'd be out of commission. Maybe I'd sleep right through Katka's death date. But if I got squished . . .

Enough thinking. My hand cupped some water and brought it to my mouth.

I drank.

Two things happened at the same time, neither of them good. The dizziness in my head came back with a vengeance. Even crouching as I was, I couldn't keep my balance and fell to the floor. At first, I thought my ears were ringing too. Then I realized it was Ajax howling. For a beast that big, his voice could get up there pretty high.

"What's wrong?" Lesana shouted above the noise. "What did you do?"

I shook my head and tried to stand up. "Nothing." On the second try, I managed to get to my feet.

The howling stopped, and so did the fountain. All noise stopped except a small burble from the spring, making it easy to hear the vodník ask in a soft voice, "What did you do?"

I turned unsteadily. The vodník stood there, running his hands through his hair and looking as crazed and close to losing control as you could imagine: eyes bugged out, licking his lips uncontrollably, nose twitching. It was all I could do not to topple right there. "Just getting the water from the spring," I said. "All done now."

He laughed. "All done. That's great. Wonderful. I'm sure that's supposed to make me relieved and happy for you. But you didn't just get the water, did you? That's all you were supposed to get. That's all you told me you wanted, and that's all you needed. I didn't want you to see it. That would have cheapened it. Made it less useful. But you didn't stop there. Greedy little—you had to go and drink it. Right from the source. *Right from the source!* Do you know what you've done? You've ruined it. Ruined it for everyone but you."

"Ruined what?" Lesana asked.

"Don't talk to me!" the vodník shouted, waggling his finger at her. "Everything I've done, I've done for you, and this is how you repay me. How could you do that? How many times did I tell you not to drink the water?"

"Never," she said.

He grunted. "Well, I should have. I should have told you a thousand times. I told him not to."

"Wait a minute," I snapped, then held up my bandaged arm. "You're the one who bit me. You said it wouldn't do anything. You lied. It'll make me like Lesana. Drinking that spring water was all I could do."

"Ha," the vodník said. "Who told you that? I have control over what happens with my bites. It would have been painful, maybe made you dizzy, maybe seeped some water, but I wasn't going to make it complete. I've learned since Lesana. But now . . . with you doing this . . . I never should have been so wishy-washy about this. You were trouble from the beginning. I could see that. I went back and forth between deciding to help you or just kill you. To kill or not to kill. Decisions decisions. I thought in the end you'd be worth it for Lesana. Well, she can wait another century until another one like you comes along. Someone else who can affect both planes. And when that happens, maybe I'll save your soul too."

"What are you talking about?" I asked.

"It's too late for that spring drinking to save you," he said. "Not if I let the effects happen all at once. And on second thought . . ." He trailed off, then melted into the floor. As soon as he did so, my ears picked up a distant creak, then rushing water.

"What's that?" I asked.

No one answered. Lesana had disappeared. Ajax was staring down at me, and the floor started shaking again with his growls. At the same time, a heavy flow of water whooshed into the chamber. The sound I'd heard must have been the vodník letting all of the water in the rest of the complex back into the room.

I tried to move toward the exit, but the flow of water was too fast. As soon as I moved, Ajax darted his head down to snap his teeth right in front of my face. It was like having sharpened elevator doors guillotine together so close you could feel the wind. I screamed and fell back, and then another sound came over the rushing water, sort of a mix between coughing and snorting. Ajax seemed to be laughing.

The water was up to my waist, my head was spinning so fast it felt like it was going to fall off, and Ajax was toying with me. Oh—and Lesana had said not to move if he became violent. So much else was happening that I completely forgot to panic at the sight of all that water coming at me. I was too busy not getting swept off my feet.

Every instinct I had screamed for me to rush to the exit as fast as I could. I had to ignore them. Ajax was staring down, looming over me, and waiting for me to make a move. The water got higher and higher. My chest. My neck.

My mouth.

I breathed it in. It had worked before; it would work now. And it did, still uncomfortable, but not deadly.

Ajax, meanwhile, began to whine. He blinked and sniffed, then put his head down close to me and bumped me squarely in the chest.

I floated backward, shooting through the water like a jet ski. My body collided with the wall, and fireworks went off in my eyeballs. Everything went black, and I worried that was the end. Then my vision cleared, and I saw Ajax floating in front of me. He must have lost track of me somewhere between playing human pinball and the water coming in. His head scanned from side to side as he searched for where I had gone. I checked my bag, which was still securely strapped to my shoulders. There was no way I was coming down here and going through all this and then losing that vial.

What followed was an experience I can only describe as life-or-death Red Light Green Light—that game we used to play in elementary school. Whenever "It" isn't looking, it's Green Light, and you can move. When It says "red light," you darn well better be frozen still, or you're out. Eaten, in this case. When Ajax turned his head for a moment, I would paddle with just my hands, trying to make it out of the chamber.

Three more times, I collided with some part of him: his tail, a flipper, part of his body. Each time, it took longer to recover from the blow. If I hadn't been in water, I'm sure I wouldn't have. Thank goodness Ajax didn't have a brain much bigger than a cocker spaniel's.

It took forever, and it was made even harder by not being able to see straight with my head spinning so much, but I made it to the exit of the chamber and down the hall to where it turned, leaving Ajax out of sight, whining and confused. In the water, the whine rippled out from him like a screechy whale.

The torches were still burning even in the water. I paused to inspect the vial. It was still intact. I shook my head, trying to clear it, and did my best to get to the exit.

I never learned how to swim, but when you can breathe water, moving through a tunnel full of it is kind of like walking on the moon. Low gravity, slow movement. Even a dizzy kid can do it.

The door to the well was open, and I emerged from the tunnel and used the wall to climb and float my way to the surface. Where was the vodník? Why hadn't he come back to take my soul?

"Tomas?" I heard a voice echo down when I surfaced about ten feet down from the top. Katka. "Is that you?"

I coughed out the water in my lungs and shouted back. "Get a bucket. Quick!"

The vodník spoke next to my ear. "Do you really think I'm going to let you get away?"

I shouted in surprise and whirled to see him sitting on top of the water, staring at me. "Leave me alone," I said.

"What?" Katka shouted.

"Nothing," I called back. "The bucket! Now!"

"You just *had* to drink the water," the vodník said. "Three hundred years, I've been saving that spring. Keeping it hidden. Keeping it safe for when it would come in handy. And one thirsty idiot of a teen was all it took. Imbecile." His voice was low and patronizing.

"I had to," I managed to say. The dizziness was increasing, and my vision was going black around the edges. If I could just hold on until the bucket came.

"You should have asked," he said. "I would have helped you."

"No—you want to kill me. You tried to. Can't trust." My mind was shutting down.

"It's too late for you, you know," he said. "Katka will die, and if I don't take your soul now, you'll be a water spirit." He took out a teacup and set it on the water's surface next to him, right in front of my face. "If I take you, though, I might still be able to save them. Lesana and your cousin."

The bucket splashed down to my right, just missing my arm. I dug around in my bag for the vial and put it in. "Pull it up," I called, just the act of shouting taking most of my energy. "Vial." The bucket started rising.

"And what's she going to do with that?" the vodník said. "You're the enchanter. She can't use it to free Lesana. With your soul in my collection, I'd be able to use your power in your stead."

"No," I said. "You lie." My arms and legs were tiring. It felt like something underneath the water was sucking me down.

"You know," the vodník said, "I don't think you're mentally with it enough right now to make a rational choice. I'd better decide for you. You'll thank me later."

I glanced from him to the cup. This wasn't fair. If Morena knew I was going to die or worse trying to save my cousin, she shouldn't have let me make the deal. I was still in the act of deciding when my strength totally gave way. Whatever was sucking me under took control, and all I saw was blackness.

CHAPTER TWENTY-SIX

BRAINS

Contrary to popular belief, zombies don't like brains. They're all about pinkie toes and gall bladders, with the occasional tonsil or appendix to spice things up a bit. Basically, zombies like non-essential body parts. Thus, when you encounter a zombie apocalypse, it's a good idea to already have all those things removed. And honestly, what are you still doing with both your pinkie toes, anyway?

I woke up surprised. Surprised I was waking up at all, for one thing, and even more surprised I couldn't move or see.

It wasn't paralysis; there just wasn't room to move much. When I tried to sit up, I conked my head.

Where was I? I remembered buying salt with Katka. Lots of salt. Why? And I had been worried about her, that she'd get another seizure. And I'd had that vodník bite . . . This couldn't be a coffin. No way. I was starting to hyperventilate, so I focused on slowing down. In. Out. In. Out.

It didn't matter how I'd gotten here. It mattered how I got out.

I felt around me with my hands and feet. I was in a box with cold smooth sides, like metal or porcelain. That was good. Coffins weren't made of metal. In fact, the whole place was pretty chilly, considering it was the middle of summer in a country with no air-conditioning. Was I in the cold room at the castle? Or the well?

The thought brought to mind the memory of panic, with water all around and something sucking me down . . .

The well. It all came back: the vodník, the virgin spring, Lesana. Everything. Wasn't I supposed to be a water spirit now? Or stuck in a teacup?

A teacup.

I scrabbled around, unable to keep the fear back. I hit at the box with my elbows, kicked with my legs—anything I could do to try and get out—until I was breathless and bruised and still just as trapped. But when I calmed down again, I noticed something else.

I had no clothes on.

How had I missed *that*? And now that I paid attention to my body, I felt something on my toe. Some sort of tag.

Wait a minute. I was naked in a cold dark box, right after an experience that almost killed me. Someone had put a toe tag on me.

I wasn't in a teacup.

I was in a morgue. Or a mortuary. Or whatever you called those places where they put dead people before they got buried.

Breathe in. Breathe out. In. Out.

This wasn't so bad. I wasn't buried yet. I was still breathing, which meant oxygen was getting in. Someone would come eventually. Until then, I'd just lie here and relax. Think things through. Maybe take a nap.

In a morgue.

I screamed and kicked off from the end of the box, trying to get enough momentum to bash open the door. In the movies, they always had the bodies in with the head closest to the door, right? Instead of opening the door, though, I slammed my head into the door end of the box and blacked out.

When I came to, my head was killing me. I edged myself down on the rolling slab and pushed off from the end again, gently. This time, instead of my head hitting the door, the slab did. Much better. I rolled back down, and pushed off hard.

Clang.

It didn't open. I tried harder.

Clang, kthunk.

The door had opened a little, then slammed shut. These things weren't designed to let the occupants out. At least now I knew I had the right end.

Clang, kthunk.

Clang, kthunk.

Clang . . . kthunk.

For a moment, a crack of light had come into the box. The biggest problem I was having was that the slab rebounded away from the door after I rammed it. I couldn't get enough momentum to shoot out of the door all at once. If I could get a hand up to catch at the door, I might have a shot.

I manipulated my arms into a position where I could use my hands more. It was tight in there, but with some contortion, I managed it. My fingers touched the door, and I started to push.

With a snap, the door opened and the rolling platform I was on shot out into the light.

I gasped in relief and stretched my arms, swinging them around me before I got off the slab and jumped around in joy. Add fear of closed places to my list of phobias. From then on, no more elevators.

The first thing I did was check my toe tag for a date. If I'd been out for more than a—

13/8. August thirteenth. I breathed a sigh of relief. I'd only lost five days. Much better than the weeks or months I had worried about. Still a week and a half to save Katka. For once, something had gone right. Sure, I'd have to explain something to my parents, but it wasn't like I had a ton of time to account for.

Actually, maybe I wouldn't have to explain anything at all. They must have thought I was dead—they'd just be ecstatic to find out I was alive. Right?

Time to look around. I was in a green tiled room, old and worn, with some of the tiles missing and others cracked, but it was clean. It had a couple of metal tables in the middle of the room, and one rolled up against a wall. When I walked over to it, I saw some shoes tucked in behind it. I stopped and frowned, then took a few steps closer.

Someone was wearing those shoes.

Slowly, shakily, a pair of hands rose above the table. Each raised a forefinger, and they came together in the sign of the cross.

Oh.

"Wait," I said, or at least tried to. My vocal cords were still rough from lack of use, and what came out was more like, "Waaargh!"

The hands shot below the table.

I cleared my throat and tried again. "Wait. I'm not . . . that." I stepped forward to peer down into a man's paper-white face. I thought about trying to explain myself, but decided against it. "Could I have your jacket?" I said instead.

He edged out of the white lab coat he was wearing. I took it from him and put it on. It came down to my thighs, but it was better than naked. "Thanks," I said, then checked around again. "Which way is out?"

His finger shook as it unsteadily pointed to a door.

Call me sick, call me twisted, but I think I was justified in what I did next. It was more from sheer joy of being alive than anything else. The guy was such a scaredy-cat, and I'd never—*ever*—have a chance like this again. I put on my best crazy expression and put out my hands, staggering toward him. "Braaaaaains," I said.

He fainted. I couldn't blame him. A Roma zombie would freak out just about anybody in Slovakia.

I left the room and worked on finding my way out. All the lights were off, and the place was empty. I checked a clock: one A.M. My footsteps echoed down the tiled corridors. After three wrong turns, I emerged into a windy night, just me in my tiny lab coat. If I didn't get arrested for indecent exposure on the way home, it would be a miracle.

Luckily, Trenčín was pretty dead. Even the cars that passed ignored me. I tried to sneak around, cutting across roads, jumping fences—anything to get there without being seen in this embarrassing outfit.

The road was rough under my feet, with stones and cracks jabbing up into my soft skin. The wind tore at my lab coat, almost ripping it off twice. And then I was standing outside my apartment block. No keys. Katka's window was just a third of a block down from mine. I jumped up to rap on it.

After my third tap, I was beginning to lose hope. Her window was right by her bed, and she should have answered after the first or second. Just before I was going to break down and try my parents' window, she parted the drapes and peered out.

Even with only the light from the street, even far away from her as I was, even without hearing her speak, I knew something was wrong. She seemed to have shrunk since the last time I'd seen her. She saw me and gasped. "Tomas?"

"Who else?" I said. "Can you let me in?"

She ducked into the room, and a few moments later, the main hall light came on, and Katka was pattering down the stairs. She opened the door, ran out, and hugged me. "You're alive!"

I wasn't sure what to do, so I hugged her back. On the one hand, she was family, but on the other, all I was wearing was a lab coat. She pushed back from me.

"I *knew* you weren't dead. Or, I didn't want to believe you were. I just . . ." She hugged me again, tight, and she didn't let go. I stood there like a lump, feeling guilty and not sure why. After a few more moments, I realized Katka was shaking. Crying.

"Come on," I said, and patted her on the back a few times. "Let's go inside."

She just kept shaking. "It's been so horrid. You have no idea."

I had just freed myself from a morgue. I thought I had a pretty clear idea of how bad things could be. "Let's go inside, and you can fill me in."

This time Katka pushed back and nodded. We went inside and into her room, both of us walking as softly as possible. I could hear Uncle Ľuboš's snores coming from his room as clearly as if he were sleeping on the couch.

Once the door to Katka's room was closed, I turned to her, holding the lab coat tightly closed. "Before we talk, would you mind getting me some clothes?"

Katka smiled and wiped at her eyes. She disappeared, and when she came back with some of her dad's clothes from the laundry, I could tell she'd taken some time to clean herself up too. Her face was less puffy from crying, for one thing.

She left again while I got dressed, and once that was taken care of, we got down to business. I started. "How bad is it?"

"What?"

"Your sickness," I said. "How bad?"

"Bad. Everything is bad. Tours have dropped off completely at the castle. No one will come, and we don't know why, and the Germans . . . That doesn't matter, though. What happened to you?"

I shrugged, trying to take it all in. "I'm not sure. I went down the well and met up with Lesana down there. We found the spring, and—" I gasped. "The vial. Did you get it? What about the potion?"

"Don't worry," Katka said. "I've been working on it. I kept notes. What happened then?"

"The vodník let all the water into this tunnel we were in, this water monster attacked me, but I managed to get away and get you the vial. The last thing I remember was getting sucked down into the well. I woke up at the morgue. What day is today?"

"The twenty-third. Or I guess the twenty-fourth, now."

My jaw dropped, my mind not quite comprehending. "The twenty-fourth? Of August?"

She nodded.

"But my toe tag," I said. "I was brought in the thirteenth. I couldn't—"

Katka smiled grimly. "I promised I wouldn't let them bury you alive, remember? I had to use every bit of persuasion I could, but I got them to put off the burial. It helped that my health has been getting worse so quickly."

"We only have *two days*?" I said. "What are we going to do? What am I going to tell my parents?"

Someone gasped behind us. "You're back!"

Ľuboš was standing there, his hair and beard all over the place and

274

looking more like a tumbleweed than a person. When had he stopped snoring? "Don't just stare." He walked over and hugged me so hard I thought my lungs would pop. "You are safe," he said. "That is good. I must admit, I began to think Katka was mistaken."

I managed to find my voice. "What—"

"I told him," Katka said. "About the vodník." Her eyes added, *And nothing else.* So no one knew about Katka's impending demise still.

Great.

"We must go tell your parents now," Ľuboš said. "When Katka told me there was a chance you would recover, I was doubtful. But I believed enough to convince your mother. Still, I could not tell her why. She . . . will not take this well." He ran a hand through his hair, then signaled for us to follow him.

I'd like to say that the reunion was a happy one, full of swooning and laughing and back slapping.

I'd also like laser vision and the ability to fly.

Mom fainted when she saw me. Fainted. As in, my dad had to catch her. Dad took things better. He just got all bug eyed and confused. It helped that he had his hands full with my fainted mother. It gave him something to do to keep from getting overwhelmed.

So the reunion was delayed somewhat while we moved into the living room and put my mom on the couch, then coaxed her back into the land of the unfainted. Dad sat next to Mom on the couch. Katka was sitting by me on the floor in front of them. Ľuboš leaned against the wall by us, his arms folded.

While we waited, I noticed the TV was back from repairs. At least there had been *one* good thing about losing all those days.

That's when the questions came.

Not huge questions. Simple ones. Like, "How did this happen?" and "How did Katka know?"

I'm not a good liar. In fact, I suck at it. And I knew if I started telling any piece of the truth, the rest of it would come out right after. "I—we—Katka? We need to tell them."

"No," she said.

"If we don't, there's no way we'll get the potion done in time," I said.

Dad said, "Potion?"

"Come on, Katka," I said. "Less than two days. We can't do this alone."

She stared up at her dad, who was now frowning at her with an uncertain expression. Then her shoulders slumped, and she nodded. When she spoke, her voice was barely audible. "Fine."

At last. I took a deep breath. My mouth dried up. Three sets of eyes drilled into mine. "Um . . . I haven't been entirely . . . *honest* with you the past few months."

It would have helped if they had responded somehow. A simple "What are you talking about?" would have been nice. Instead, they waited silently for me to continue. It would be easier to take this in stages. First the visions, then the problems with Katka. I took a breath and spit it out.

"There's a vodník trying to kill me."

Sometimes it's amazing how simple it is to state complex problems. Even then, I figured their response would be one of confusion, or denial, or shock—anything but what I got.

Outrage.

"No!" Mom shouted. Shouted. She stood up. "No! This is not happening again."

"Quiet," Ľuboš said. The walls might be concrete, but the neighbors could still hear shouting, especially in the middle of the night. "Whether we want it to or not, it is."

She shoved her finger in his face. "You. You knew this was happening. You encouraged it." Her head whipped back to me. "Tomas, you're delusional. It's the only—"

Dad tried to take her hand and pull her back down to the couch. "Maybe we should let him tell us a bit more."

She stopped and frowned. Behind that anger, I thought I saw a good dose of fear too. "Explain," she said.

I stood up and snapped back at her, "Oh, sure. Now you want me to explain. Now it's suddenly all okay, since I have your permission. What is it with you? Do you know how much easier things would have been on me the past few months if it weren't for you freaking out and going all silent whenever anyone came close to giving me answers? Each way I tried, you'd cut me off ahead of time. You and your idiotic 'no talking about it' rules."

My mom stepped toward me. "Those idiotic rules are for your own damned good."

"Maybe I should decide what's for my own good and what's not. Ever think about that?"

She sputtered a few times, then shook her head and turned away, apparently too furious to talk. It served her right.

"Okay," I said, trying to calm down. Where to begin? "The first time I noticed something was the night we arrived." It took a while to go through it all, mainly because there was too much for me to keep it straight. I'd be talking about Ohnica, only to jump to Starenka, and then that made me think about Morena (being careful to avoid any mention of Katka's situation yet), and each jump was followed by a slew of questions from Dad and Ľuboš: what things looked like, how they spoke.

Mom, on the other hand, clammed up. It took a while for Dad and Ľuboš to notice, but eventually they saw what was happening, and their questions died.

Mom was crying and shaking her head. "It's happening again," she said.

No one spoke. "What is?" I pleaded. Seeing her cry like that made all my resentment at her shrivel. A little.

She cried harder.

Ľuboš cleared his throat. "He should be told."

Mom closed her eyes and nodded. It seemed like that agreement took even more out of her. She shrunk in her chair and kept crying.

On the other hand, my father and uncle sighed at the same time; a heavy load had been taken off their backs. "Tomas," Ľuboš said. "Remember when you and Katka asked me what happened to your grandmother?"

So that's what this was all about. Finally. "Yes."

Ľuboš went on. "I told you some then. Now I can tell you all. When I was ten, my father died. My mother was a hard worker. She did her best to keep the family together, and she succeeded for the most part. When I was sixteen, things began to change. She lost interest in her work and began having complaints from her supervisors. But this was Communism, so nothing changed at first. Many people didn't work hard—it was normal. Then, my mother told us something. She was seeing things. Creatures. Not just seeing them, either. Talking to them."

Mom stopped crying now and watched her brother, a stony expression on her face.

Ľuboš continued. "I thought she was only telling us stories. These sorts of things did not happen, speaking with dwarves and vílas. But it was not make-believe to her. In fact, this other side of her took over her life. And then she was murdered by one of these things."

Mom scoffed. "She was mugged, kidnapped, murdered maybe, but not by some fairy tale, Ľuboš. If she hadn't been delusional, she would still be with us."

"No," Ľuboš said. "You didn't talk to her like I did. You didn't want to believe. Didn't want to investigate. Instead you threw yourself into school work. But I studied. I've researched. I talked with our mother about who she thought she was talking to. This was real. Maybe the same vodník who has been talking to Tomas is the one who was speaking with our mother."

"We don't need more of this," Mom said. "Tomas needs to see a doctor. A psychiatrist. When she went, they said it was hereditary. Remember all the tests we were put through, Ľuboš?"

"Mom," I said. "I'm not crazy. I know what I've seen."

"It's not possible," she said.

"Wrong," Ľuboš said. "It's the only explanation."

Mom frowned. "Unexplained things happen all the time. That doesn't mean fairies cause them."

I got up and went to my room. Deep in my closet, underneath the clean clothes pile, was *Death in the Modern Day*. I brought it back to the room and plopped it on the kitchen table. "Then how do you explain that?" I asked.

"What do you mean?"

"That popped up in the middle of the street one day while I was out walking. Morena sent it. If I were crazy, how would that explain things appearing out of thin air?"

Then I realized, *Oh crap.* They'd only see a dictionary.

Mom picked up the book and leafed through it. "That's silly," she said. "Anyone could have written this. Look at these silly pictures. Cartoon reapers?"

Dad took the book from her, his brow furrowed in confusion. "What do you mean? It's a dictionary. Of course anyone could have written it, but what does that matter?"

Well, that was a strange development. I hesitated, but then pushed forward. "What do you see, Mom?"

Dad handed it back to her. She folded her arms and refused to take it. "A dictionary. Just like everyone else."

"You can see them too," Ľuboš said. "Just like Mama."

"That's silly," Mom snapped. "Just because I see some stupid book about death doesn't mean—"

"No," I said. "It's only visible for people who either can see the mythological creatures on their own or who have taken a potion to let them."

"Then it just means I've inherited this insanity too. But we don't have to give into it, Tomas. We can—"

"Dana," Dad started, half sitting up from the couch.

"You know what, Mom?" I said. "It doesn't matter what you think. Because we don't need to be arguing about this. If you think I'm nuts, then we'll see. Katka's going to die in two days if I don't save her."

That brought shock all around. And silence. "What?" Ľuboš said. He sounded hollow, like someone had just punched him in the stomach, hard.

I hung my head. "I found out from Morena when Katka's going to die. If I can find a substitute soul before then, then Death will spare her."

He sat back in his chair, all the blood gone from his face.

Mom plopped down on the couch next to Dad, whose jaw was still slack. Katka had her head in her hands. Her shoulders were shaking.

I felt like I had to say something—do something to fill the silence. "That's where I've been the past two weeks. The vodník said he had a plan to help. If we released a water spirit, since she used to be human, that would fill the contract. But then he tried to kill me, and things got . . . complicated. But if we can release the water spirit, then we can still fulfill the pact. Katka will be saved."

It didn't seem to matter to anyone. Mom and Dad were confused, Katka's shoulders were only shaking harder, and Ľuboš seemed to have popped. All the words in the world wouldn't fix this. We had to start *doing* things.

"Where's the potion, Katka?" I asked. "We can finish it, and—"

Mom spoke. "You're really seeing these things?"

"That's what I've been saying, Mom. And if we don't—"

"It's why we moved in the first place," she said. It didn't seem like she realized anyone else was there. Her hands fiddled with the hem of her blouse, her eyes frozen open. "When you had the accident, and we knew what had happened to Babka, we had to move. But then the fire, and the insurance. We shouldn't have come back. We should have sacrificed. Stayed poor. Then we wouldn't have had to risk losing you."

I moved to sit next to her, trying to snap her out of it. "But if we'd done that, I wouldn't have found out about Katka. And now we still have a chance to save her. I'm not dead, okay? The vodník tried to kill me, and he failed. That makes me stronger."

She blinked, then looked at me. "How?"

"It's a long story. I'll explain later. But this doesn't have to be like with Babka. This can be a good thing. We can save Katka's life."

Mom shook her head. "When I lost my mother, I thought life couldn't get worse. But if I were to lose you too . . ."

"Not going to happen," I said. "I'll teach that vodník a thing or two. You'll see. But we need to focus on Katka." I turned back to my cousin. "Now, where's that—"

Katka's head shook once more, and her whole body fell over. Her eyes were rolled up into her head, and she was twitching.

CHAPTER TWENTY-SEVEN

RAIN

When filling out paperwork, please at least use a red pen. Writing in blood, while not strictly necessary, is always appreciated.

When everyone heard me cut off, it didn't take more than a moment for them to realize what was happening. We went into panic mode, Ľuboš snapping out of his stunned state to get his daughter on the floor on her side while Mom cleared space for them. Dad called the paramedics.

Usually when she had a seizure, she came out of it soon. I told myself that, while the seconds ticked by. Ľuboš whispered to his daughter and stroked her forehead. Dad sat next to Mom and rubbed her back. Time slowed down. It was taking too long. Any second, Katka would be back with us.

But if anything, the seizure got worse. She went from mildly twitching to full spasms, her arms flailing at her side. Ľuboš held them down, still speaking to her in a calm voice. "It's going to be okay," he said. "I'm here. I'm here." His lower lip was quivering, the movement causing his whole beard to shake.

She'd come out of it. She had to. I didn't know where the potion was, or what still had to be done. I couldn't do it alone. Why hadn't I been paying more attention to her earlier? I'd thought she was just crying. I was too focused on how I was feeling. Too angry with my mom. This was all my fault.

It wasn't until the paramedics arrived that I had to face the facts. Time hadn't slowed down. Katka was still deep in her seizure, for far too long.

"She'll come out of it, right?" I asked Dad as we watched Ľuboš and Mom drive away with Katka in the ambulance.

He licked his lips. "I don't know. That looked like *staticus elepticus*. Permanent seizure. It's exactly what happened to her mother before she . . ." He took a deep breath. "Tomas, you said we can fix this. What do we need to do?"

"This is my fault," I said.

"What?"

"It's all my fault. She didn't want to tell people what was happening. If I hadn't forced her to help me with the potion, then maybe she wouldn't have been so stressed out. Maybe she wouldn't have gone into that seizure, and she'd still be fine. What if what I did pushed her over? What if she dies because of me?" Instead of massaging my burn, I found myself rubbing the bite mark, where a new scar had formed.

Dad hugged me. "It's not you," he said at last, letting me go. "She's been sick for a long time. But if you're right, and there's a way to help her, what do we need to do?"

I took a deep breath and nodded. "First, we need to find that potion. Until we've got that, I don't know what we can do. It should be outside somewhere, open to the elements. Also, Katka said she'd been taking notes on the potion. It's a little complex, and if we mess it up, it might not work. So we need to find those notes."

"Good," Dad said. "It's three thirty in the morning. It won't be light out for two hours, but we can start by searching inside for the notes. Come on—they're bound to be in there somewhere."

We got to work in Ľuboš's apartment five minutes later. I started in Katka's bedroom, while Dad headed for the living room bookcase.

A big part of me thought I'd find it right away. I knew Katka, and I knew where she liked to hide things from her dad. I went straight for her dresser, her desk, her closet, her nightstand—nothing. Not under the socks, not shoved back on the hard-to-reach highest shelf—I even checked in the underwear drawer. Nada. When I went out and checked with Dad, he hadn't found anything, either. Ransacking the rest of the apartment brought the same result. We moved bookcases, flipped through books, checked under the fridge and stove. *Nič.*

By the time we had finished, the sun was rising, and worry was gnawing through my stomach. Every time I'd glance at a clock, there was that much less time left before Katka would die. Seven o'clock: forty-one hours to finish the potion, find the grave, and get this done. We'd already blown three and a half hours, and we still hadn't even gotten her notes.

At half past seven, Dad hit pay dirt: Katka's makeup compact. It made sense, I guess. She was in an apartment where the only other occupant was male. Speaking as a male with some experience in the matter now, the compact was pretty much the last place a man would think of to look. Dad brought it in to me and together, the two of us read it. She had basically rewritten the instructions into list form, and checked off things as they were done.

Katka had gotten a lot farther than I had feared she would: the potion had been transferred to the crystal basin and she had added the Dubak, walnut, and blood. All that was left was to put it into the cherry wood cup precisely at dawn tomorrow morning and then spread it on Lesana's grave before Katka died tomorrow night.

"But it doesn't say where the potion is," Dad pointed out.

I shook my head. "She would have hidden it somewhere outside, where it wouldn't be messed with. And we still don't know about the grave, either." And we had no clue if the potion would actually work. I had assumed all along that I was the one who was supposed to complete all the steps. I was the "enchanter." Would it work the same with Katka having done so much? There had been that disclaimer at the bottom of the instructions saying if we screwed it up, it could cause "severe consequences."

Dad said, "According to the notes, we have until tomorrow morning to complete the potion. Why don't you help me get started on finding the grave, and while I'm on that, you can find where Katka was keeping it. You said it was outside somewhere?"

I nodded. "It has to be. That's how it's made."

We rushed back to our apartment, and Dad went straight to the computer. He quizzed me at first about everything I knew about Lesana, peppering me with questions. What the legend was, when she was supposed to have lived—anything that might help him in his search. He was a librarian. This was what he did. When he had drained me dry, I was released to go find that potion.

Outside, the clouds hovered close to the ground, almost scraping the apartment buildings. It was going to rain. I hurried around the building, checking all the windowsills and glancing at all the trees and low branches, hunting for a gleam of crystal. Nothing. I thought about making the circuit again, but there wasn't time. The only place I could think of that Katka would place the basin was the castle. There was nowhere else she could be sure it would be safe, and the castle had a ton of nooks where a basin could be stashed.

When I was halfway into town, running for all I was worth, I practically collided with Draco. He was coming out of the bakery and his eyes about popped out of his head when he saw me. It probably would have been better if the Bigot Gang had kept thinking I was dead until after this thing with Katka was over, but whatever. I dodged and missed him by a few inches. I checked to see if he was following me. He wasn't. Maybe he thought he'd seen a ghost.

Thirty feet later, a fat raindrop splashed into my face. Another hit the ground in front of me. And then it was raining in earnest, an enormous downpour that soaked me in seconds.

I didn't care. There were more important things in life than worrying about being wet, or wondering what other people were thinking about you. And anyway—all that worrying about water and fire hadn't done me any good.

It rained harder, my feet splashing through puddles that had formed in seconds. My lungs were aching, but I kept pushing myself. Halfway up the hill to the castle, I had to slow down. Getting there fast and then falling over from exhaustion wouldn't help anything, and no matter how much I wanted to get this done quickly, I had to pace myself. I wondered what Dad was doing—if he'd had any success—and how Katka was. Maybe Ľuboš or Mom had called with an update.

Once I'd caught my breath, I started running again, up the hill and to the castle gate. Janči was in the ticket booth again, and I stopped to question him, though I could barely talk. "Have you—seen Katka—"

"No," he said.

I shook my head, droplets falling off my face as the rain continued to pour down. "Crystal basin. Have you seen her with a crystal basin here recently?"

He frowned. "No. What's the matter? Hey!"

I was already running again, scanning the walls and the windows—anywhere the basin might be. By the time I was at the castle's first court-yard, I realized how futile this was. It was one thing to think "the basin's at the castle," but I could search the place for a day and still not look everywhere. Just finding the note in Katka's room had taken my dad and me over three hours.

Some water flicked in my face, as if I'd been splashed. I glanced around to see where it had come from. No one was there.

It came again, like the rain had decided to curve in for a moment and hit me straight in the eyes. I blinked the water clear, and when I could see again, I could see her.

Lesana.

A shiver went down my spine. She was standing in front of me, her body outlined by the falling rain. I had assumed she wouldn't be around to help—that the vodník would have captured her or locked her up to keep me from getting help. But then again, he must think I was dead. Why would he worry about Lesana helping me now?

She pointed to her throat and shook her head. No talking. The vodník kept her on a pretty tight leash. The only reason she was as visible as she was now was likely because of the rain.

I stepped toward her. "Do you know where the basin is?"

Lesana nodded.

"Can you show me?"

She nodded again, then turned and started to run.

I followed after her, glancing up at the sky, for once in my life hoping as hard as I could that it wouldn't stop raining. It was going full blast right then, but the way Slovak weather was, it might turn off at any moment.

Following a figure made out of rain—in the rain—is even harder than it sounds. I had to keep pausing to be able to make her out again. Each time, she was motioning me frantically to continue. She led me to the right, to a house-sized wooden tower that hugged one of the castle walls.

We climbed up two flights of steps, and then Lesana walked out onto the wall, like a gymnast on a balance beam.

We weren't supposed to go up there. Katka must have put the basin there at night. No one was out right now, but the wall was slick, and it wasn't wide, with crenellations built into it, so the top of the wall wasn't smooth: it had those little spaces for archers to fire out from. A fall from thirty feet could kill me. About twenty feet down the wall, I could just make out the basin. It had been risky for Katka to put it there in dry weather. In wet weather, getting it back was borderline suicidal.

I got up and followed the water ghost.

Now I couldn't go quickly. The rain was still pelting down, and I got down on my hands and knees to creep forward toward the basin. Each time I came to a space on the wall, I had to reach out, balancing only on my knees for a second, and praying I didn't fall. On either side of me, the ground dropped down, and the farther out I went, the longer the drop became as the hill fell away below, making me dizzy every time I forgot and looked down. The wall was rocky and jagged in my grip, and my knuckles were white with the effort of keeping my balance. The image of the other section of the castle wall—the one lying in crumbled ruins— flashed through my mind. There was a reason we weren't supposed to go on the walls: they were unstable.

Lesana was waiting by the basin. I got up into a crouch so I could use my hands and pick it up. It was overflowing with rain water. That didn't matter—the spell had said to leave it open to the elements. I slowly stood up and did my best to turn around on the narrow wall without sloshing any of the water out. I wobbled, losing some of the contents, but I managed to complete the turn and glance back the way I had come.

Crawling out had been hard enough. Now I had to go back walking, and I couldn't use my hands for balance. The wooden observation deck seemed miles away, and I was no gymnast.

Pace yourself, Tomas. It's no good if you drop it, and no good if you die. Just get there.

Inch by inch, I started back. All my instincts wanted me to let go of the basin and get better balance. I tried to imagine I was just on a street curb, but there was all that empty space on either side of me, and my imagination wasn't up to the task. Now wasn't the time to get afraid of heights.

It was inevitable, really. Halfway back, I slipped. For a few seconds, I was teetering on one foot, high above the ground. I pressed the basin to my chest, trying to throw my weight around and regain balance. Water sloshed out and fell to the courtyard below, but I recovered in time to make sure some of it stayed in the container. And I had regained my footing with that move too. That had been too close.

I took a few deep breaths, closed my eyes, opened them, and then kept going. I had to do this. I had no other options. I came to another crenellation and stepped across it, shifting my weight more smoothly. It was one of the longest twenty feet I've walked in my life, but I made it.

Once I had my feet back on a surface wider than six inches, I faced Lesana. "Thank you," I said.

She nodded. I thought she might be smiling. I bent down and set the basin on the floor in front of me. "Lesana, I need to know where you're buried."

She shook her head, then shrugged.

"You really don't remember?"

She nodded. The rain was slowing down.

Come on! This had to work. She'd told me before to ask the vodník, but he and I hadn't exactly parted on speaking terms. "It was in a crypt," I said. "I saw it in one of the visions. You were buried alive. Remember!"

She paused for a while, thinking perhaps. Then she shook her head again and pointed to the ground.

"What? Here?" I said. "You were buried at the castle?"

"No," she mouthed, then disappeared down to the lower story of the observation deck.

I picked up the basin and followed. Down there, the rain couldn't penetrate, and I couldn't see Lesana anywhere. I was about to continue on to the ground when some water flicked in my face again. When I turned, I saw she had managed to write something on the dry wood.

Try the archives.

The archives? What archives? I went to ask her, but the rain was stopping in the way only Slovak rain could. "Lesana?" I asked.

It took me a bit to spot her now that the rain was slower, but after a moment I did. She was standing outside, just within the reach of the rain so I could see her. "What do you mean?" I said.

She pointed at her throat, then shrugged and pointed at the message again. Now her body was only outlined by drops here and there. I watched in frustration as she disappeared altogether. I felt a tug on my hand, like someone had brushed it with their own. It shouldn't have meant much to me, but it did. Why couldn't she have been alive? I didn't even know Lesana, but I still found myself thinking about her, wanting to get to know her, wanting— *Focus, Tomas.* Those kinds of thoughts weren't going to get me anywhere.

I *could* do this. I was meant to do this.

Tomorrow night, Katka would be back to normal and Lesana would be free of the vodník, no matter what.

CHAPTER TWENTY-EIGHT
ANTISEPTIC

Hospitals are wonderful places. A home away from home for the weary Death. You can always get a warm meal, kick your feet up and read a magazine, then go out and collect a few souls—all in a one-stop-shop.

Getting home was an ordeal. I didn't want to cover the basin, for fear of further violating whatever rules the potion was supposed to follow. So I had to go as fast as I could without spilling any of the leftover contents, ignoring the strange looks other people threw my way. Who cared what they thought? I caught a glimpse of Gollum, sitting on a park bench and chowing down on an ice cream, but I didn't think he'd seen me. Please, just give me a day free of the Bigot Gang. I couldn't deal with them right now.

I took the basin to the canal across the street from our apartment. It still had to be left outside, but it wasn't like I could just leave it outside one of our windows. Maybe I'd been living in Slovakia too long and had become as paranoid as the rest of them, but anyone could steal it or knock it over. The BGs would love to get their hands on anything I valued. This was probably why Katka had put the basin in such a hard-to-reach place to begin with.

The canal was nestled between manmade hills on either side of it.

On the side by the city, there was a path at the top of the hill and one at the bottom. Trenčín spread out behind me, but across the canal was nothing but fields and a few houses. It was still surprising to me how quickly Slovak cities ended. Urban sprawl didn't exist in this country.

Having seen Gollum, I'd taken extra care to make sure I wasn't being followed to the canal. All I needed was for the Bigot Gang to ruin everything. I descended the hill to go to the path right by the canal. Every so often, the canal had a road that crossed it, and you could walk under the bridges when you were on this route. I checked again to see if anyone was watching. The path was clear. I stuffed the basin on top of one of the girders in the bridge closest to my house. When I was done, I didn't think anyone would find it unless they were searching for it: to reach it, I'd had to clamber on top of a garbage can I'd dragged over.

It was as safe as I could make it for now. And even if it wasn't outside under the stars, it was still technically outside. It would have to do. The instructions said it had to stay outside for a week, and that meant tomorrow morning. If only we could just use it now. But first we had to find Lesana's grave anyway. Maybe Dad had had some luck.

I rushed back to my apartment and straight to Dad's office. He sat hunched over the computer, a light breeze blowing in from the open window next to him, a serious expression carved into his face.

"Have you found it?" he asked when he saw me.

I nodded, breathless. "It's all set for tomorrow at dawn. You?"

He shook his head. "Not yet." There were books everywhere, all of them opened to different pages and spread out all over the floor. "I've found all the local cemeteries, and I've seen references to the legend of her death, but nothing that says where she was buried." Dad liked to keep a running commentary going when he searched—it was the librarian in him coming out again. The man was always in Teach Mode.

He continued in English—in our urgency, we'd been slipping in and out of Slovak to avoid wasting time thinking of the right words. "One problem we're coming across is that Slovak graveyards simply aren't online. In America, you can actually have quite a bit of success at finding grave sites, particularly of famous or more notable people. There are whole websites devoted—"

"Dad?" I said.

"What?"

"Can we get back to the search?"

He pushed his glasses back up his nose. "Right. In any case, I thought we might be able to find at least *some* graves online, but I'm not having any luck with that. And even if we could, there's no guarantee her burial place is in a graveyard. From what I've learned, back then the rich could decide to be buried anywhere. Churches, the forest, a favorite travel spot—even in their basement. Lesana belonged to a wealthy family, and there's no way to tell where the family crypt is. At least no way I've found."

"What about the archives?" I asked.

"What?"

I shook my head. "That's all I know. Lesana said to try the archives."

Dad frowned. "I'm not sure. I've never heard of something like that."

"Then call Ľuboš. Has he gotten in touch with you yet? How's Katka?"

My father looked sheepish, then took out his cell phone. Sometimes librarians get so used to checking sources they forget they can get answers from people too. I looked at the clock. 5:08 P.M. Less than thirty-one hours to go.

Dad dialed, then put it on speaker.

"What?" Ľuboš said. Slovaks aren't big on the whole "Hi, howya doin'?" routine, even when they aren't in the middle of a crisis.

"It's Brian," Dad said. "I'm sorry to disturb you, but Tomas and I are having trouble finding some information here, and we were wondering if you might be able to help?"

Silence on the other end, then, "Hold on. I'll call you back." He hung up.

It took him about five minutes, minutes my dad and I spent making fruitless attempts at Internet searches. The phone rang.

"Sorry," Ľuboš's voice came out from the speaker. "I didn't want to disturb Katka."

"How is she?" Dad asked.

"She's . . . they've put her into a coma. Said it would be better for her. The doctors, they know nothing. They're so . . . They won't . . ." He was quiet for a moment, then said, "How can I help you?"

"We need to find a grave," Dad said. "An old grave."

"Why?" Ľuboš asked.

I answered. "It's about what I was saying before Katka went into her seizure. If I can release a soul to replace Katka's, then Morena will spare her. We need to find the grave of the girl I asked you about before. The one who was buried alive?"

"Andricka," Ľuboš said.

"Right," I said.

Ľuboš grunted. "Finding a grave that old . . . very difficult. And I'm not even sure Andricka was the name of this girl. It's only a legend I heard, one of many. Based on fact, maybe, but how to tell?"

I nodded at the phone. "Right. But I've been haunted by this girl's ghost, so I'm pretty sure it's a real legend. You said she died in the late 1700's? Are there graves that date back that far in the city graveyard?"

"Possible." He trailed off, apparently deep in thought.

I cleared my throat. "I heard we might want to check the archives?"

I held my breath, hoping he knew something about this.

"Of course!" Ľuboš said. "If this is an event that really happened, and is not just some legend, then there is a place that would have it written down. The city chronicle."

"Great," I said. "Where's that kept?"

He grunted again. "The most recent years are at the Trenčín city museum, but for something so old, you'd have to go to the Slovak National Archives in Bratislava."

The archives. Bingo.

"Is there any restriction on who can view the chronicle?" Dad asked.

"It depends. Bureaucracy, you know. Sometimes, they let you in with no trouble. Other times, you need to have what you need in writing and wait a month for them to approve it. Stupid."

I broke in. "So we just call down there, ask someone to look it up for us, and that's it?"

"Tomas," my dad said. "It's not that simple."

"Hold on a sec," I told my uncle, then muted the phone and asked my dad. "What do you mean?"

"You can't just call up a librarian and wave a wand. It would take time to find this out. Archives that old aren't going to be digitized, and they're not going to be indexed. We'd have to search them, page by page."

This was a nightmare. It didn't happen this way in movies. If this were a movie, my father would have conveniently been studying grave locations for the past few months as research for his writing, and he would have led us straight to the grave. Then again, if this were a movie, Nazis would probably be in there somewhere too. Or ninjas. I unmuted the phone. "My dad says we need to go down there in person. Will they let us see them?"

"If we are lucky, yes." Ľuboš said. "But they are closed now. It's Sunday.

No one will be there."

"What?" I said. "We can't wait clear till tomorrow."

"You must," my uncle said. "Finding the right volumes on your own would be impossible, and you can do nothing if you break in and they arrest you."

"Then we'll try the cemeteries in person," I said. "Maybe we'll get lucky."

Ľuboš was silent for a moment, then said, "Come and pick me up. I will go with you."

"But Katka," Dad started.

"Can only be saved by this," Ľuboš said. "The doctors can do nothing, and I can do nothing waiting here. I'd rather be with you two, trying to get something done."

"Fine," I said. "We'll be there soon."

Dad and I rushed out to the car and were speeding through the streets of Trenčín in no time.

"It's for things like this that Google was invented," I told my dad on the way over.

"It's for things like this that we still need librarians," he said. Trust Dad to never miss a chance to put in a plug for his profession. He was in his element, sure and confident. "Don't worry, Tomas. We can do this. I'm sure of it."

After that, the drive over to see Katka was as silent as it got. I had lost all the optimism I had felt when I found the crystal basin. There was too much left to do and not enough time to get it done. If it hadn't been for that cursed vodník, I would have had plenty of time. I could have helped Katka with the potion, and taken the time to find Lesana's grave. Of course, when the vodník had given me the recipe for the potion, I hadn't thought finding the grave would be an issue.

The hospital was straight out of a horror film, full of long corridors and unfriendly people. There was no central reception area; Dad had to ask when we parked what section to go to, and once we were there, we had to walk up and down the halls searching for the right room. Even after calling Ľuboš and getting directions, we still got lost twice. The whole building had that sick taste unique to old folks' homes and hospitals: antiseptic, dirty bodies, and death.

Ľuboš was waiting for us outside the room. When he saw us, he walked over, his shoulders slumped and bags under his eyes.

Dad hugged him, and for a minute I was worried Ľuboš was going to fall down where he stood. I'd never thought I'd see the day when my dad was the stronger of the two of them. Right then, seeing my father comforting Ľuboš, I had a flash of real pride.

"Can we go in and see her?" Dad asked.

Ľuboš nodded and turned around to go back into the room. A large part of me didn't want to follow him. I didn't want to have a picture in my mind of her in this place, helpless. But if I didn't go in—and I failed tomorrow—then I wouldn't have a chance to see her again. She'd want to know I came. I swallowed and entered the room, a nauseous feeling deep in my stomach.

Katka lay on a bed in a room with five other patients; there weren't even any curtains separating everyone into their own spaces. Her eyes were closed, her cheeks sunken. She didn't look anything like the girl who had become my best friend over the summer. She seemed dead.

This was too much. I ran down the hall to a bathroom we had passed, barely making it into a stall before I threw up. I stayed there for a few minutes, trying to get myself under control. If I let myself, I was going to start crying, and I wasn't sure I'd be able to stop. Someone came into the room and walked over to the stall I was in. A flowing black robe and staff peeked underneath the door. I opened up to see Morena grinning down at me.

"It's not easy, is it?" she said.

I was too depressed to even want to argue. "Come to gloat?"

She sniffed. "Gloating's not my style, boy. I show up for the victory, then go on to the next one. I just saw you were in the neighborhood and thought I'd drop in between appointments to see how things were going."

"Yeah, well, they're not going, but I'm sure you knew that already, didn't you?"

Morena snapped her fingers, and a three legged stool appeared behind her. She perched on it, leaning her weight forward onto the pole of her scythe. "I think you've been doing a marvelous job, if that makes you feel any better. I haven't had this much fun in ages, and I mean that literally. Throat lozenge?"

I shook my head. "Do you know where she's buried?"

"The water girl?" Morena asked, then sniffed. "I suppose I could look into it, if I really wanted to. But I don't. Better to see what you come up with on your own."

I didn't say anything to that. The woman was a sick, twisted person, with no regard for human decency.

She cleared her throat. "I could end it now, you know."

"End what?"

"Katka. I could take her now, if you'd prefer. It's close enough to her death time that I'd just have to fill out some extra paperwork. It's been so much fun watching you struggle, that's the least you've earned."

"You've *enjoyed* watching me struggle?" I said. How could she just dismiss people's lives so easily?

"You don't watch sports much, do you?" Morena asked.

"What's that got to do with it?"

"I love sports. Especially your American football. You can get it over here, you know. Not all the games, but enough. I think it exemplifies everything I like about the human race. Your drive to win at all costs. There's nothing as good as a comeback, and that's the one sport where a comeback—a victory over seemingly impossible odds—is always a real possibility, right up to the very end. I don't even care if the team I'm rooting for is beaten by that comeback. It's a joy to watch."

I wiped at my mouth, trying to get the foul taste out. "This isn't football," I said.

She grunted, then stood up. "Well, duty calls. Just remember. Life is very much a game, at least in my way of thinking. I'll see you tomorrow night."

She walked back out of the room. A stranger came in moments later. "You going to use that, or you just resting?" he said.

I stood up and flushed, then washed my hands, rinsed out my mouth, and left the bathroom. Mom, Dad, and Ľuboš were sitting around Katka's bed, but they stood when I walked in.

I tried to resist it, but my eyes kept getting drawn to Katka. Mom came over and gave me a hug. "I'm sorry, Tomas."

I nodded and cleared my throat. "We should get going."

Ľuboš grunted, then went to his daughter and kissed her gently on the forehead before whispering something to her, standing, and striding out the door.

"Good luck," Mom said. "I'll stay here with her."

I turned from her to Katka, then the other patients in their beds. It wasn't right; a person should at least be able to die among family, not with strangers. I went over to Katka and took her hand. I squeezed it, then set it down on the bed again. She seemed dead already. If I'd told her dad what was going to happen before, then at least they would have had time to say good-bye . . . But that hadn't been my choice to make.

"Mom," I said, catching her eye with a gaze I hoped was confident. "Eleven fifty-six, tomorrow night. If she lives past then, you'll know we succeeded."

I left the room.

The graveyard was across town, over in an area named Juch. It was about as pretty as it sounded—meaning not. The buildings were massive Communist housing projects that stressed cement and straight lines and kept windows to a minimum, like they were made of giant, square Legos. The cemetery parking lot was shared by a convenience store. Classy.

We got there at seven and spent a good two and a half hours of daylight and dusk walking up and down the rows of graves, but we didn't have any luck. The graves in Slovakia were much better taken care of than I was used to: neat and orderly, with lots of flowers. Each grave had a large upright marker, but instead of burying the bodies, they kept them in stone boxes lying on the ground next to each marker. It made each grave look like a twin-sized bed, complete with headboard, which made me feel sort of like we were searching a large dormitory or furniture store instead of a cemetery.

I remembered *being* in Lesana's crypt—not just a normal grave—but Ľuboš pointed out that her body might have been moved at some point, so we were stuck looking at everything, just in case. No "Lesana Andricka" or anything like that on anything, although Ľuboš continually reminded us that legends change, and there was no guarantee the name attached to the legend was correct.

"I'll know it when I see it," I kept saying. I had been in the place in one of my visions, after all. I knew her first name was Lesana. I had seen the monk begin to carve it. That was a start.

But the longer we went with no success, the more depressed I became. If the grave wasn't here—if it was in some basement, or off covered in vines in the woods—then we'd never find it.

The evening wore itself out. I was so focused on our task that it was only when I caught myself squinting to make out a grave name that I realized the sun had set and night was well on its way to falling. Even then, I kept pressing, only stopping when Ľuboš came over and put a hand on my shoulder.

"It's not here," he said.

"But I haven't—"

"No," he said. "You have. This is the second time you've gone through the cemetery. We should go home and sleep."

I shook my head. "I can sleep tomorrow night after this is all over."

Ľuboš sighed. "And if tomorrow, when we are at the archives and have an actual chance of discovering the grave site, you fall asleep? What then? No. Wandering in circles now won't do us any good. We go home, and in the morning you complete the potion and we go to the archives."

He had a point, no matter how much I didn't want to acknowledge it. I surveyed the cemetery. In the falling dusk, crickets were out and the area seemed peaceful—until I realized Katka would be here in a few days if we failed.

CHAPTER TWENTY-NINE
BOOK DUST

Robes are dry-clean only. We have a standing account with Paul's Dry Cleaning, a little place in New York over in Chinatown. Failure to use this union-approved cleaning facility is punishable by Birth.

I had my alarm set for five A.M. Sunrise was at 5:56, and I didn't want to miss it. I shouldn't have worried; I couldn't sleep. Why was it that on all the days when it didn't matter if I had a full night's rest or not, I got one, but whenever I knew the next day was going to be important—and that I needed the sleep—all I did was toss and turn? I eventually gave up, choosing to spend my time searching the Internet for clues that might help us the next day.

I didn't find any.

At 5:15 A.M., I was out the door and heading to the canal, cherry wood cup in hand and ready to complete the potion. It was brisk out, and I was wearing a light jacket.

I got to the bridge, moved the garbage can into place, and fished around for the basin. It was right where I had left it. Why had I feared it wouldn't be? Probably because everything else in my life had gone wrong, so why not that too?

When I turned, basin in hand, the Bigot Gang were standing at the top of the hill, silhouetted against the city. How in the world? I thought

293

about running, but I couldn't—not without risking spilling the potion everywhere. A wave of adrenaline washed through me, my heart rate quickening. *Embrace the fear. Use it.* A glance at my watch showed me I had thirty-four minutes until the potion had to be completed. If I missed that time, then I'd have to start the whole thing over from scratch. And we didn't have that kind of time.

I started walking back to my apartment, sticking to the lower path. It was still dark down there, and I hoped they'd miss me in the pre-dawn gloom.

The BGs came down to meet me, splitting up to surround me.

"What are you doing out so early, Gypsy?" Draco asked, his voice snide and particularly Slytherinish.

"I'd like to know the same thing about you," I said, still walking.

Jabba reached the path in front of me and folded his arms, standing there like the Balrog. Draco was behind me, and Gollum to my right on the hill. The only way out was the canal.

"Your kind isn't so bright," Gollum said, then snorted up a particularly large piece of nose blockage. "I saw you yesterday, slinking around and looking suspicious. I followed you. Lost you for a bit, but I found you again at your apartment. What in the world was the crazy Gypsy up to? You and your Yankee father were right by an open window while you talked. It was English, but I caught enough. You're not the only one who can speak English. Going on about completing potions at dawn. Some sort of superstitious black magic? I thought you were dead."

"They're like roaches," Jabba said.

I clenched my jaw and took a step forward. "Leave me alone."

Jabba shoved me in the chest, the water in the basin splashing. Some of it spilled over the side.

"Not until we teach you a lesson," Draco said, taking a few steps closer to me.

Gollum coughed, then smiled slyly as he took out a small bottle of lighter fluid. In front of me, Jabba was lighting a cigarette.

"Afraid of fire, aren't you?" Draco said. He was right behind me. So this was their master plan. Burn the Gypsy.

And suddenly the fear was gone, turned into anticipation. They were messing with the wrong Gypsy.

But I had to get them away from that basin. I set it on the ground, then tried to run between Gollum and Jabba. I got about five steps before Jabba caught my arm and twisted it behind me, then grabbed the other. I might have tried one of the moves Ľuboš had taught me, but I didn't want to get away. Not this time. Running away from a group of guys who practically stalked you only delayed the inevitable.

I had to do something more extreme, keep them scared of me until I knew enough self defense to protect myself no matter what. *Thanks for bringing the lighter fluid, boys.*

Draco had left the basin lying on the ground untouched, thank goodness. We were now huddled in a bunch about ten feet away from it. I struggled, pretending to try to escape, but really just doing my best to get us farther away from the potion. It earned me another five feet and a punch to the face from Gollum.

"Stop struggling," Draco said, "and we might go easy on you. Put your ugly arm forward."

Jabba manhandled my scarred arm, making me hold it out. Draco nodded to Gollum, who took the lighter fluid and squirted it all over my jacket arm. How could people do this to another human being?

"They burned one of your families in the east." Draco took out a lighter and clicked the flame to life. "I read about it online. The whole house up in flames. Be glad we're not doing that to you. This won't kill you. Probably." He nodded to Jabba, and the brute released me right as Draco touched the fire to my doused jacket arm.

It ignited with a *whoosh*.

I screamed and whirled in circles, always away from the basin. I waved my burning arm, acting like I was trying to put out the fire in a panic, though it only made it brighter. The Bigot Gang backed away from me, Gollum glancing up the hill toward the city, but down here this early in the morning, no one could see us unless they were already on the path.

When I was far enough away from the basin, I stopped screaming. Stopped running in circles. Instead, I stood to my full height in the middle of the path, blazing arm at my side, where it caught some of the rest of my clothes on fire. I lit up the path in the pre-dawn twilight, where Draco and the rest stood there in confusion, their eyes wide, a frown on Draco's face.

"Seriously?" I asked, my voice calm. The fire guttered on my clothes, flames eating the fabric greedily. It was just mildly warm, though the lighter fluid smelled pretty awful. "You were going to burn me? What was next on your plan? Drowning?" I smiled and held my burning hand in front of my face, watching the tongues of flame pulse up and around it. I made a fist.

"You've got to ask yourself one question," I said, going for my best Clint Eastwood. "Do I feel lucky?"

I took one step toward the gang, and Gollum and Jabba took a step back. Draco, on the other hand, rushed me. I hadn't seen that coming. He barreled straight into me, and we thudded to the ground, rolling around. But where the flames weren't hurting me, Draco didn't have that protection. I punched him in the side, a quick small jab that left a burning imprint on his shirt. He landed several blows on my kidneys, the pain sharp and clear. We tussled some more, each of us fighting for position, until I got my burning right hand free and placed it right over his face, pushing him away. I felt his skin sizzle where my hand made contact.

He screamed in pain, the truth of what was happening finally sinking in. He pulled back, and I let him go. He frantically brushed at his face, and the fire went out. A hand-shaped burn covered his cheek, the skin red and black, but it had missed his eyes, I thought. They were wild with terror, and he stumbled back away from me, running into his cronies. That was all the encouragement Jabba and Gollum needed. They grabbed Draco by the arms, turned, and fled up and over the hill and out of sight.

I grinned. I felt like the Human Torch, only cooler.

Of course, extinguishing flaming clothes is still a bit of a bother. And if I didn't put them out soon, I'd have another nearly-naked walk home ahead of me. I beat my arm against my side, then ended up rolling around in the dirt some to finally get the flames out.

I'd melted my watch. So much for knowing exactly when dawn was. It still wasn't quite light yet, though the horizon had started to pinken.

It didn't matter. I'd complete the potion the second a beam of sunlight hit me. That was as close to the definition of "sunrise" as you could get.

I waited there, the cup carved from cherry wood in my left hand, the basin in my right. My jacket had burned completely through on my right arm, and I was covered in dust from the ground, but I completed the potion right on time.

I dipped the cherry cup into the basin and drew it out full of dirty water with some chunks floating in it that I was pretty sure were bird crap. It didn't do anything. No explosion, no bright flare of power, no

297

confidence-boosting noises to show it was complete. Time to go back to the apartment.

Ľuboš was waiting for me inside. I nodded to him. He frowned at my appearance, but I shook my head. "Just a bit of trouble. I took care of it."

He shrugged and held out some saran wrap and rubber bands. "Put this on top of the potion."

Dad met us at the door, dressed in a shirt and tie. He glanced at Ľuboš in his T-shirt and jeans and me in my burned jacket. "Are you okay?" he asked me.

I rolled my eyes. "I'll explain on the way. Let's go."

"No," Dad said. "If we've only got one chance at this, we're going to have to dress to impress."

Where did parents get those lines? Was there some book they all had a copy of? He had a point, though: we were going to a research institution, and we wanted to make sure they let us in. Ľuboš and I hurriedly washed up and changed clothes. My skin wasn't hurt at all from the BG's little stunt, but my burnt clothes had left black smudges all over me. I didn't have time for a full shower, but with a bit of water and soap, I was at least presentable. My uncle looked like a bear in a suit, with his beard bursting out of the collar. How impressive could we be? A kid and a caveman? Good thing Dad was so sharp in his suit. We packed ourselves into the clown car and headed off to Bratislava. The archives opened at eight. We were right on schedule. An hour or two to find the grave's location, an hour and a half back home, and we should be done with all of this before noon.

As long as there were no more hiccups.

Not many other cars were on the road; most people in Slovakia traveled by train or bus. But even with the drone of the engine, I was too wired to go to sleep. Ľuboš, on the other hand, dozed off. The man was way too pragmatic.

"What's it like?" Dad asked after a while, speaking over Ľuboš's snores.

"What?" I said.

"Seeing all these things. Talking to them. What's it like?"

"I don't know. Strange. Cool. A real pain."

"I'll bet it was frightening at first."

I nodded. "No kidding." Terrifying was more like it, for some of it, at least—though I wondered whether I'd found it scary when I was a little kid. I still had no memories of that time period, despite all I'd learned in the hunt for answers to Katka's problem.

"I wish you'd come and talked to us about it."

"I tried, but you and Mom shut me off every time. I didn't want to cause problems."

Dad cleared his throat. "You're not a problem. Never. I'm sorry we weren't more available to you. I'm sorry we . . . I'm sorry. Maybe we could have come up with a different solution together, if your mom and I had been more available to you." He hesitated. "Do you regret coming here?"

I didn't even need to think about it. "Not a bit."

That seemed to satisfy him. "Get some rest if you can," he said. "I'll wake you up when we get there."

I settled in for the drive, but sleep stayed far away. Every time my eyes started to drift shut, the image of Katka lying helpless in her hospital bed came into my head, and I jolted awake again.

One way or another, time passed, and then Dad was tapping Ľuboš on the shoulder. "There it is," he said.

My uncle grunted and sat up. In front of us was the complete antithesis of a castle. The building was as big as one, but it was shaped like four giant vertical books held together by a horizontal one. The architect must have been as high as Mount Everest when he designed it. "That's it?" I asked.

"Ugly, huh?" Dad said.

"No kidding." Now that we were there, the ball of anxiety grew bigger in my stomach. If we didn't get in . . . or if we couldn't find what we were searching for, then it all ended now. We at least needed some sort of a hint to proceed.

"You two are my research assistants," Dad said. "Let me do the talking. Okay?"

Ľuboš and I nodded. Whatever worked.

We parked and walked into the building. This one at least, unlike the hospital, had some signage showing us where to go. In no time, we were standing in line at the archives desk. We'd thought we'd get there early enough to be first in line, but there were still three people in front of us, all of them looking bored to be there. Even worse, the guy behind the desk seemed like he was about as happy to be there as he would be to shove toothpicks under all his toenails. He gruffed his way through the line, turning away two people and pissing off the one he helped. And then we were up.

"And?" the guy said.

Dad cleared his throat. "Yes. I'm here to study the population increases in Trenčín from 1600 through 1850."

The man sniffed. "America?"

Dad smiled. "Yes, how'd you know?"

"Your accent is horrendous. These books you need to study, they are for a scholarly paper?"

Dad nodded.

"Then I'll have to ask you to fill out an application to request them. They're far too old and fragile for us to simply lend them out to anyone."

"How long will that take?" Dad asked.

"It shouldn't be more than a month."

I felt my stomach drop. Ľuboš cleared his throat to say something, but Dad frowned. "A month? Just to corroborate some facts? I'm sure it won't take longer than a few hours."

The man shook his head. "Not possible on such short notice."

"The conference I'm presenting at is next week," Dad said. "I need the information today. Can't you make an exception?"

If anything, the man became more sure of himself. "You Americans can't expect to waltz in here and do whatever you want. There are rules."

Ľuboš practically growled, and Dad had to reach over and put a hand on his arm to keep him quiet. Dad sighed. "I'd like to talk with your manager."

"I am the manager."

"Who do you report to?" Dad asked.

"He's not here."

"What's his name?"

Now the man seemed less sure of himself. "There's no need to—"

Dad leaned forward and read the man's name tag. He reached into his jacket pocket and took out a notepad and started scribbling. "Your last name?"

The rest of the people in the line were beginning to edge forward for a better view, and the man glanced at them, then licked his lips and looked back at my dad. "What was it you needed again?"

Within fifteen minutes, we were waiting in a private room for someone to bring the Trenčín city chronicle. "How'd you get around that guy so easily?" I asked my dad.

He smiled at me. "I've had coworkers like that guy. Some people think they own the world as soon as you put them behind a desk. Usually they get away with it, but there aren't many librarians who are stubborn or brave enough to put up with a patron who gets belligerent. Push too hard and we call security. Push the right way, and we fold. I mean, come on. We're just librarians."

I smiled back. Thank goodness he had been there. Adults don't treat belligerent teenagers with the same sort of respect. Maybe there were times when being a librarian was cool.

Ľuboš certainly seemed impressed with Dad. My uncle laughed and slapped him on the back, saying, "Very good. Very."

The books came—tons of them, each three inches thick. Each time one plopped to a table, another cloud of dust billowed into the air until there was so much you could taste it. I checked the clock. 8:45 A.M. Dad went right to work, examining each book to get a sense of its contents. "She supposedly died in 1796, correct?" he asked.

Ľuboš nodded.

"All right," Dad said. "We'll start there. Much later than that, and I would think the story wouldn't be a legend—people would know it as fact. I'm betting it's earlier. Tomas, you take 1796 and go forward to about 1810. I'll work back from 1796, and Ľuboš can go from 1750 forward. If someone finishes sooner and we still haven't found anything, then they start helping the others. Okay?"

The chronicles were boring reading. There were maps of the city, lists of prominent citizens and what they did from year to year, discussions of flu outbreaks and floods. How much so-and-so inherited from his uncle. Pretty much everything that happened of importance in the town, they wrote down. "Why do they keep all these records?" I asked.

"State law," Ľuboš said, his nose still in his book. "I suggest you start by looking for Andricky in the list of prominent citizens. If we can be sure when they lived in the area, then we'll be able to focus our search."

It was a good idea, in theory. In practice, it didn't pan out. It wasn't that Andricky was a common name. There were few enough of them that it wasn't like looking up all the Smiths in a phone book, but there weren't any with a daughter named Lesana. And no stunning records of anyone being buried alive jumped out at us. Between the three of us, we had processed over a hundred years' worth of chronicles, and it had taken two hours, even pushing ourselves to go as fast as we could.

I slammed another book closed in frustration.

"Stop that, Tomas," Dad said. "If we start mishandling their books, they'll kick us out, no matter what we do."

"This is ridiculous," I said, rubbing the bite scar on my hand. "We haven't found anything."

"We just need to be more thorough. The legend could have the date wrong. Hurrying us up won't help—we might miss something important."

"But we've already skimmed through the entire century," I said. "And it's past eleven. We only have a little over twelve hours before—before it'll be too late. And we still need an hour and a half to get back to Trenčín and find the stupid grave in real life. Finding it on paper won't do us any good. What if the building's locked? What if the grave is in a different country, or off hidden in the woods? What if—"

"What do I always tell you?" Dad said. "When you have a big task, focus on getting one thing at a time done. It's the only way." He handed me another book. "The more we talk about not having time, the less time we have. Keep searching."

I read those books until my eyes bled. They were handwritten, and although they had been neatly scribed, there was only so much Slovak cursive you could read before everything began to blend together.

The more time it took, the more often I checked the clock. Noon went by. So did one o'clock. I felt like I was in the open book test from hell, and of course it was timed. Ľuboš and my dad, meanwhile, were like machines. They stayed focused and on task.

I sat back again. "I'm not even sure I'm seeing what I'm reading anymore."

Dad sat back as well. "Maybe we need to have lunch. We'll think better on a full stomach."

That didn't feel right, either. I grabbed another book, and flipped through it casually. Some of the chronicle pages had some pretty well-drawn sketches. I didn't want to give up, and going to have lunch would sacrifice a lot of time, but I also didn't quite have it in me to keep trying to do what seemed so pointless. We'd never—

I froze, staring at the page in front of me.

Dad noticed my surprise and leaned forward. "What is it?"

Ľuboš heard this and glanced up as well. I tapped the picture I was looking at. It was of a small city house, sort of what you'd expect Sleeping Beauty to stay in when she was slumming it as a peasant. "This house here. I've seen it before. This is where Lesana lived."

Dad took the book and stared at the picture. "How can you be sure? Did she show it to you?"

"It was in one of the visions. I'm sure. This is it." I read the caption below it. *Mierové Námestie 17, 1718.* "Peace Square," I said. "That's where the plague pillar thing is, right?"

Dad nodded. "Let me see the book for a moment." He leafed through to the map of the city, and then pointed out number seventeen. "That's it. It's two or three houses down from the church. But it's listed here as being empty."

It took us a bit to piece together what happened. In 1710, half the city died from cholera. In 1716, another third died or moved away. The place was a death trap. A new family didn't move in until 1719, but the chronicle said they did extensive renovations on the house before they entered, including altering the facing.

"That can't be them, then," I said. "*That* was the house she lived in. Who lived in the house before?"

Give my dad a whiff of the right direction for information, and he's a bulldog. He ripped through the chronicle like a man obsessed. In five minutes, we had a clearer picture. Before the cholera struck, the house had been in the Laurinsky family for almost a century. They were wealthy merchants who had been important in the city until they were wiped out by cholera.

"So we had the wrong name all along," I said.

"It gets better," Dad said. He peered at me over his glasses and tapped on the page in front of him. "Lesana Laurinská died in October of 1709 and was buried in the family crypt under the house."

"Under the house?" I asked, closing my book and pushing back my chair. I still couldn't get used to the idea of people who weren't serial killers burying their dead in their basements.

"Don't complain," Ľuboš said. "This makes finding the grave easy. Most of the current buildings are still resting on the original foundations. Some of them date back into the 1600s."

"Wait," I said. "One of those stores in that square has a crypt in the basement?"

Dad stood. "Maybe more than one."

"So what are we going to do?" I asked. "Indiana Jones our way down into the catacombs?"

We rushed out the door, leaving the books behind. Dad answered. "Sounds like a plan. There's a hardware store just across the square. We can pick up a sledgehammer there if we hurry. If not, we'll have to break in and steal one."

CHAPTER THIRTY
ROTTING FLESH

Never underestimate the value of a good sledgehammer. In most situations, they're even better than duct tape.

The race back to Trenčín was intense. Dad pushed our little two-door as fast as physics would allow, the doors shaking hard enough I thought they might fall off. We were behind schedule, and we all knew it.

Then we hit traffic.

Slovak roads aren't exactly designed for high speed car chases. In America, freeways crisscross the country. Anywhere you want to go, you can drive fifty-five or higher to get there, for the most part—usually on roads that are in fairly good repair. Slovakia had freeways that started and then ended fifty miles later, going back to country lanes. The government was trying to build the freeway network, but it took time and money. The freeways in existence weren't particularly wide—two lanes at most, with not a whole lot of shoulder.

All of this is just to say that when we hit that traffic, we didn't have any other alternatives. It was wait it out or nothing. My dad groaned in disappointment. Ľuboš slammed his fist into the dashboard. I sat back in my seat, stunned. The traffic would clear soon. It had to.

Or not.

As it turned out, the traffic jam was from two semi trucks jackknifing in the middle of the road. It took us five and a half hours longer to get back to the city than we'd planned. Where was the good luck when you needed it?

By the time we got to the city, it was almost nine o'clock. Three hours left. Dad parked the car right in the city center—Ľuboš had a special parking pass—and the three of us ran the rest of the way, me carrying the potion. With each step, it sloshed against the saran wrap, but the rubber bands held it tight to the cup. I hoped it didn't spill.

We got to the square, the buildings lit up for the evening. A few people were out strolling, but for the most part, the place was empty. Ľuboš was analyzing the buildings and counting. Then he pointed at the electronics store, its lights off and clearly closed. "That's the one," he said. "I'm going in."

Dad caught his arm. "We need supplies. The crypt entrance has likely been covered over by renovations. We'll need a sledgehammer at least. And we can't be too obvious about this. If the police show up . . ."

Ľuboš grunted and I nodded, nervous. It wasn't the getting caught that had me jumpy—it was what that would do to our schedule if we did. There was no time for a police investigation.

I stared at the building. It was old, but it was much more flowery than it had been in the picture in the chronicle. What if we were wrong? The one to the right seemed closer to what I remembered from the vision. It wasn't like they'd kept the same house numbers for the past three hundred years. Then again, a lot of renovation could happen in that time. The façade wouldn't still be the same as it had been then.

Ľuboš went to find some tools—I didn't ask where he'd get them. It was too late to buy anything at the hardware store down the street. Dad and I examined the electronics store. Shattering our way in through the glass front door would attract an audience, no matter how few people were on the square. The store was essentially one large room filled with aisle upon aisle of gadgets and televisions, from what the city lights illuminated. Farther back in the store was nothing but darkness.

We circled around back to check for a delivery entrance. For once, we lucked out. The door in the rear was steel, but it had the store name clearly labeled in stenciled paint.

Ľuboš met us out front, loaded up with a sledgehammer and a couple of high powered flashlights. "Ready," he said.

We took him back to the service entrance. Two resounding medieval-knight-infused sledgehammer blows later, and the doorknob and lock had fallen off. Did I ever mention how strong my uncle was? I glanced around nervously, looking for people peering out to see what the racket had been. The buildings were all right next to each other, after all. Nothing but row houses, really: apartments up top and stores on the street level. No lights came on. Everything stayed silent.

We crept in, shutting the door behind us and clicking on the flashlights.

Boxes stuffed with CDs and DVDs filled every available piece of shelf space and much of the floor too. I felt like I had to breathe in just to navigate the hallways. The first room we came to was an office, and around the corner was a staircase leading down to the basement.

Jackpot.

The stairs were old, with little smooth grooves worn into the centers where centuries of feet had stepped. We switched on the overhead lights. No one would see these from outside. The basement was just as crammed as upstairs. From working at the castle, I could recognize older architecture, and this basement was full of it. The stones they had used to build the wall were large and roughly cut, with little mortar between the cracks.

It took a different kind of skill and craftsmanship to do that than was needed to build things today, when concrete and rebar gave you all sorts of shortcuts.

Then again, there was also no sign of any crypt entrances. Certainly no "Dead People Here" signs. If the crypt were down here, the sledgehammer would be the only way to get to it. Or dynamite.

"Nothing," I said.

"Not to worry," Dad said. "If the family died of cholera, I'd think whoever moved into the house afterward did everything they could to forget about the crypt. They wouldn't have moved the bodies—too worried about getting the disease as well—but I could see them covering up the entrance to the family's burial site."

Then it was a matter of knocking on walls and the floor with the sledgehammer, searching for a place that sounded hollow. Part of me didn't think such a simple approach would work, and I grew more certain of that the longer we went without hearing anything. Dad kept banging away, always with the same sound.

Thunk thunk thunk.

I was hunting for anywhere the masonry seemed newer, but it was hard to see the bigger picture when you had to keep shoving boxes out of the way.

Thunk thunk thunk.

Maybe I could just sprinkle the potion on the basement floor. Would it be close enough to Lesana's grave to count? I checked the shelf where I'd put the potion, just to make sure it was still safe. It was.

Thunk thunk boom.

We all froze. Dad tapped that last spot again.

Boom. The sound echoed beneath us, promising a large open space, most likely filled with dead relatives of Lesana.

I asked, "There isn't a chance of that cholera still being around down there, is there?"

Dad shook his head. "It's transmitted by drinking or eating contaminated water or food, so . . . no. Step aside. This should only take a few blows." He seemed eager to try his hand at the sledgehammer, maybe inspired by Ľuboš's herculean performance earlier. Ľuboš and I crouched behind some boxes to be out of the way of flying concrete shards, followed by signs of brick farther down. The sledgehammer made a sound loud enough to blow out eardrums, but nothing happened.

Just as I was about to suggest librarians might not be the best equipped for breaking into crypts, the bricks Dad was standing on shattered all at once, and his body fell through the hole like a stone into water.

Ľuboš and I rushed to the edge and looked over. All I could see was black, but a foul stench was coming up out of the hole. It smelled so bad I could taste it: making me think of ancient bones and rotting flesh. I stumbled back from the opening and coughed, then leaned forward again when it felt like I could breathe. I fumbled for my flashlight and turned it on.

The hole led to a stairwell. Dad had fallen through and tumbled to the bottom of the stairs. "Dad?" He wasn't moving.

"Quick," Ľuboš said. "I'll lower you down."

I tucked the flashlight—still lit—into my belt, then grabbed my uncle's hands and he lowered me into the hole. Once I was down, he gripped the edge and swung down into the opening. I ran to check on my father.

He was breathing, but it smelled even worse down here. Whatever had been in the air, his lungs were full of it. I checked him for injuries. If my dad died because of this, I didn't know what I'd do. He wasn't bleeding, but I was afraid to move him. What if his back was broken?

"We have to call an ambulance," I said.

"No," Ľuboš said. "Not from here. We must get him out ourselves."

"We can't do that. His spine—"

"Stay calm," Ľuboš said. "I have training in this—a requirement for the joust in case of injury. Stay here." Without another word, he grabbed the remaining flashlight—Dad's had fallen in with him and broken in the fall—went back to the opening, and hoisted himself through it.

I stayed there in the dark, my eyes straining to see my dad. What if he was paralyzed? This was all my fault. I should have been the one to use the sledgehammer. Or we should have found out more about what we were trying to do. Or—

A board dropped down through the hole, followed by Ľuboš. "Here," he said. "We must roll him onto the board, but it is important we do it at the same time. I will roll the shoulders, you will roll him at the waist. Okay?"

"But what—"

"No buts," Ľuboš said. "The medics would have to do the same in any case. We must get him to where the ambulance can help him. Come on. Go to his side. Ready?"

Not a bit. But he was right, and he seemed to know what he was doing. I nodded.

"Okay. When we roll him, it is important to keep his head, neck, and back in line. Follow my lead. One. Two. Three."

I don't know what I was expecting—maybe to have my dad scream in pain or an alarm to go off that we were doing something wrong. But we rolled him without him making a sound, and Ľuboš used some cord he had found to secure Dad to the board. "Now come," Ľuboš said. "We need to get him up through the hole. Move carefully and quickly."

He took the lead, showing me when to lift the board and how to maneuver it the right way. My mind was in a haze, and I just did what I was told, although all through it, I kept wondering what would happen. What if Dad couldn't move? Couldn't type? Couldn't—

"Good," Ľuboš said.

I blinked and discovered we were outside, with my father still on the makeshift stretcher, laid out a little way down the alley behind the store. "What now?" I asked.

Ľuboš checked his watch. "You have an hour and a half. Was that the right crypt?"

My jaw dropped open. As soon as I'd seen my dad get in trouble, everything else in my mind had gone blank. "I—I don't know."

"Go check. I'll stay here with your father."

I grabbed the flashlight and darted back into the building. It didn't take more than a few seconds for me to rush down the stairs, duck my head into the hole in the basement and shine the light around before I recognized the place. I knew right where Lesana's grave ought to be. Sure enough, when I shone my flashlight down the middle aisle, I recognized the false wall that had been built to house her body. Carved into it were the words

Lesana Laurinská
March 18, 1693–October 17, 1709

As soon as I saw the inscription, I ran back out to Ľuboš. "This is it."

"Good," he said. "Go down and complete the spell. I will take care of your father."

I stared at my dad, lying helpless on the ground. "But—"

"Please, Tomas. This is something I can do, finally. I can do nothing

313

about saving my daughter, nothing about saving the castle from being turned into a spa, but I can do this. You do what you can do. Help Katka before it is too late. Here. Take my watch and go. Quickly."

He was right. I took a final glance at my dad before grabbing the watch, heading back down to the basement, collecting the potion on the way, and then lowering myself into the crypt. I put on the watch, clicked on the flashlight. Now that it was just me there, the place was silent, and I could hear each shuffle my feet made on the floor. The room was large, with low vaulted ceilings. Sarcophagi lined the walls and were placed throughout on the floor, rows of sleeping stone faces and folded arms. It made me think of Katka's hospital, with so many people sharing the same place for something that should be a private affair.

I shook my head clear and bent down to grab the sledgehammer, its wooden handle smooth and cold in my hand. The walled-off portion —where Lesana had been entombed—was about twenty feet in front of me. I could still remember hearing her scream from behind that wall in my vision, and I pictured her trapped behind there, crying until her body died and her soul transformed. I shuddered and looked around with the flashlight again, just to make sure I was alone.

Then I clenched my teeth, hefted the sledgehammer, and did my best to smash the wall apart with one blow.

Hitting a thick stone wall with a sledgehammer hurts you more than it hurts the wall. The hammer felt like it was trying to leap out of my hands, and all it did to the wall was make a tiny little chip. I grunted, took a tighter grip on the handle, and tried again.

This time I was ready for the shock, and I made a bigger dent. I didn't know what they had made that wall out of, but it took me fifteen minutes to break through. I stepped back and let the bad air rush out. No sense breathing more of the foul stuff than I had to. After that, things went more quickly, as the hole widened with each blow.

I paused and went over to pick up the flashlight from the floor where I had set it to give me some light. Before I shone it into the opening, I steeled myself for what I might see. Rotting clothes, decayed flesh, a pile of dust—it wouldn't be pretty.

I wasn't prepared to see a girl about my age, sleeping on a pedestal in an alcove of the crypt, which had been turned into a small room when it was walled off.

There was no doubt it was Lesana. After all these years, she could have been asleep. Her clothes were in much worse shape, the cloth brittle and aged, but she herself looked like Sleeping Beauty, ready to waken with a kiss. She was still pretty, nose and all. In fact, now that I knew her—well, comparatively—she was even more attractive. As soon as I saw her like that, I felt a jolt through my heart. I know it sounds corny, but that's as good as I can describe it. Like I was wishing for what could never be. It had been one thing to meet Lesana as a water spirit, but to have her lying there— *Focus, Tomas.* It wasn't fair what had happened to her. That vodník had a lot to answer for.

I went back to work until the hole was big enough for me to squeeze through without too much struggle. My palms were sweating, and blisters had formed on both hands. I threw the sledgehammer through the opening—to enlarge the hole on my way out, when I had more time—and got the potion.

In a few seconds, this would all be over.

I clambered into Lesana's burial site, one hand holding the potion, the other holding the flashlight. I could stand and walk around in there—the room was about ten feet by ten feet. In the unsteady light, I could almost see her breathing.

I took a few deep breaths and stepped closer to her corpse. I managed to get the rubber bands off the cup, and then took off the cellophane. I studied the contents.

With a silent prayer, I poured the potion into her mouth, hoping for all I was worth that I got more of a result than dirty water splashing on her skin.

I didn't.

No flashing lights, no sudden explosions—just dirty water on Lesana's non-decayed skin. Nothing else. She was a three-hundred-year-old corpse, if perfectly preserved. If the potion had done what it was supposed to, I should have seen something—massive decomposition, something. Maybe it was unrealistic to expect to see her crumble to dust like a vampire on *Buffy*. But at the very least, I would have expected Morena to come tell me "mission accomplished."

It hadn't worked. Either we'd screwed it up, or the vodník had been playing a trick, or—

I screamed in frustration and hurled the cup at the wall. What was I supposed to do now? I had maybe forty-five minutes until my cousin died, my father might have been paralyzed, and I was covered in the dust of an ancient crypt. It was all for nothing.

This wasn't supposed to happen. This was supposed to be where I released Lesana's soul in a wonderful display of pyrotechnics, at which point Katka would race in, cured. It wasn't the scene where the hero fails after trying everything. There had to be something else I could do. Anything else.

A series of ideas flashed through my mind as I paced around in the small space. Maybe Lesana's soul stayed on earth because her body was in such good shape. Maybe she was like a vampire, and I could stake her through the heart or behead her or—too bloody. Maybe I could run up to the church and grab some holy water. That could do something, right? Holy water?

What did they do in fairy tales when this happened? They certainly didn't take household ingredients, stick 'em in a cup, and dump them on a corpse. No. The prince waltzed in, kissed the princess, and they all lived happily ever after.

I looked back at Lesana, lying there as if she had been waiting for me.

It could work.

I'd try the kiss, and if that didn't work, I'd—I'd think of something else.

I walked to her pedestal and shone my light on her face. Her lips were even moist. Maybe she wasn't dead. *No,* I reminded myself, *that's just where the potion poured over her.* I checked for breathing, just in case. Nothing.

I licked my lips and tried not to feel like a pervert. This was for Katka. My first kiss was going to be with a girl who'd been dead for three centuries.

Come on, Tomas. You're stalling. I bent down and put my lips right on top of Lesana's. At first, it was like pudding mushing into oatmeal.

Then a jolt like electricity arced through my lips. I yelped in surprise and stumbled backward.

Lesana gasped, coughed, and sat up.

CHAPTER THIRTY-ONE
BACON

This book is dedicated to Plato, Ramses II, Edgar Allen Poe, Emily Dickinson, and the Backstreet Boys.

I stared at Lesana.

She looked down at her clothes and wiped her mouth, no doubt wondering why it was full of watery bird poop taste and boy spit. "Tomas?" she said. "What happened? Where am I?"

It was one thing to wish for something, another to get it. Part of me was happy Lesana was alive and, well, datable, but a large part of me was furious at myself for feeling that way. With her alive, it meant there was no soul to take Katka's place. I sank to the floor and sat down, letting the flashlight fall. It rolled to shine back at the hole I had smashed in the wall. The vodník was glaring at me through it.

"What the hell's the matter with you?" he said.

I blinked at him, confused. "What?"

"You teenagers these days. Nothing but hormones. Is that all you can think about?"

"The potion didn't work," I said. "I—"

"Didn't work? You're hormonal *and* illiterate? Sixty seconds. The potion needed sixty seconds to work its course."

He was right. I remembered that now. "So if I had waited longer, then—" Then I could have saved Katka.

"Then Lesana's soul would have gone straight to my teacup, where she's supposed to be," the vodník said. "It's a good thing I'm a genius, or I might be more than irritated at this point."

"Stop," Lesana said, looking down at her body with a panicked expression. "What's going on? What happened to me?"

I stood up and stalked over to the opening where the vodník was peering in. "What do you mean she'd be in a teacup?"

"Now," he said. "If I could just remember where I put that teacup. Always carry one around with you, you know. Don't leave home without it."

"I'm human again?" Lesana said behind me.

"Wait a minute." I rushed up to the opening and grabbed the vodník by his collar. "Her soul was supposed to be released."

He twittered, then tried to tug his collar out of my hand. "You're—I can't—would you mind?"

I tightened my grip and jerked the vodník toward me so he was pressed up against the edge of the opening. With me standing between him and the beam of the flashlight, his face was cast in shadow.

"Fine," he said. "I suppose I can understand why you're slightly irate. But see it my way. Can't you see how much extra work you've made for me? Now I'll have to take her soul the—"

"Shut up," I said, shaking him. "My cousin's set to die in forty-five minutes, and you'd better have a damn good explanation about how this is all going to work out."

"Ah," he said. "Here it is." He brought up his other hand and smiled as he showed me a teacup. "I knew it was there—"

I grabbed it from his hand and threw it on the floor. It shattered. A soul-stealing teacup. Broken at last. I held my breath for a moment.

The vodník snarled, his eyes glowing blue for a moment. "Get off me.

My patience is wearing—"

"I don't understand!" Lesana wailed from behind me.

"Did I do it?" I asked, staring at the teacup. "Did I let a soul go?"

"You're so stupid," the vodník said, the snarl gone from his face. "How many times do I have to tell you? Once I've loaded a teacup, I make sure it can't break." He peered past me to Lesana. "Never mind all this," he said again. "Don't you worry your pretty little head about a thing, Lesana. Not a thing. I'm here now, and I'll take care of you."

"No," she said. She had a tremble of panic in her voice. "Get away. I don't want anything to do with you."

"Look," the vodník said. "I realize I haven't always been the perfect gentleman. But I never intended this to happen. I didn't mean to bite you—I was just barely a vodník back then, and you were hurting me. How was I supposed to know a little nibble would turn you into a water spirit? It was self-defense. Bite or be killed. And besides, it's all better now, right? You're back to being human and everything, and as soon as I can go get another *teacup*"—he glared at me again—"we'll be ready to go. You don't have to worry about a thing from here on out, because Ond—"

I shook him by the collar. "I think the lady said she wanted nothing to do with you. You're going to show me where your teacups are, and then you're going to release some of your souls. And you're going to do it right now."

The vodník tried to back away from the hole. "You-you-you-you stay out of this. You've done your part, even if you did manage to hormone it up. But I'll overlook that, and now I'll let you go, and I think I'm being rather generous about that too."

"You do, huh?" I said.

He nodded. "Yes. Very. Extremely. You were the only one who could have brought Lesana back to me. Make her soul suitable for extraction, so to speak. It had to be someone who could affect both worlds. So what if love's first kiss did the trick instead of a magical potion." He shrugged. "Moot point. Now she's back to life for a bit, but I can take her soul the old-fashioned way. Just an extra step. And sure, maybe for a bit I thought I'd steal your soul and force you to do what I wanted, but this way worked so much more neatly. You didn't have to die, and Lesana could come and be safe with me."

"What about Katka? What about all that crap about this solving all my problems?"

The vodník cleared his throat. "Right. About that. You see, I was going to explain—after this all calmed down, maybe over a nice hot tea. Your cousin will be taken care of. I'll go get her soul and give it to you, free of charge. You can talk to her whenever you want. She'll never get old, never die, never nothing. No pain, no seizures, no racism. Easy. Simple. I'm a very generous vodník."

"Yeah?" I asked. Something was building inside me. All the nerves and the worries and the frustrations that I'd had since I got to Slovakia—especially since I found out about Katka's fate—were bubbling up from deep down. A low subwoofer was thumping somewhere deep in my ears.

"Yes," he said. "I'm practically a philanthropist. I love people. All people."

"You don't love people. You kill them."

"Tomas, I don't kill people. I've told you that already. I help people."

"Not anymore, you don't. I'm going to kill you. You said I could affect both worlds. Maybe you should try helping yourself for once."

He melted into liquid and dripped through my fingers, only to reform out of my reach, in the darkness outside Lesana's room. "Don't be ridiculous, Tomas. Kill me? That won't do anyone any good. My death wouldn't fill the deal you made with Morena. It has to be a human soul, and my soul's been tainted. I've got a whole shelf full of wizards who can assure you of that. No killing vodníks. Bad idea."

"It doesn't have to fill the deal for Katka," I said, pointing at him. "I'll break every teacup you have, and that'll do the trick. But you let us think this would work. You told us it would. And you're going to pay for it even if I have to shove your face into a salt mine."

"Tomas," Lesana said from behind me, "be careful, he's much stronger than he lets himself appear."

"So am I," I said. The subwoofer was getting louder.

"Listen to the girl," the vodník said. "You wouldn't like me when I'm angry."

I lunged through the opening, but before I could get more than my hands through, a membrane of water sprang from the vodník's hand and blocked the entrance. Where it touched my skin, it burned.

"I think we need to calm down," the vodník said. "Deep breaths. You're being very hasty."

"Let me out!" I slapped at the membrane again, and my skin hissed where it touched it.

"Not right now," he said. "I'll just go grab a few extra teacups. Everyone's calmer with tea. Or *in* tea or—whatever."

The vodník ran up the stairs and leaped through the hole into the basement, as easily as if he were hopping from one stair to the next.

I slapped the wall in frustration.

"Tomas."

I turned to Lesana, who had walked over to me. "Calm down."

"There's no time," I said. "We have to go after him. If I can't get my hands on one of those teacups . . ."

"How?" she said. "We're trapped."

I glanced around the room and the sledgehammer caught my eye. "Not for long." I picked up the hammer and attacked the membrane. As soon as the steel hit it, the membrane fell in a splash to the floor. I rushed through the hole.

Outside, my father and Ľuboš were gone, hopefully to a hospital or an ambulance. Ľuboš would take care of Dad. I had to trust him, just as he was trusting me with Katka.

It wasn't until I was running down the street that I noticed I wasn't alone. Lesana had caught up to me. For someone who until a few minutes ago had been dead for centuries, she was remarkably fast. She was pumping her legs as quickly as they would go, her dress streaming back behind her and making her look backlit in the street lights.

"Wait, Tomas!"

I shook my head and kept running.

"You're going the wrong way!"

If I were going to run to the castle, yes. But I wasn't going to run. I'd drive. In a few more seconds, I was at the car, my hand fumbling in my pocket for the spare keys. It took some time to open the door and take off the bar on the steering wheel, but it was still faster than I would have been able to make it up to the castle. I leaned over and opened the door for Lesana. "Get in."

The engine roared to life and we were off, the car rattling on the cobblestones as I steered around pedestrians and through the narrow streets. I wasn't the world's best stick-shifter, but even I could manage a short drive (as long as I didn't come to a complete stop going uphill).

In less than a minute, we made the final turn, and the castle gates came in sight. They should have been locked for the evening, but they were wide open and the vodník was nowhere in sight. The only person on the castle plateau this late was the other night watchman, and if he was running on schedule, he was off somewhere patrolling the main keep right now.

I drove through the gates, the car scraping against them, since it was barely wide enough to squeeze through. Dad would understand the damage.

At the top of the hill, by the steel and glass visitor's center, I put the car in park and got out. So did Lesana. Ahead of us, the moon picked out the Well of Love in hazy detail. Standing beside it was the vodník. The steel grate that locked the well was wide open, and as I watched, something flew out of the well and into the vodník's outstretched hand. He looked at us, then motioned for us to come closer.

"It's a trap," Lesana said. "He has another teacup."

Since when did a teacup become a lethal weapon? "That's what I want," I said and started walking toward the well. Lesana followed.

The vodník smiled when we were within speaking distance. "I really appreciate you coming here so quickly. Very considerate. Thoughtful, even. Look, Lesana. I got the master cup for you. Straight into the lap of luxury. Come. Into the cup. You'll be happier with me."

"No," Lesana said.

The vodník frowned, his face taking on more emotion than that response should have generated. "I don't believe I gave you a choice."

"What's a master cup?" I asked.

"Boys should be seen, not heard," the vodník said.

"It's his first cup," Lesana said, putting her hand on my arm and trying to pull me back. "He doesn't need to prepare it to take a soul, and he stores his most choice souls inside it."

"What—all at once?" I asked.

The vodník grunted. "Think of it as a soul motel. Souls check in, they don't check out. Now, I've been more than reasonable, but the time for reason is finished." Water shot out of the well behind him, spilling over the sides and quickly making a shallow pool.

A reptilian head erupted from the middle of the water, crashing upward through the awning that covered the well. It was attached to a long sinuous neck, dark blue in the moonlight, covered in scales. The neck was followed by an arm, then another, each heavily muscled, with strong paws ending in curved claws. They swiped at what was left of the awning, scattering splinters across the plaza. Thick wings emerged from the well, as if the beast was just being born, fresh into the world. It all happened in a matter of moments.

Ajax. The water dragon was free, and he was pissed.

As I stumbled backward from the explosion, a tendril of water snaked out to loop around Lesana's leg. In a flash, she was swept from her feet and dragged into the well. The vodník jumped in after her, and then it was just me and the monster. He sniffed at the air, huge gulps of breath that caused the leaves on the tree to get sucked forward with each intake. His eyes glowed in the moonlight.

Right about then, all those thoughts about "doing this no matter what" didn't seem quite as reasoned as they had. *He can't see you if you don't move,* I reminded myself. I'd just do what I did when I'd been in the well last time: stay still and wait to move. Red light, green—

Ajax lowered his head, opened his mouth and unleashed a blast of water. Picture getting hit with about twenty fire hoses going full blast.

I flew backward through the air and landed in the tree behind me.

I would have fallen to the ground, but I had been impaled by two branches, one through my unscarred arm, the other through my side. Where was the pain? I glanced down to see bloody leaves still attached to the tree limbs.

Meanwhile, the water beast tromped over to me. Up in the tree, I was almost at eye level with him. The monster's gaze was two glowing hurricanes. Ajax flicked out his tongue once, then leaned forward and flicked the tongue out again.

His head couldn't fit within the branches, and he couldn't tell where I was in the middle of all those moving leaves. His arms weren't long enough to bat at me. The overall effect was like watching a T-rex trying to get something out of a vending machine. And the beast did what any sentient predator would try—he rattled the tree.

His tailed whipped out and lashed at the trunk. The tree withstood the blow—it was thick and old and had seen abuse from storms before. But it shuddered, and the branches impaling me cracked, shifting my weight. I slipped forward off the branch.

I must have been in shock; there was still no pain. The fear of what would happen when I hit the ground, however, was too real. I scrabbled at the branches around me, but my left arm—the one with a branch through it—was next to useless, and the other—the one with my burn— couldn't get a grip. I fell.

The branches below me cushioned most of my fall, but I still hit the ground with a resounding thud that knocked the wind out of me. I lay there, the moon shining through the tree above me as I waited for the monster to squish me.

But Ajax was still searching the tree. He had missed me falling down, and with his attention focused elsewhere, maybe I had a chance. He kept whaling at the tree with his tail, and with each blow, there were a few seconds where the tail was between me and the monster's eyes. That was when I moved, bit by bit at first, then more when I was farther out of the thing's line of sight.

When I couldn't wait anymore, I broke out into a run. It wasn't like I had time to do nothing. I checked my uncle's watch—twenty-five minutes left. I did my best to sprint up the hill toward the keep, praying the beast wouldn't spot me. It didn't. I had an idea, but I'd need wood to do it. And matches.

My lungs felt like they were on fire, but I kept going. Halfway up the hill, I ran into the other night watchman, Julo. He was pale and his eyes were round as cherries. "What's going on?" he said.

I shook my head. "Run. Just run and hide. Find someplace safe, and don't come out until morning." He didn't need encouragement. Julo fled, his longer strides outdistancing me easily. When I made it into the keep, I headed up the stairs into the watchman's apartment.

As soon as I was through the door, I rifled through everything, looking for matches. I found a couple of bottles of vodka in the process, and I added handkerchiefs when I found those. Still it took me a couple of minutes to finally come across a lighter. When I had it, I clutched it to my chest, then realized that there was still no pain from my puncture wounds. How long did shock last? I felt at them.

The wounds had scabbed over already.

No time to question how.

The thudding noises coming from below had stopped. The monster must have figured out I had gone.

I edged my way out of the apartment and peeked around. No water dragon. I snuck down the stairs and back in the direction of the well, cradling the vodka bottles in my scarred arm. I crept down the path, through the gates and into the well courtyard.

The beast was nowhere to be seen.

I opened up one of the vodka bottles and poured some of the alcohol onto a handkerchief before stuffing the cloth down the neck, then I repeated the process with the other bottle. I wasn't an ammunitions expert, but hopefully my immunity to fire would protect me from any really stupid errors. I took out the lighter, and on the second try a tiny flicker appeared. Just touching it to one of the cloths was enough for the fire to crackle to life.

Molotov cocktail time.

"Here, Ajax," I called out. I'd rather have the thing bellow out and rush me—and me know where it was—than try to sneak around without knowing when I might get attacked. My mouth was dry and my vision a bit blurry, but I tried to act calm and stride confidently out into the open, waving the flaming bottle above my head. "I've got a snack for you."

From somewhere ahead of me, I heard sniffing. Great bellows of lungs inhaling the night air. I kept walking.

In an instant, the dragon surged out from the path leading down to the city, barreling toward me. I touched the flames to the other bottle, then cocked my arm back and threw.

If the monster hadn't kept running at me, I'm sure I would have missed. I'd thrown too soon. But he could move even faster than I had guessed, and the bottle crashed into his neck, fire blossoming all over his chest, splashing in flaming drops to the ground.

Ajax roared in pain and shook himself before spitting water all over the wound—he wouldn't be distracted for long. I sprinted past the monster and toward the house-sized wooden structure opposite the tour guide office. When I was close, I hurled the other cocktail at the beams. Once again, glass shattered and fire went everywhere, licking at the wood and becoming a blaze in seconds.

"Ohnica," I shouted. "I don't know if you can hear me, but I need you now!"

The fire kept snapping and growing, but there was no sign of the víla. Something hit me from behind, and once more I was sailing through the air, landing next to a bench in the amphitheater.

The water dragon had put out his fire, and now he knew where I was. I rolled onto my back to see him bearing down on me, his eyes narrow slits with blue light streaming from them. If anything, he smiled as he reared his head back and inhaled for what I was sure would be a strong gush of water, shot right at my head.

I rolled at the last instant, and the water spout didn't hit me straight on, instead propelling me into one of the other benches. Now I was on my feet, and I turned to face the beast. His head lowered, and the tail came around for another blow. I ducked down to the ground, the tail passing inches above me. I struggled to my feet and faltered my way toward the beast. I couldn't let him have the space for another go with that tail.

"Ohnica!" I called out again. "Help!" Could she even hear me?

Ajax backed up a single step, taking away all the ground I'd gained. The tail finished its swing and started back for the return blow. This time he overcorrected: maybe he wasn't as competent on land as he was in water. The tail swung low to make sure it made contact with me. It hit the ground first, sending up a shower of dirt and slowing the blow enough that I didn't go sailing.

The beast roared again. He reared back his head in the same move-ment he had made right before he jetted me with water, and I held out my right arm in a feeble gesture to block what was coming. Just then, something sailed up from behind the beast, arcing through the air.

Something bright and orange and flickering.

Something that sailed straight into the monster's head.

The beast yelped in surprise and recoiled. The back of his head was . . . melting. Great globs of fat dripped down to the grass around him, and I could hear the frying sound. It smelled like bacon. The wound didn't seem to be mortal, but the monster was clearly in pain.

The beast turned to see where the fireball had come from, and when he moved, I saw as well. Ohnica was standing in front of the burning beams, and she had dialed her heat up to the max. Looking at her was like staring at the sun.

And suddenly, I remembered. Not everything. But I'd seen her like that before. Blazing with fury. I remembered her grabbing hold of my hand, and me screaming in pain. Just that one image, clear as day. And maybe a hint of terror? Had I been *afraid* of her then? She held up her hands and sent another comet blazing toward the monster. This time where it hit, the flame spread out, catching the beast on fire in the middle of his chest. He roared even louder, craned his long neck, and spat water on the flames, which went out. The thing growled at Ohnica.

"Get over it," she said. She whipped her arm toward the monster in a full-on throw, and another basketball-sized globe of fire hurtled out.

The beast couldn't dodge that, but he could spit water at it. Water and flame connected in midair, bursting into a ball of steam. Ohnica started throwing fireballs as fast as her arm would go. The dragon managed to intercept each one. His water kept coming, and so did the víla's fire. But she was on the offensive, and she had the advantage for the moment.

I got up and started edging my way to the well, but it was slow going. Fireballs and water blasts were being thrown every which way, and it was all I could do to avoid getting hit by accident.

Ohnica started walking toward the monster, keeping up the throws but reducing the amount of space they had to go before they reached the beast. She was smiling wickedly, clearly enjoying the challenge. Almost toying with the beast to make it last longer. Behind her, I could see the wooden structure was burning fast. She was using up a lot of energy, very quickly. Maybe it wasn't enough fire to free her. Maybe I'd get lucky and have her beat Ajax, but not be freed. The beast backed up as well until it reached the castle wall. Then it had nowhere to go. One fireball connected full on, splashing flames across its shoulder. Ajax craned his neck to get an angle to extinguish it, and in that moment, Ohnica wound up another fireball and threw it straight at the beast's head.

She didn't miss.

The water dragon inhaled in surprise, and that was all it took. There was no roar of pain or anguish this time. I think the lungs burned at the same time as the beast's brain. A strip of flesh along the monster's throat sloughed off and fell to the ground. The whole body collapsed in on itself.

A wave of grease rushed over the scene and swept over my feet, running down the steps of the amphitheater. It all headed down the hill back toward the well, where it joined up with the water that had spilled out into the well plaza. I couldn't help but feel sorry for Ajax. Yes, he'd tried his best to kill me, but he was just doing what his master had wanted.

Ohnica burned stronger than ever. She came over to me and grinned, but her expression seemed off. She was gloating. Maybe because she'd gotten some revenge on the vodník. Or maybe because she didn't have to pretend to be nice anymore. "We're even now, mortal."

"Um . . . thanks?" I said, taking a step back. Her attitude had changed too. Less friendly. More arrogant.

She breathed in deeply, flames burning bright through every part of her. Behind her, the huge bonfire had gone out completely. "Free at last. It's been decades." She hurled a fireball up into the air fifty feet. It hit a seagull, which burst into flames and fell to the ground. Ohnica's smile grew wider.

I cleared my throat. "Um . . . the vodník has—"

"You're on your own now, kid," Ohnica said. "Be thankful I don't feel like killing you anymore. After this long, being freed by the witch's grandson is far better revenge than killing you would have been. Maybe the vodník was right to stop me, after all. But next time I see you, all bets are off." She exploded in a gust of fire that burst straight up into the sky, leaving me an afterimage of her figure burned into my vision.

Ever get the feeling like you'd just made a big mistake?

Magnify that by fifty. But I didn't have time to think about that right now.

I checked Ľuboš's watch again.

Seventeen minutes left.

One problem at a time.

CHAPTER THIRTY-TWO

TEA

Many of the myths surrounding Death have their roots in simple everyday occurrences. The story of the toll Charon charges to cross the River Styx all started when he was a few drachmas short on his lunch money one day. He asked a passenger for a loan, and a legend was born.

I ran to the well as fast as I could. My breaths came in gasps, and my muscles felt like gelatin. But I wasn't going to let Lesana get captured by the vodník on the same night that I'd let him trick me out of the one chance I had of saving my cousin. And there were still seventeen minutes left. Could I hope for a last-minute miracle?

The well was still full of water, perhaps to let Ajax go back to his master once he had finished with me. I took a breath—for habit's sake— and dived in. At first I did my best to swim downward, but it wasn't until I exhaled and took my first breath of water that I began to make serious progress.

The water was inky black, and it was only the feeling of the algae-covered walls passing by on my side now and then that showed I was still going down. Then I caught a glimpse of blue light, light that increased in intensity the closer I got. The entrance to the vodník's lair was open.

I pushed myself harder. The wounds from the branches that had impaled me were fully healed now. I didn't know how or why, but I wasn't complaining. Once I was in the vodník's tunnel system, I had no clue where to go.

Thankfully, the vodník had lit the torches only on the path he had taken. All hail laziness. The tunnels zigzagged every which way, but I kept following the light until I emerged in midstroke into a waterless tunnel.

I fell flat on my chest, water bursting from my lungs as I made the switch back to air, a process that involved a lot of hacking. I got up and hurried down the passage, trying to make as little noise as possible.

After fifty feet, I heard voices—faint, but heated. I tried to listen as I continued, hoping to have a clue what was going on before I burst out into Lesana and the vodník's confrontation.

"All that I did, I did for you." That was the vodník.

Lesana said something I couldn't catch.

"What do you mean I should have asked you first?" the vodník said. His voice was shaking, on the edge of raving. "You were a water spirit. You were miserable. I didn't have to ask you that. It was obvious. I was the one that put you in that state. I had to fix it."

"You shouldn't have put Tomas into—"

"Tomas." The vodník snorted from a room ahead of me. The room was comfortably furnished, with two stuffed easy chairs next to a coffee table, as well as a rolltop desk bursting with papers. Overflowing bookshelves lined the walls. A cozy study compared with the Gothic flair the rest of the place had going. "That idiot," the vodník continued. "And to think there was a time when I actually wanted him to be one of us. Not that I don't want him in my collection, what with his powers and all. They would come in very handy these days, if they make the transition into the teacup. Very convenient, especially if there were someone like me—

someone with more than a quarter of a brain, I mean—controlling those powers. Of course, he might be kind of squishy once Ajax gets through with him. But once I have his soul, I'll—"

"You'll what?" I stepped into the room.

The vodník and Lesana turned to me in surprise. The vodník recovered first. He frowned, then stood on his tiptoes, looking behind me. "I'm sorry," he said. "I was just wondering, have you seen a gigantic water monster around? About as tall as a building, with glowing eyes?"

"He's dead," I said.

The vodník rolled his eyes and groaned. "Oh great. This is just fantastic. First you screw up a simple potion, and now you kill my pet. Friends don't kill friends' pets, Tomas."

"Friends don't kill friends," I countered.

"How many times do I have to tell you?" he said. "You wouldn't 'die.' I left a cup there for you. Your soul would have been captured, no trouble. Easily. And Ajax would have brought me the cup. He was under strict orders about that. 'No eating the cup,' I told him. 'And don't stomp on it, either.' I was very specific. You have to be with water monsters."

He picked up his master cup from the walnut rolltop desk and ran his index finger around the lid. "And if you had done what you were supposed to do, Tomas, then by now, you, Lesana, and Katka would all be comfy and cozy on a shelf downstairs. Three little teacups, meeting new people, discussing new ideas. Isn't that what you wanted? Instead, Ajax is dead, Katka's got about"—he glanced at his watch—"ten minutes, Lesana's not in a teacup, and I'm not even sure if I want you anymore."

"I—"

"Don't interrupt me when I'm complaining," the vodník said. "You might think you're great because you resisted my bite and didn't become a water spirit yourself. When I summoned that undercurrent in the well to suck you out to the river, I just thought I was getting rid of a corpse. So you survived. My bad." He straightened his tie and cocked his head to the side for a moment, like a wannabe gangster. "You're a high and mighty Rasputin, but there are other ways to die. I have the power of fifty wizards, seventeen witches, four Rasputins, and two kings at my beck and call. You think all of them just wandered into teacups willingly? Do you? Well, they didn't. They struggled. They kicked. They threw lightning bolts at my head. But I didn't hold that against them. They're happier now, and they've apologized too."

His eyes narrowed and he stepped toward me, holding the teacup out. "They all come around in the end. They all see what's best."

I wanted to say something, but I couldn't take my eyes off the cup. Was there something glimmering in the bottom? My feet moved on their own. My arm reached out. I'd just take the cup from him. That would be best. Have it close to me, safe.

Lesana lunged to smack the cup from the vodník's hand, releasing me from the spell he had been weaving. The vodník scowled at her, but the teacup dropped to the floor without so much as chipping. "Now I have to reset it," he said. "Stop delaying the inevitable." He melted into a puddle that slipped from the room faster than I could follow it, taking the teacup with him.

Lesana was after him at once. "We must hurry," she said. "It takes him some time to prepare the cups before he can use them."

We raced after him to a stairwell going down. The two of us took the stairs as fast as we could, and soon we had reached the end. This time, when the door opened to a room about the size of a rich man's living room, I was momentarily stunned.

The room was littered with shelves. Hutches lining the walls, mantels over fireplaces, shelves standing in the middle of the room, all of them brimming with teacups. Even more incredible: stuffed in, around, and over all those shelves was treasure.

Lots of treasure.

Gold coins, sparkling jewelry, paintings, ornate woodcarving, tapestries, mounds of iPods (probably broken, if the vodník had acquired them by drowning their owners), expensive stereo equipment—you name it, it was there. It was like someone had gone to a library and dumped a dragon's hoard all over the place, then updated some of it for the twenty-first century. Lying in the middle of it all was a stone sarcophagus, carved into the shape of a sleeping king. The grave of Matúš Čak. No wonder humans had never found it—the vodník had probably drowned anyone who came close. Everything was lit by the same guttering blue torches the vodník used elsewhere, giving the whole place an eerie underwater feel.

The vodník stood between two tall shelves, holding the master cup and muttering over it. I cocked my arm back like I was going to throw something, hoping I could bluff the vodník into submission. "Stop," I said. "I'll kill you if I have to."

"What's that going to do?" he asked, sneering.

"Ask your pet," I said.

The vodník froze, then smiled at me. "Tomas. You wouldn't. You couldn't. I mean, you killed Ajax, so obviously you're not an animal lover, but to kill your own friend?"

I shook my head, stepping around a pile of antique goblets to get a better angle on him. "Maybe we were friends before, but you're no friend of mine now. Put the cup down."

He looked over at Lesana. "You'd let him do this? After all we've been through?"

I didn't take my eyes off the vodník, so I couldn't see her expression, but she didn't say anything back.

He cleared his throat. "I told you. Everything I've done, I've done for you, Lesana. Well, maybe not *everything* everything. I made myself dinner a few times, and there was this little crystal vase I bought once for myself, but other than that, it's been all for you. I'd say we were *like* brother and sister, but that would be a lie, because we are."

"What?" Lesana asked, startled.

The vodník nodded, then started fumbling inside his vest for something. "Right. Brother and sister. You and me. I was going to save this revelation for a more relaxed atmosphere, perhaps over tea, but your boyfriend over there seems a little kill-happy right now, so . . ." He took out a small glinting something and held it out to Lesana. "See?"

She stepped forward to examine whatever it was, and I put out my other arm to stop her. The scar on my hand from the vodník's bite caught my eye.

"No," she said. "I need to see this."

I let her go. My mind was racing, thinking about that scar. The vodník had tried to take my soul through the bite, and that hadn't worked—and had given me a new scar—which meant I was immune to that now, right? Did the same apply to soul-stealing by teacup? I tried to remember if I'd ever read anything about it in *Death in the Modern Day*. What would happen when two magics collided? Rasputin vs. vodník? One would have to win.

Lesana snatched the glittering thing, then rushed back out of reach of the vodník. I spared a glance to see what it was—a bracelet.

"Where did you get this?" Lesana asked.

"Where did I get it?" he said. "I got it from the boat the two of us stole when I was captured by the vodník. The other vodník. You were there."

I remembered that vision; it had been the first one I'd had, when I'd just got to Slovakia. I remembered *being* that boy. "That's ridiculous," I said. "Don't listen to him."

The vodník laughed. "Ridiculous, he says. It didn't feel ridiculous when I got pulled under the water. It didn't feel ridiculous when my soul was ripped from my body and took on this new form. I was lost, confused—terrified, even. Out of my mind."

His face became progressively more serious, and he continued. "I had all these new instincts rushing through me, and I didn't know what to do with them. So I went to the one person I trusted. My sister. I didn't realize what I'd look like when she saw me. She got scared, I got scared, and I did something stupid. I tried to make her a vodník too. Is that so wrong?"

Lesana seemed to be believing him.

"No," I said. "No no no. You can't buy that. A vodník killed your brother, and that vodník would have the necklace your brother had. None of this proves anything."

"Don't listen to him, Lesana," the vodník said. "Ask me anything. I know it all. What was your dog's name? What was the name of that annoying neighbor who was always peeking into our windows? Ask me everything."

"Wrong," I said. "He stole your brother's soul. He's had centuries to find out those answers."

The vodník stomped his foot. "Will you stop that? You're so negative. What do you know? You're only sixteen. Lesana and I are so old, we're measured in centuries."

"All he wants to do is figure out a way to put you in a teacup, Lesana.

Are you going to let him?"

It took her a while to respond. "I don't know," she said.

We stood like that for what must have been a full minute. None of us saying anything, none of us moving. It was like a showdown in a Western movie. I was only watching the vodník, who was splitting his time between glancing at me and Lesana, probably trying to gauge what we were thinking and whether Lesana was buying his story.

Finally the vodník must have decided things weren't going his way. He opened the teacup and pointed it straight at Lesana. A beam of light shot out from it, connecting with Lesana, who gasped. I made my choice. It probably wouldn't work, but it was the last chance I had at saving everyone. I stepped into the beam. As soon as I did, it felt like a hook landed in my heart and someone started pulling. All my energy disappeared, and my lungs felt like they were filling with water—but not water I could breathe.

Behind the vodník, Morena had appeared.

"What are you doing?" she asked.

I opened and closed my mouth, trying to find strength to say something, but the pulling and drowning sensations were getting stronger. My soul was leaving my body.

Morena snorted and walked over to me.

"You stay out of this," the vodník said. "No geriatrics allowed." Lesana was standing still, her forehead wrinkled in confusion.

Death ignored him and studied me. "Sacrificing yourself isn't going to do anything. I already told you that. I ought to snap the connection he's put on you, just so I can harvest your stupid soul myself."

I shook my head and slumped to the floor.

"That's not fair," the vodník said. "I got him first. He's mine. That's how things work. Anything else is cheating. There are laws against this."

"Bah!" Morena waved her hand at the vodník in disgust. "So, Tomas. Your time's almost up, and I find you here playing with a vodník."

"Shouldn't you be off collecting his cousin?" the vodník asked. I still couldn't speak. A white speck of *something*—not light, not solid—left my chest, followed by another, then another, then a flood of them.

Morena shrugged. "I had a bit of spare time, and I thought I'd check in to see what you were up to. Whether there were any last minute heroics worth watching." She checked on Lesana, who seemed to be recovering from the teacup spell's effects. "I must admit you got fairly inventive. If you'd released her soul instead of restoring it, I think you would have filled the contract fairly enough." She turned back to me. "You came close. Closer than most have come. But in the end it hardly ever works."

Lesana spoke up. "Is she here for—"

"No," the vodník said. "She isn't here for anybody. She was just leaving. Just passing through."

"You don't shut up, do you?" Morena said. "I'll stay as long as I like. I have sixty seconds left before the deal's over, and if I want to be here, here's where I'll be."

Whatever was *me* left my body, and I could see myself, lying there on the floor as a steady flow of white light left my chest and gathered in a ball above my body. I didn't feel like I was drowning anymore. I didn't feel . . . anything. The ball started to swirl around, and I grew dizzy. So much for this final plan—it had only been a hunch to begin with.

The spinning increased, and I was drawn toward the teacup. I came closer and closer, the invisible current increasing as the vodník watched in satisfaction.

"I'll take Lesana after you, anyway," he said, his arms folded and a smirk on his face. "And it'll be too late for your cousin. This is what you get for getting in my way."

Now it was as if I was at the bottom a vortex. The master cup loomed larger than life in front of me, and—

I felt a prick from where the bite scar on my hand would have been, if I still had a body. My soul paused at the edge of the brim.

The smirk left the vodník's face. "Hey. That's not right," he said in a flat voice.

The current reversed, and now I was being drawn back to the scar on my physical body.

The vodník set the cup down and backed away from it. "Stop. I take it back."

With a flash, I was in my body, breathing again. The white lights were streaming back into my chest.

I stood up and walked over to the master cup, which had begun to shake—first just a tremble, and then more violently. The last white light went back into me, and the master cup jumped into the air with the worst shake of all. I caught it in midair, stared at the vodník, then hurled the cup to the floor.

It shattered, pieces scattering across the floor.

Morena and the vodník fell silent.

The vodník started edging to the exit. "Well, this has been fun, hasn't it?"

A light gray mist rose from the remnants of the teacup.

"Maybe next time we should do a potluck," the vodník said. "Bring your own beef." He was halfway to the door now, skirting us and the shelves.

The gray mist thickened, and from the center of it came the noises of murmuring voices. It sent a tendril out to grab at the vodník, then sent another branch to slip into one of the ordinary teacups.

The vodník dropped to his knees and crawled over to Morena. "This doesn't have to be the end now, does it? Just take the souls. All of them. I promise, I'll never keep another for as long as I live."

Morena cackled. "That's a promise you'll keep." She held her scythe out, and some of the mist started heading toward it, as well. The sound of murmuring increased.

The ordinary teacup exploded, sending china flying. I shielded my eyes with my arm, and when I looked again, two orbs of mist were forming. They worked faster this time. Mist entered cups and exploded them and then reformed and did it again more quickly than I could follow, doubling every time. Was Babka's soul in there somewhere? The room was filled with the sound of breaking cups and the angry shouts of a disembodied mob. More mist gathered around Morena's scythe and the vodník's feet.

The vodník yelped in surprise, seeming to see what was happening for the first time. All the cups shattered at once, shards flying everywhere, peppering my skin with tiny porcelain bits. Then the mist attacked the vodník. He was surrounded in swirling, glowing vapors, each one distinct and yet part of the greater whole, like a school of fish clumped together. But deadlier. The vodník screamed, and then I couldn't see him anymore. All was churning mist, and everything got brighter. The muttering of the mob increased, and so did the vodník's screams.

Then the screams stopped.

The mists froze. After several heartbeats, they shot over to Death's scythe, which devoured them all in an endless stream. All that was left of the vodník was his top hat, sitting in a puddle.

Morena broke the silence by cackling again. There was no other way to put it. She was beaming at me. She clapped her hands and rubbed them together. "Finally! Well done, Tomas," she said. "Some minor hiccups, but understandable. Improvisation at the end—I love it! Contract fulfilled. I hope you take the job. It would be a pleasure doing business with you."

She disappeared.

CHAPTER THIRTY-THREE
VICTORY

Many have asked if death is just the beginning of something far more wonderful. The answer is simple. Of course! Death is the beginning of a long and beautiful career. What else is there in life?

Lesana and I stared at each other, then down to the puddle on the floor, then around us at all the treasure. She rushed over to me and hugged me, hard. "Thank you," she whispered into my ear.

Suddenly everything felt better. The world was brighter. Katka was going to live, and I was getting hugged by a fully living, breathing, warm-blooded Lesana.

"Do you think he was telling the truth?" Lesana asked after a moment, separating from me but still holding onto my shoulders.

"About what?"

"About being my brother."

I thought about it. "I don't know." Vodníks *were* created by drowning children, but . . .

Lesana didn't answer that, and I had something more pressing on my mind. "Do you think Katka's better already?"

"She's fine," a voice said from behind us. Lesana yelped and let go of me, darting her hands behind her back. We turned to see the old candy cane–backed granny, Starenka, hobble into the room. She smiled at us, then cleared a pile of coins off an old throne and sat down. "It'll take her a bit to come to, but she will. Don't worry."

"Who are you?" Lesana asked.

"An observer," the granny said. "And that was some nice creativity at the end there, Tomas."

I shrugged, uncomfortable with the praise. "I didn't really know if it would work."

"What *did* you do?" Lesana said.

"He's a Rasputin," Starenka said. "When the vodník bit him, he started taking his soul, and when Tomas overcame that bite, he became immune to the vodník's soul stealing. It was one magic versus another at the end there, and the Rasputin magic won out. Frankly, I had no idea that would happen. After that, because he'd escaped from the vodník's teacup, Tomas was able to free the other souls, and they took care of the rest."

I hadn't known, either—I'd just hoped. I looked down at the hat sitting in the puddle, and Starenka followed my gaze.

"In a way," she said, "I'm sorry to see him go."

"You knew him?" I asked.

The granny nodded. "He saved my life, once." She straightened. I don't mean she sat up straighter; I mean she sat up, removing the candy-cane angle of her back and appearing about a hundred years younger. Her face lost most of the wrinkles, and my jaw dropped. I recognized her. Her face had been in a picture frame on the mantle every day of my life.

"Babka," I said.

She smiled at me and bobbed her head. "It's because of that vodník that much of my life changed from the course it had been heading. Ohnica attacked me back then. I was supposed to be dispatching her in the same way you just took care of the vodník. She surprised me with a last-minute burst of flame right as I'd bound her to her element—a binding you've now loosed. That'll cause trouble, but we can worry about it later. Back then, the vodník exploded a water pipe in the basement to save me. Of course, doing one good deed hardly makes up for all the other people he murdered over the years. But still . . ." She walked over to the hat, picked it up, and put it on one of the shelves, now empty of teacups. "When Ohnica tried to kill you when you were little, he saved you too. Tried to do it by drowning, but he always did have a warped sense of right and wrong."

"But why didn't you go back?" I asked, suddenly feeling guilty somehow, and trying to mask it. "What about Ľuboš? My mom?"

Babka sighed and brushed away some dust from her blouse. "I couldn't. Your mother didn't approve of what was happening to me, and Ľuboš was already far too obsessed with it. Imagine how he would have turned out if I had stayed? He's mostly a knight as it is. And there was the danger to worry about. They were only children, and around me, things aren't safe."

"Are you a Rasputin too?"

"No," she said. "A different type of magic user, more like your friend there." She jerked her head toward Lesana. "But you don't need a lecture now. I'm here on assignment from Morena."

"Do you work for her or something?" I asked.

"Of course," she said. "I'm Death's Assassin. Or at least I am for now." Lesana gasped.

"Think of me like a hit man for Death," Babka said, then shrugged. "Or hit woman, I suppose. My job was to kill the magical creatures that refused to let Morena win."

I remembered that from *Death in the Modern Day*. "What do you mean, that *was* your job?" I asked.

"I mean it's your job now."

I blinked. "Mine?"

She nodded. "If you'll take it. If you don't, I'm stuck with it some more, and I'm worn out. Fresh blood would help the position, and being a Rasputin wouldn't hurt, either. Not to mention being the first drinker of a virgin spring. Eternal regenerative power will come in very handy in this line of work."

So that was how I recovered from those tree branch puncture wounds so fast. In all the rush, I hadn't had time to think about it too much. "But—but—I can't. Me? I couldn't be a hit man. I've never killed anything before in my life."

Babka sniffed. "What do you call that puddle over there, then?"

"That was an accident. I just guessed. And I only did it because I had to."

"Tomas," Babka said. "Don't start getting a guilty conscience. Getting rid of the vodník was your first assignment. He's been escaping Morena for decades, and this was just the opportunity we needed to take him out, regardless of your history with him."

"Assignment?" I said. "What about Katka, then? Was that some sort of—"

"No. Katka's death time was real. We didn't alter that. We just made sure you knew about it so you were properly motivated."

"You *used* me."

"Semantics," Babka said, picking up a painting that looked vaguely like a Van Gogh. "The vodník was a bad egg. It was because of him the whole city of Trenčín won't go near water. You fixed all that, or did for the most part. I just had to send you a few notes now and then, to keep you on track. You should be proud."

It clicked. So that's who the notes had come from. "A" stood for Alena, Babka's first name. I was quiet for a while. What do you tell someone when they start prattling off things like that? "What about you?" I said at last. "If I become this Death's Assassin person, what do you do?"

She smiled and set the painting down. "I get to go home. Take up my life where I left off. Maybe do some consultation for you on the side, but I'd retire."

"And if I don't take it?"

"Then I'm stuck," Babka said. "Somebody's got to do the job, and if you don't, then we'll just have to wait for another candidate before I'm through."

My mind was racing. There was just too much to think about at once. "Would I have to go into hiding too?" I asked. The thought of disappearing from the world wasn't too appealing—not right after I'd just ironed things out in my life.

"I doubt it," Babka said and stood. "Not if I'm there to keep you headed in the right direction. And not if you don't want to, though it might get kind of hairy at times, being Death's Assassin while you're still in high school."

"What about me?" Lesana said.

I had completely forgotten about her, and that was saying something. She was standing there with wide eyes, her face pale as snow.

Babka grunted. "You. You weren't really foreseen, to tell the truth. But I think something can be arranged, if you don't mind living with an old lady."

"With you?" Lesana asked.

"Why not? I'll be needing an apartment, and I'd rather not stay in it alone. I've had enough of solitary life for now. A girl your age needs a guardian, especially with boys like Tomas running around."

I blushed and was more than a little relieved to notice Lesana blushing too.

Babka laughed. "Oh, to be young. Don't worry, I think if Tomas behaves himself, I might approve a little courtship now and then. But we can sort that out later. For now, I think there's someplace Tomas ought to be."

"Katka?" I asked.

Babka nodded. "She'll be waking up soon. You should be there."

"Can you, like, magic us there or something?" I asked.

"You know," Babka said, "that's the problem with you kids today. You're all so lazy. You left your car up by the castle gate. We can drive, as long as Ajax didn't squish it."

I don't know how we would have gotten out of the well if it weren't for Babka. She led us out through the passages, all of which were now clear of water, though the magic torches still burned. "The vodník had to force water to come here," Babka explained. "With him gone, it'll dry out quickly."

At the door to the complex we paused. The water had receded to just below the edge of the door, and without its presence, I had no idea how we'd get out of the well.

"Not to worry," Babka said. She leaned out of the door and felt around on the well wall for a moment before she scraped away a chunk of dripping algae. "There are handholds. I'll go first."

"Handholds" was putting it liberally. A more accurate description would be "slick death traps." The climb was long and there were a few times when I was sure I'd fall back down, but somehow we made it. Babka helped Lesana and me get out once we reached the top. She was pretty spry for someone who had been masquerading as a candy cane–backed granny.

"What about the vodník's tunnels?" I asked. "All that treasure."

"It's not going anywhere," Babka said. "Maybe mention it to Ľuboš—I'm sure he'll figure out something to do with it all. I can't wait to see what the rest of the town does when they find out a Rom has fallen into that much treasure. I always hated how mean my countrymen were to my husband." I hadn't really thought about the position that Babka had put herself in by marrying a Roma man. It only increased my admiration of her, and it made me wonder what sort of man my grandpa had been.

Ajax hadn't squished the car, although there were deep scratches on either side from where I'd scraped against the gate on the way in. I opened the driver's door to get behind the wheel, but my grandmother stopped me.

"Do you have a license?"

I stopped. "Well . . . no."

"Didn't think so," she said. "I'll drive."

We all piled in, and Babka revved the engine and raced down the castle road in reverse. The tires screeched when she whipped the car around at the bottom of the hill and shifted back to drive. She drove like a maniac, weaving from lane to lane and taking turns so tightly I worried we'd tip over. All the while, she had a grin on her face as wide as a half moon.

"I love cars," she said after she noticed my white-knuckle grip on the door handle. "I never got one when I was your age, and the ones they have today handle so much better than those Communist ones."

By the time we got to the hospital, I thought our tires might have melted. Babka pulled up to the front door. "Okay," she said. "Here's your stop."

"You're not going to come in?" I asked.

She shook her head. "I think there's been enough excitement for one day. I can get caught up with my children when it's not so hectic, and we can explain Lesana later too."

Maybe she had a point. I looked over to Lesana. "You'll be okay?"

"Of course," she said. "Go see your family."

Finding Katka's room this time wasn't nearly as difficult as it had been last night. Had it really only been last night I was here? I walked down the hall at first, then broke into a run. I needed to see Katka—know she was okay.

As I approached the room, I was alarmed to see a swarm of nurses and doctors milling around. Had something gone wrong? I elbowed my way through the crowd.

"—don't understand it," a doctor was saying.

I heard Ľuboš's voice. "You don't need to."

At last I emerged into the room. Katka was sitting up, her eyes alert and bright. They'd rolled the other patients out, probably to let them avoid all the commotion. I was also relieved to see my dad standing by the bed. No paralysis—not even a sling or a neck brace. Only some bruises. Ľuboš ran over and hugged me so hard I thought my eyeballs would pop out. "Thank you," he whispered.

I would have said something in response, but I couldn't breathe. He let me go and then bellowed for all the hospital staff to leave the room. They didn't want to, but when Ľuboš starts yelling he can move things by his voice alone. In no time, it was down to just family. I finally reached Katka's side and leaned over to give her a hug.

Katka smiled. "I take it the potion worked?"

"Not exactly," I said. "But I came up with something else."

"What?" she asked.

"I'll explain later."

"I missed it all?" Dad asked on my left. He sounded disappointed.

"Be glad you did," I said.

"Glad?" His shoulders slumped. "That was going to be my plotline for the book. Now what am I supposed to do?"

I rolled my eyes. "I'll fill you in on how it turned out. Don't worry."

He grumbled something about "missing out on the first-hand experience." The fall hadn't changed him a bit. Thank goodness.

After that, there was one of those uncomfortable pauses where no one can think of anything to say. The last couple of days had been crazy for all of us. My return from the dead, Katka's coma, getting the potion. But it was over now. It had worked, as hard as that was to believe. Ever since the fire that burned our house down, it felt like I had been shoved from one mess into another. Now maybe I could just be a normal guy again. Then I thought of Babka, Lesana, and the whole Death's Assassin thing. Not to mention being a Rasputin and having new regenerative powers.

Well, maybe not a *normal* guy, but that would probably have been boring anyway.

My mom hugged me again. "Tomas, I am so sorry."

"It's okay. I—"

"No," she said. "It's not okay. I've . . . behaved badly. It might not be easy for me, but I want you to know, I'm starting a no-secrets policy from now on. You can tell me anything."

A pang of guilt struck me. "Anything?"

She nodded.

Well, technically I hadn't agreed to this policy yet, so I figured I could wait to tell her about Babka. At least until morning. Maybe I could say it had slipped my mind. But some things had to be addressed sooner. I thanked my mom, then pulled out of her hug and faced my uncle. "Ľuboš," I said. "The . . . uh . . . castle courtyard got a little trashed."

"Trashed?"

"Well, I'm not sure what normal people will see, but when I left it last, there was an enormous water dragon melting in the middle of it. And I kind of burned down that wooden tower across from the tourist guide office."

"Where was Julo during all of this?"

"The night watchman? He ran away."

"Typical," Ľuboš said. "Well, I suppose I can forgive you, under the circumstances. But repairing it all . . ." He tried to smile. "It doesn't matter now, anyway. The Germans are making their final preparations for the buyout. At least this way, they'll have to pay more to fix it all."

"About that," I said. "Have you ever thought of suggesting someone search inside the well for Matúš Čak's grave?"

He frowned. "Inside the well? I think people have tried that already."

I grinned. "I don't think they looked hard enough. When I was down there cleaning it, I think I might have seen something kind of like a door. Maybe we should check it out. There might be a lot of treasure down there. It would be sure to attract tourists. Lots of tourists. And I've got a hunch people are going to stop complaining about Roma curses in the town pretty soon too."

It's not every day you get to witness someone go from troubled to carefree in a matter of seconds. Ľuboš had been happy before, but now he stood up straighter, his shoulders seeming to swell and a smile breaking out on his face that was as genuine as I'd ever seen. He laughed and slapped me on the back. "You were born to be here in Trenčín, Tomas. Check the well? That's a great idea. I'll do it first thing in the morning."

I beamed back, doing my best not to wince from the back slapping. Ľuboš was right about one thing, though. It did feel like I was born to be in Trenčín. Even with everything I had to put up with from storekeepers, strangers, and the Bigot Gang. Thinking about my family—and Lesana— I felt like I belonged. Like I fit in, in a way I'd never felt in America.

Like I was home.

AUTHOR'S NOTE

I've been to quite a few cities in Europe, big and small. But when I first visited my wife's hometown of Trenčín, something seemed different right away. I've always been a fan of cities that have their very own castle, and Trenčín's is a real doozy, having endured everything from marauders to Communists. I went to the joust, took the tour, and had a barbecue by firelight next to the tower. I toured the city, ate the ice cream, and had a wonderful time. I've tried to recreate that experience in this book. All the places described in it actually exist. Trenčín is a beautiful old city, with a rich history and friendly people.

When I lived in former East Germany for a few years, I was surprised at how different the perception of Communism is to people who had lived with it for decades. In America, we'd like to believe everyone in a Communist regime is miserable and wants to be free. In reality, many people missed the days of Communism, when prices were low and work was plentiful—but sometimes you couldn't buy bananas, televisions, cars, or even toilet paper. I believe Communism set Slovakia back by at least a decade, maybe two. But it's a resilient country, and it's emerging stronger and more beautiful than ever.

As far as folktales go in the book, I tried to base as much as I could on real Slovak mythology. Vodníks are as widely represented in Slovakia as vampires are in the United States: sometimes portrayed as tricksters and occasionally villainous, with competitions with each other to see who can steal the most souls. Vílas are Slovak fairies, typically associated with a different element (fire, water, etc.). Matúš Čak did indeed rule from Trenčín castle, and his grave remains a mystery. The Well of Love gets many visitors each year, and has been the site of various proposals, as well as a wedding or two.

Ajax the water dragon, Rasputin powers, and Lesana the water spirit are all my own fabrications, although the story of the girl who dropped dead when her father forbade her marriage is a real Slovak legend that I adapted to my own purposes. Morena is the traditional Slovak goddess of winter and death. Starenka is a popular figure throughout Eastern Europe, although sometimes she goes by different names.

Capturing the Roma elements of the book proved more difficult. I had seen some Roma on my first trip to the country, but Trenčín doesn't have a very big Roma population, and so it took a trip to more southern and eastern parts of the country for the situation to become real. It's a complex situation, with Slovaks resenting Roma for what they perceive as an inherent lack of desire to be self-sufficient, and Roma resenting Slovaks for what they see as centuries-long oppression. While I haven't been able to go into too much depth on the many facets of the conflict, hopefully what I've presented gives you an idea of the sort of struggles facing the Roma—not just in Slovakia, but throughout Europe.

FURTHER READING

Slovakia

Hurn, Margaret. *A Foreigner's Guide to Living in Slovakia*. Modra Publishing, 2007.

Mallows, Lucy. *Slovakia: The Bradt Travel Guide*. Guilford, CT: Globe Peqout Press, 2007.

Spiesz, Anton, and Dusan Caplovic. *Illustrated Slovak History: A Struggle for Sovereignty in Central Europe*. Bolchazy-Carducci, 2004.

Slovak Language

Lorinc, Sylvia, and John M. Lorinc. *Slovak-English, English-Slovak Dictionary & Phrasebook*. New York: Hippocrene, 1999.

Naughton, James. *Colloquial Slovak: The Complete Course for Beginners*. London: Routledge, 2003.

Slovak Folktales

Cooper, David, ed. *Traditional Slovak Folktales*. M.E. Sharp, 2001.

Dobsinsky, Pavol. *Slovak Tales for Young and Old*. Bolchazy-Carducci, 2002.

Roma

Hancock, Ian F. *We are the Romani People*. Hertfordshire, England: University of Hertfordshire Press, 2002.

Yoors, Jan. *The Gypsies*. Prospect Heights, IL: Waveford, 1967.

ACKNOWLEDGMENTS

This book has been a long time in the making, but it wouldn't have gone anywhere if it weren't for two key people: Denisa Križanová, who introduced me to Slovakia in the first place, and her brother, Miloš Križan, who provided volumes of information and insight on Slovak folklore, history, and anything else I might need an answer for. Special thanks also go to my editor, Stacy Whitman, and my agents: Joshua Bilmes and Eddie Schneider. Isaac Stewart is a giant among men, and he did a fantastic job designing this book and helping it be the best it could be. Thanks to Nikolas Rybár, who evaluated the Roma cultural pieces of the book. My writing instructors at BYU also helped me in many ways: Louise Plummer, Dave Wolverton, Chris Crowe, and Doug Thayer. I'd like to thank members of my writing groups: Brandon Sanderson, Janci Patterson, Kimball Larsen, Holly Venable, Heather Kirby, Eric James Stone, Sally Taylor, and Bradley Reneer. In addition, I've had a variety of readers for this book: Robb Cundick, Ted Cundick, Wilson Coltrin, Audrey Stone, Emilia Križanová, Kristy Kugler, Molly Reed, and Betsey Hyde. Also, Reed Nielsen, who really ought to be a bigger BYU fan. Thank you all so much! Writing can be a very solitary experience, and having friends there to cheer you on makes all the difference.

DEMCO